Also by Derek Landy:

Skulduggery Pleasant

Skulduggery Pleasant
PLAYING WITH FIRE

Skulduggery Pleasant
THE FACELESS ONES

Skulduggery Pleasant
DARK DAYS

Skulduggery Pleasant
MORTAL COIL

DEREK LANDY

HarperCollins *Children's Books*

First published in hardback in Great Britain by HarperCollins *Children's Books* 2010
First published in paperback in Great Britain by HarperCollins *Children's Books* 2011
HarperCollins *Children's Books* is a division of
HarperCollins*Publishers* Ltd
77-85 Fulham Palace Road, Hammersmith, London W6 8JB

Visit us on the web at www.harpercollins.co.uk

Skulduggery Pleasant rests his weary bones on the web at
www.skulduggerypleasant.co.uk

Derek Landy blogs under duress at
www.dereklandy.blogspot.com

1

ISBN 978-0-00-732601-3

Typeset in Baskerville MT by Palimpsest Book Production Limited,
Falkirk, Stirlingshire
Printed and bound in England by
Clays Ltd, St Ives plc

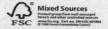

This book is dedicated, with great reluctance, to my editor, Nick Lake, because he is forcing me to.

Personally, I would have liked to include Gillie Russell and Michael Stearns who, along with Nick, really welcomed me into the publishing world with my first book.

Unfortunately, because Nick is now my sole editor, he has threatened to edit this dedication down to an unrecognisable mess of blacked-out lines, and so as a result this dedication is to him, and him alone.

Personally I think that this shows a staggering amount of ███████████ and ████████████, which proves that Nick is nothing but a ████████████████████████████ with ████████████ for ████████████, but hey, that's just my personal opinion.

Here, Nick. You finally get a book dedicated to you. Hope you're ████████████ happy.

████████████.

(Editor's Note: Nick Lake is a great guy.)

1

WREATH'S TASK

The doors swung open and High Priest Auron Tenebrae strode into the room, his robe swirling around his tall, narrow frame. To his right was Quiver, a miser with words, but overly generous with withering glares. To Tenebrae's left, Craven, a bland sycophant, possessed of an uncanny skill to worm his way into his superior's good graces. Solomon Wreath had been seeing far too much of all three lately.

"Cleric Wreath," Tenebrae said, nodding imperiously at him.

"Your Eminence," Wreath responded, bowing deeply. "To what do I owe the honour?"

"Why do you *think* we're here?" Craven said, almost sneered. "You're late with your report. Did you think the High Priest would forget? Do you think him a fool?"

"I do not think him a fool, no," Wreath answered calmly. "But as to the intelligence of the people who accompany him, I'm afraid I cannot say."

"An insult!" Craven screeched. "How dare you! How dare you use a derogatory tone in the presence of the High Priest!"

"Enough," Tenebrae sighed, "both of you. Your constant bickering tries my patience."

"My humblest apologies," Craven said immediately, bowing and closing his eyes, his lower lip trembling on the verge of tears. A magnificent performance, as usual.

"Yes," Wreath said. "Sorry about that."

"Despite Cleric Craven's overt dramatics," Tenebrae said, "he is quite correct to point out that you are late with your report. How is Valkyrie Cain progressing through her studies?"

"She's a fast learner," said Wreath. "As far as the practical side goes anyway. She's a natural at shadow casting, and every time I see her she's improved."

"And the philosophical aspect?" Quiver asked.

"Is not progressing nearly as smoothly," Wreath admitted. "She doesn't seem to be at all interested in the history or the teachings of the Order. It's going to take a lot to open her mind to it."

"The skeleton has already poisoned her against us," Tenebrae said bitterly.

"I fear you may be right. But I still think the effort is worth it."

"And I have yet to be convinced."

"Just because the girl is a fast learner," Quiver said, "does not mean she is the Death Bringer."

"Cleric Quiver speaks the truth," Tenebrae nodded.

Wreath did his best to look humble, keeping his comments to himself. He'd been searching for their saviour, for the one who would save the world from itself, for most of his life. He knew full well the danger of false hope and blind alleys – he'd had his fair share of both. But Valkyrie Cain was different. He felt it. Valkyrie Cain was the *one*.

"She troubles me," Tenebrae said. "Does she have potential? Absolutely. With training and with study, she could be the best of us. But the best of us still falls far short of what the Death Bringer should be."

"I'll keep working with her," Wreath said. "In two years,

maybe three, we'll have a better understanding of what she's capable of."

"Three years?" Tenebrae laughed. "A lot can happen, as we have seen, in a short space of time. Serpine. Vengeous. The Diablerie. Dare we risk being sidetracked by a mistake? While we are busy testing Miss Cain, another one of Mevolent's disciples might actually succeed in their insane goals and bring back the Faceless Ones for good. What if, as you yourself fear, Cleric Wreath, Lord Vile returns to punish us all? If that happens, our plans mean nothing. There will be no world left to save."

"Then what does His Eminence suggest?" Wreath asked.

"We need to know if we are wasting our time with this one."

"A Sensitive," Craven nodded.

"We've tried this before," Wreath argued. "None of our psychics are able to tell us anything."

"Reading the future has never been a particular talent of the Necromancer Order," Tenebrae said. "Our Sensitives are somewhat lacking when it comes to fortune-telling. But there is another I keep hearing about. Finbar something..."

"Finbar Wrong," Wreath said. "But he knows Valkyrie personally. It would raise too many questions. Even if he didn't know her, I doubt he'd ever aid our cause. As I keep reminding you, nobody out there likes us."

"We're working to save them all!" Craven barked, and this time not even the High Priest paid him any attention.

"The psychic will help us," Tenebrae said, "and afterwards he will remember nothing about it. Cleric Wreath, I want you to take the Soul Catcher and release the Remnant we have trapped inside it."

Wreath's face slackened. "Your Eminence, Remnants are highly dangerous..."

"Oh, I trust your ability to handle any situation," Tenebrae said with an airy wave of his hand. "Have it possess this Finbar person, and if he sees a future where Valkyrie Cain is the Death Bringer, and he sees her saving the world, then we can put all our energies into making sure she fulfils her potential. If he does not see this future, we forget about her, and our search continues."

"But using the Remnant..."

"Once the job is done, simply return it to the Soul Catcher. What could be easier?"

2

THE SMILING DETECTIVE

Christmas was a few days away, and all but one of the houses on this suburban Dublin street had lights in the windows. Three of the most competitive neighbours had filled their small gardens with flickering Santas and frolicking reindeer, and some idiot had even wrapped a cable of fairy lights round the lamp post outside his gate. There was no snow, but the night was cold, and frost clung to the city like glitter.

The big car that rolled to a stop outside the house with no lights was a 1954 Bentley R-Type Continental, one of only

208 ever made. It was an exquisite car, retro-fitted with modern conveniences, adapted to the needs of its owner. It was fast, it was powerful, and if it received even the slightest of dents, it would fall apart.

That's what the mechanic had said. He'd done all he could, used all his knowledge and all his abilities to bring this car back from the brink so many times – but the next dent, he promised, would be its last. All the tricks he'd used to keep it going, to bend it back into shape, would be counteracted. The glass would shatter, the metal would rupture, the frame would buckle, the tyres would burst, the engine would crack... The only way to avoid complete and utter catastrophe, the mechanic had said, was to make sure you weren't *in* the car when all this happened.

Skulduggery Pleasant got out first. He was tall and thin, and wore a dark blue suit and black gloves. His hair was brown and wavy, and his cheekbones were high and his jaw was square. His skin was slightly waxy and his eyes didn't seem capable of focusing, but it was a pretty good face, all things considered. One of his better ones.

Valkyrie Cain got out of the passenger side. She zipped up her black jacket against the cold, and joined Skulduggery as he walked up to the front door. She glanced at him, and saw that he was smiling.

"Stop doing that," she sighed.

"Stop doing what?" Skulduggery responded in that gloriously velvet voice of his.

"Stop smiling. The person we want to talk to lives in the only dark house on a bright street. That's not a good sign."

"I didn't realise I *was* smiling," he said.

They stopped at the door, and Skulduggery made a concerted effort to shift his features. His mouth twitched downwards. "Am I smiling now?"

"No."

"Excellent," he said, and the smile immediately sprang back up.

Valkyrie handed him his hat. "Why don't you get rid of the face? You're not going to need it in here."

"You're the one telling me how much I should practise," he said, but slid his gloved fingers beneath his shirt collar anyway, tapping the symbols etched into his collarbones. The face and hair retracted off his head, leaving him with a gleaming skull.

He put on his hat, cocked at a jaunty angle. "Better?" he asked.

"Much."

"Good." He knocked, and took out his gun. "If anyone asks, we're scary carollers."

Humming 'Good King Wenceslas' to himself, he knocked again, and still no one answered the door, and no lights came on.

"What do you bet everyone's dead?" Valkyrie asked.

"Are you just being incredibly pessimistic," Skulduggery asked, "or is that ring of yours telling you something?"

The Necromancer ring was cold on her finger, but no colder than usual. "It's not telling me anything. I can only sense death through it when I'm practically standing over the dead body."

"Which is an astonishingly useful ability, I have to say. Hold this."

He gave her his gun, and crouched down to pick the lock. She looked around, but no one was watching them.

"It might be a trap," she said, speaking softly.

"Unlikely," he whispered. "Traps are usually enticing."

"It might be a very rubbish trap."

"Always a possibility."

The lock clicked open. Skulduggery straightened up, put his lock picks away, and took his gun back.

"I need a weapon," Valkyrie muttered.

"You're an Elemental with a Necromancer ring, trained in a variety of martial arts by some of the best fighters in the world," Skulduggery pointed out. "I'm fairly certain that *makes* you a weapon."

"I mean a weapon you hold. You have a gun, Tanith has a sword... I want a stick."

"I'll buy you a stick for Christmas."

She glowered as he pushed the door. It opened silently, without even a creepy old creak. Skulduggery went first and Valkyrie followed, closing the door after them. It took a moment for her eyes to adjust to this level of gloom, and Skulduggery, who had no eyes for this to be a problem, waited until she tapped him before moving on. They passed through into the living room, where she tapped him again. He looked at her, and she pointed to the Necromancer ring. It was buzzing with a dreadful kind of cold energy as it fed off the death in the room.

They found the first dead body sprawled across the couch. The second was slumped in the corner, amid the wreckage of what once had been a side table. Skulduggery looked closely at each of them, then shook his head at Valkyrie. Neither was the man they were looking for.

They moved into the kitchen, where they found a third corpse, face down on the floor. Were his head not twisted all the way around, he would have been looking up at the ceiling.

A bottle lay beside his hand, smashed against the tiles, and the smell of beer was still strong.

The rest of the ground floor was clear of corpses, so they went to the stairs. The first one creaked, and Skulduggery stepped back off it. He wrapped his arms around Valkyrie's waist, and they rose off the ground and drifted up to the body on the landing. It was a woman, who had died curled up in a foetal position.

There were three bedrooms and one bathroom. The bathroom was empty, as was the first bedroom they checked. The second bedroom had scorch marks on the wall and another dead woman halfway out of a window. Valkyrie guessed this woman was the one responsible for the scorch marks – she'd tried to defend herself, then tried to run. Neither attempt had worked.

There was someone alive in the last bedroom. They could hear whoever it was in the wardrobe, trying not to make a sound. They heard a deep breath being taken as they approached, and then there was absolute silence for all of thirteen seconds. The silence ended with a ridiculously loud gasping for air. Skulduggery thumbed back the hammer of his gun.

"Come out," he said.

The wardrobe burst open and a shrieking madman leaped

17

out at Valkyrie. She batted down his arm, grabbed his shirt and twisted her hip into him, his shriek turning to a yelp as he hit the floor.

"Don't kill me," he sobbed as he lay there. "Oh God, please don't kill me."

"If you had let me finish," Skulduggery said, slightly annoyed, "you would have heard me say, *'Come out, we're not going to hurt you'*. Idiot."

"He probably wouldn't have said *idiot*," Valkyrie told the sobbing man. "We're trying our best to be nice."

The man blinked through his tears, and looked up. "You're... You're not going to kill me?"

"No, we're not," Valkyrie said gently, "so long as you wipe your nose right now."

The man sniffled into his sleeve and she stood back, trying not to shiver with revulsion. He got up.

"You're Skulduggery Pleasant," he said. "I've heard about you. The Skeleton Detective."

"Season's greetings," Skulduggery nodded. "This is my partner, Valkyrie Cain. And you are...?"

"My name is Ranajay. I live here with my... with my friends. It's so nice, living next to all these normal people. We really liked living here. Me and my... Me and my friends..."

Ranajay looked like he was going to start sobbing again, so Valkyrie cut in quickly. "Who did this? Who killed everyone?"

"I don't know. A big guy. Huge. He wore a mask, and spoke with an accent. His eyes were red."

"What did he want?" Skulduggery asked.

"He came here looking for a friend of mine."

Valkyrie frowned. "Ephraim Tungsten?"

"Yes," Ranajay said. "How did you know?"

"That's who we want to talk to. We believe he's been in contact with a killer we've been tracking for three months."

"Davina Marr, right? That detective who went bad, blew up the Sanctuary? That's why the big guy wanted Ephraim too."

"Do you know if Marr has been in touch with Ephraim?" Skulduggery asked.

"Oh, she has, yes. Paid him to make her a false ID and arrange to get her out of the country. That's what Ephraim does. When people have to disappear, he takes care of it. Only this time he didn't. I think after he realised what she'd done, he didn't want any part of it. The detective, Marr, she came looking for everything she'd paid for after the Sanctuary fell into the ground, but he was gone. She tore this place up three times in the same month looking for him. Haven't seen her since then. Haven't seen Ephraim either. We all thought it'd be

19

safer if we stayed away from him, you know? Fat lot of good that did my friends."

"The man who killed them," Skulduggery said, "did you tell him where Ephraim is?"

Ranajay shook his head. "Didn't have to. *I* knew what he wanted to know. I think that's the only reason he didn't kill me. Ephraim had told me, ages ago, that the only thing he'd done for Marr was to set up places for her to stay in three spots across the city. That's all the information the big guy wanted, just to know where Marr was staying."

"Can you tell *us* the three spots?"

"Are you going after him?" asked Ranajay.

"Our main priority is Davina Marr, but the man who killed your friends has just made it to number two on our list."

"You'll stop him?"

"If we can."

"You'll kill him?"

"If we have to."

"Yeah. Yeah, I'll tell you."

3

TESSERACT

He was a giant of a man, his thick-set muscles stretching the dusty black coat he wore, but he was quiet, she had to give him that. Smart too, to get this close to her without setting off the alarms. *Probably dismantled them as he came*, she thought as she flung herself through the window into the cold air. Taking his time, doing it right, the way any good assassin should. She knew who he was, of course. Killers that size tended to be conspicuous, and only one of them wore a metal mask over his scarred and misshapen face. The Russian, Tesseract.

She hit the ground and rolled, shards of broken glass accompanying her down. She reached into her jacket, found the trigger device, flicked the safety off with her thumb and pressed the red button without even taking it out of her pocket. He was up there, right now, and she would only get one chance at this.

But when there was no big explosion, she looked up to see him climbing out of the window overhead. He'd dismantled the explosives. Of course he had. Davina Marr didn't even bother to curse. She just ran.

The ground was wet with recent rain, and she slipped in the mud and scrambled up again. All that time and effort spent fortifying this pitiful excuse for a dwelling, all for nothing. The security measures she'd placed at every conceivable entrance to the disused construction site had turned out to be useless. The traps she'd set on the metal stairs to the foreman's office in which she'd been living had turned out to be *less* than useless. The big brute had entered silently and it had only been pure luck that she'd happened to look up in time.

She ran to her car, but if he was as meticulous as she thought he was, he'd already have sabotaged the engine, so she broke left, running for the tall fence that bordered the east side of the site. She heard quick footsteps behind her and decided to try to lose him in the maze of cargo containers. It was a moonless night, too dark to see much of anything, and she hoped he was finding it as difficult in this gloom as she was. There was a heavy *clang*, followed by footsteps on metal, and he was moving above her, across the top of the containers, aiming to cut her off before she reached the fence.

Marr doubled back, wishing that she'd had time to grab her gun off the table before she'd made that jump. Magic was all well and good, she often thought, but having a loaded gun in your hand was a reassurance like no other.

She ducked low and crept along, keeping her breathing under control. She couldn't hear him any more. He was either still up there and not moving, or he was down here, in the muck and the mud and the dark, with her. Possibly sneaking up on her right now. Marr glanced over her shoulder, saw nothing but shadows.

She tried to remember what Tesseract's chosen discipline was. He was an Adept, she knew that much, but beyond that, his magic was a mystery to her. She hoped it wasn't the ability to see in the dark. That would be just typical, and it'd fit right in with how her luck had been going these past few months. All she'd wanted to do was go home, for God's sake. Marr was from Boston, born and raised, and that's where she wanted to die. Not here, in wet and muddy Ireland.

She got on her belly and crawled through a gap between pallets. She took another look behind her, to make sure he wasn't reaching out to grab her ankle, and then considered her options. They weren't great, and they weren't many, and hiding wasn't one of them. He'd find her eventually, probably sooner rather than later. She could try the east fence again, or she could go all the way back to the entrance at the south. Heading west was out of the question, seeing as how there was nothing there but acres of flat ground with no cover.

Marr propped herself up on her elbows, the cold wetness seeping through her clothes, and looked straight out in front, due north. There was another fence there, higher than the east side, but it was closer, and at least there were pallets and machinery she could duck behind if she needed to.

She inched forward, out through the gap, coming up on her hunkers. There were a couple of barrels stacked up on top of each other, and she hurried to them. Still no sign of Tesseract.

Running bent over, she came up around a bulldozer and made a mad dash for the next piece of cover. The chain-link fence was maybe twenty strides away. It was tall, as high as a house, taller than she'd remembered, but Marr felt sure she could jump it. She allowed herself a moment to envy the Skeleton Detective and his newfound ability to fly. That would really come in handy right about now. She gauged the distance and felt the currents in the air, reckoning that she'd need a running start to clear the fence successfully.

She looked back, making sure Tesseract wasn't anywhere nearby. She scanned her surroundings carefully, methodically, pivoting her head slowly, on the alert for the slightest movement. It took her a full second to realise that she was looking straight at him as he ran at her. She couldn't help it – she gave a short yelp of fright and stumbled back, tripping over her own feet.

Slipping and sliding on the wet ground, Marr scrambled for the fence. She flung her arms wide, hands open and grasping, then pulled the air in around her and lifted herself up, away from the mud. She wasn't even halfway to the top when she realised she wasn't going to make it. She managed to steer herself closer and reached out, fingers slipping through the links just as she started to drop. Her body swung into the rattling fence, her fingers burning. She looked down, saw him looking up, silent behind his metal mask. She started climbing, using only her hands. She glanced down. Tesseract was climbing up after her.

God, but he was quick.

It started to rain again, and the droplets soon began to sting against her face. Tesseract was closing the gap between them with alarming speed, his long arms reaching further than hers, and his great muscles hauling his body after her without tiring. As for Marr, her muscles were already complaining, and as she neared the top, they were screaming. Still, better them than her, she reckoned.

Below her, Tesseract had stalled. It looked like he'd snagged that coat of his in the fence somehow. Marr couldn't spare the time to be smug about it, but she promised herself a smirk when this was all over.

She clambered over the top, pausing a moment to estimate how high up she was, and then let herself fall. The street rushed towards her, and as she prepared to use the air to slow her descent, she glanced at Tesseract. In an instant she saw that he hadn't stalled, but had been cutting through the links with a knife.

As she passed him on her way down, he reached through the fence and grabbed her arm. Her body jerked and twisted. She cried out and he held her for a moment, then let her fall. She tumbled head over heels to the street below. Her shoulder hit the pavement first and shattered, and her head smacked against the concrete. Marr lay there, waiting for Tesseract to jump down and finish the job. And then a familiar car came screeching around the corner, and she blacked out.

4

GRANDER SCALES

Skulduggery braked, the Bentley swerving to a perfect stop on the slippery road. Valkyrie threw the door open and jumped out. Davina Marr lay in a crumpled heap on the pavement, several bones obviously broken.

A man landed behind Marr, a big man in a metal mask, and Skulduggery appeared beside Valkyrie, gun in hand.

"You're Tesseract," he said. "You are, aren't you? Who hired you? Who are you working for?"

The man, Tesseract, didn't even look at him. His red eyes

were focused on Marr. He moved towards her and Skulduggery stepped into his path. Immediately, Tesseract grabbed the gun, twisting it from Skulduggery's grip. Skulduggery grabbed the bigger man's elbow and wrist and wrenched, and the gun fell back into his hand.

"Get her to the car!" Skulduggery ordered, and Valkyrie grabbed Marr and started dragging her away.

As they struggled for control of the weapon, Tesseract kicked Skulduggery's leg and Skulduggery kneed Tesseract's thigh. They headbutted each other as they locked and counter-locked, using moves Valkyrie had never seen before. She heard the gun *click*, but their hands were covering it so she couldn't see what was happening. Finally, Tesseract flipped Skulduggery over his hip, but Skulduggery took the gun with him. He rolled and came up, aiming dead-centre for Tesseract's chest, and the fight froze.

Valkyrie shoved Marr into the back seat of the Bentley, and looked back in time to see Tesseract hold out his fist, and slowly open his hand. Six bullets fell to the ground.

"I *thought* it was a bit light," Skulduggery muttered, putting the gun away.

Valkyrie considered helping, but she'd never even heard of this guy Tesseract, and she knew how dangerous it was to charge into a fight without knowing who your enemy was. Instead, she slipped in behind the wheel of the Bentley.

The priority here was Marr, and they had her, after all this time. Valkyrie wasn't about to risk letting her escape again. She put the Bentley in reverse, like she'd done a hundred times before under Skulduggery's tutelage, then yanked the wheel. The car spun and she put it in first. She sped away from the fight, rounded the corner and kept going. There was no other traffic on the road.

Valkyrie took another corner a little too sharply, but maintained control. Something moved in the rear-view mirror, and then Skulduggery was flying alongside the car. He nodded to her and she braked and slid over to the passenger side. Skulduggery got in behind the wheel and they took off again.

She frowned. "Are we not going back for him?"

"For Tesseract?" Skulduggery said. "Good God, no."

"But he's in shackles, right? You beat him?"

"I like to think I beat him in a moral sense, in that he's an assassin and I'm not, but apart from that, no, not really."

Valkyrie turned in her seat, looking at the dark street behind them, then settled back. "Who is he?"

"Assassin for hire, is all I know. I recognised him from his sheer size, and the fact that he wears a metal mask. I've never encountered him before. That's probably a good thing. But let's not dwell on the new enemy we might have made tonight. Let's dwell instead on the old enemy we've got in the back seat. Hello, Davina. You're under arrest for multiple counts of murder. You have the right to not much at all, really. Do you have anything to say in your defence?"

Marr remained unconscious.

"Splendid," Skulduggery said happily.

The Hibernian Cinema stood old and proud and slightly bewildered, like a senior citizen who'd wandered away from his tour group. It had no part in the Dublin that surrounded it. It hadn't been refurbished or refitted, it didn't have twenty screens on different floors and it didn't have banks of concession stands. What it did have were old movie posters on its walls, frayed carpeting, a single stall for popcorn and drinks, and a certain mustiness that agitated long-dormant allergies. The one screen it did possess only ever showed one thing – the black and white image of a brick wall with a door to one side.

But beyond that screen were corridors of clean white walls and bright lighting, rooms of scientific and mystical equipment, a morgue capable of dissecting a god and a Medical Bay that Valkyrie visited on a worryingly regular basis.

Kenspeckle Grouse shambled in, dressed in a bathrobe and slippers, what remained of his grey hair sticking up at odd angles. He looked grumpy, but then he always looked grumpy.

"What," he said, "do you want?"

"We have a patient for you," said Skulduggery, nodding to Davina Marr on the bed beside him.

Kenspeckle glared at the shackles around her wrists. "Don't know her," he said. "Take her to someone else. She's your prisoner, isn't she? Take her to one of those Sanctuary doctors, wake *them* up in the middle of the night."

"We can't do that. This is Davina Marr. She's the one who *destroyed* the Sanctuary."

Some of the grumpiness vanished from Kenspeckle's eyes, replaced by a kind of disgusted curiosity. "This is her, then? You finally found her?" He walked closer. "She's a bit the worse for wear, but I have to admit I'm surprised she's still alive. Are you getting less ruthless as you get older, Detective?"

"We didn't do this to her," Valkyrie said, not comfortable with where Kenspeckle's questions were heading. "We saved her, actually. She'd be dead if it wasn't for Skulduggery."

Kenspeckle pulled back one of Marr's eyelids. "I put that down to your good influence, Valkyrie. But that still doesn't explain why you haven't taken her to the authorities. You are, after all, Sanctuary Detectives once again, are you not?"

"We want to keep this quiet," Skulduggery said. "Things are too volatile at the moment. If we hand her over to the Cleavers, I doubt she'll even get a trial. They'll execute her on the spot."

Kenspeckle traced his hands lightly around Marr's head. "From what I remember, you've executed your fair share of guilty people in the past."

"I'm not here to argue with you, Professor. The fact is, I don't believe she was working alone when she decided to destroy the Sanctuary, and I fear that her allies, or her *bosses*, will try to have her killed before she can name them. I'm fairly confident they're the ones who hired the assassin."

"Ah," Kenspeckle said, "so it's not mercy that stays your hand – it's a grander scale of ruthlessness."

Skulduggery cocked his head. "This woman is responsible for the deaths of fifty people, but there are others who also share that responsibility. They're all going to pay."

"Well," Kenspeckle said, "justice can wait, can it not? Your prisoner has a serious head injury. She's staying with me until she's out of danger. It should be a few hours. A day at the most."

"She's going to need someone to stand guard over her."

"You think she poses a threat? She'll be unconscious until I say otherwise."

"And what if the assassin comes looking for her?"

"First he'd have to know who she's with, then where to find me, and lastly he'd have to get past my defences, for which he'd need an army. Leave me now. I'll get in touch when she's strong enough to answer your questions."

With nothing left for them to do, they walked back to the Bentley. Valkyrie buckled her seatbelt as they pulled out on to the road. Skulduggery was using the façade again. Ghastly Bespoke's façade gave him his own face every time, minus the scars, but Skulduggery hadn't been able to decide on one look, so China made it so that *his* façade changed every time. Same cheekbones, same jaw, but all the rest was brand-new.

"Could you drop me off at Gordon's?" Valkyrie asked.

Skulduggery raised an eyebrow – a newly acquired skill. "You don't want to go home to Haggard?"

"It's not that, it's just that I haven't been to Gordon's in a while, and it's nearly Christmas. Around this time every year when I was a kid, we'd go up there, to his big house. I loved that part of Christmas, because, finally, someone would talk to me like I was a person, you know? A grown-up person, not a child. That's what I loved about him the most."

"Ah, there it is," Skulduggery said, and nodded.

"Sorry?"

"That, right there. That story you just told. That little excerpt from your life. That's the most annoying thing about Christmas. Everyone has these little stories about what Christmas means to them. You don't get that at any other time of the year. You don't get people telling you what Easter means to them, or St Patrick's Day. But everyone opens up at Christmas time."

"Wow," Valkyrie said. "I never noticed before, but you're a grouch."

"No, I'm not."

"You're a Grinch."

"I am neither a Grinch nor a grouch. I like Christmas as much as the next person, so long as the next person is as unsentimental as I am."

"Sentimental's nice."

"You *hate* sentimental."

"But not at Christmas. At Christmas, sentimental is a perfectly fine thing to be. It is allowed. In moderation, naturally. I don't want anyone, you know, being sentimental around *me*, but in principle I have no problem with... uh..."

"What? What's wrong?"

"Um, the façade..."

Skulduggery tilted his head, and the left side of his face drooped down off his skull, looking like melted rubber.

"I think something's going a bit wonky," said Valkyrie.

Skulduggery felt his ear flapping against his lapel and took hold of his face with one hand and hoisted it back up again. He gathered a thick fold around his forehead, trying his best to manoeuvre an eye back into its socket. "This is a tad undignified," he murmured. "Do please tell me if we're about to crash into something."

"Maybe you should let me drive."

"I saw how you drove a few hours ago. I'm not letting you behind the wheel of this car ever again." His voice was muffled because his lips were sliding down his jaw. "Do I look better now?"

"Oh, much."

He did his best to keep his nose in one place.

"So will I pick you up from Gordon's once your lapse into sentimentality is over? We have that meeting to go to, in case you've forgotten."

"How could I have forgotten?" she asked dryly. "I've been looking forward to this incredibly boring meeting for days, I really and truly have, oh boy oh boy."

"You appear to have found a new level of sarcasm," Skulduggery nodded. "Impressive."

"And no, you don't have to pick me up. I'll get Fletcher to pop by. Of course, if you change your mind and decide I don't have to go to this incredibly boring meeting, I can take my time about it all, and really get the sentimentality out of my system for good."

"And deprive you of your chance to be there? I actually think you'll be surprised by how interesting it all is."

"I actually think I'd be *very* surprised."

"But we'll be electing a new Grand Mage. This is history in the making, Valkyrie."

"And how long do you think the new Grand Mage will last before he's either murdered or imprisoned?"

"You're too young to be so cynical."

"I'm not cynical. I just happen to *remember* the last four years. You give me one good reason why I should go. One good reason why I would be even remotely interested in attending."

"Erskine Ravel will be there."

"Well, OK then."

Skulduggery laughed, and let go of his face. After a dangerous quiver, it settled down and stopped misbehaving, apart from the ear that was slowly drifting towards his chin.

5

VALKYRIE'S DILEMMA

With the morning sun barely making an effort to leak through the windows, Valkyrie's dead uncle made a steeple of his fingers, and peered at her over the topmost peak. When he was alive, he would often do this while sitting in an armchair with his legs crossed, giving him the air of a wise and contemplative man. Now that he was dead and could no longer interact with the physical world, it merely gave him the air of a man in desperate need of a chair.

"You've discovered your true name," he said.

"Yes," Valkyrie responded.

"And your true name is Darquesse."

"That's right."

"And Darquesse is the sorcerer that all the psychics are having visions about – the one who's going to destroy the world."

"Correct."

"So *you're* going to destroy the world."

"It looks like it."

"And when did you discover all this?"

"About three months ago."

"And you're only telling me about it *now*?"

"Gordon, it's taken me this long to stop freaking out about it. I need your help."

Gordon began to pace the room. It was a big room, lined with bookcases and Gothic paintings. An oil portrait of a semi-clothed Gordon, his body rippling with muscles he had never possessed when he was alive, hung over the vast fireplace, glaring down at all who passed like a great and terrible god. Even though this house and the land around it had been left to Valkyrie, she still couldn't bring herself to take the painting down. It was far too amusing.

"Do you realise what this means for you?" Gordon asked, as

his slow pacing took him towards the corner of the room. "A sorcerer who knows their own true name has access to power other sorcerers can only dream about."

His image began to fade away, and Valkyrie cleared her throat loudly. Gordon stopped and swung round, pacing back the way he had come. Immediately, he became solid again. The Echo Stone which housed his consciousness sat in its cradle on the coffee table, glowing with a soothing blue light.

"I don't care about any of that," she said. "I saw one of these visions, OK? I saw a burning city and injured friends and I saw Darquesse – I saw *me* – kill my own *parents*."

"Now, just wait a second. From what you've told me about Cassandra Pharos's vision, your future self and Darquesse seem to be two distinctly separate entities."

"That's just because at no time in that vision was I ever seen hurting anyone. We saw *fragments* of what's going to happen. We saw Darquesse, *me*, as a figure in the distance, fighting and killing and murdering, and then we saw me, my *future* self, close up, feeling pretty bad about it all, which was nice of her, but she's undoubtedly a little fruitloops. Listen, it's taken a while for me to look at this and be logical about it, but obviously *someone* finds out what my true name is, and they use it to control me."

"Then you're going to have to seal your name," Gordon said.

"Do you know how I can do that?"

"No," he admitted. "I wrote about magic, but as you are aware, I never had the aptitude for it. Something like that, sealing your true name, is knowledge only a certain breed of sorcerer would have."

"I can't ask Skulduggery," Valkyrie said quietly. "I don't want him to know."

Gordon stopped pacing, and looked at her kindly. "He would understand, Valkyrie. Skulduggery has been through an awful lot."

"If he's so understanding, how come you still won't let me tell him you exist?"

"Well," Gordon said huffily, "that's different. That was never about him or anyone else. It was always about me, and my insecurities."

"Which you are now cured of, right?"

He hesitated. "In theory..."

"So you'd be fine with me telling Skulduggery that I talk to you on a regular basis?"

Gordon licked his lips. "I don't think that now is the perfect time for that. You have a lot on your plate, and I think

I can be of more use to you without the distraction of other people."

"You're scared."

"I'm not scared, I'm cautious. I don't know how my friends would react. I am not actually Gordon Edgley after all – I am merely a recording of his personality."

"But...?" Valkyrie raised her eyebrows.

"But," he said quickly, "that doesn't mean I'm not a person in my own right, with my own identity and value."

"Very good," she smiled. "You've been working on it."

"I have a lot of time for self-affirmation while I'm sitting in that little blue crystal, waiting for you to drop by."

"Is that your subtle way of telling me I should call round more?"

"I practically cease to exist when you're not here," Gordon said. "There's nothing subtle about it."

The alarm on Valkyrie's phone beeped once. "Fletcher will be here soon," she said, picking up the Echo Stone and its cradle. "We better get you back."

Gordon followed as she led the way out of the living room and up the stairs. "The big meeting is this afternoon, isn't it?"

"Yeah," she scowled. "Even after everything that's been happening, with everything that's hanging over me, I still have

41

to waste my time at this stupid thing. Skulduggery says it's important to see how this kind of politics works."

"You're lucky," Gordon said wistfully. "I would have loved to have been invited to something like that when I was alive."

"It's going to be a bunch of people talking about what we're going to do about setting up a new Sanctuary. What do I have to contribute to *that*?"

"I don't know. A general air of grumpiness?"

"Now *that* I can do."

They passed into the study, but instead of following her through the hidden doorway to the secret room where he kept the most valued pieces of his collection, Gordon went to a small bookshelf beside the window. "And how is Fletcher these days?"

"He's grand."

"Has he met your parents?"

Valkyrie frowned. "No. And he's not going to."

"You don't think they'd approve?" Gordon asked as he scanned the books.

"I think they'd start asking all kinds of awkward questions. And I don't think they'd like the fact that my boyfriend is older than me."

"He's eighteen, you're almost sixteen," Gordon said. "That's not *drastically* older."

"If I need to tell them, I will. Right now, Skulduggery has taken responsibility for asking every single awkward question that my parents could ever *possibly* ask, so you needn't worry."

"This one," said Gordon, pointing to a thin notebook. "In here there are directions to a woman who might be able to help you."

"She can seal my name?"

"Not her personally, but I think she knows someone who can."

"Who is she?"

"*Who* isn't important. *What*, however, is. She's a banshee."

"Seriously?"

"Most banshees are harmless," Gordon said. "They provide a service, more then anything else."

"What kind of service?"

"If you hear a banshee's wail, it's a warning that you're going to die. I'm not sure of the advantage of such a service, but it's a service nonetheless. Twenty-four hours after you hear it, the Dullahan gets you."

"What's a Dullahan?"

"He's a headless horseman, in the service of the banshee."

"Headless?"

"Yes."

"Seriously?"

"Yes."

"So he has no head?"

"That's usually what headless means."

"No head at all?"

"You're really getting hung up on this headless thing, aren't you?"

"It's just kind of silly, even for us."

"Yet you spend your days with a living skeleton."

"But at least Skulduggery has a head."

"True."

"He even has a spare."

"Are we going to get past this now?"

"Yes. Sorry. Carry on."

"Thank you. The Dullahan drives a carriage, the Coach-a-Bowers, that you can only see when it's right up beside you. He is not a friendly fellow."

"Probably because he has no head."

"That may have something to do with it."

"So this banshee," Valkyrie said, "is she one of the harmless ones, or the harmful?"

"Now *that* I do not know. Banshees are an unsociable bunch

at the best of times. If she isn't too pleased to see you, though..."

"Yes?"

"I'd recommend putting your hands over your ears if she opens her mouth."

Valkyrie looked at him. "Right," she said. "Thanks for that."

"When do you plan to approach her?"

"Soon, I suppose. I mean, as soon as I can. I want this over with. I think I'll... Tonight."

"Really?"

"Yes. I have to, Gordon. If I put it off, I'll never do it. I'll give Skulduggery some excuse. He won't miss me."

"Valkyrie, from what I know of it, sealing your name is a major procedure. You have to be sure, going in, that this *is* the best thing to do."

"I'm *going* to be sure. You remember when Dusk bit me? He tasted something in my blood, something that marked me out as different. I think that whatever he tasted has to do with Darquesse. So I'm going to get a second opinion."

Gordon frowned. "You're going to get someone else to taste your...? Oh, I see. You're talking about *him*."

"Caelan will be able to tell me what Dusk sensed. If it's bad,

I won't need any more proof or prodding. I'll know this is something I have to do."

"Right," Gordon said gently.

Valkyrie nodded, feeling an unwelcome mixture of apprehension and uncertainty. She left the Echo Stone in the hidden room and took the notebook from the shelf, flicking through the pages until she got to the part about the banshee. She put the notebook in her jacket pocket and went down to the living room. Her phone beeped again, and a moment later Fletcher Renn appeared beside the fireplace. Blond hair standing on end, lips always ready to kiss or smirk, one hand behind his back, the other with a thumb hooked into the belt loops of his jeans.

"I'm gorgeous," he said.

Valkyrie sighed. "Are you, now?"

"Do you ever just look at me and think, God he's gorgeous? Do you? I do, all the time. I think *you're* gorgeous too, of course."

"Cheers."

"You've got lovely dark eyes, and lovely dark hair, and your face is all pretty and stuff. And I love the way you dress in black, and I love the new clothes."

"It's a jacket, Fletch."

"I love the new jacket," he insisted. "Ghastly really made a lovely, lovely jacket." He grinned.

"You look wide awake," she said. "You're never wide awake at this hour of the morning."

"I've been researching. You're not the only one who likes to read books, you know. Apparently, my power will increase if I work at it a little, so I thought I'd give it a try. I was told there was this book in Italy, written by a famous Teleporter – dead now, obviously – that could really help me, so I went there and got it."

"Good man."

"But it was written all in Italian, so I left it on the shelf and went to Australia for ice cream." He brought his other hand out from behind his back, holding an ice-cream cone. "Got one for you."

"Fletcher, it's winter."

"Not in Australia."

"We're not *in* Australia."

"I'll take you to Sydney for five minutes, you can eat the ice cream while we watch the sunset, and then we'll come back to the misery here."

Valkyrie sighed. "Your power is wasted on you."

"My power is brilliant. Everyone wishes they had my power."

"I don't. I quite like being able to hurl people away from me just by moving the air."

"Well, every *non-violent* person wishes they had my power, how's that?"

Valkyrie frowned. "I'm not a violent person."

"You punch people every day."

"Not *every* day."

"Val, you know I think you're great, and I think you're the coolest chick I've ever met, and the prettiest girl ever – but you get into a hell of a lot of fights. Face it, you lead a violent life."

She wanted to protest, but no argument sprang to mind. Fletcher stopped holding out the ice cream, and started licking it instead, already forgetting what they'd just been talking about. Valkyrie checked the time, forcing her attention back to the here and now.

"Are you getting me anything for Christmas?" Fletcher asked, and Valkyrie found herself grinning despite everything.

"Yes. You better be getting *me* something."

He shrugged. "Of course I am."

"It better be amazing."

"Of course it is. Hey, this time next year, you'll have someone *else* to buy presents for. When's your mum due?"

"Middle of February. I'm going to be asked to babysit, you know. How am I supposed to do that?"

"Get your reflection to do it."

"I'm not leaving the baby with the *reflection*. Are you nuts? But I don't even know how to hold a baby. Their heads are so big. Aren't babies' heads abnormally large? I'm not sure I'm going to be a good big sister. I hope she doesn't take after me. I'd like her to have friends."

"You have friends."

"I'd like her to have friends who weren't hundreds of years older than her."

"Have you realised that you're referring to the baby as 'her'?"

"Am I? I suppose I am. I don't know. It just feels like it's going to be a girl."

"Do you think she'll be magic?"

"Skulduggery says it's possible. Of course, that doesn't mean she'll ever *find out* about magic. Take my cousins, for example."

"Ah, the infamous Toxic Twins."

"They're descended from the Last of the Ancients the same as I am, but we'll never *know* if they can do magic, because they don't know magic even *exists*."

"So if you don't want your sister involved in this crazy life of

49

yours, you can just not tell her. And in twenty-five years, she'll be looking at you, going, 'Hey, sis, how come we look like we're exactly the same age?' Will you tell her *then* that magic slows the aging process?"

"I'll probably just tell her that my natural beauty makes me look eternally young. She's my little sister – she'll believe anything I tell her."

"To be honest, Val, I love the fact that this is happening. Once you have a sister, or a brother, that looks up to you and needs you, it might make you stop and think before rushing into dangerous situations."

"I do stop and think."

"And then you rush in anyway."

"There's still stopping and thinking involved."

Fletcher smiled. "Sometimes I just worry about you."

"Your concern is touching."

"You're not taking me even a little bit seriously, are you?"

"I can't take you seriously, Fletch, you have a dollop of ice cream on your nose. Besides, we can have this conversation a thousand times – it's not going to stop me going out there and doing what I do."

Fletcher finished off the cone and wiped the ice cream from his face.

"Are you so determined to be the hero?" he asked softly.

She kissed him, and didn't answer. He was wrong, of course. It wasn't about her being the hero – not any more. It was just about her trying not to be the villain.

6

THE NEW MESSIAH

Sneaking up on someone who can see into the future is not as impossible a task as many people think. For one thing, the future changes. Details shift, circumstances alter, and while the universe is struggling to realign itself into some semblance of balance, opportunity has its moment to present itself. The trick is to be a constant destabilising influence in a world that really just wants to be left alone.

Solomon Wreath was confident that he could be just such a destabilising influence. Leaving many of his decisions open to chance, he had approached the tattoo parlour three times already, and by the toss of a coin he had walked on by. The fourth toss of the coin, however, brought him to the door, and had him climbing the narrow stairs, black bag in one hand, cane in the other. No sound coming from above him. No whine of the tattooist's needle. No chat, laughter or yelp. He could practically sense the trap waiting for him, but this didn't slow his step.

At the top of the stairs he turned and walked through the doorway, and that was when the skinny man with the Pogues T-shirt came at him with a cushion. Not being the world's deadliest weapon, the cushion bounced softly off Wreath's shoulder, and the skinny man did his best to run by. Wreath dropped his cane, caught the man and threw him against a chair that looked like it belonged in a dental surgery. The skinny man fell awkwardly over it.

"Finbar Wrong," Wreath said, putting the black bag on a nearby table. "May I call you Finbar? I assume you know who I am."

Finbar sprang to his feet, hands held out in front of him, fingers rigid. "I do," he said, "and I feel I have to warn you, man, you can't beat me. I've seen this fight already, and I know every move you're gonna make."

Shadows curled around Wreath's cane, and brought it up off the floor and into his waiting hand.

Finbar nodded. "I knew you were gonna do that."

Wreath went to walk around the chair. Finbar moved in the opposite direction. Wreath turned, went the other way, and so did Finbar.

Wreath sighed. "This is ridicul—"

"*Ridiculous!*" Finbar interrupted quickly. "See? I've already lived through this encounter. You'd better walk away now, dude, save yourself a whole lot of pain."

"If you *have* seen this fight, if you knew *precisely* when I would arrive, then why did you attack me with a cushion?"

Finbar hesitated. "I'm... I'm toying with you, is what I'm doing. Hitting you with a *cushion* instead of my fists of fury is gonna, like, take *longer*, draw out your agony. Kinda like water torture, with cushions. Cushion torture."

"It doesn't *sound* very painful."

"Well, I haven't really settled on a name for it..."

"You're a trained fighter, I take it?"

"Oh, yeah."

"You're a bit thin, aren't you? You're practically malnourished."

"Looks can be deceiving, man. After all, the strongest muscle in the human body is the *brain*."

"Well then, as along as you don't hit me with your brain, I should be OK."

Finbar suddenly broke for the door. Wreath came up behind him, whacked the cane into the back of his legs. Finbar crashed into the wall.

"Ow," he moaned.

Wreath took a hold of him and dragged him back, threw him into the dentist's chair. "When did you first have a vision that I would be paying you a visit?"

"Last night," he moaned.

"And what did you do?"

"I sent Sharon and my kid away. I was gonna join them, but the vision changed, and you weren't gonna come."

"But then a few minutes ago..."

He nodded. "Had another one. Told me you were about to climb the stairs. Only weapon I had was the cushion."

"Which is not technically considered a weapon."

Finbar glared. "A true master can make *anything* into a weapon."

"But you're *not* a true master, Finbar." Wreath prodded him with the cane, forcing him to sit back. "Did your vision tell you *why* I was coming to see you?"

"I didn't really get that far."

"I need you to do me a favour. I want you to look into Valkyrie Cain's future, and tell me what you see."

"Why don't you just ask her?"

"I need something more than what you've already seen. I need you to look harder."

"Can't do it," Finbar said, shaking his head. "I won't do it. Val's a friend of mine. You can torture me all you want."

"Can I?"

He paled. "Metaphorically speaking."

Wreath smiled, and shadows crept up the chair, wrapping themselves around Finbar's arms and legs before he could even struggle. Wreath went to the black bag on the table. "It's OK. I know it would probably take a lot for you to betray a friend like that. So I'm taking the option away from you."

From the bag, Wreath took a glass sphere, encased in a stone shell.

Quickly realising that he couldn't break his bonds, Finbar settled back into the chair. "You're bribing me with a snow globe?" he asked. "That's a bit... insulting, don't you think?"

"This isn't for you."

Now Finbar could see the darkness swirling in the sphere, and his face slackened and his voice cracked. "That's a Soul Catcher."

"Yes, it is. And its occupant is the Remnant who caused everyone so much trouble a few months ago. This is the little guy who possessed Kenspeckle Grouse, who went on to repair the Desolation Engine that destroyed the Sanctuary. This is not a very nice Remnant."

Finbar licked his lips nervously. "You can't put it in me. You just *can't*, man. No, listen, that thing is, it's *evil*, right? Once it's in me, it'll lie to you, tell you whatever it thinks you wanna hear."

"It will tell me whatever I want to *know*, Finbar, which is not quite the same thing."

"Aw, please, don't do this." The man was almost crying.

"I'll take it out of you immediately after," Wreath assured him. "You'll black out; you won't remember a thing."

"I don't want it in me. It'll change me."

"Only for a few minutes."

Wreath turned the sphere in the stone, and stepped back.

The darkness drained out of the Soul Catcher as the Remnant flitted straight to Finbar. He turned his head and shut his eyes and clamped his mouth shut, but the Remnant would not be denied. Things that may have been hands prised his jaws apart. Wreath watched, fighting the urge to suck the foul creature back into its prison.

Finbar tried to scream as the Remnant, no more than a streak of twisted darkness, clambered its way down his throat. The scream choked and the throat bulged. Finbar's body thrashed, but Wreath's restraints held. Finbar suddenly went limp. A moment passed, and dark veins spread beneath his skin and his lips turned black. Then his eyes opened.

"Why is it," Finbar said, "that every time I'm set free, I have to share a body that isn't in the peak of physical perfection? Last time it was an old man. Now it's... this."

"I didn't release you for a casual conversation," Wreath said. "I just want to know what I want to know."

"And why would I help *you* dig up information on my good buddy Valkyrie?"

"She isn't your friend," Wreath said. "She's *Finbar Wrong's* friend."

"And there you go, man, making the mistake that everyone makes. I *am* Finbar Wrong."

"No, you're a Remnant."

"To be honest with you there, a Remnant isn't really much more than *intent*. It flies around being angry and doesn't think too much about anything, y'know? It doesn't have a personality, or a real consciousness to speak of. But when it inhabits a body, that all changes. It's whole again. I *am* Finbar Wrong, but I'm also the Remnant inside him. We're very happy together, as you can see." He smiled, and the black veins receded and the darkness disappeared from his lips.

"It's easy for you to pass for normal, isn't it?" Wreath asked. "To hide the tell-tale signs that mark the possessed?"

"We can hide it when we need to, yeah."

"And it's good to be out of the Soul Catcher, yes?"

"Oh, yeah," Finbar laughed. "That thing is even worse than being in that room in the Midnight Hotel where they kept us locked up."

"Now that you've tasted freedom, do you want more? I can give you more. I can let you go."

"A few moments ago you said you were gonna separate us immediately after."

"I'm a Necromancer. I lied to make it easier on... you. The old you. Look into the future for me, and tell me what you see."

"And what makes you think I'll be able to see anything new?"

"Because you and I both know that Sensitives are wary about pushing themselves too hard. Seeing the future is a dangerous line of work. Minds can snap."

"That they can."

"But your mind is reinforced now, isn't it? It's stronger. So you can look further, and harder, until you see what you need to see."

"This is all very true," Finbar nodded. "But why should I trust you? The last people to ask me a favour put me in an old man's body. Now, I'm not denying I had fun being Kenspeckle Grouse for a day, especially when it came time to hammer nails through Tanith Low's hands, but they cheated me. They wouldn't let me go when they said they would."

"Scarab has never been a trustworthy man."

"And *you* are? You're a *Necromancer*."

"Then how about this? You look into the future for me, or I'll kill you. Remnants can't survive in something dead, am I right? So the moment Finbar's body dies, the Remnant inside him dies too. Do you want to die? Either of you?"

Finbar smiled. "You're talking like there are two of us in here, man. There's not. You had Finbar, you had the Remnant, and when you put them together, you get me. And I happen to think that the world would miss me too much if you killed me."

Wreath smiled back. "I thought you'd see it my way."

"I'm gonna need a few things before I start, though. Herbs, potions, a backrub..."

"You have three seconds to begin."

"A very *quick* backrub, then."

Wreath raised the cane, and Finbar laughed. "OK, OK! I

suppose I could do without the luxuries, just this one time. You're gonna have to back off – I'm not gonna be able to attain the required level of relaxation if you're hovering over me."

Wreath nodded. "Get it done, Remnant, or you're going back in the bottle."

"Chill," Finbar breathed, closing his eyes. "My old buddy Val," he murmured. "Are you going to show me why everyone's so interested in you, are you? Are you going to show me what's in store for you...?"

Wreath suppressed a sigh while Finbar prattled on, his voice growing softer and softer. He'd never had much time for Sensitives. They'd deliberately chosen a branch of magic where you reached out with your feelings instead of your fists. They were, in his opinion, a bunch of spaced-out, peace-loving hippies, and he'd *never* liked hippies. The 1960s and 70s had been particularly annoying times for him.

"There she is," Finbar said, a slight smile on his face. "Found her."

"How far ahead are you?" Wreath asked quickly.

"Hard to say, man... She looks a little older... She's got a tattoo..."

"Is she a Necromancer?"

Finbar's brow creased over his closed eyes. "Don't know..."

"What's she doing?"

"Walking..."

"Where?"

"In the ruins."

Wreath shook his head. "That's with Darquesse, right? I'm not interested in that. You need to find out if Valkyrie is the Death Bringer."

"I can only see what I see," Finbar said in a sing-song voice. "My sight is drawn to the big moments..."

"Then look away," Wreath snarled, but his impatience went unnoticed.

"I've never seen this much detail," Finbar continued, deep in the trance. "I've always flinched... But now I can see it all... So many dead... It's wonderful..."

Wreath held his tongue.

"I'm looking at Darquesse now... She's magnificent... She's striding through the city, death all around her... You'd like this, dude. So much death..."

"I didn't ask for a vision of Darquesse, I asked for a vision of Valkyrie." Wreath's eyes narrowed. "Unless..."

Finbar smiled in his dream-state. "Unless?"

"Is Valkyrie still there? Can you see her?"

"I can sense her presence, but all I can see is Darquesse."

"Maybe that's it," Wreath said, sudden excitement burning through him. "Maybe that's how she does it. If Valkyrie *is* the Death Bringer, maybe she's the one who steps up and fights. Maybe she's the one who stops Darquesse and then *this*, her victory, is what leads to the Passage. This is how she saves the world."

"I don't see any of that," Finbar said. "All I see is Darquesse." His smile was replaced by a grimace. "This is painful, by the way..."

"Keep looking."

"It hurts my head."

"Keep looking or you'll *lose* that head."

"I'll keep looking then."

Blood dripped from Finbar's nose. Wreath said nothing.

"I've found her again," Finbar said happily.

"Valkyrie?"

"Darquesse. I'm... I'm drawn to her... I don't have a choice. She is... everything. She's so cold. I'm trying to get in closer, but she's... She's unlike anything I've ever *seen*..."

"Can you see a weakness? How can Valkyrie destroy her?"

"Darquesse will *not* be destroyed!" Finbar snarled suddenly. "She is everything!"

"Tell me her weakness."

"She has none! She is perfection!"

"Then who is she? Where does she come from?"

Finbar strained harder, and blood began leaking from his ears. "The shadows are heavy around her... I'm trying to see her face... She's looking away from me... No, wait, she's turning, she's turning, I can see her..."

Finbar stopped talking.

"Well?" Wreath pressed. "Can you see her face? What does she look like? Who is she?"

Finbar's eyes opened. He blinked up at Wreath. "This changes everything."

Wreath leaned in close. "Who is she, damn it?"

"You Necromancers have your messiah," Finbar said, "now we Remnants have ours."

The black veins appeared again, and his head shot forward and crunched against Wreath's nose. Wreath stumbled back, cursing, feeling his shadow restraints collapse under Finbar's Remnant-enhanced strength. Hands grabbed him, and suddenly he was flying into the far wall. He crashed through a shelf and sent equipment spilling out across the floor.

"Hope you don't mind, man," Finbar said, smiling at him, "but I'm gonna take you over for a bit. I have a brand-new mission, and I need an upgrade."

Wreath tasted his own blood. His cane was on the floor behind him. There were two ways out of this room – the door and the window. The window was closer.

Finbar opened his mouth wide. Wreath glimpsed the Remnant start to climb out and then he spun, snatching up his cane and using the shadows to smash the window. He leaped through the broken glass without the slightest hesitation, landing painfully on the cobbled street, sending people scattering all around him. He didn't look at their shocked faces. He didn't look back at Finbar, standing at the window. He just ran.

7

BLOOD

Valkyrie took a taxi to St Anne's Park, which was still covered in a fine frosting of white that the weak sun was failing to melt away. She passed over the gurgling stream, smiling at a dog that was being taken for a walk. Her breath came out in puffs of cloud, and her hands were jammed in her pockets. She moved off the well-worn trail into the trees. Dead twigs cracked under her boots.

Caelan was standing on an embankment that dipped five metres down. He didn't look round as she approached. Instead, he kept his gaze on an old couple below him, out for a brisk midday stroll. Valkyrie wondered, briefly, if he was hungry.

"I need your help," she said, and watched him turn his eyes to her. Being held in his gaze had become an electric experience that was as addictive as it was unsettling. She didn't like this power he had over her. Being around him was like being around China, but with China she at least had the knowledge that the attraction was coerced through use of magic. With Caelan, though, the attraction was real, and so it was a lot more dangerous.

"I'm waiting," he said, with a slight smile, and she realised she hadn't spoken a word for the last few seconds. She looked away, letting her hair fall over her face to hide the blush creeping through her cheeks.

"You're probably not going to like it," she said, "so it'd be a huge favour I'd have to pay back. The problem is that I can't really tell you why I need this done. You've just got to trust me when I say I have my reasons."

"What do you need?"

Valkyrie hesitated. "I need you to taste my blood."

Caelan's smile froze on his lips. "You can't be serious."

"Dusk bit me," she said. "You know how much he wanted to kill me, and he had his chance, but he didn't take it. Haven't you ever wondered why he let me go?"

"Because I stopped him," Caelan replied gruffly.

"No. You arrived after he'd pushed me away. He told Billy-Ray Sanguine that he tasted my blood and... I don't know. Whatever happened, whatever was in my blood, it changed his mind. He no longer wants to kill me. They both think it's a lot crueller to let me live."

"You want me to tell you what's so special about your blood?"

"Yes."

"Dusk is hundreds of years older than me. He could detect a thousand different nuances in your blood that I couldn't *begin* to identify. Dusk is a connoisseur. I'm not."

"But you can try."

"There's no point."

"Caelan, there's something wrong with me, do you understand? There's something wrong with who I am and Dusk knew straight away, from one tiny bite. You might not have his experience, but I need you to *try.*"

"You don't know what you're asking. It's far too dangerous."

"I'm used to dangerous."

"For *me*, Valkyrie. It's too dangerous for *me*. I don't know how Dusk managed to deny himself, but I'm not that strong. If I bite you, I won't stop feeding until you're dead."

"Then don't bite me. I'll cut my finger – you can taste a drop."

"Would you please remember who you're talking to? I'm a vampire! There's a reason I'm classed as a monster! You really think that letting me taste a drop of your blood is a good idea? Really? You think that won't drive me insane? One drop and I'd need the rest. I'd need all of it."

"You've still got a mind. You don't lose the ability to think, do you? You're not an animal."

"That's precisely what I am. You look at me while the sun is shining, and you think this is me. This is Caelan. You think the vampire is the thing that comes out at night, then goes away in the morning and Caelan comes back. You don't understand yet that the vampire *is* Caelan.

"This face is a mask. This skin is a disguise. Beneath it is the real me, Valkyrie. I'm not a tortured soul. I'm not a brooding romantic figure. I'm a monster, and not a moment goes by when I don't want to rip your throat out. No other vampire on the planet wants anything to do with me, and I really don't want to be cornered by the Skeleton Detective and his vengeance-hungry friends after I'm done feeding on your corpse. I quite like immortality. You get very used to it after a while."

Valkyrie looked at him, but didn't speak, and the anger slowly left him, until they were just two people, standing there in silence.

"You know," she said at last, "that's the most words I've ever heard you speak."

Caelan nodded. "I was just thinking the same thing."

"You feeling OK?"

"Vocal cords are a little sore."

"You might want to sit down."

He smiled, and she smiled back.

"I need you to do this."

His smile vanished. "I'm telling you, no."

"Listen to me, OK? I'm working on something, something to help me, something that could hopefully solve all my problems. But the thing is, it's dangerous. And I mean really dangerous. I might not live through it. And I can't tell Skulduggery or Tanith or Fletcher because they'll try to stop me."

"But you can tell me because you think I won't try to stop you?"

"No, I'm not telling you either. But before I do this, I have to know if this is the right thing to do. I need to know what Dusk saw, or what he felt, or what he sensed. If it's as bad as I think it is, then I'll go through with this dangerous thing because it'll be my only option. If it isn't as bad as I think, I won't. Simple as that."

Caelan turned away, and didn't speak for a long time.

"Fine," he said at last. "But afterwards, it would probably be best if we never saw each other again."

"That's a bit dramatic, isn't it?"

"Perhaps."

"But that's stupid. Why should we never see each other?"

"You say that like you'd miss me."

"Of course I'd miss you. You're my friend."

"No, I'm not."

She frowned. "You're not?"

"You and me could never just be friends, Valkyrie. We were fated to either be nothing to each other, or everything."

She stared at him, struggling to make sense of what he was saying. "Uh…"

"Eloquent as usual."

"I mean… Caelan, I'm with Fletcher. And I *like* Fletcher, and I don't want to hurt you, but I… I don't know how I feel about you. This is a bit of a surprise to me, to be honest."

"You truly didn't know how I felt?"

"I really and truly didn't. I'm sorry if you think I did."

"I see."

She looked at him as he stepped back. "And now I feel awful."

"Don't," said Caelan.

"I can't help it. Do you... I hope you don't think I was leading you on, or anything."

He shook his head, but kept his eyes down. "Of course not. This is my fault."

"It's no one's fault, Caelan. You didn't do anything wrong. It's just, you know, I'm with Fletcher, and I never really thought about... the possibility of you."

"Because I'm a vampire," he said softly, like he was cursing his very soul.

"That's part of it," admitted Valkyrie. "But most of all it's because I'm fifteen and you're, like, a hundred."

"Ah," he said, cracking a smile. "I'm too old for you."

"Ever so slightly."

"And there is no part of you that wonders what it would be like?"

She swallowed. "I didn't... I didn't say *that*..."

"You need me to do this?"

"Yes. I do."

"Very well." He stepped up to her, one hand at her shoulder, the other sweeping her hair slowly from her neck. "I'm sorry to say this will hurt."

"I've been bitten before," said Valkyrie, and gritted her teeth.

Caelan pulled her towards him and she waited. When she was this close to Fletcher, she could feel his warmth, the heat emanating from him with each rapid heartbeat, but there was no warmth coming from Caelan. He was cold as smooth stone. Even though his mouth was a centimetre from her bare skin, she felt no breath. The fingers of his right hand curled in the collar of her jacket, the fingers of his left in her hair. She waited for his teeth. His cold body sagged, and he stepped back.

"I can't," he murmured. "I'd tear your throat out." He took a penknife from his pocket, slid the blade free, and gave it to her. "Just a drop. No more, Valkyrie, OK? I should be able to handle a drop. I think."

She pressed the blade into the pad of her fingertip, wincing as it pierced the skin. A drop of blood swelled up, and she brushed it with the knife and handed it back to him. Caelan hesitated, then brought the knife to his lips, running his tongue the length of the blade. He worked the blood around in his mouth, and as he did so, he folded the penknife and put it away. His movements were slow and deliberate; his eyes were closed. He swallowed, and licked his lips, like a lion standing over a felled deer.

Valkyrie had a sudden urge to step away.

"Caelan?" she said softly.

He was on her, lifting her off her feet and driving her back, teeth bared and diving for her throat. She twisted in his grip and hit a tree and he moved from her throat to her mouth and kissed her, his mouth crushing against hers. The kiss took her by complete surprise, and she hung there for a long moment before she realised she was kissing him back. She felt her arms wrap round his neck, felt his hard chest press against her. Then something sparked in Valkyrie's mind.

She pushed off against the tree with one foot while she tripped him with the other. They both fell to the ground, and she rolled off him and got to her feet. She tried to speak, but he was already behind her, his cold hands on her face, turning her head to kiss her again. Valkyrie folded into him, weakness flooding her body, before she forced strength back into it. She broke off the kiss and leaned away.

"This is not going to happen," she breathed.

"It already is," he said, his eyes dark.

"What did you see? Caelan! My blood. What did you see?"

He smiled. "Nothing. I tasted your blood and saw nothing."

"You're sure?"

"I don't know what insight Dusk gained, but I gained nothing. The only difference between your blood and anyone else's is... history."

"What do you mean?"

"It's old blood. It stretches back to power."

"To the Last of the Ancients?"

"That's probably it." His hand reached out to her and she slapped it away. His smile broadened. "But everyone knows you're descended from the Ancients. I can't see why it should come as such a big revelation to Dusk."

"Maybe he saw something else."

"Very possible. I've changed my mind, you know."

"About what?"

"About how we should spend some time apart."

"Caelan..."

"Now I think we should spend more time *together*."

"I think I need to go now."

Valkyrie went to walk by him and he laughed, and grabbed her hand. When she swung back to face him, his laugh was gone. "Fletcher's a boy," he said.

"That's why they call it a boyfriend."

"We're meant for each other."

"Holy God," she said, "do you always come on this strong?"

Caelan looked like he was about to sneer, then he frowned, and backed off. "I told you," he murmured, looking away. "I'm not... I'm not always in control."

Valkyrie took the opportunity to hurry away.

"Thank you," she called over her shoulder.

Caelan didn't answer.

8

THE ZOMBIE KING

The refrigerated van pulled in to the side of the road. Seconds passed, and the driver got out. He was a middle-aged man with bad skin. He wasn't very bright and tended to say stupid things that annoyed his master. His master was a great and terrible man. His master was the Killer Supreme. His master was the Zombie King.

Thrasher opened the rear door and Vaurien Scapegrace, the Zombie King, stood there majestically, blinking against the cold afternoon sunlight.

"We have arrived?" he asked imperiously.

"We're here," Thrasher said, nodding his idiot head. "We got lost for a little bit. I took a wrong turn, had to stop and ask for directions. I had a map with me, but it's pretty old, and with all these new one-way systems it's pretty hard to..."

And he prattled on, annoying the Zombie King with mind-numbingly boring detail. Not for the first time, Scapegrace wished he'd picked someone else to be his first zombie recruit. Every recruit *after* Thrasher decayed at the normal speed for a dead body, but Thrasher had – unfortunately – inherited some of Scapegrace's longevity.

But even the great Zombie King was looking poorly these days. Months earlier, his face had been badly burned by Valkyrie Cain. He had tried to peel the burnt skin off in giant flakes, but that only made things worse. His body would not repair itself, and so the disfigurement stayed, and occasionally another bit of him would fall off or stop working. Survival had become his only ambition. He went everywhere in this refrigerated van, he stayed out of the sun as much as possible, and he covered himself in car fresheners that struggled to mask the stench of rotting meat with sickly wafts of pine.

Survival. That's what it was all about. And that's why he was here today. Scapegrace stepped out of the van, on to the road.

"What do you need me to do, Master?" Thrasher asked, eagerness ripening his features.

"Stay here," Scapegrace replied, "and don't annoy me. How is my face?"

Thrasher hesitated. "It's... good. Fine. The make-up is... it really hides the, uh, the worst of the scarring."

"And my suit? Do I have any bits on it?" His ear had fallen off the day before. He'd stuck it back on with glue.

"It looks clean, sir."

"Excellent. Back in the van you go, Thrasher."

"Yes, sir... only..."

Scapegrace sighed. "What?"

"Don't you think I should be the one to talk to these people, Master? They are civilians, and I don't have the... distinguishing features that may alarm them..."

"Nonsense. I have it all worked out. I have my plan, and I've accounted for every single possibility. Every question they are likely, or even not so likely, to ask, I have prepared an answer for. My backstory is rock solid. My lies are intricate and one hundred per cent infallible. You'd only mess it all up."

"Yes, Master."

"Back in the van, moron."

Thrasher bowed, and did as he was bid. Scapegrace

79

adjusted his tie, then strode purposefully along the pavement. The road was a cul-de-sac, with only three buildings on it – a funeral parlour on either side, and a large house at the end with a car outside.

Scapegrace entered the first funeral parlour. A man in a sombre suit hurried up to him, took one look at his face and faltered.

"It looks worse than it is," Scapegrace chuckled good-naturedly.

"I... see," said the man.

"It was the same accident that killed my brother," Scapegrace continued, realising that he should probably stop chuckling. "It's a tragic shock. We're all very saddened by his loss."

The funeral director shook Scapegrace's hand, and gave him a sad smile. "Would you like to sit down?" he asked gently.

"I would, yes. I'm feeling quite faint, because of the loss of my dead brother."

The funeral director showed him to a comfortable chair, then sat behind his big desk and solemnly opened a ledger. He picked up what looked to be an expensive pen, and raised his eyes to Scapegrace. "May I ask your name?"

Scapegrace had rehearsed this part a dozen times, coming

up with answers for every possible question. This was an easy one. "Elvis O'Carroll."

The funeral director hesitated, then nodded, and wrote it down. "And your brother's?"

"I'm sorry?"

"Your brother's name?"

Scapegrace froze. It had all been going so well. "My brother's name," he managed, "is... a name that makes me cry every time I hear it. His name, my brother's name, my dead brother, is..." His mind raced, careered off walls and stumbled over hurdles. A name. A simple name. All he needed was a simple name to get to the next stage of the conversation, and he could not think of one. Aware that he was staring at the funeral director with a perplexed look on his face, Scapegrace seized a random name from history. "Adolf," he blurted.

The funeral director stared at him. "I'm sorry?"

"Adolf O'Carroll," Scapegrace continued, trying to be as calm as possible. "That's with two L's at the end."

"Your brother's name was Adolf?"

"Yes. Do you find something wrong with that? It's a common name in my family. I had an uncle Adolf, and a great-aunt Adolf."

"A great-aunt? You realise, of course, that Adolf is traditionally a man's name...?"

"Well, that makes sense, as my great-aunt was traditionally a man."

"You do seem to have an interesting family, Mr O'Carroll," the funeral director said politely as he scribbled notes.

"Please," Scapegrace said. "Call me Elvis."

"Indeed. May I inquire as to what service you wish us to provide for you, during this trying time? The funeral, of course, is what we specialise in, but we also—"

"Embalming," Scapegrace said. "Do you do your own embalming?"

"We prepare the departed for their final resting place, yes."

"And you do that here?"

"On the premises, yes. We have a staff of professionals who take care to treat each individual with the utmost respect. We have found there to be dignity in death, as there is in life."

"How long does it take?"

"The embalming process?"

"How long does it take to stop the decomposition?"

"I'm not sure I understand... What exactly are you asking us to do?"

"I want him preserved."

The funeral director put down his pen, and interlaced his fingers. "Are you... Are you asking us to perform taxidermy?"

"Am I? What's that? Is that when an animal is stuffed and mounted?"

"It is."

"That's it!" Scapegrace said happily. "That's what I want! Can you do that?"

"No."

"Why not?"

"Because the actual animal body is not *used* in taxidermy. The animal is skinned, and the skin is stretched over a *replica* animal body. Note, I keep saying *animal*. That is because taxidermy is not done to humans. It might be seen as somewhat barbaric."

"Wouldn't suit me anyway," Scapegrace murmured. "It needs to be the original body. So can you embalm it and just give it to me?"

"I'm afraid that we do not provide a take-away service."

"Maybe the place across the road does."

"That wouldn't surprise me," the funeral director said huffily, "but I doubt even *they* would stoop to that level. Mr O'Carroll—"

"Elvis."

"Elvis, I think the death of your brother has affected your judgement. You're not thinking clearly. What you're asking for is... unsettling."

"It's what Adolf would have wanted."

"I'm sure he would have appreciated a more peaceful resting place."

"His last words to me were, '*Don't bury me*'."

"We also provide a cremation service."

"And then he said, '*Don't burn me either*'."

The funeral director sighed. "Elvis, I don't think we are the people to help you. It is not often I recommend our rivals across the road, but I feel they would be more suited to your needs. I'm sure they'd be happy to deal with your... requests."

He smiled.

Scapegrace left the funeral parlour and crossed the road, dousing himself with a half-can of deodorant as he went. He was greeted by another sombre funeral director, explained his injuries without the chuckling this time, and was shown to another comfortable chair. He skipped through the tragic loss stuff quickly and got down to specifics.

"Adolf was a devout Catholic," he said. "And I mean, devout. Oh, he was crazy for that religion. He'd be praying every day, sometimes twice a day. It was all *Our Father* this and *Hail Mary* that. Rosary beads and signed pictures of the Pope. He went nuts for the whole thing. He thought priests were great altogether."

The funeral director nodded slowly. "So at least he was comforted in his time of need. Then it will be a traditional funeral you're looking for?"

"Not at all. Have you read the Bible?"

"I have, yes. I find great strength in its words."

"Did you read the bit about the zombies?"

"Uh..."

"The bit at the end, where God raises the dead for Judgement Day."

"Um, I... I'm not sure I..."

"It's when God decides who gets into Heaven and who doesn't, and all the dead climb out of their graves and they all wait there to see who gets in. That's in the Bible, right? That's what Adolf wants to do, but he wants a head start on all the others. He doesn't want to waste time crawling out of a hole in the ground. He wants to be ready for the sprint. So I want you to preserve him."

The funeral director paled. "*Preserve?*"

"I was thinking, if you pump all that embalming fluid into his veins, then I can take him away, store him somewhere cool, and he'll be ready to go at the end of the world. What do you think?"

"Are you... being serious?"

"I've got my dead brother in the back of my car. Of course I'm being serious."

"Mr O'Carroll..."

"Elvis."

"Elvis, what you're saying makes no sense."

"Do not deride my brother's religion."

"I assure you, I am doing no such thing. But what I *am* saying is that... your plan is nonsensical. A dead body will rot, sir, no matter how much embalming fluid is injected into it. Over time, everything decays."

"Adolf is particularly resilient."

"Even if Judgement Day happened before he started to decompose – say, if it happened on Thursday – embalming fluid would actually be a hindrance. It suffuses the muscles, stiffens them until they can't be moved. Do you understand, Elvis? He wouldn't have a head start on anyone. He'd actually be left behind, unable to move."

Scapegrace frowned. "So... So there's nothing you can do to stop decomposition?"

"I am sorry."

"What about those bodies they find in bogs, hundreds of years old?"

"Do you really want to lay Adolf to rest in a bog? Elvis, unless you're prepared to mummify your brother, he is going to decompose."

"What's that? Mummify? He'd be a mummy?"

"We don't do that sort of thing here."

"Well, who does?"

"Nobody."

"What about the Egyptians?"

"Nobody apart from the Egyptians," the funeral director nodded. "Take him to an Egyptian funeral parlour. They'll wrap him in bandages and put him in a sarcophagus and he'll be right as rain come Judgement Day."

"Really?"

"No. Those morons across the road paid you to come in here and waste my valuable time, didn't they?"

"Of course not."

"Did they tell you to act so stupid?"

"I'm not acting," Scapegrace responded.

"Tell them if they want to start this practical joke war again, then I'm fine with that. I've still got a few tricks up my sleeve. If it's a war they want, it's a war they'll get."

Scapegrace left the funeral parlour, confused and disheartened. It was as if the universe was closing off every avenue just as he was realising it was there. He had pinned all his hopes on being embalmed, and what was he left with, now that science had let him down?

He stopped in the middle of the road. Magic. Of course. He hadn't considered it before because, quite honestly, he had no sorcerer friends. But surely there *must* be something a mage could do. They were always coming up with new and exciting ways to live for as long as possible. Would it really take that much power to stop meat from rotting?

He was no expert – even in life, his grasp of magic had been negligible at best – but this seemed possible. All of Scapegrace's magic was used to animate his body and keep him thinking, but there was nothing stopping anyone else from performing magic *on* him.

There was a name that his old master Scarab had once mentioned. He had been talking about an expert in science-magic... Grouse, that was it. Kenspeckle Grouse, who had a

Medical Facility somewhere in Dublin. Butterflies of excitement fluttered within Scapegrace's stomach. He just needed to find out where it was, and all his troubles would be over.

A car horn beeped right behind him and he jumped in fright, then stalked to the pavement, muttering curses. The car carried on past him. Scapegrace saw it out of the corner of his eye, and froze. He knew that car. The first time he'd seen it, he had been thrown into the backseat in handcuffs. The second time, he was thrown into the trunk, in another set of handcuffs. It was the car Skulduggery Pleasant drove.

Scapegrace suddenly forgot how to walk like normal people. How had Pleasant known he was here? Had he been following him? Was this the day his existence ended? He was sure he hadn't been recognised, because he had been facing the other way and he was dressed in a suit, but all it would take was one glance and it would all be over. He staggered to a large bush and fell into it, then crawled around to take a look through the leaves. The black car turned the corner and was gone.

This didn't make any sense. Was it all an elaborate trap? An ambush? Pleasant had driven right by him. Had the great Skeleton Detective made a silly mistake? Or maybe he *hadn't* been searching for him after all. Maybe this was just a coincidence. Maybe the house...

Scapegrace looked back at the big house. Pleasant's car had been parked outside it. In the driveway in fact. Pleasant had parked his car in the driveway of the house like... like... like he'd *owned* the place.

Scapegrace stared. He knew where Skulduggery Pleasant lived.

Now all he had to do was figure out who'd pay the most for the information.

9

THE NEW GRAND MAGE

Valkyrie followed Skulduggery as he strode briskly through the alley. It was so cold it was almost painful, and for once, she was glad of it. It meant she had something else to think about other than kissing Caelan. She regretted it now. She'd regretted it the moment after it happened, but she couldn't stop replaying it over and over in her head.

Skulduggery came to some steps leading down below street level, and an iron door swung open to let them through. The corridor they walked into was warm, with fantastic images carved into the walls on both sides. In places the paint was cracked and peeling, but the years had not diminished the sheer lushness of the colours used. Valkyrie bent to examine a tiny running figure. Even the light glinting in the figure's eyes had been painted in.

"What is all this?" she asked.

"History," Skulduggery answered. "It's all here, for those who know how to look." He nodded to a carving of two men and a woman, holding light in their hands. "These are the Ancients, discovering magic for the first time. The clouds above them represent the Faceless Ones, and the grass at their feet represents the people."

"Regular people are represented by a lawn?" Valkyrie asked with a raised eyebrow. "How nice, and not at all insulting."

"The people are represented by individual blades of grass," Skulduggery said, a smile in his voice. "Born of the earth, as natural and integral a part of life as magic. You can see the Ancients protecting the grass from the unnatural storm clouds."

"All I see are the Ancients *standing* on the grass, being rained on, and not one of them thought to bring an umbrella. Not the smartest, were they?"

"Don't be *too* harsh – you're descended from one of them, remember."

"Any ancestor of *mine* would have brought an umbrella," Valkyrie muttered, and crossed to the other wall. The scene depicted there disturbed her, like a hook that had found its way inside her belly and was now tugging gently at her guts. A city in ruins, the dead scattered like dry leaves fallen from a tree on a still afternoon. At its centre stood a man, burning with black fire. "And this?" she asked. "Is this meant to be Mevolent?"

Skulduggery stood at her elbow. "These chambers were built before the war with Mevolent even started. No, that's not Mevolent. That's his master. That's the Unnamed."

Valkyrie looked at him. "Was his *name* the Unnamed, or did he just not *have* a name?"

"He didn't have one."

She frowned. "But how does *that* work? All our magic comes from our true name, right? I've been reading all about this. So if he didn't *have* a true name, where did he get his magic from?"

"To every law of nature, there are the aberrations. I'm very impressed that you're doing a little research, by the way."

"After Marr ordered Myron Stray to kill himself and destroy the Sanctuary, I thought it might be a good idea to learn a little more about the whole name thing."

"You're worried that someone might learn *your* true name?"

Worried was such a weak term for something so coldly terrifying. Valkyrie nodded, but didn't speak. She didn't trust herself to answer him.

Skulduggery started walking again. "So what did you learn?"

She walked beside him, forcing herself to remain casual. "Our true names are names of magic, from the oldest of the magical languages. Virtually all of us go around without knowing what that name actually is, but we can still use the magic it provides."

"And?"

"If you find out what your true name is, it's kind of like going straight to the source. You'd become more powerful than even the Ancients were. You'd be able to take on the Faceless Ones without needing a weapon."

"If that is so," Skulduggery said, "then how come Myron Stray became a puppet, and not a god?"

"Someone, in this case Mr Bliss, found out his true name before he did, so he never had time to seal it."

They walked into the Great Chamber and the conversation died away. Thirty or forty people stood around on the marble floor, talking quietly. The walls in here were splendid, the elaborate carvings continuing up to the domed ceiling.

Erskine Ravel smiled as he came over. Valkyrie had met him a few times before – he had fought in a special unit with Skulduggery and Ghastly during the war. She liked Ravel. He was charming and nice and quite beautiful, in a manly sort of way.

"Erskine," Skulduggery said, shaking his hand.

"Skulduggery, good to see you," said Ravel, shaking Valkyrie's hand next. "Valkyrie, you're looking well."

She actually blushed, and turned her head so it wouldn't be noticed. Then she spotted an old man with a grey beard, and frowned. "Why is he here?"

Ravel put his hands in his pockets. "Like it or not, we need representatives from all the major groups in order to elect a new Grand Mage, and the mages in Roarhaven have as much say as anyone."

"But why does *he* have to be here?"

"You don't like the Torment?"

"He doesn't like me."

The Torment scowled at Valkyrie when he met her eyes. There was a woman beside him, in a black dress that flowed on to the ground at her feet. Her face was covered by a veil, and her hands were gloved.

"He's here with his sister," Ravel said, anticipating her next question. "Not his real sister, of course, but another Child of the Spider."

Valkyrie had seen with her own horrified eyes the way the Torment could vomit black spiders the size of rats, with talons for legs. He also had the disconcerting habit of transforming into a spider himself – a huge monstrous thing that liked to haunt her dreams every once in a while.

"Madame Mist," Skulduggery said, eyeless gaze on the woman in the black veil. "She lives in Roarhaven now too? Since when? I didn't even know she was in the country."

Ravel shrugged. "We really weren't chatting long enough for me to get the details. I try to stay away from Children of the Spider, you know? They tend to give me the creeps. And speaking of creepy..."

High Priest Tenebrae entered the hall, flanked as always by Craven and Quiver. Tenebrae nodded to Valkyrie as they swept by in their black robes.

"Well now," Ravel said, catching the nod. "You seem to know more people here than *I* do."

Valkyrie smiled. "I'm still going to need some help with the boring ones."

Ravel laughed. "I'm sure they'd love to hear themselves being called that. In this hall, you have the usual suspects.

Sorcerers of particular power or age or standing. That lady over there is Shakra, and beside her is Flaring. You probably know them from the Sanctuary. They were lucky enough not to be there the day the Desolation Engine went off. To their left are assorted sorcerers you may not know – they work behind the scenes mostly, and do their best to stay out of the spotlight.

"Over here we have Corrival Deuce," Ravel continued, indicating a portly old man in a colourful coat. "He's more or less retired now, but we dragged him out of his house for this little get-together. He's a good man."

"A very good man," Skulduggery agreed. "We took orders from him during the war. There aren't many people I'd take orders from. He's one of them."

Valkyrie had heard Skulduggery and Ghastly mention Corrival Deuce in their conversations, always with real affection and respect. She decided she liked the old man very much, even though she'd never met him.

"The two people ahead of us," Skulduggery said, "are Geoffrey Scrutinous and Philomena Random." Scrutinous had bizarrely frizzy hair and a goatee, and despite the cold weather outside, he was wearing sandals. Random's appearance was altogether more sober – she had short hair, a warm coat, and none of the beads or rings or bangles that decorated her colleague's wrists and hands.

"They're public relations officers – it's their job to convince the mortals they didn't see what they thought they saw. The five people glaring at the Necromancers call themselves the Four Elementals. They see themselves as being in harmony with the world around them, and because of this they're astonishingly self-righteous."

"The Four Elementals?"

"Yes."

"But there are five of them."

"I know."

"Can they not count?"

"They started off with four, but then Amity, the man with the unusual chin married the heavyset woman with all the jewellery and insisted she be allowed to become the fifth member of the quartet."

"Couldn't they just rename themselves?"

"And become the Five Elementals, when there are only four elements? They didn't want to lose their precious synchronicity."

"It's better than everyone thinking you can't count."

"That it is," said someone at Valkyrie's elbow. She turned,

surprised to see Corrival Deuce standing there. She hadn't heard him approach. "You're Valkyrie Cain," he said, smiling. "I've heard so much about you. This is indeed an honour."

She shook his hand. "Hi," was all she could think to say.

"Erskine," Corrival said. "Skulduggery. Good to see you again."

"I didn't think you'd come," Ravel said to the older sorcerer.

Corrival barked a laugh. "What, after a solid three weeks of you pestering me about it?"

"I thought I was being subtle."

"You don't know the meaning of the word. Where are the others, then? Where's Ghastly, and Vex?"

"Ghastly hates these things," Skulduggery said, "and I don't know where Vex is."

"Probably having another adventure," Corrival said with a little sigh. "That boy needs to grow up one of these days, he really does. What about Anton Shudder?"

"Shudder likes to stay in his hotel," Ravel said. "Besides all the Remnants trapped in there, he also has a vampire guest to contend with. If I were him, I'd want to keep a close eye on things too."

The memory of Caelan's kiss came flooding back into Valkyrie's mind, and she fought against it in vain.

Corrival looked around. "So is this it? Is everyone here? Erskine, maybe you should start the ball rolling. I have places to go and things to do."

"Me?" Ravel asked. "Why do I have to start it? You're the most respected mage here. You start it. Or Skulduggery."

Skulduggery shook his head. "I can't start it. I don't like most of these people. I might start shooting."

Ravel scowled. "Fine."

He turned, cleared his throat, and spoke loudly. "Everyone who is going to be here is here," he announced. The other conversations died down, and all eyes turned to him. "We all know why we've gathered. If we can elect a Grand Mage today, then we can immediately start work on forming a new Council and finding a new Sanctuary."

"Before we talk about the new Sanctuary," Geoffrey Scrutinous said, "I think we should discuss the old one. In particular, I think everyone would like to ask how the search for Davina Marr has been going."

"As far as we know, she's still in the country," Skulduggery said. "Any more than that, I'm afraid I can't disclose."

"Why not?" asked the Elemental named Amity.

"It's an ongoing investigation."

"She has evaded you for three months already, Detective

Pleasant. Maybe we should be entrusting somebody else with the task of tracking her down."

"Then by all means, Amity," Skulduggery said, "find someone else."

"The damage has been done," the woman called Shakra said in a Belfast accent. "Marr isn't important, not any more. What is important is how weak we appear. The Sanctuaries around the world are waiting to pounce, did you know that?"

"That's a slight exaggeration," Scrutinous said.

"Is it? The Americans have already announced how they will no longer stand by and watch as Ireland struggles against the legacy that people like Mevolent have left us. That's what they said, word for word."

"It was a gesture of support," Amity said.

"No," Shakra responded, "it was a threat. They're telling us they're getting ready to step in and take over if something like this happens again."

Amity shook his head. "Nonsense. Ireland is a Cradle of Magic. No one would dare disrupt the delicate balance that holds the world in check."

Shakra scowled. "You're a moron."

"Being rude does not make you more intelligent than I."

"No, being more intelligent than you makes me more intelligent than you, you goat-brained simpleton."

"I did not come here to be insulted."

"What, do you have somewhere special to go for that kind of thing?"

"Can we please focus?" Corrival asked. Immediately, everyone shut up. "In the last five years alone, two of our Elders have been murdered, the third betrayed us, and the Grand Mage who took over has been revealed as a criminal. Two out of Mevolent's Three Generals returned, and the Faceless Ones actually *broke through* into this reality.

"Amity, you and your Four Elementals may not want to believe this, but Ireland is under attack. We have enemies both obvious and hidden. The war with Mevolent was fought largely on Irish soil. His actions, and the actions of his followers, have created an instability that is impossible to be rid of. This is where the agents of unrest are drawn. There is blood in the water here."

"That's right," Flaring said. "Dark sorcerers like Charivari in France, or Keratin in the mountains of Siberia, hate us and plot against us with every moment that passes. And what about all the visions of this Darquesse person, laying waste to the world? We need to be ready."

Valkyrie saw the nods and the looks in the eyes. If any one of them knew the truth, they'd have torn her apart right there and then.

"Then we need to get down to business," High Priest Tenebrae said. "The task ahead is not an easy one. We'll have to set up a new Council, elect a Grand Mage and two Elders, build a new Sanctuary and consolidate our power base. Even though it will add greatly to my responsibilities and workload, I am willing to put my own name forward for the role of Grand Mage."

There were some rolled eyes and cruel whispers, but Corrival held up a hand to silence them. "Thank you, High Priest. Who are the other nominees?"

"Some of us have been talking about this among ourselves," Scrutinous said, "and we'd like to suggest Corrival Deuce as a candidate."

Corrival raised an eyebrow. "Excuse me?"

"You're well-respected and well-liked, Corrival, and—"

"I know what I am," Corrival interrupted, "and what I am is retired. Even if I wasn't retired, I've never been interested in the job. That's for people like Meritorious, not people like me."

"Your country needs you," Flaring said.

"My country needs better taste."

"You're the only one who can do it."

"This is ridiculous," Corrival said. "I don't have the experience or the training, and I'm always getting into arguments. Not many sorcerers agree with my point of view, you know."

"Even so," said Philomena Random, "you're one of the few people who could bring the Irish magical community together in its time of need."

"Nonsense. There are plenty of others."

"We don't make this suggestion lightly, Corrival. We've considered this a great deal."

"And all you could come up with was me?"

"I'm afraid so."

"But I'm really enjoying my retirement. I get to sleep in every day. I do crossword puzzles and eat cakes."

"Duty calls, Corrival."

"Then we'll vote," Flaring said. "Right here, right now. Let's forgo the usual pomp and circumstance and have it as a simple *aye* or *nay*. All those in favour of High Priest Auron Tenebrae as the new Grand Mage, say *aye*."

Craven and Quiver both said *aye*. Tenebrae clenched his jaw against the overwhelming silence.

"OK then," Scrutinous said. "All in favour of Corrival Deuce as the new Grand Mage, say *aye*."

Ayes filled the room. Only the Necromancers and the Roarhaven mages stayed quiet.

Scrutinous grinned. "I think it's decided."

"Fine," Corrival said. "I'll accept the position, on the condition that as soon as someone more competent comes along, you'll all let me retire in peace."

"Agreed," said Amity. "So now we need to talk about nominations for the other two seats on the Council, and where the new Sanctuary is going to be built."

"Don't need to start building," the Torment said in his dreadful croaky voice. "We have a Sanctuary, ready and waiting."

"In Roarhaven?" Tenebrae said, disgust in his voice.

"Yes," the Torment glared back. "A fine building, built especially for this purpose."

"Built for a coup that failed," said Ravel.

"That may be so," the Torment said, "but the fact remains. There is a new Sanctuary building with all the rooms and requirements. Do any of you have any proper objections, apart from the fact that it's outside your precious capital city?"

There was silence.

"It's a good suggestion," Corrival said. Valkyrie looked at him in surprise. She wasn't the only one. "The fact is," he continued, "it's there, and it's available. And if someone sets off another bomb, we won't have to explain it to the civilian authorities. And as for the other two seats on the Council, I already have my nominees. I nominate Erskine Ravel and Skulduggery Pleasant."

Someone barked a laugh. Valkyrie turned to Skulduggery, really wishing he was wearing a face so she could see his reaction.

"Ah," said Ravel.

"Oh," said Skulduggery.

"Sorry, fellas," Corrival said, "but if I have to suffer through this ridiculousness, then so do you. Both of you are controversial figures, but I fought with your unit on the battlefield, and I've never known such bravery and honour. Erskine, you like spending money way too much, but you've been my trusted confidant for the last hundred years, and I don't think there is anyone who is going to deny that you would make an excellent Elder. You're wise when you need to be, and impulsive when you have to be.

"Skulduggery, my old friend, I daresay a lot of people are going to object to your nomination."

"Myself included," Skulduggery answered.

"You make more enemies than friends, which isn't saying an

awful lot, but you also make the difficult decisions. You always have. That's all I'm going to say on the matter. The rest is up to the voters. As duly elected Grand Mage, I now call a halt to proceedings, as I have a crossword to do and some cakes to eat."

Without waiting for a response, Corrival turned and walked from the room.

"I was not expecting *that*," Ravel said in a low voice.

"I'll vote for you," Skulduggery said, "so long as you promise *not* to vote for me."

Ravel grinned. "And let you miss the fun? Not on your life, dead man."

As they were walking for the Bentley, Valkyrie caught sight of a pretty blonde girl standing by a long, black car. "Back in a minute," she said to Skulduggery, and jogged over to the girl, trying her best not to smile too broadly.

"Hi Melancholia," she said brightly.

Melancholia scowled. She was four years older than Valkyrie, tall, and she wore black Necromancer robes. From the very start, Melancholia had never made a secret of the fact that she despised Valkyrie utterly. Valkyrie, for her part, thought this was astonishingly amusing, and revelled in the many opportunities she had to annoy the older girl.

"What you doing?" Valkyrie asked, smiling a friendly smile.

"I'm standing here," Melancholia responded, not looking at her.

"And a fine job you're doing of it, too. Do you know where Solomon is? He said he was going to come today, but I didn't see him."

"Cleric Wreath is on an assignment."

"Cool. What kind?"

"I don't know."

"Is it exciting?"

"I don't know."

"Right. So you're just waiting here for the others, then? Waiting for ol' Tenebrae?"

Melancholia stiffened. "You should show more respect for the High Priest. You should use his full title when referring to him."

Valkyrie shrugged. "High Priest Tenebrae just takes so long to say, you know? I usually just call him Tenny. He likes that."

"If you were truly one of us, you would be severely disciplined for such behaviour."

Valkyrie frowned. "Do you really talk like that, or are you just putting it on?"

Melancholia finally looked at her. "You are mocking me?" she snarled.

"Is that a statement or a question?"

Melancholia was taller than Valkyrie, and she loomed over her. "I should punish you myself, on behalf of the High Priest."

"I don't think Tenny would like that very much."

"You are *not* our saviour."

"Solomon seems to think I am."

"Cleric Wreath has spent too long out in this decadent world. He's lost his objectivity. He looks at you and he sees the Death Bringer, whereas everyone else looks at you and sees a pathetic little *child*."

Valkyrie grinned. Despite how sinister it sounded, the Death Bringer was a title that she was beginning to actually like. She found Necromancers creepy on a very fundamental level – Solomon Wreath aside – but even so, it was nice to be thought of as a possible saviour. Certainly, it was a change from having to think of herself as Darquesse. The chance, no matter how slim, that instead she might turn out to be the Death Bringer was a source of comfort to her. Two possible destinies – one where she saves the world, and one where she ends it. Her future couldn't get any starker than that. "Maybe I *am* the Death Bringer," she said.

"Don't be absurd. You've been studying Necromancy for just over a year. I've been studying death magic since I was four years old. You're nothing compared to me, or anyone like me."

"And yet," Valkyrie interrupted, "I'm the one they're all making a fuss of."

Melancholia scowled. "You're nothing but an Elemental *playing* at being a Necromancer."

"And you're a Necromancer, through and through. You've wanted to be nothing else your entire life. And yet, I've been invited to all the important meetings and you get to stay out here and mind the car. I've been told things about your art and your religion that you won't be told for another year or two."

"Ridiculous."

"Is it? When were you told about the Passage?"

Melancholia hesitated. "I learned about the Passage when I was ready, when I had completed my studies on over three dozen—"

"It was pretty recently, wasn't it?"

Melancholia gritted her teeth. "Yes."

"See, I was told about it ages ago. Now, I'm not saying I'm an expert. In fact, I have loads of questions about the whole thing. You must have noticed that some of it just doesn't seem to make any sense. Your religion is based on the idea that when you die, your energy passes from this world to another one, right?"

"It's not an *idea*," Melancholia said tersely. "It's a scientific *fact*."

"It's little more than a theory," Valkyrie countered. "But I'm OK with that. So you guys are waiting for the Death Bringer to come and collapse the wall between the two worlds, so the living and the dead can exist in the same place, at the same time, meaning that there will be no more strife, no more war, and everyone will live, or at least exist, happily ever after."

"Yes," Melancholia said.

"And yet, no one has told me how this is possible."

"You can hardly expect to understand the advanced stages of our teachings, if you do not have the patience or the skill to master the basics."

"Do *you* know how it's possible?"

"I will. Soon. Once I experience the Surge, once I am locked into Necromancy for the rest of my life, all of its secrets will be laid open for me."

"Oh, that'll be nice. I still don't know if it's for me, though. I really don't want to draw my power from death, and that's basically what Necromancy is. I'd rather not have to rely on other people's pain to use magic."

"I hardly think it will be up to you. The sooner the Clerics realise what a mistake they're making, wasting their time on you, the better. Then you can run along with your skeleton friend and have lots of fun together, and you can leave the important stuff to us."

"Sometimes I get the feeling that you don't like me."

"Trust your feelings."

"So we're not going to be friends?"

"I'd rather gouge my own eyes out."

Valkyrie shook her head sadly, and started to walk back to the Bentley. "Your leaders are looking to me to be their saviour, Melancholia. You might have to learn to love me."

Melancholia's voice was laced with venom. "You are *not* our saviour."

Valkyrie looked at her over her shoulder, shot her a smile. "Better start praying to me, just in case."

10

THE BONEBREAKER

Back when Vaurien Scapegrace was alive, he had briefly owned a pub in Roarhaven that catered, almost exclusively, for sorcerers. That had been before he'd found his true calling as a Killer Supreme and, later, as the Zombie King, but he'd enjoyed it nevertheless. He knew there were pubs and clubs and bars around the country, around the world, whose clientele were magical, but he liked to think that his pub offered something a little different. A home away from home perhaps. A refuge from the pressures and stresses of modern living.

But now that some time had passed, now that he was viewing it all with a more objective eye, he realised what it was that his pub had really offered. It had offered dim lighting, bad drinks, grumpy bar staff and a toilet that smelled of wet cabbage. There was absolutely nothing to take pride in. Nothing to feel good about. But that, of course, was the whole point. Sorcerer pubs were bad pubs by necessity. If they were good pubs, *everyone* would be going to them.

Sitting in this particular sorcerer pub in Dublin, Scapegrace reflected on the trials and tribulations he had gone through as a living man, and hoped that by the time this night was done, he would be a step closer to being a living man once again.

Thrasher came through the sombre crowd, spilling someone's drink and apologising profusely before arriving at Scapegrace's table. "Some men are here," he said urgently. "They say they know you."

Scapegrace leaned back in his chair. "Let's see them."

Thrasher nodded, turned, but the crowd was already parting for the six newcomers. Scapegrace did indeed know them. Lightning Dave sidled up on Scapegrace's right, playing with a bright stream of electricity that crackled between his fingertips. His hair stood on end, and his features had settled into a permanent smirk.

Beside him was Hokum Pete. Hokum Pete had been born in Kerry, but harboured a well-known and widely ridiculed desire to be seen as a Wild West outlaw. He liked to wear cowboy boots and long duster coats, and today he had a six-gun holstered low on his right leg. His hand flashed and the gun cleared the holster. He started to spin it around on his finger, like that was going to impress anyone.

Thrasher gave a delighted "*Oooh*", and Scapegrace fought the urge to hit him.

To Scapegrace's left was a pair of sorcerers who had never managed to garner much of a reputation for themselves. They weren't powerful and they weren't smart, and Scapegrace could never remember their names.

Brobding the giant, bringing up the rear, had to hunch over to even fit in here, and the man who stood right in front of Scapegrace was Hieronymus Deadfall. Deadfall had been a mercenary, had fought in a few wars, both magical and mortal, before returning to Ireland and settling down in Roarhaven, where he had stolen Scapegrace's pub from under him. Not that Scapegrace held a grudge or anything.

"Hello, moron," said Scapegrace.

"My God," Deadfall responded. "It's true. Everything they said is true. You're a shambling pile of decomposition."

Hokum Pete sniggered, and Scapegrace sat up a little straighter. "I am the living dead, if that's what you mean, yes. What can I do for you, Hieronymus? I assume you've heard about the auction."

"We heard," Deadfall nodded. "So you know where the Skeleton Detective lives?"

"Yes, I do. You want revenge, for the time he smacked you around your own pub? This is how you do it. Catch him unawares. Or you can sell the information to someone else. His little partner will probably be there too."

"Cain," snarled one of the sorcerers whose name Scapegrace couldn't remember.

"This information is worth a lot," Scapegrace continued, "but all I'm looking for is information in exchange. Kenspeckle Grouse. I want to know where to find him."

It was all going so perfectly, and Scapegrace had to resist grinning in case any more teeth fell out. He'd give up the Skeleton Detective's location, and in return he'd find Kenspeckle Grouse and get himself fixed. It was, he had to admit, one of his more brilliant plans.

"Grouse..." Deadfall said. "The scientist? How the hell would I know that?"

"If you don't know it, you're of no use to me. Next! Anyone know where Kenspeckle Grouse is?"

Deadfall smiled. "Tell me, Vaurien, what's to stop us from just pulling you apart, limb from limb, until you tell us the skeleton's address?"

Scapegrace didn't really have an answer for that one.

There were mumblings and mutterings in the crowd as a large man in a long coat passed Deadfall and approached the table. He had his hood up, and beneath it Scapegrace could see metal, like a mask.

"I need to know where Skulduggery Pleasant lives," the big man said with an accent. Eastern European maybe, or Russian. Scapegrace decided on Russian. It was, like many sorcerer's accents, one that came from a lot of places over the years.

"Do you have what I need in exchange?" Scapegrace asked, ignoring Deadfall's scowl.

The head beneath the hood shook. "I have heard of this Grouse person, but I do not know where he lives."

"Then why are you wasting my time?"

The Russian didn't answer for a bit. Then he placed both hands on the table, and leaned in. "Because I'm giving you a chance to avoid bloodshed. Tell me where the Skeleton Detective lives and we can all walk out of here. You are a dead man, but there are ways to kill even dead men."

The conversation had tilted wildly out of Scapegrace's control in a remarkably short amount of time, with an astonishingly small amount of words.

It was the tone the big Russian was using, a tone that implied that violence was a mere afterthought. Scapegrace didn't like that one bit. Anyone who did not give violence its careful and rightful due was someone to whom violence was an old pair of shoes – slip on, slip off, think nothing more about it. That wasn't Scapegrace's style at all.

"Maybe," he said, "we can reach a compromise."

"No way," Deadfall said to the mysterious Russian. "Listen, pal, a funny accent and a funny mask don't scare me. We were here first, so you, take a hike."

The big man turned to him slowly. "You do not want to make trouble with me."

Deadfall actually chuckled in disbelief. "Scapegrace, take note. After we deal with the funny man here, you're next."

Hokum Pete was still showing off with his six-gun. His finger in the trigger guard, he spun it until it blurred, then flipped it, reversed it, slid it into the holster. It barely had time to settle before it flashed out again. He tossed it into the air and caught it as it spun, tossed it to his other hand, still spinning. He threw it over his shoulder and caught it, reversed the motion and that was when the Russian reached back, snatched it from the air, and shot him point-blank.

Hokum Pete flew backwards, there were screams and yells and cries, and suddenly everyone was moving.

Lightning Dave snarled and electricity burst from his fingers. The Russian dodged behind the giant, and Brobding shrieked as the stream hit him instead. Scapegrace toppled backwards over his chair, saw Thrasher dive to the floor. Panic spread, and there was a stampede for the exits.

The Russian shot Lightning Dave twice in the chest. Deadfall, his fists already turning to hammers, knocked the gun from the Russian's hand and swung for his head. The Russian ducked under the swing and moved past him, towards the two sorcerers with the forgettable names.

The first of them had glowing hands, ready to discharge a blast of energy. The second had opted for the up-close-and-personal approach, drawing a long dagger from his sleeve. Scapegrace watched as the Russian bent the second sorcerer's arm back, stabbing him with his own blade. The poor, unmemorable fool gurgled in astonishment, and the Russian took the dagger from him and whipped it across the throat of his friend. Then he turned, saw Brobding coming for him and flicked the dagger to the ground. It impaled itself through the giant's foot, pinning it to the floor. Brobding shrieked.

Deadfall came at him. The Russian swayed back out of range, watched the hammer swing uselessly by his face, then leaned in. His knuckles met the hinge of Deadfall's jaw, and Deadfall's legs gave out from under him.

Brobding pulled the dagger from his foot with a self-pitying squawk of pain. He fixed his face with a snarl, and charged. He didn't have far to charge, but he did have to keep himself stooped, so it resembled more of a stumble. Still, the intent behind it was unmistakable.

The Russian ducked under the giant's arms. Brobding's great fist came around, but the masked man avoided it easily. Brobding lunged and the Russian snapped out a pair of jabs that broke the giant's nose and split his lip. Brobding bellowed and the Russian kicked his knee. The bellow became a howl, drawn-out and horrified, his huge hands clutching at his leg.

The Russian tapped a single fingertip lightly against Brobding's chest. There was a terrible crack of bone, and Brobding fell, dead. It was like a great oak falling in a forest.

Deadfall was up again, preparing to swing his hammer-fists, but the Russian just stepped close and pressed his hand against him. Every bone that comprised the skeleton of Hieronymus

Deadfall gave a slight tremor, and then came apart with a violence that ruptured his body. Bone shards burst both organs and skin, spraying blood into the air. His corpse dropped, contorted and disfigured beyond recognition. The Russian turned to look at Scapegrace, his eyes red beneath his mask.

"I'll tell you," Scapegrace said, hands high above his head. "I'll tell you where Skulduggery Pleasant lives. Just please, don't explode me."

11

THE ROARHAVEN MAGES

The closer you got to Roarhaven, the sicker the trees looked, the browner the grasses, the blacker the lake. Its streets were narrow, its buildings hunched, their windows squinting. Paranoia and hatred, seething resentment and bitter hostility – these things leaked through the town like its lifeblood. It was a creature, a mangy, diseased dog, afflicted with fleas and ticks and lice, kept alive by its own loathing.

The man with the golden eyes stood by the stagnant lake, his coat buttoned up against the cold. "Marr?" he asked.

"Still alive," said the old man behind him.

The veiled woman in black spoke quietly. "I thought we hired the best."

The old man didn't bother to keep the irritation out of his voice. "We did."

"She needs to die," said the woman. "She's far too dangerous to be languishing in chains."

"Tesseract assures me she will be dead soon." The old man looked away from the woman. "Do they still think the Americans are to blame?"

The man with the golden eyes shrugged. "Who knows what Skulduggery Pleasant thinks? We can only stick to the plan. If he begins to suspect us, we'll deal with him then. For the moment, though, we're on schedule. This town will hold the new Sanctuary. From here, we're going to change the world."

12

KEEPING A
STRAIGHT FACE

China Sorrows wasn't in the library that took up an entire half of the tenement building's third floor, and neither was she in her apartment across the hall, which took up the other half. China's assistant, the thin man who never spoke, merely cast his eyes downwards when Skulduggery asked him her whereabouts, but apparently, this was sufficient.

Valkyrie followed Skulduggery down the dank staircase. His façade was up, but still refused to settle. She watched as his face started to drift round to the back of his head.

"Where are we going?" she asked. A pair of dull green eyes floated slowly through Skulduggery's hair.

"To the basement."

"I didn't know this place had a basement."

"There wasn't one until China bought this building and commissioned the work to add a sub-level. Even the people living here don't know about it."

"You've got eyes in the back of your head, you know, and I don't mean that as compliment."

"I know," said Skulduggery sadly.

"How can you even see right now?"

He glanced back at her. The mouth of the façade was gaping wide over his left eye socket.

"That is so wrong," she murmured.

They continued walking.

"There's only one reason why China ever goes down into the basement," Skulduggery said. "Well, it's also where she keeps her car. OK, so there's only two reasons why she ever goes down there, apart from the fact that it's secure and dry and it works well as a storage area. So that's three, only three reasons why she ever goes down there, and apart from the car and the storage, the main reason is privacy. Seclusion. Why does she need privacy and seclusion?"

"Don't know."

"She needs privacy and seclusion when she catches someone trying to steal from her." They reached the ground floor.

"How do we get there?" Valkyrie asked. "Is there an invisible elevator? A trapdoor? Oh, is it one of those fire station poles that we get to slide down?"

Skulduggery went to the broom closet, and opened the door. There were no brooms in there, and no floor. There were only—

"Stairs," Valkyrie said, disappointed.

"Not just ordinary stairs," Skulduggery told her as he led the way down. "Magic stairs."

"Really?"

"Oh, yes."

She followed him into the darkness. "How are they magic?"

"They just are."

"In what way?"

"In a magicky way."

She glared at the back of his head. "They aren't magic at all, are they?"

"Not really."

The basement was cold. A dim bulb struggled valiantly

against the darkness. They walked down a narrow corridor between chain-link walls, passing stacks of boxes and crates. Rusted pipes crossed the ceiling, the failing light making them look like boa constrictors, liable to drop down and snatch the pair of them up and slowly squeeze the life out of them. Out of *her*. Skulduggery had no life to squeeze.

They heard voices ahead. Finally, the chain-link maze came to an end, and they stepped into a wide-open space, illuminated only by the headlights from an idle car. A man was on his knees, doing his best to shield his eyes. Whether he was shielding his eyes from the blinding light or the blinding beauty of the woman who stood above him was hard to tell.

China Sorrows was cast in half-shadow. Her raven hair was tied off her face in a simple ponytail. The light hit her back and made her clothes shine and her skin glow. She held a book by her side. Skulduggery and Valkyrie stayed where they were, watching silently.

"I'm sorry!" the man sobbed. "Oh God, Miss Sorrows, I'm so sorry! I didn't mean to do it!"

"You didn't mean to hide this book under your jacket and leave without telling me?" China clarified. "This is a very valuable edition, and would be sorely missed from my collection."

"Please. Please, I have a family. They're starving."

"And so you planned to *feed* them the book?"

"No... No, but..."

"You planned to sell it then. To whom, I wonder?"

"I don't... I can't..."

"If you tell me who the interested party is, I will let you go." At a wave of her hand, a section of wall opened up at the top of a concrete ramp – obviously the means of exit for her car – and daylight flooded the gloom. "You will never be allowed back here, and you will cross the street and run away to avoid me, but I will take no further action. Against *you*. The actions I will take against the interested party, however, will be quite severe, even by my standards. I never ask twice – my patience is quite short. You will tell me now."

He sagged. "Eliza Scorn."

If there was any reaction shown in China's face, the shadows hid it. "I see," she said. "You may leave."

"I... can?"

China sighed, and the man scrambled up, wiped his eyes, and hurried towards the ramp.

"Wait," China said. She looked at him for a long moment.

"If you return to Eliza Scorn without this book, she will most likely kill you *and* your pathetic starving family." She held it out. "Take it."

"Really?"

"I have three more around here somewhere. Take it before I change my mind."

He scurried back to her, accepting the book. "Thank you," he wept. "Thank you for your kindness and your, and your beauty. I... I love you, Miss Sorrows. I've never loved anyone as much as—"

"You have a pathetic starving family to get back to, you grubby little man. Get back to them."

He tore his eyes away from her and ran, wailing, up the ramp and out into the alley. The wall closed up behind him, and China turned, allowing the light to cast itself over her perfect features.

"An act of kindness," she said, "purely for your benefit, Valkyrie. I know how much you dislike me being mean to people."

Valkyrie stepped out of the shadows, smiling. "Kindness suits you."

"Really? I think I'm quite allergic to it. Now what can I do for you both? Perhaps you are here seeking my opinion on matters discussed at this top-secret meeting to which I was not invited?"

"You may not have been there," Skulduggery said, "but I'm sure a woman of your resources has heard detailed accounts of everything that was spoken about."

"Nonsense. That meeting was highly confidential. Congratulations, by the way."

Skulduggery grunted. "There's nothing to congratulate."

"Don't be so modest – I haven't laughed so hard in years. Erskine, possibly, has the makings of a good Elder, and Corrival Deuce is an inspired choice for Grand Mage. But you? Skulduggery my dear... that is inspired lunacy."

"Yes, well, we'll see how it all pans out, but I'm afraid we're here on matters much more cosmetic." Skulduggery took a step out of the gloom, and China saw his drooping face.

"Oh dear," she said.

"It gets better when I do this." He began slapping himself and shaking his head violently, causing the face to tighten slightly.

"Well," China said, "at least you're keeping your dignity. Come. Keep the façade active."

She touched the car and the headlights went out. They followed her out of the basement and up the stairs.

"What have you heard about Tesseract?" Skulduggery asked as they climbed. His bottom lip hung over his chin like a dead slug.

"The Russian killer? Why on earth would you want..." China looked down at them, her pale blue eyes narrowed. "He's in the country?"

"You didn't know?" Skulduggery asked, actually sounding shocked.

There was a brief flicker of annoyance on China's perfect face, and then it evaporated. She turned, and resumed climbing to the third floor.

"Here is what I know about Tesseract. Born and raised in Russia, somewhere between three and four hundred years ago. He is an Adept, nobody knows who trained him, and nobody knows how many people he's killed. He wears a mask – again, nobody knows why. He lives in a truck of some description. He's self-sufficient, doesn't need to resupply for weeks at a time. His method of communication is a mystery to me – how those who require his services get in touch with him, I confess, I do not know.

"What all this means is that he could be living across the street from me and I'd never know it. It means that I have not heard one single rumour about him in twenty years, and the fact that he is here and I didn't know about it causes me no small amount of alarm and drives me to unimaginable fury. I am, however, hiding it well. You are *sure* he is here?"

"We saw him," said Skulduggery.

They reached the third floor and stopped talking as a man and a woman passed. The man stared at China, entranced by her beauty. The woman stared at Skulduggery, repulsed by the face that was slowly sliding down his head. China led them into her apartment – to Valkyrie it was as beautiful and elegant as China herself – and shut the door after them.

"He went after Davina Marr," Skulduggery said.

China's eyebrow raised. "Did he kill her?"

"He came close."

"Do you have her?"

"She's somewhere safe and secure – you don't have to worry about her. This can't be repeated to anyone, of course."

"Who do you think I am, some cheap and tawdry gossip-monger? Sit. Loosen your tie."

Skulduggery did as he was told, and China took a small black case from her desk. From the case she withdrew a calligraphy pen that reminded Valkyrie of a scalpel. She dipped it in black ink before taking a monocle from a side pocket. She crossed to Skulduggery, undid a few shirt buttons to expose the symbols carved into his collarbones, and examined them using the monocle. "Have you questioned Marr yet?" she asked.

"She remains stubbornly unconscious," he answered. "However, the very fact that someone sent an assassin after her has told us an awful lot. Up until now I was almost prepared to believe that Marr acted alone. She could have enslaved Myron Stray of her own volition, put the Desolation Engine into his hands, and arranged for Valkyrie and myself to get caught in the blast. I was close to putting her actions down to pure anger and a petty need for revenge that escalated into something terrible. But that doesn't hold up. Not any more."

"Because of Tesseract?" Valkyrie asked.

"Tesseract was put on her trail, which leads me to believe that she had co-conspirators who have since abandoned her, and now want her silenced."

China put down the monocle, pressed the pen against the symbol on Skulduggery's left collarbone, and applied pressure. "If there is a conspiracy, who would gain from the destruction of the Sanctuary? There has been a three-month period where there has been no Sanctuary, no Grand Mage, and yet from what I can see, there has been no dramatic upsurge in antisocial activity. Whoever organised this seems to have missed their opportunity."

"Unless the scale is far grander than we imagine," Skulduggery said.

"Now you just sound paranoid." Whatever China was doing to the symbol was having an effect on Skulduggery's face. It tightened until it almost split, then loosened again. "If you're right about this grand conspiracy, by the way, you might want to consider the possibility that Marr never really stopped working for the American Sanctuary."

"We've thought about that," Skulduggery said. "Valkyrie?"

"OK," Valkyrie said, "so two years ago, Marr is working for the American Sanctuary. Thurid Guild offers her a job in Ireland, thinking she won't be able to resist the chance to work at a Cradle of Magic because, let's face it, every day here is an adventure. She tells her bosses, they tell her to accept the job, but to work undercover for them. Any Sanctuary around the world would want to gain a foothold in a country with this much raw magic at its core, and America is no different.

"She starts work, proves to be as good at her job as everyone expects, but all the time she's looking for a way to bring down the Sanctuary. The Americans need a crisis so they can swoop in. Marr eventually gives them that crisis."

"The problem with that theory," Skulduggery continued, "is that once the Sanctuary is destroyed, the Americans do nothing, and then Corrival Deuce gets elected as Grand Mage, with Ravel and myself as possible Elders. I really can't see how that would benefit the Americans, or anyone else, in the slightest."

"That should do it," China said, stepping back. Skulduggery looked up at her, his face staying put. "It was off by a millimetre in depth," she explained. "An unforgivable mistake on my part, and yet I think I shall manage to forgive myself. Could you deactivate the façade now?"

Skulduggery tapped the symbols, and the face slid away. "You want me to use it only when I have to?" he asked.

"Not at all," China said. "It's just that talking to you when you have a face is quite disconcerting. I much prefer you as a skeleton."

"Me too," Valkyrie agreed.

As Skulduggery stood up and buttoned his shirt, China began to pack away her equipment. "Then maybe it *isn't* the Americans," she said. "Maybe Marr was working undercover for somebody else."

"It could be someone who just doesn't like us," said Valkyrie. "We've already had Dreylan Scarab and Billy-Ray

Sanguine come after us for revenge, so what about other bad guys we've beaten? What about Jaron Gallow? No one's heard from him since he chopped off his own arm and ran away from the Faceless Ones. And Remus Crux. If there's anyone crazy enough to want to kill that many people, it's *that* lunatic."

"It's not Remus Crux," China said.

"How do *you* know?"

"Because Davina Marr would never work with someone so unstable."

"Then what about the Torment? Roarhaven stands to benefit a lot from this. They get the Sanctuary right in the middle of their creepy little town."

"But that still doesn't grant them any great degree of power," Skulduggery argued, fixing his tie. "There will still be a Council of Elders, and an entire staff of non-Roarhaven sorcerers. All they gain is the proximity of location."

"Which is not a good enough reason to set off the Desolation Engine," China said. "The Children of the Spider *are* known for their cunning, but the fact is, this may have nothing to *do* with Roarhaven."

"I still think the Torment is behind this," Valkyrie muttered.

Skulduggery's smile was in his voice. "Is that because he tried to get me to kill you?"

"I think he's behind this because he's a horrible old man who turns into a giant spider. But mostly because he tried to get you to kill me. There are still plenty of others to choose from, though. And don't forget, we only have Scarab's word that *he* wasn't behind it. This might be his last bid for revenge before he dies in prison, to make us think there's someone else out there."

"So," Skulduggery said, "to sum up: Davina Marr's co-conspirators could either be the Roarhaven mages, the Americans, or anyone else who just doesn't like us."

China smiled. "I'm just glad we could narrow it down." She walked from the room, Valkyrie and Skulduggery following her into the library. "And may I say what a privilege it is to be involved in this investigation at its inception. It fills my heart with warmth to know that, finally, you trust me enough to bother me with things at a much earlier stage than I am used to or am, indeed, happy with."

"They say sarcasm is the lowest form of wit," Valkyrie said.

China glanced at her. "They've obviously never met *me*."

"The fact is," Skulduggery said as they walked through the labyrinth of bookcases, "over the past few years you've proven yourself to be someone who can be depended on."

"And the unfortunate side effect of that," Valkyrie

continued, "is that you get to join our little crime-fighting club, whether you like it or not."

China stopped, and turned to them, a slight frown on her face. "Does this mean... Please don't tell me this means we are all now *friends*. I have done very well without friends up to this point and I have no intention of developing any *now*."

Valkyrie frowned. "You make us sound like a rash."

"An irritation that shows up when you least want it? I think the analogy is quite apt."

"You do realise that I know what all the big words you're using *mean*, right?"

"And there I was, trying to baffle you with my verbiage."

"Understood *that*, too." Valkyrie glimpsed a familiar face in among the stacks. "Be right back," she said. They walked on and she approached her friend. "This is where we first met," she said.

Tanith Low looked up, and smiled. "God, that seems like a hundred years ago. You were so small."

"I was never small."

"And so narrow. Now look at you. How are the arms?"

"I'm not showing you."

"Yes, you are."

"No, I'm not. We're in the middle of a library."

"A library frequented solely by freaks and other assorted weirdos. I haven't seen the arms in weeks. Come on."

Valkyrie tried to sigh, but ended up grinning. She unzipped her jacket and took it off.

"*Damn*," Tanith said, drawing the word out. "I hope Fletcher appreciates all the work I've put in to making his girlfriend rock solid."

"I've told him I'm aiming to have shoulders like yours. He kind of dribbled when he heard that." Valkyrie put her jacket back on. "But I was never small."

Tanith laughed, slid the book she'd been reading back on to the shelf. "You were so unsure and innocent and wide-eyed and shy... Well, maybe not shy."

"Never shy."

"But definitely unsure. I knew from the moment I met you we'd be friends, you know."

"Really?"

"I didn't know we'd be quite so close, but I saw you and I went, yeah, she's cool. Hadn't a clue you had anything to do with why I was over here, though. Things kind of worked out quite well, didn't they?"

"Yes, they did."

"My folks say hi, by the way. And my brother wants to meet you. He's heard so much about the great Valkyrie Cain."

"Your parents are lovely, and I've seen a picture of your brother. I definitely want to meet *him*."

Tanith wagged her finger. "You, my dear, are a one-man woman. Stick with Fletcher, and stay away from my *older* brother." Tanith's smile faded slightly. "What's wrong?"

"What do you mean?"

"I said 'one-man woman' and you... you practically *flinched*."

"No, I didn't."

"Everything OK with Fletcher?"

"Yes," said Valkyrie. "Things are great."

"And you're happy with him? Still having fun?"

"Sometimes it's like leading a child around, but yes, absolutely, still having a laugh."

"Then what's wrong?"

"Nothing's wrong," Valkyrie said, and laughed.

"What did you *do*?"

"I didn't do *anything*."

"Who is he?"

"I don't know who—"

Tanith looked into her eyes.

"Oh no," she breathed.

"Oh no what?"

"Not him."

"Tanith, I really don't know what you're on about."

"The *vampire*, Val? *Really*? The *vampire*?"

"He has a name."

"He's a vampire!"

"I don't know what you're talking about, OK? Nothing happened!"

"Oh, that's a big old lie right there."

Valkyrie prepared to argue, but she knew there was little use. She sagged. "Fine. OK. We kissed."

Tanith covered her face with her hands. "No. No no no. You can't do this."

"I'm not doing anything. It was a one-off. It's not going to happen again."

"He's too old for you."

"I know that."

"And he's a vampire."

"Tanith. Caelan has problems, but he's not like the others."

"Valkyrie. You're insane. He's *exactly* like the others. This isn't some brooding Gothic rubbish."

"I swear to God, I know all this. I explained to him, it'll

never happen again. I'm not in love with him, for God's sake. It meant basically nothing."

"It might have meant nothing to *you*," Tanith said, "but I can tell you that it meant a lot to *him*."

"That's not my problem."

"It will be. Val, I hate to disapprove of *anything* that you do. We're friends. I shouldn't lecture you. I should support you. And I will. And I do. But something like this, you're just going to have to forgive me, because I'll keep going on about it until it's over for good."

Valkyrie nodded. "I understand that."

"I take it Fletcher doesn't have any idea?"

"God, no."

"Good. There's no point in hurting him and destroying your relationship when you don't have to. It was a mistake."

"Yes, it was," said Valkyrie.

"And it'll never happen again."

"No, it won't."

"But if it does, you can talk to me about it and I won't shout at you too much."

"Thanks."

"I'm not even going to ask if Skulduggery knows. If Caelan's still alive, that means he doesn't."

Valkyrie nodded her agreement, the truth of that statement making her uneasy. They walked out of the stacks, to where Skulduggery and China were talking.

"Oh, good," China said without enthusiasm, "Tanith's here."

Tanith's smile made no effort to reach her eyes. "Hello China. You're looking radiant as ever."

"And your leather seems to have shrunk since the last time I saw you," China responded. "Don't you all have somewhere else to be? It's not that I want you to go, it's just that I don't want you to stay."

13

SUFFERING

leric Craven was in no hurry as he walked the cold corridors of the Temple. He'd always disliked the cold, but such was the Necromancer way. Hardship and suffering, misery and discomfort. The Temple was, almost to its last metre, cold and dark and dank, lit only by sputtering torches in rusted brackets on the walls. *To suffer is to live*, as the saying went – one of the basic tenets of his faith. Who was Craven to object to that? Who was he to demand special consideration? Who was he to forgo the suffering, when so many of his fellows shivered and rattled and didn't complain?

Beneath his robes he was wrapped in thermals.

He knew for a fact that High Priest Tenebrae wore thermals beneath *his* robes. Cleric Quiver didn't, as far as he could tell, but then Quiver was the kind of man who enjoyed the odd bit of suffering. As for Cleric Wreath, he didn't even *wear* his robes, and his clothes *always* looked warm. Craven would expect no less from a Cleric who had spent so many years out *there*, in the world. The house where he lived was furnished, insulated and warm no matter how cold it got elsewhere. Decadent. Indulgent. How Craven envied him.

He reached the iron door of the High Priest's office and let himself in. Shelves of books and papers. Cabinets of trinkets. Bare walls, bare floors. A single desk. Two chairs. No decoration. The bare necessities – nothing more.

Tenebrae, seated at his desk, glanced at him, scowling, before returning his eyes to Wreath. Behind him, the White Cleaver stood, scythe strapped to his back. Quiver stood by the far wall, hands clasped beneath the sleeves of his robe. Immediately, Craven regretted his tardiness. Wreath was agitated. Craven fought to contain his grin.

"Cleric Wreath," Tenebrae interrupted, "I understand your concerns, but we are quite safe here in the Temple."

"The Remnant is loose," Wreath said angrily. "The moment they realise this they'll be coming here to ask questions."

"Let them come."

"Your Eminence, with all due respect, they are going to want to know how the Remnant escaped. Skulduggery Pleasant will work out that we attempted to use it to control someone."

"Nonsense. We can tell them one of our acolytes set it free, quite by accident. We'll tell them the acolyte has been punished and will never do it again. You're getting upset over nothing, Cleric."

Craven stood by the door, enjoying this immensely. It wasn't often he got to see Solomon Wreath being patronised.

"Having a Remnant loose out there is a good enough reason to be upset," said Wreath. "If we are going to tell people it got free by accident, then at least let it become public. Sorcerers have to know of the danger."

Tenebrae sat back. "Solomon, for all we know, the Remnant will leave the psychic's body and fly off somewhere to be alone, and never bother anyone ever again. Why invite scrutiny and derision when we don't have to? If it makes a nuisance of itself, and if the Skeleton Detective or anyone else comes here asking questions, we can feign surprise and shame upon learning of this terrible, accidental oversight on our part."

"What did he see?" Quiver asked.

Wreath looked at him. "What?"

"The Sensitive. What did he see when you put the Remnant in him?"

Wreath sighed, and pinched the bridge of his nose. "Nothing. Nothing useful. He got sidetracked."

"By what?" Tenebrae asked.

"He saw a vision of Darquesse. Seemed quite enamoured with her."

"So he saw nothing about the Cain girl?"

"Actually, I think there's a reason Darquesse intruded upon his vision. I think Valkyrie is going to be the one to defeat her. I think that will be the start of her journey to becoming the Death Bringer."

Craven cleared his throat, pleased with the anger that flashed in Wreath's eyes. "If I may, High Priest?"

Tenebrae waved a hand. "Of course."

"Cleric Wreath, I admire your tenacity, and I admire your faith in Valkyrie Cain. I do think, however, that you have allowed yourself to focus on her to the exclusion of all others. You say it is now your opinion that Miss Cain defeats Darquesse. And yet every vision we have heard about has Darquesse *killing* both Cain and Pleasant, before starting in on the rest of the world."

"The future can be changed," Wreath growled.

"Oh, yes, indeed it can. I'm not arguing with you there. I'm just wondering about your interpretation. Have you considered the possibility that the Sensitive saw a vision of Darquesse because there *was* no Valkyrie Cain to see? She is obliterated. Wiped from existence. That, to me, would seem the logical interpretation."

"Cleric Craven makes a valid point," Tenebrae nodded. "Solomon, I wanted proof that Cain is strong enough. We have not had that proof."

"What we *have* had," Quiver said, "is a warning. We can't waste any more time on candidates who are going to fall short of what is required. This Darquesse woman is coming. Unless we find our Death Bringer before she arrives, this world will be destroyed."

Wreath's jaw clenched and his face flushed. Craven's grin was itching to spread.

"And the Remnant?" he asked. "We're just going to let it go free?"

"What would you have us do?" Tenebrae asked, almost laughing. "Form a search party? Track it down? Cleric Wreath, that is not the Necromancer way. The Remnant, at this moment, is not our problem. Let others deal with it, if they have to."

"Your Eminence—"

"You are not to involve yourself in this matter any further. Do you understand me, Cleric?"

Wreath stopped himself, and bowed. "Yes, sir. Of course, sir."

Craven walked into the depths of the Temple, allowing the grin to consume his face. That had been most enjoyable. That had been altogether *thrilling*. Not only had Solomon Wreath been humbled before him, but also permission had been given, in a way, for Craven's own plans to commence. The need was apparent. The time frame inescapable. Tenebrae didn't know about it, of course, but then His Eminence was too cautious a leader. In times of strife, victory favoured the bold.

Craven came to a section of the Temple that he had quietly, and secretly, sequestered for his own use over the years. This was the darkest and dankest and coldest part of the Temple, at its lowest point beneath the graveyard. He took a long key from his robes, slotted it through a door and turned. A heavy *clunk* rewarded him, and he stepped in. Melancholia was already standing beside the chair he had given her. She waited with her head down, hands by her sides.

"You may raise your eyes," Craven said. "Cleric Wreath has returned. His mission, unfortunately, a failure."

Melancholia's eyes sparkled. "Then Cain isn't the Death Bringer?"

"We can't be sure, and my fellow Cleric has not been forbidden to continue her lessons... but it is looking increasingly unlikely. You never believed she would be the one, did you?"

Melancholia hesitated. "No, sir, I'm sorry. I didn't."

"Neither did I."

She frowned. "Cleric?"

"Even if Valkyrie Cain does have the power to usher in the Passage, I don't think she would. She's the wrong person. Just like Lord Vile was the wrong person. But you, Melancholia, you might just be what we've all been waiting for."

"Me?"

"You may not have Cain's natural gift, but you make up for it in passion and dedication – attributes I value much more highly. What age are you?"

"Twenty, sir."

"And you haven't reached the Surge yet."

"No, sir."

"You're sure it's Necromancy you want, then? When your

power surges, in a month, in a year, whenever it happens, your choice is over. From that point, you will be locked into one, and only one, discipline, for the rest of your life."

"Necromancy is all I've *ever* wanted."

"Good. Good. I have been waiting for someone with the right qualities, of the right age, on the cusp of the Surge. I've been waiting for *you*, Melancholia."

"You really think I can be the Death Bringer?"

"With my help, yes. I do. We will need to work hard. It won't be easy and it will be painful. We're going to have to prepare you, so that when the Surge happens, you will be infused with shadow magic."

"Is that... is that possible?"

"I'm not going to lie to you. This has never been done before. It's never even been thought of. My research into the language of magic has opened up possibilities that we had never considered. But I've grown tired of waiting. My patience has ended. If we can't find someone powerful enough to assume the mantle of the Death Bringer, then we will *make* someone powerful enough. You, Melancholia, will be the one to save the world. Do you accept?"

"Yes, sir," the girl said, her eyes gleaming. "Oh yes, sir."

14

DEAD MEN

It always surprised Valkyrie whenever she realised just how close the weird and the wonderful, and the fierce and the frightening, lived to the rest of the non-magical, *mortal* world. She'd visited Dublin streets where every house held a sorcerer. She'd been thrown from the balcony of a block of flats that was home to a dozen vampires. She'd had tea with a psychic in a tattoo parlour, fought a blade-wielding assassin beneath the Waxworks Museum, and she'd dodged bullets at a football stadium. And the latest example of how close her two lives ran came in the form of an address for a banshee who, apparently, lived within a half-hour's drive of Dublin.

Valkyrie had decided that she was going to take a taxi to see her – so all she had to do was make her excuses to Skulduggery and leave. It would have been simple if, when she followed Tanith into Ghastly's shop, Erskine Ravel hadn't been there to greet them.

"I don't believe I've had the pleasure," Ravel said when he set eyes on Tanith.

"I think I would have remembered," she replied, smiling as they shook hands. "I'm Tanith Low. You must be the notorious Erskine Ravel. I've heard stories about you."

"Did any of them paint me in a flattering light? Because if they did, they are probably lies."

"Just the usual Dead Men tales."

Despite her pressing need to be elsewhere, Valkyrie frowned. "Dead Men?"

"That's what they called us during the war," Ghastly said, carrying a broken mannequin into the backroom. His shirtsleeves were rolled back off his thick forearms. His muscles, added to the ridges of scars that ran vertically down his entire head, plus the glare he sent Ravel's way, would have been enough to make practically any man back away from Tanith. But it only made Ravel's smile widen.

"They were legends," Tanith told her, missing the glare completely. "Skulduggery, Mr Ravel here, Shudder, Dexter Vex. And Ghastly of course. They called them the Dead Men because they went on suicide missions and always came back alive."

"Not all of us," Skulduggery reminded her as he came in behind them. "Erskine, so good to see you again after so short a time."

"I was in the neighbourhood," Ravel shrugged. "I thought I'd drop in and say hi to Ghastly. I kind of hoped you'd stop by, actually. Has it sunk in yet?"

"Has what sunk in?" Skulduggery asked. "The insanity of what Corrival asked, or the stupidity?"

Ravel shook his head. "It's ridiculous, isn't it? I was just thinking that and... It *is* ridiculous. The two of *us*, on the Council of Elders? Do you realise how boring that job would get? We're not used to jobs that... peaceful."

"I hear Elders don't even get to punch anyone," Skulduggery said miserably. "Apparently, we'd have people to do that for us."

"We're just not suited to it. We've commanded people on the battlefield, we've issued orders during investigations... I mean, being a leader is one thing, but..."

"But being mature is something else entirely," Skulduggery nodded. "I agree completely."

"So you're not going to do it?" Tanith asked. "Really? You're both going to turn this down?"

"What would we be turning down?" Skulduggery asked. "It's only a nomination. It doesn't mean anything."

"What about Corrival?" Valkyrie asked. "If he'd said no to the Grand Mage position, would you have accepted that?"

At that, both men hesitated. Finally, Ravel shrugged.

"I don't know. The chance to make a difference? To make some real and lasting changes? He's perfect for the job."

"And it's going to be really nice to have someone in the Sanctuary we can trust," Skulduggery said. "If he said no, I wouldn't have stopped until I'd convinced him to change his mind."

"So you're saying that you wouldn't have *allowed* Corrival Deuce to turn down this opportunity," Tanith said, "but the pair of you are just too *cool* to say yes?"

"Well, we're rogues," Ravel informed her.

"Mavericks, one might say," Skulduggery added. "Also, we don't appreciate our own arguments being used against us. It's self-defeating in the worst possible way."

Tanith raised an eyebrow. "And also tremendously hypocritical?"

"If I'm a hypocrite," Ravel announced, "I haven't noticed. I've never cared much for introspection. I've done my best to leave that for the bleakest of poets and the most self-pitying of vampires."

Valkyrie was going to point out that not all vampires were self-pitying, but she didn't feel like getting a glare from Tanith. Also, she wasn't entirely sure she believed it.

Ghastly came out of the backroom. "When are you going to tell him you're saying no?"

"I'm planning on delaying it," Skulduggery said. "The longer it goes on, the more ridiculous it will seem, and the more people will complain about it. They'll do my job for me. Erskine, of course, doesn't have that luxury."

Ravel looked at him. "What? Why don't I?"

"Because not enough people dislike you. And Corrival trusts you implicitly – he always has. Erskine, to be brutally honest, it doesn't sound like a completely stupid idea to have you as an Elder."

"Take that back," said Ravel.

"He's going to need your help. As he goes on, he's going to make a lot of enemies. He's prided himself on being a man *of* the people, *for* the people. His greatest priority has always been the safety and protection of the mortals. I can see him restricting sorcerer activity even more than it already has been. That's probably a wise move, too. The way things have been going, it's only a matter of time before one of our secret little battles explodes across the mainstream media, and then not even Scrutinous and Random will be able to smooth things over."

Ravel shook his head. "Not everyone is going to be as understanding as you, Skulduggery. I've been by his side for the last hundred years, and even I'm going to have trouble with some of the things he'll introduce. He has this glorious vision of sorcerers as humanity's guardian angels – silent, invisible..."

"Exactly what they need."

Ravel laughed. "I suppose you're right."

"The new Council needs to be strong," Ghastly said. "Without a strong leadership with a clear purpose, I have a feeling that our friends around the globe won't be content to just sit back and watch."

"They'd try to take over," Skulduggery said.

"Could they?" Valkyrie asked. "I mean, would they be allowed?"

"Who'd stop them? The fact is, they don't trust us to take

care of our own problems. They're not our enemies. If the Americans *were* involved in the destruction of the Sanctuary, it's not because they want to destroy us – it's just because they think that things would be better if they were in charge."

"So... they'd invade?"

"It would be quiet, vicious, and sudden."

"You two would probably be the first to be killed," Ravel said.

Valkyrie stared. "What?"

"Sorry, but it's true. The amount of damage the pair of you have inflicted on anyone who's crossed you over the past few years? They're not going to take a chance on leaving you alive."

"He's right," Skulduggery said. "We're just too good at our job."

"Damn it," Valkyrie scowled. "I hate being too good at our job."

The conversation drifted. Ravel was charming and funny, and he certainly amused Tanith, even if Valkyrie sensed a hesitancy in her laugh whenever Ghastly walked by. Valkyrie checked the time, and the butterflies began fluttering in her belly. She'd have to leave soon. Her phone rang.

"Marr will be ready to be moved in the morning," Kenspeckle told her.

"Is she conscious?"

"She regained consciousness and I sedated her. I have no intention of talking with that woman. Tell the detective he can collect her first thing. I don't want her here one second longer than she has to be."

"Is everything OK?" Skulduggery asked when she'd hung up.

She nodded. "Kenspeckle says we're to pick up Marr in the morning."

Ravel looked surprised. "What? What's this? You know where Marr is?"

Valkyrie closed her eyes and groaned.

"Ah," Skulduggery said. "Yes. That was supposed to be a secret, Valkyrie."

"I know," she said miserably. "I'm sorry."

"You have Marr?" Ravel said. "She's in custody? Why is it a secret? This is great news!"

"We're not telling anyone until we've had a chance to question her," Skulduggery said. "Or that was the *plan*, at least."

"I said I'm sorry," Valkyrie muttered.

"Well let's go," Ravel said. "She's with Kenspeckle Grouse? Let's go question her."

"Professor Grouse has made it clear," Skulduggery said, "that he's quite happy to help us and heal us, but he doesn't want his facility used as a headquarters. No, tomorrow we'll take her somewhere else. We're going to need somewhere secure."

"How about *your* house?" Tanith said.

Skulduggery tilted his head. "That's not a bad suggestion, actually." He looked at Ravel. "Erskine, seeing as how you are now part of this incredibly well-kept secret, do you want to tag along?"

Ravel glanced at Tanith, and smiled. "Sounds like fun. Ghastly? You in?"

"I'm busy," Ghastly said, a little gruffly. "These dresses aren't going to make themselves, you know."

"Well, all right then," Skulduggery said. "Tomorrow morning, we get the answers we've been looking for."

Valkyrie managed to keep her mouth shut until they were outside, and walking for the Bentley. Tanith was heading for her bike, and Ravel had fallen a little behind.

"I have to go," she blurted.

Skulduggery turned his head to her. "Sorry?"

She smiled, hoping he wouldn't see the nervousness in her eyes. "I have to go. Sorry. I should have told you. I've got something else on. Other stuff. Personal business stuff."

"I see. Is everything all right?"

"Yes," she laughed. "Everything's fine. I just should have told you."

He shook his head. "No, nonsense, you don't need to explain. Will this business be finished by tomorrow?"

"Oh yes, God yes. Absolutely. I really don't want to miss out on interrogating Davina Marr if I can help it. I kind of owe her for when she interrogated *me*."

Skulduggery nodded. She had the feeling he was waiting for her to tell him where she was going. When she didn't, he nodded again and picked a loose thread off his sleeve. "You're OK for a lift?"

"I have Fletcher."

"Of course you do. Well, I'll see you later, then."

She gave him a little wave, and walked away, a hollow feeling growing in her gut. She didn't keep much from Skulduggery. Up until three months ago, Gordon's Echo Stone was the only significant truth she'd kept from him, and that wasn't even her choice. But this was different. She had an urge to run back to him, tell him everything, tell him that she was

Darquesse, that she was on her way to talk to a banshee, and she was sure he'd understand, sure he'd help her, make things easier on her...

But Valkyrie didn't run back to him. She just kept on walking.

15

THE BANSHEE

Down by the river, sheltered from the wind by the ancient trees that grew unhindered by city or road, the cottage sat in its patch of darkness and shadow. The river, no more then a stream really, flowed down from the hills and bisected the fields and meadows, and even from her vantage point Valkyrie could hear the gentle rush of water.

She didn't like doing things like this without Skulduggery, but she couldn't see that she had a choice. She stuffed

Gordon's notebook into her jacket and started down the hill slowly, trying her best not to slip on the grass.

And then she heard the scream.

Valkyrie looked up, eyes wide. There was another scream and she took off running, sprinting down to the river and splashing through it, soaking her clothes in the freezing water. She emerged from the other side and saw a narrow road ahead, and a woman stumbling to her knees.

Valkyrie called out and the woman glanced back. Relief washed over her face, and that's when Valkyrie heard the thunder of many hooves, and a creaking and a trundle. She looked around. They were alone out here, but the sounds were getting louder...

And then it materialised in front of her, a great black coach driven by four headless horses, the colour of night. Valkyrie leaped out of the way as it hurtled by. It vanished from sight, but she could still hear it, and now the woman was screaming again. Valkyrie scrambled to her feet and sprinted.

The woman tried to run, but was sent sprawling as if hit from behind. Valkyrie ran closer and the carriage appeared, as the headless horses drew to a stop. The driver climbed down. He was dressed in traditional coachman's attire, though he, like his horses, had no head. He didn't seem quite so ridiculous now.

"Leave her alone!" Valkyrie yelled, running up to him.

He turned to her as she summoned fire and threw it, the ball of flame exploding against his chest, but dying away instantly. She ran right into him, charging him with her shoulder and he stepped back under the collision, but gave no more ground. She felt a cold hand around her neck and she was flung into the air, and she hit the ground hard.

"Help me!" the woman cried as the driver, the Dullahan, strode towards her. He took hold of her arm and pulled her back to the carriage as she begged and screamed.

Valkyrie launched herself at the Dullahan, pushing outwards at the air and making him stagger and then driving a kick into him. He swiped at her with his free hand, but she ducked under it and punched, and her fist met his side and it was like punching a wall. The back of his hand caught her and she spun like a top and dropped to one knee. The Dullahan carried on towards the carriage.

She could only watch as the Dullahan shoved the woman up against the carriage, the door of which opened silently behind her. The woman kept her eyes on the headless driver, tears running down her face, and then a dozen pale hands grabbed her and pulled her, screaming, into the carriage. The door swung gently closed and the Dullahan climbed back to his seat.

Ignoring Valkyrie completely, he flicked the reins and the headless horses took off at a trot, the Coach-a-Bowers trundling behind them. It vanished from sight, though Valkyrie could still hear the hooves, fading into the distance.

She stood up, still a little dizzy from when he had struck her.

"You can't defeat the Dullahan," said a voice from behind her.

She turned. A woman walked up, her black hair hanging over her lined face, her ragged dress trailing on the grass behind her. Her feet were dirty and bare and her hands were thin.

"He is not a man," the woman continued, "he is not a beast, he just is. You cannot defeat what just is."

"Who was she?" Valkyrie asked, forcing herself not to be intimidated. "The woman he took."

The answer came in a voice that was almost fond. "Her name was Margaret. She was the last of her family. She heard my cry and now that family is no more, wiped from the world like a stray tear."

"Why?"

"Because it was her time."

"Who are you to decide?"

The old woman looked up and her hair parted, showing

more of her face. All Valkyrie could make out were wrinkles and lines and one hazel flecked eye, blinking at her. "I'm not the one who decides," she said. "Now then, who are you, and why have you sought me out?"

Valkyrie looked down at her, her anger bubbling right beside her needs. She made herself calm down. "My name's Valkyrie Cain. I was told you could help me."

"Who told you this?"

"My uncle. Gordon Edgley."

"Gordon," the banshee said, smiling. "I haven't heard from him in years. How is he?"

"Dead."

"Give him my best, won't you?"

"I need to seal my name. He said you might know someone who could do something like that."

"You know it, then? Your true name?"

"Yes, I do."

"Impressive. And Gordon was right – I know of one who could do what needs to be done. Its name is Nye – a doctor, and quite a curious creature. I wouldn't trust it, but then, I don't have to. Of course, there is no guarantee that Nye will agree to help. Its time is taken up with experiments and... procedures. It depends how busy the good doctor is, if it can fit you in, and if you make it curious. Luckily for you, I *do* think you will make it curious. Tell me, my dear, do you know what the sealing of your name would entail?"

"I only know that it's dangerous."

"Oh, it is. You're absolutely sure you want me to arrange it?"

Valkyrie thought of her mother, her father, the baby on the way. She thought of what she'd seen and the screams she'd heard. "Yes," she said.

The old woman turned to go. "Then I will be in touch shortly."

"Wait," said Valkyrie. "What *will* it entail? Do you know?"

The banshee smiled. "I only know that the first thing you will have to do is die. Once you've done that, Nye's work will begin."

16

THE INTERROGATION
OF DAVINA MARR

er teeth gritted against the cold of the morning, Tanith followed Skulduggery and Ravel into the Hibernian, fantasising about what it would be like if her clothing of choice was waterproof fleece instead of tight leather. She wouldn't cut such a striking figure, it's true, but the comfort and warmth and sheer cosiness would more than make up for it. The door unlocked for them and they passed through, into the relative warmth of the dark and musty cinema.

Skulduggery had let Ravel do all the talking on the drive over, while he'd stayed quiet. She knew he was wondering about the personal business that had delayed Valkyrie. She'd never chosen personal business over the job before, at least not that Tanith was aware, and it was an unsettling development. Back when Skulduggery was trapped in a world overrun by Faceless Ones, Valkyrie was single-minded in her dedication to rescuing him. But since then, it seemed, she'd been distracted. There was always something going on, something she didn't want to talk about.

Was it Caelan? Was she feeling guilty about the kiss? Was there something more, something she hadn't told Tanith? Was she with him now, despite the promises she'd made? Tanith knew full well how things could get confusing at that age. She had been a teenager once, and she knew that, despite the apparent contradiction, a person's teenage years lasted well into their fifties. It had only been at age sixty that *she'd* managed to gain some control over herself, after all.

These days she was a fine young woman of eighty-three, and even though she was still astonishingly immature for her age, the allure of bad boys had faded somewhat. They were still all around her of course – in her line of work, she had her pick of them. But bad boys would always disappoint. It was inevitable. Whereas nice guys tended to surprise you.

The only parts of her that weren't numb with cold were her feet, because she was wearing boots Ghastly had made for her. He hadn't needed any special occasion to do it either. He'd just presented them to her one day, mumbled something about the importance of circulation, and wandered into the backroom of his shop. She grinned at the memory.

But as for Valkyrie... Tanith was willing to give her the benefit of the doubt. She might *not* have been with the vampire last night. It may have been *family* business – it *was* Christmas time, after all. Or Fletcher. Maybe they'd had a date.

Tanith frowned. Did people still go on *dates* any more? She was sure they did. They probably called it something different though. She tried to think of the last date she'd been on. The last *proper* date. Did fighting side by side with Saracen Rue count as a date? They ended up snuggling under the moonlight, drenched in gore and pieces of brain – so it had *probably* been a date. If it wasn't, it was certainly a fun time had by all. Well, not *all*. But she and Saracen had sure had a blast.

Tanith needed a date. She needed a lot of things, but above all she needed a date.

It didn't help to be reminded of that fact every time she saw

Valkyrie and Fletcher together. Valkyrie didn't like public displays of affection, but she wasn't allergic to them either. The hand-holding, the sitting close together, Fletcher's hand on the small of her back... These things did nothing to take Tanith's mind off the subject. And then there were the talks, Valkyrie filling her in on details Tanith could have done without. But that was her role, she supposed. Best friend and big sister, all in one.

Her eyes drifted to the back of Skulduggery's head. Maybe not *best* friend, she corrected. But close enough.

They climbed on to the stage and passed through the door in the screen. Clarabelle met them in the corridor, wearing her white lab coat over a summer dress, and a huge black gas mask contraption on her head.

"Good morning," she said, her cheery voice muffled. "Are you here to pick up the patient? She's not very nice. She said some harsh words about my intelligence before the Professor made her go unconscious again."

"Why are you wearing that?" Tanith asked.

Clarabelle's head dipped heavily as she looked down at her dress. "Because it's pretty."

"No, I mean the gas mask."

"Hmm? Oh, *this*. I just wanted to see what it would be like to live in a bubble. Professor Grouse is busy elsewhere. He said the patient should be awake in about half an hour, and then he asked me to escort you to her."

"It's OK," Skulduggery said, "we know where she is."

"Good, because I think I'm lost." Clarabelle caught sight of the doorway nearest to her and she wandered through it, bashing her head against the doorframe on the way.

"Delightful lady," Ravel said as they walked on.

They got to the Medical Bay, where they found Davina Marr sedated and unconscious. Skulduggery undid the restraints, then shackled her hands behind her back. He pulled her into a sitting position, and suddenly she started levitating. For a split second, Tanith was ready to spring into action.

"You were going to carry her?" Ravel asked, manipulating the air to float Marr gently to the door. "Why make things more difficult than they have to be?"

Tanith relaxed, and Skulduggery shook his head as they followed Ravel out into the corridor. "I like to keep magic for special occasions. I don't use it simply to show off." He caught the grin Tanith threw his way. "Shut up."

She laughed.

They put Marr in the boot of the Bentley and drove to Skulduggery's house, with Tanith following on her motorbike.

By the time they got there, Tanith's teeth were chattering with the cold.

Skulduggery carried Marr into the living room, where he secured her to a chair. He left his hat and gun on a coffee table and Ravel hung up his coat. Tanith turned the heating on, and when she walked back into the room, Marr was awake, and smiling.

"You look happy," Skulduggery said.

Marr shrugged. "Not happy, just surprised."

"At your surroundings?"

"At the fact that I'm still alive. I thought Tesseract would have tracked me down by now."

"I assure you, you're quite safe."

"No I'm not, and neither are you. Any of you."

"In that case, we better talk fast before we're interrupted. You've been betrayed. Tell us what we want to know and we'll protect you."

Marr laughed. "You can't protect me. This is Tesseract we're talking about."

"You may not have noticed, but there are more of us than there are of him."

"I'm startled that you think it'll make a difference."

"Tell us who you were working with," said Skulduggery.

"I wasn't working with anyone. Why is Erskine Ravel here, anyway? Have you joined this merry band of detectives, Mr Ravel? Have you got nothing better to do with your time?"

"Things have been happening since you've been away," Ravel said. "You don't know what you've been missing."

"You claim that you decided to destroy the Sanctuary all by yourself," Skulduggery said. "Why, Davina? Were you bored that day?"

"Well, it sounds silly when you say it like *that*..."

"You don't owe these people your loyalty. They want you silenced. They want you dead."

"I sincerely don't know what people you're referring to."

"If you don't help us," Skulduggery said, "all the blame lands at your feet. You will be tried, *alone*, for multiple counts of murder and terrorism."

She shook her head. "Terrorism. Everything is *terrorism* lately. Such an overused word."

"Those whose spread terror are terrorists by definition."

"But don't you think that word misses out on the subtleties that separate these acts from each other? Why do they have to be terrorists? Why can't they just be criminals and murderers? The spreading of terror isn't a motive – it's a means to achieving a goal. Labelling an act of atrocity as terrorism instantly dismisses the nuances of human behaviour as regards hatred, anger and greed."

Skulduggery folded his arms. "The destruction of the Sanctuary, then. This wouldn't be terrorism?"

"Not at all."

"It would simply be murder?"

"Now you're getting it," Marr said with a nod.

"So you're a murderer."

"Finally, we agree on something."

"You forced Myron Stray to take the Desolation Engine into the Sanctuary and set it off. You wanted Valkyrie and myself to be there when it happened."

"Sorry about that. Purely personal."

"Why did you do it?"

"I was disgruntled."

"You were having an off day?"

Marr smiled. "Again, you make it sound so silly."

"I think you're lying."

"I am deeply hurt."

The front door opened, and they all spun. Footsteps approached, and Valkyrie walked in.

"Hello, sweetie," Marr smiled.

Immediately, Valkyrie scowled. "Is she talking?"

Marr chuckled. "Do you really think you're going to get anything out of me? I've been where you are, remember. I've been the one asking the questions. This doesn't intimidate me."

"Well, yeah," Valkyrie said, "you asked the questions, but you weren't very good at it, were you? I mean, I was interrogated by you, and you failed so spectacularly that you had to try to *beat* a confession out of me."

"Very true," Marr nodded. "I didn't get a confession though, did I?"

"No, you didn't."

"But I did get you to beg."

The look of anger that came over Valkyrie's face was startling, and Marr laughed. Tanith silently willed her friend to stay calm.

"That's enough," Skulduggery said. "Davina, you have this one chance to help yourself. If you don't seize it now, you will die in prison. Were you working for the American Sanctuary? Did they orchestrate the destruction of the Sanctuary to destabilise the country?"

"This country is already destabilised."

"You were reporting back to them, weren't you?"

"Maybe the odd postcard."

"I've never known you to make so many jokes."

"You've never known me. You thought you did. You thought many things. You know your problem? You think you're smarter than you actually are. It becomes very annoying to the people around you. You agree, don't you, Valkyrie? Or maybe I'm asking the wrong person. How about you, Tanith? You're not besotted with him like Valkyrie is, are you? You've got far too many other romances to be thinking about. You're a very popular girl, from what I hear."

Tanith frowned. "Are you coming on to me?"

"How's the tailor, by the way? Are you still torturing him by pretending not to notice how he feels?"

The retort died on Tanith's tongue, and she just glared.

"Struck a nerve, did I?" Marr asked. "Deeply sorry. You can continue your interrogation now, if you want. It's a fun way to pass the time while we wait for Tesseract to find me."

"Why are you protecting them?" Skulduggery asked. "They want you dead, Davina."

"The whole country wants me dead."

"I can't understand this. You've been abandoned. By your own admission, your life is in incredible danger. Why won't you help us stop the people responsible?"

"Because this is more amusing."

Skulduggery shook his head. "No. That's not it. That's not why you're refusing to help. I think you're refusing to help because you can't."

"I see," Marr said. "Yes. That's exactly right. Well done."

"Think about the people responsible."

"I told you—"

"Yes, yes, you told us you were working alone, and we don't believe you. What I want you to do, Davina, is to think of the people you were working with. You don't have to tell us their names. I just want you to think about the people. OK?"

"You want me to think about no one?"

"I don't care if you keep up the charade – the only thing I want you to do is see them, in your mind. Picture them. Think of their names."

Skulduggery paused, then tilted his head. "You can't, can you? You can't picture them. You can't think of their names. You try to. You've probably been trying to for the last three months. But you can't."

Marr wasn't smiling any more.

"They've blocked themselves from your memory," Skulduggery continued. "The harder you try to remember, the further away they get. Given time, with the right people and the right procedures, we could break through that wall. But we don't have the time."

Marr shrugged. "So you've worked out my little secret. Big deal. Now you can stop repeating the same questions, right?"

"What do you remember?"

"You've just figured out that I don't remember anything."

"You don't remember anything specific. What about generalities? Vague impressions? How many of them were there?"

"Don't know."

"Five? Ten?"

"One," Marr said. "A man. I think."

"A man contacted you?"

"Yes."

"Told you his plan, asked if you were interested?"

"That's as much as I remember."

"He left the finer details up to you?"

"He told me why he wanted the Sanctuary destroyed. Whatever it was he said, it made sense, I remember that much. I agreed with him. I came up with how to go about it, and I set the plan in motion."

"You can't remember anything about him?" Skulduggery pressed. "Height? Accent? Hair colour? Age?"

Marr sighed. "Nothing. Whatever he dazzled me with, it dazzled me good. I've been trying to remember the finer details since it happened, but all I get is a very confused fog."

"If we can get you remembering, will you help us?"

"No point. I'll be dead before the day is out."

"If we keep you alive, will you help us?"

"And what do I get out of it? Immunity? Do I get to walk free?"

"No," Ravel said. "We can't give you that. But we can make sure that the people who set this up are brought to justice."

"What kind of justice? The kind of justice where I'm tied to a chair in someone's living room? I don't see any officials here, or anything stopping you from executing me the moment I tell you what you want to know. Would they be brought to *this* kind of justice?"

"*Exactly* this kind of justice."

She smiled. "Well, why didn't you say so? Call whoever you have to call – let's get my memories unlocked."

Skulduggery made a few calls, and Tanith and Valkyrie went into the kitchen to chat. A few minutes later, Tanith excused herself and walked into the bathroom. She shut the door behind her, unbuckled her belt, and looked up into the mirror just in time to see a colossal man in a metal mask reaching for her.

17

THE JOB

Tesseract spent three hours getting into the Skeleton Detective's house. First he dismantled the magical defences, then he turned his attention to the technological. He worked quickly but without hurry, allowing himself to be impressed with the attention to detail in the security arrangements. Before this visit to Ireland, he had never personally encountered Skulduggery – Tesseract liked to be on a first-name basis with the people he would probably end up killing – and he was glad to see that all the stories about his professionalism appeared to be true. A worthy opponent, if ever there was one.

Of course, Tesseract wasn't especially interested in worthy opponents. He was not on a crusade to prove himself, or test himself, or needlessly risk his life or his freedom. If he had the choice, he always preferred to kill someone when they were distracted, or when their back was turned, or when they were sleeping. He had even, on one memorable occasion, killed a man who was already dead. A heart attack had taken his target's life before Tesseract had even reached him, so he stabbed him once, not too deep, and returned to his employer to claim his payment. Tesseract was not above a little foul play. He was, after all, an assassin.

And so his current situation was not resting easily in his mind. He didn't like the fact that, in order to find out where Davina Marr was being kept, he would have to go through Skulduggery Pleasant, and probably Valkyrie Cain, and whoever else they might have along with them. The numbers were against him, but his employers at Roarhaven had given him a deadline. Tesseract's hand, as they say, had been forced.

He wasn't nervous. He wasn't excited. He wasn't looking forward to the blood he had to spill, but neither was he dreading it. Two, or even three, against one were not good odds, and yet he felt no fear. He was a professional, and he was quite capable of killing three sorcerers in one go, even sorcerers as powerful and experienced as Skulduggery, provided he took them by surprise.

Neither was he dismissing Valkyrie Cain. He had files on everyone he was likely to go up against, and he had one on her too. She had a habit of upsetting the plans of her enemies – through either luck, skill, or pure bloody-minded determination. She was not to be underestimated.

His face itched under the mask. He had chosen an angular one for today, with deep cheekbones cut into the metal and three small holes at his mouth. He took a knife from the sheath under his arm, poked the tip through the left eyehole and manoeuvred it down to give himself a good scratch. He grumbled with satisfaction, but put the knife away when he heard the car.

He went to the window, saw Skulduggery and Erskine Ravel get out of the Bentley. Tanith Low rode up after them on her bike. Three powerful sorcerers. These weren't good odds, but he'd faced worse. Under the cover of night, Skulduggery lifted something large from the boot of the car. For once, luck was smiling on Tesseract. They'd brought Davina Marr *to* him.

He left the room, staying away from the other windows. He stood behind the door in the bathroom, his breathing as calm and as quiet as ever. The front door opened and they came in. He heard Davina's voice as they questioned her.

If he was lucky, Davina would be allowed a bathroom break. Then all Tesseract would have to do was step out and implode her skull, and vanish before anyone came knocking. If he was *un*lucky, he'd have to kill Tanith or Erskine first, and work through them one at a time. If he was *really* unlucky, no one would need to visit the bathroom at all, and he'd have to confront the whole lot of them at once.

He stayed behind the door for twenty-three minutes. He heard Valkyrie arrive, which brought the tally to four against one. The odds were getting worse. There was a break in the questioning, and Valkyrie and Tanith moved to the kitchen. Another minute passed before one of them left, their footsteps getting closer. Tanith Low walked into the bathroom, already unbuckling her belt, and swung the door shut without seeing him. The first to die, then.

He stepped up behind her, reached for the back of her head, and looked into the mirror over the sink at the same time as she did. Her eyes widened. He promised to curse himself later for making such a grievous error.

She whirled, whipping the belt from her trousers as he lunged. The belt wrapped around his wrist and she tugged it, tried to pull him off-balance, but he was already adjusting. He rammed his shoulder into her, driving her through the open doors of the shower. Before she could call for help he kicked her. She wasn't expecting it. In his experience, fast people rarely expected to encounter someone faster than they were. The toe of his boot sank into her belly and lifted her off her feet, doubling her over and forcing all the air from her lungs. She dropped forward and he cracked his knee into her chin, and caught her as she fell.

He didn't kill her. Unconscious, she was no longer a threat, and so he saw no point to it. Also, he tried not to do freebies if he could avoid it.

Tesseract moved to the door and listened to the low murmur of uninterrupted conversation – Skulduggery was talking to Davina Marr again. Tesseract stepped out, walked silently to the kitchen. Valkyrie had her back to him. She was making a pot of tea. How very Irish of her.

Even as he crossed the floor, he acknowledged that he had an opportunity to leave her alive, but decided against it. The encounter with Tanith had simply turned out that way. The simple truth was that it was easier and quieter to kill this girl than to subdue her. Tesseract was nothing if not a practical man, and so he went for the spine.

She must have felt the air shift, because she started talking, assuming he was a friend. His fingers closed around her neck, and her body jerked and she made a noise like someone had kicked her in the throat. Then she twisted out of his grip and stumbled to the floor.

"Help!" she barked.

Tesseract narrowed his eyes, looking at the jacket that she was wearing, realising too late the magical properties it must possess. His fingertips had pressed against the collar, not her skin, and the collar had protected her. Another mistake, in a day that was becoming chock-full of them.

Skulduggery Pleasant burst into the kitchen and Tesseract went to meet him head on. He ducked under a punch and slammed an elbow into Skulduggery's side. He felt the framework under the skeleton's clothes flex inwards, and then the rewarding crunch of elbow against ribs. Skulduggery staggered away and Erskine came next. He pushed at the air, but Tesseract moved around it. Credit where it was due, Erskine switched to a physical attack without blinking. Not that it was going to do him any good.

Tesseract blocked a punch with his forearm, then smacked Erskine in the mouth and followed him as he stumbled back. Too late, Tesseract saw it was a ruse. Erskine kicked at his leg, and if Tesseract hadn't managed to move slightly, he was in no doubt that the kick would have smashed his kneecap.

The air shimmered and hit him like God's own punch. He was thrown across the room, landed on the table and rolled off the other side.

Erskine threw a handful of fire that Tesseract had to sidestep to dodge, and as he did so Valkyrie caught him in the chest with a stream of shadows. He tumbled into the living room. Davina was shackled to a chair, staring at him with wide eyes. She started struggling against her bonds.

Before he could move towards her, Skulduggery and the others barged in behind him. Skulduggery gestured and his gun flew from a coffee table towards his gloved hand. Tesseract flung his knife. The tip of the blade slid through the trigger guard and pinned the gun to the wall.

"Let me free!" Davina yelled.

Tesseract ran at Valkyrie, hurling the coffee table at Skulduggery to distract him. Valkyrie whipped a tendril of shadows at him, but he dived under it, rolled and came up, grabbed her black clothes with both hands and lifted. He slammed her against the wall and then spun her around, throwing her like a rag doll to the window beside them. Her legs smashed through the glass, and he released her and the momentum kept her body turning. Her back hit the edge of the window frame and she rebounded and fell, cracking the shards of glass beneath her. She lay half in, half out of the window, folded over the sill. If it weren't for those clothes, she'd have been slashed to bloody ribbons.

He turned as Skulduggery rushed him, a snarl behind that impassive skull. Tesseract dodged a punch and swung into him, throwing him over his hip to the ground. He heard a finger click, and Erskine sent flames bursting across his back. Tesseract stumbled, but Skulduggery was already on his feet. His coat on fire and his skin burning, Tesseract caught Skulduggery's fist in his hand, his fingertips curling around the glove, making the bones underneath tremor. Skulduggery cried out as they snapped apart. Tesseract's power could only be transmitted through his fingertips, so when his knuckles broke Skulduggery's jaw, it wasn't magic that did it, it was a combination of pure strength, the right angle, and a happy piece of luck.

Skulduggery went down, just as a wall of air slammed into Tesseract and sent him hurtling over the couch. He ripped off his fiery coat and turned to meet Erskine's charge, saw the Elemental's hands pushing down by his sides, and knew what was coming next. He grabbed a floor lamp with both hands, and as the air shimmered and Erskine shot towards him, he swung the lamp like a baseball bat. It splintered on impact, catching Erskine perfectly and sending him crashing to the ground.

And then a kick came from nowhere, right into his face, and Tesseract tripped over the broken coffee table and went sprawling. Tanith Low dropped from the ceiling. He should have killed her. He should have killed her when he had the chance.

She jumped at him, aiming to finish the fight with another kick to the head. Tesseract raised an arm to block it, but she flipped over him. He rolled sideways, avoiding the foot stomp, and got up in time to block the next attack and give himself some room. He had never been one for talking during a fight, but he would have loved to ask her a question right now. Once she'd regained consciousness, had she run immediately to help her friends, or had she done the smart thing and delayed for a moment, long enough to call for reinforcements?

Tesseract darted forward, catching her off guard, the heel of his palm striking her in the chest. He tried to follow it up with a grab, but she demonstrated a most impressive aerial cartwheel and got away from him. She backed off, and his eyes flickered behind her and saw where she was headed. Her coat lay over a chair, and upon that chair lay her sword. She ran for it.

Tesseract wrapped an arm around the music system that was on a shelf beside him. He yanked it free of the wires and cables and hurled it across the room. Tanith grabbed her sword and turned and the music system hit her square in the face. She twisted as she fell, and the system clattered to the ground beside her.

If she *had* taken a moment to make that call, he knew she would undoubtedly have called Fletcher Renn, told him to bring help. Tesseract strode to where Davina Marr struggled.

"No," said Davina, real fear in her eyes. "Not like this. At least let me stand up. Please, not like this."

He would have liked to grant her wish, but the Teleporter would have gone to either Ghastly Bespoke or China Sorrows – most likely the former. The question then became, if Fletcher had been alerted, how long would it take him to find Ghastly? Thirty seconds? A minute? Tesseract just didn't have the time to waste.

He placed his hand on Davina's chest and her breastbone shook and the ribs splintered inwards, piercing her heart. She died with her eyes open.

Tesseract turned, and a heavy fist caught him in the hinge of the jaw, right where his flesh met the mask. If Ghastly Bespoke hurt his hand with the punch, he gave no sign as he pressed forward.

Tesseract absorbed the punches, swung one of his own that Ghastly swayed away from. Three jabs rocked the mask against his face, then Ghastly went low, working the body. He surprised Tesseract with a kick that buckled his leg. Tesseract went down, but was helped back up again with an uppercut to the chin.

Fletcher Renn was across the room, carefully lifting Valkyrie down from the shattered window. The moment she was clear of the glass, they both vanished. A moment later, Fletcher was back, alone. Eye blink by eye blink, he disappeared with Skulduggery, Tanith and Erskine.

Tesseract had worked out Ghastly's rhythm by now, and dodged three more jabs before responding with a punch that sank into the muscle in the boxer's right side. Ghastly fell back, gasping for air, eyes suddenly wide. A good punch would do that to you, Tesseract knew. A good punch did more than deliver hurt – it disrupted an offensive, shook a fighter. Ghastly was shaken. He wasn't expecting a punch that fast, that hard. Tesseract could tell by the way he was circling that Ghastly was wary now, and unsure.

Fletcher appeared. "You ready?" he asked. Ghastly kept his eyes on Tesseract and didn't answer. "Ghastly. You ready to go?"

"Yeah," came the grudging reply.

Fletcher nodded. He took Skulduggery's gun down from the wall, tossing the knife away. He teleported to the chair and picked up Tanith's sword, then Skulduggery's hat, and then he appeared at Ghastly's elbow. They both vanished.

Tesseract let his fists uncurl. His back was burnt, the skin bloody and charred, but his mission had been a success. He found himself hoping that his Roarhaven employers would hire him to kill Skulduggery and the others. He'd quite like to finish this.

18

LICKING WOUNDS

Valkyrie lay in a tub of cold mud, its healing properties working on the damage Tesseract had inflicted on her back. A curtain separated her from the others. Skulduggery was on the bed to her right, mumbling instructions while he waited for his jaw to set. His hand, she had seen, was wrapped in gauze until his bones realigned. Ravel was to her left, healing up from his smashed ribs. Across the room, behind another curtain, was Tanith. Her jaw had been broken, her cheek shattered, nose crushed and four teeth had been knocked out. It was taking Kenspeckle Grouse a little longer to heal her.

Valkyrie lay in the tub and listened to the conversation go on around her.

"One man?" Kenspeckle was saying. "One man did all this?"

"We weren't ready," Ghastly said, and she could hear the quiet anger in his voice. "I should have gone with them. Should have been there at the start."

"Then who would Fletcher have gone to for help?" Kenspeckle asked. "No, Ghastly, I think it's just as well they had you as back-up. The man who did this, Tesseract. He wouldn't happen to be Russian, would he?"

"That's him," she heard Fletcher say. "You know him?"

"I've read reports of some people he's killed. He's a bonebreaker – he can break bones with the gentlest of touches. Highly unusual ability, but extremely effective. I daresay, actually, that he'd be the only person in the world who would be assured of killing Detective Pleasant here, if he so desired."

Skulduggery murmured something that sounded like, "Your bedside manner is dreadful."

"I thought I told you not to talk."

Skulduggery grunted.

"Tesseract could kill him?" Valkyrie asked, sitting up.

"Oh, yes," came Kenspeckle's answer, "and quite easily, too. We've seen how my grumpiest of patients can survive being dismembered, but it has long been my theory that if there isn't a large enough section of him that remains intact, his consciousness would dissipate. Just drift away. Tesseract has the ability to splinter an entire *skeleton*. I doubt there'd be anything left of the detective to think *with*."

Valkyrie lay back in the mud. She had come to regard Skulduggery as unkillable – mainly because he was already dead. She didn't like the idea of someone utterly *destroying* him.

She heard Ravel get off the bed to her left, and saw his shadow under the curtain as he moved to join the others.

"Mr Ravel," Kenspeckle said sharply, "I must insist that you allow yourself time to heal."

"I'm fine, Professor," Ravel responded. He groaned slightly, and Valkyrie heard the rustle of fabric. He was putting on his shirt. "I need to report this to Corrival. The upside is that we caught Davina Marr, which shows the Councils around the world that we can take care of our own messes. I don't think we should mention that Tesseract was the one to kill her though."

Skulduggery murmured something that could have been, "Agreed."

"We'll say she died resisting arrest, or she took her own life or something. Leave it with me. I'll take care of it."

"And what about Tesseract?" Fletcher asked. "He's still out there."

"His job is done," Ghastly said. "Unless he has another target, he'll slip away like he's always done."

Skulduggery murmured something that nobody understood. He made a few grunts that sounded like threats, and then Kenspeckle's voice moved closer to Valkyrie.

"Fine," Kenspeckle said. "I'll remove the bandage, but if your jaw falls off, you're going to the back of the queue."

Everyone waited a moment.

"OK," Kenspeckle said. "Open your mouth. Close it. Move it side to side. Very well, you can speak."

"Thank you," Skulduggery said. "Ghastly's right – Tesseract is probably gone already. And with him, any hope we have of finding out who his employers were."

"If he even remembers," Ravel said. "They could have dazzled him the same way they dazzled Marr."

The curtain by Valkyrie's tub parted, and Kenspeckle came through. He motioned her to lean forward, and checked her spine.

"I don't think so," Skulduggery said. "You wouldn't take the chance of double-crossing someone like Tesseract, not unless you planned to kill him. And we all know that's not exactly an easy thing to do."

"So he's collected his payment and gone," Ghastly said. "And Marr is dead, and her co-conspirators are safe. Where does that leave us?"

"Your back is healed and the swelling is going down," Kenspeckle said to Valkyrie. "There's a robe by the chair."

She nodded her thanks and waited until he had left before climbing out of the tub. She listened to the conversation as it developed into an argument for and against Roarhaven's involvement. She put on the robe, feeling it squelch against the mud covering her, and slipped her feet into the slippers. She was a little stiff as she walked through the curtain.

"The fact is," Skulduggery said, "we have nothing. No clues, no evidence. The only thing we know is that one of the people involved has the power to cloud memories. That's all."

Valkyrie looked at him. "Did we lose this one?"

"Of course not. We just didn't win it."

Ravel grabbed his coat. "I have to go. Grand Mage Deuce needs to know what we know."

"We don't know an awful lot," Skulduggery said.

"Then it's going to be a short meeting."

Skulduggery and Valkyrie drove back to Haggard in glum silence. It was dark again – they'd spent practically an entire day recovering from their injuries. Valkyrie's parents were undoubtedly asleep by now, which meant she had missed her chance to spend Christmas Eve with them, and this put her in an even worse mood than before. That heartless, soulless reflection had been there instead, smiling its fake smile. She sank into her seat and glowered.

"How are you?" Skulduggery asked.

"Fine," she muttered.

"You don't sound fine."

"I'm as fine as could be expected then, for someone who was in a fight in which one guy beat four of us at the same time, and then got away."

"We were the ones who fled, actually."

"You didn't have to point that out. I could have done without you pointing that out. He killed Marr with a touch. We'd probably all be dead if he'd been paid to kill us."

"That's a possibility."

"I don't like the fact that there's someone out there who can do that."

"We're not unstoppable, you know," said Skulduggery.

"Sometimes we are."

"Not tonight."

"No, not tonight. I'm glad she's dead. That's probably really horrible, isn't it? But I am. I'm glad Marr is dead."

"She killed a lot of people."

"Is that it, then? Is it over?"

"It appears to be. For now. Are you going to tell me what else is upsetting you?"

"What? Nothing." He cocked his head and she rolled her eyes. "Fine. I missed Christmas Eve with my parents. Happy? This is my last Christmas Eve as an only child, and I wanted to bask in my parents' love one final time."

He sounded amused. "They're not going to stop loving you just because you have a new brother or sister."

"You don't understand. When I was seven, Mum bought me a rabbit, Mister Fluffy. For two weeks, Dad paid more attention to that rabbit than he did to me. He played with it, he took it on walks, he practically tucked it in at night. And that was a *rabbit*. Imagine what he's going to be like with a *baby*."

"But after those two weeks, once the novelty wore off, he was back to normal, wasn't he?"

"I don't think it was because the novelty wore off. I think it was because he stood on Mister Fluffy."

"Pardon?"

Valkyrie sighed, her head lolling back on the seat. "He stepped on it. Squished it. Squashed it. Killed it. Cut it down in its prime. It kicked the bucket, turned up its toes, shuffled off this mortal coil. It was... an ex-rabbit."

"He's a dangerous man, your father."

"The baby better learn to dodge."

The windshield wipers activated, and Valkyrie looked out at the swirling snow caught in the headlights.

"That's pretty," she said. She lowered the window and stuck her head out, getting a freezing blast full in the face. She brought her head back in, slightly dazed.

"Fun?" Skulduggery asked.

She brushed the snowflakes from her hair. "It lightened my mood. I still have tomorrow off, right?"

"That's our deal."

"No matter what happens, Christmas Day is off-limits. It's a day for presents under the tree, turkey for dinner, and dozing off on the sofa while we watch Indiana Jones on TV."

"Sounds lovely."

"What are you going to do?"

"The same, except completely different."

Valkyrie managed a smile. "I love Christmas. I'll never understand anyone who doesn't."

"Plenty of people don't enjoy Christmas. It can be a lonely time of the year."

"But it's when all the family gets together," she said, speaking too fast to stop herself. Skulduggery dipped the headlights as a car passed in the opposite lane, then flicked them back up.

"Sorry," she said quietly.

He turned to her slightly. "What for?"

"You know. The family thing."

"Oh," he said. "You mean because my family is dead."

She winced. "Yeah."

"You know, I'd completely forgotten about all that until you brought it up."

She stared at him, horrified. They passed a sign for Haggard.

"I'm joking," he said at last.

"Oh, my God. That was mean."

"You shouldn't feel guilty about enjoying something that other people don't. Well, apart from torture, but that's probably the only exception. You love Christmas, and that's wonderful. Keep in mind that not everyone does, but don't let that take away from how you feel."

"Wow," she said. "It's like you're teaching me something and being all wise."

"You are not easy to get along with," Skulduggery said.

They got to the pier in Haggard and Valkyrie unbuckled her seatbelt. "Tomorrow is off-limits and everything, but... you're still going to drop by, aren't you?"

"Of course. I have to give you your present, don't I?"

She grinned. "Yes, you do. Merry Christmas, Skulduggery."

"Merry Christmas, Valkyrie."

She got out, and ran home through the snow.

19

CHRISTMAS MORNING AT THE MIDNIGHT HOTEL

Anton Shudder knocked on the door to Room 19 as he unlocked it. He waited a few moments, and then the door opened and the vampire looked out, wearing its human skin.

"Good morning," Caelan said. "Did I... I'm sorry if I was loud last night."

"Not at all," Shudder said. "The walls are still sealed. No sound escapes."

"I'm afraid I broke some furniture. The chain snapped and, well... I'll pay for it, of course. Some of the walls are scratched, too."

"We've discussed this. Snapping your chains or damaging the walls means nothing if you can't leave this room – and once I've locked this door, you don't even have the option. You're safe in there, and everyone else is safe out here. You are a guest in the Midnight Hotel. You have no need to apologise."

"Thank you. Where are we, by the way?"

"Scotland."

"Are we scheduled to appear in Ireland today?"

"In just under an hour. You have business there?"

"Some," Caelan said.

"I'll let you know when we arrive."

"Thank you, Mr Shudder."

Shudder walked to the stairs, nodding to a guest coming the opposite way. He climbed to the second floor on his usual morning rounds. All but two of the rooms on this floor were occupied, but none of the guests were awake yet. He stopped outside Room 24, as he always did, and tested the handle. It turned, but didn't open. Locked tight, as it always was.

Satisfied, he returned to his office on the ground floor. He busied himself with paperwork, barely noticing the location shift. Had anyone been standing outside, they would have seen the Midnight Hotel suddenly come apart, and then sink into the earth within the space of a few seconds. For those within the hotel, however, there was a slight tremor and nothing more.

He reached for the phone and called the vampire's room as another tremor passed, and the hotel sprouted and grew in a wood just outside Dublin. He told Caelan they'd arrived, and a minute later, the vampire left the hotel.

Shudder worked for another hour, then took the keys for the car he kept parked here and walked out. He needed supplies, food and cleaning materials. Also, some new furniture for the vampire's room. And some decent chains.

The forest was chilled as he passed through the trees. Twigs cracked dully under his weight, his steps tossing wet leaves from his path. He got to the clearing beside the road that acted as the hotel car park, and stopped.

A man lay unconscious on the ground in front of him. Despite the cold, he was only wearing jeans and a T-shirt. He had tattoos and piercings.

Something caught Shudder's eye, and he turned just as the Remnant flew at him. He stumbled back, tried in vain to stop it from prying his mouth open and slithering in. He gagged, throat bulging as the Remnant forced its way down. Shudder fell to his knees, feeling it spread out inside him, rushing through his body, its darkness seeping into his bloodstream. The pain stopped. His fingers and toes were buzzing.

Shudder got to his feet. He looked over at Finbar Wrong, who lay unconscious in the wet grass and leaves. He remembered being Finbar, and he remembered all the things he'd seen in the vision. Before Finbar, Shudder had been Kenspeckle Grouse, and before that... Well, before *that* he'd spent a long time trapped in a room in the Midnight Hotel, with all the other Remnants.

Shudder took the key from the chain around his forearm, and walked back to the hotel to free his brothers and sisters.

20

'TIS THE SEASON

There had been a time, not too long ago, when Christmas morning was a big deal. A morning when Stephanie Edgley would wake up and rush to her parents' room, practically dragging them out of bed. Her father would go downstairs first, to check that Santa Claus was gone. When he gave the all-clear, Stephanie and her mother would hurry into the living room, and all three of them would dive under the tree, squealing with delight as each present was torn open. Her dad squealed the loudest, for some reason, especially when he got packs of brand-new socks. Her dad *loved* new socks. It was almost disturbing how he looked forward to slipping each pair on.

Her mother found each and every Christmas morning hilarious. Some of Valkyrie's fondest memories were of her mother, doubled up with laughter upon receiving her gift from her husband. Like the year she'd been given a hammer. Valkyrie could still see her dad's face, proud that he had managed to get his wife a present without help from anyone, and then the look of puzzlement that crept over his features as his darling Melissa slowly collapsed to the carpet, laughing so hard she was completely silent.

Valkyrie hadn't missed a Christmas Day yet. With all the time she spent away from home, she felt it was important to spend this day with her family, doing normal Christmas things like a normal daughter. Skulduggery would usually drive up in the evening, and she'd slip out to meet him at the pier. They'd exchange presents as the sea crashed beside them.

His presents were always much better than hers. Last year she'd given him a mug with a picture of Betty, a neighbour's one-eyed mongrel (and officially *Ireland's Best-Loved Dog* after she won a competition), printed on the side. Valkyrie feared she may have inherited her dad's dreadful present-buying prowess, but Skulduggery didn't seem to mind too much.

For so long, she'd been an only child at Christmas, and it was fair to say that she'd been a little spoiled by it all. But the idea that next year she'd have a little brother or sister made her smile as she lay in bed thinking about it. Having a kid around to get excited, to whoop and squeal like she had done, would ensure that Christmas stayed as special as the ones she remembered. They'd have to alter the routine, of course. The kid would have to wake *her* first, then they'd *both* wake their parents, drawing out the excitement, prolonging the anticipation. She couldn't wait.

Her mother knocked on her door and peeped in. "Steph?"

"Mum."

Immediately, her mother broke out into a smile and came in, her dressing gown closed over her round belly. "Happy Christmas, sweetheart," she said, sitting on the bed and leaning down to kiss Valkyrie's cheek. "Are you getting up? Desmond got impatient. He's downstairs, waiting to check that Santa is gone."

Valkyrie chuckled. "Oh, I'm so sorry. I've just been lying here."

"Thinking heavy thoughts?"

"Thinking about the baby we'll have around this time next year."

Her mum grinned, patting her bump. "It'll be fun, won't it? You promise you won't get jealous, now?"

"I think I can manage that."

They heard heavy footsteps coming up the stairs, and her dad appeared in the doorway. "Hurry up!" he whined.

"Speaking of babies," her mum muttered. She heaved herself off the bed and walked over to him as Valkyrie threw off the covers. Even as they were flying from her she remembered the massive bruises all over her body, and she yanked the covers back and held them tight against her.

"Didn't see anything!" her dad cried, his eyes squeezed shut. "Didn't see one little thing! Not one!"

Valkyrie laughed as her mum shooed him away. His eyes still shut, he allowed himself to be manoeuvred through the door.

"Please God," she heard him say, "let the next one be a boy."

Once she heard them on the stairs, she let the covers fall and examined herself. The bruises were angry purple and yellow and blue, but they looked more painful than they felt. She pulled on a T-shirt and grabbed her dressing gown, rooted out her fluffy bunny slippers and hurried downstairs, just in time to watch her father lunge into the living room.

"He's gone!" he proclaimed. "Santa Claus has gone, and he left me presents!"

Valkyrie got clothes, and a little money, and a new music device that was smaller than her thumb. She opened an envelope and a card slipped into her hand. She frowned at it. "Gym membership?"

"For a year," her mother said. "It's the good place, beside the Pavillions. They have a pool, and a sauna, and you can take in one guest for free. And I *really* like saunas."

"And I really like *pools*," her dad smiled.

Her mother looked at him. "She can only take in one guest at a time."

"I know, so what's...? Oh. You mean *you*. So... what am *I* going to do?"

"You're a big boy, Des, you can make up your own mind. Maybe you can stand outside and listen to the splashing."

"I can listen to splashing in the *bath*," he pointed out, somewhat sulkily.

"Excuse me?" Valkyrie said. "Um, the gym. Why?"

Her mother shrugged and smiled. "You're working out *somewhere*, so we thought why not do your training where all the instructors know first aid and everything's clean and nice?"

"I'm not *working out*, Mum. I'm... I play sports in school, that's all."

"What kind of sports?" her dad asked. "Badminton? Rugby? Cage-fighting?"

"Just sports. I run a lot. And swim."

"The gym has a *pool*."

"Yes, Dad, I know."

"If you don't want it, that's no problem," her mum said, reaching out to take the card back.

Valkyrie held it close to her chest. "Oh, God, no," she laughed. "I'm using this!"

Her parents smiled, turning to the next present on the pile, and Valkyrie wondered why she'd been so defensive. She was fine about accepting observations concerning her physique from sorcerers, from anyone in that part of her life, but apparently she wasn't so relaxed about it out here. Maybe she didn't want her family noticing how different she was. She liked the idea of blending in once she was home, of sinking into the background and becoming something unexceptional. Here, she wasn't a potential Death Bringer. Here, she wasn't Darquesse, the World Killer. Here she was Stephanie Edgley – daughter, schoolgirl and soon to be big sister.

In the weeks following the glimpse of her future self, she had hated the thought of getting older, of getting stronger. The older and stronger she got, the more like her future self she'd become. But when she'd realised there was a way of sealing her name, of making sure she would never turn into the monster who would go on to kill her own parents, all that had changed. She was back in control and looking forward to becoming more like Tanith. Toned. Streamlined. Efficient.

She didn't need a gym membership to do it, either, but it was a nice gesture from her folks. It showed they were taking an interest without interfering. She appreciated that.

They went visiting. At midday every Christmas, her mother's side of the family would meet up at Valkyrie's grandmother's house over in Clontarf. Valkyrie used to dread this visit, but now she loved it. Her cousins were so much more interesting than they had been as children, and her aunts and uncles revealed personalities that all their head-patting and cheek-pinching had obscured over the years.

Her nana reminded her of a silver-haired Tasmanian devil, whirling from group to group, making sure everyone was enjoying themselves, or at least had a paper plate piled with food in their hands. Valkyrie chatted and laughed easily, feeling like a normal fifteen year old.

After an hour of good times, it was time for the bad. They drove from her mother's side of the family back into Haggard, to her father's side. They found a parking space on the road outside, and walked like condemned prisoners up the garden path to the front door.

"Knock," said Valkyrie's mother.

Her dad shook his head. "Don't want to."

"They're *your* family."

"I can't knock. I have no hands."

"Stephanie, would you be a good girl and knock on the door, please?"

But Valkyrie was busy pretending she was deaf.

Her mother sighed, said "Fine", and raised her knuckles. She hesitated. Her hand lowered. "Would they miss us?" she wondered.

"They wouldn't," Valkyrie's dad said immediately.

"It's probably packed in there," his wife continued. "It'd be pretty difficult to see anyone. We could be in there an hour and not get through half of them. I doubt we'd even be noticed."

"We should go home and wait for the turkey to be ready."

And then the door opened, and Beryl looked out at them, and any hopes of escape were dashed.

"Happy Christmas," Beryl said, her mouth twitching into a rigid smile. "Won't you come in?"

Valkyrie let her parents go first, and trudged in after them.

The heat in the living room was on full blast. That, and the hot air being emitted from the assembled guests, was probably eating a hole in the ozone layer. There were some Edgleys here, but most of the crowd were Beryl's lot, the Mullans. They talked long and they talked loud, and Valkyrie guessed that half of the adults were already on their way to full drunkenness.

She headed for a gap in the crowd near the Christmas tree, gaudily decorated in different-coloured lights and streams of tinsel. It wasn't a particularly big tree, nor was it particularly nice. It was lopsided, lacking that ideal Christmas tree shape that her father always managed to find, no matter how late he left it.

Carol and Crystal broke through the crowd, practically stumbling into her.

"Oh," said Carol.

"Ah," said Crystal.

Perfect. "Merry Christmas," Valkyrie said.

They responded in kind, with as much enthusiasm as Valkyrie had mustered. They had changed so much since the last time she'd seen them. They were almost nineteen, and Carol was heavier, looking like she'd been insulated and left to wander around on her own. Her dress was designed to seize as much of that extra weight as possible and shove it out in front. The result was possibly not what she had intended.

Her twin had gone the other way. From what Valkyrie's mother had told her, Crystal had become obsessed with counting calories, and flitted from one diet to the next, gradually getting skinnier and skinnier. She was close to losing all shape except straight. Carol was still bottle-blonde, Crystal was a redhead, and neither looked healthy.

"You're looking well," Valkyrie lied.

Carol nodded and Crystal grunted, and Valkyrie prepared for the sarcastic comments to start flying.

Instead, Carol sighed, and said, "Get anything nice?"

"Uh... mostly clothes. You?"

"Same. We got money too."

"Dad said he'll buy us a car," Crystal added. "He says as soon as the economic climate picks up a little more."

"Right," Valkyrie said. "Can you drive?"

"Like, right now? No. But when we have the car, we'll have a reason to learn."

"Makes sense. How's college?"

"Boring," said Crystal.

"It's not too bad," said Carol.

Valkyrie nodded. She hadn't a clue what to say. They'd

never gone this long without flinging insults before. And then she saw it, the looks the twins were getting from their other cousins. She saw smirks and sneers, right behind their backs. The twins were doing their best to ignore it all and concentrate on the one person who wasn't mocking them.

Valkyrie felt a sudden, and quite surprising, need to protect them, so she plastered a big smile on her face and forced herself into conversation. She laughed and joked, and basically acted like Carol and Crystal were the two most interesting people alive.

It was quite a performance.

When it was time to go, she said her goodbyes and hugged the twins, promising to meet up soon, and then she allowed herself to be dragged out of the house. Her parents stared at her as they walked to the car.

"Do not ask," Valkyrie sighed.

They got home, and she helped her mother with the turkey and ham and roast potatoes while her dad lit the fire. They sat down to Christmas dinner, pulled crackers and told the awful jokes they found inside. Valkyrie was stuffed after dinner so turned down the offer of Christmas cake. Her phone rang and she walked into the kitchen as she answered.

"Is that Valkyrie?"

It was a woman's voice, sounding very distant, and the line crackled.

"It is," Valkyrie said. "Who's this?"

"Nye is ready for you."

It was the banshee. Valkyrie frowned. "What, *today*?"

"Yes. Today. Now."

"But it's Christmas."

"Doctor Nye cleared his schedule for you. Unless you've—"

"No," Valkyrie said quickly, "no, that's OK. I can do it. Where do I go?"

"You'll be picked up," said the banshee.

"Where?"

"Wherever you are. You have exactly ten minutes."

The banshee hung up. Valkyrie felt sick. Some advance warning would have been nice. It was bad enough she had to leave her parents on Christmas Day, but now this had to be the day she died? Granted, it wasn't permanent death. At least, she hoped it wasn't. All at once she felt glad this was happening so suddenly. If she had time to consider all the possibilities, she might not go through with it.

She walked back to her folks. They were sitting at the fire, talking. If something went wrong, if Nye killed her but was unable to revive her, this would be the last time she'd ever see them. She hugged her dad, and then went and hugged her mum.

"Thanks for a great Christmas," she said.

"Aww," said her mum, "you're welcome, love."

"I'm going to lie down for a bit," she said. "I think I ate too much."

"That gym membership is really looking like a good idea now, eh?" her dad winked.

She smiled and left, and the moment she was out of the room her smile disappeared. She'd had a lot of practice at closing off the part of herself that felt sad about things like this. Now it came naturally, and she felt the wall go up and didn't stop it. She climbed the stairs to her bedroom and called Skulduggery.

"I can't meet up later," she said.

"Oh," came his reply. "That's a pity."

"Yeah. There's a family thing on that we're all going to. Hopefully it won't happen every year, but I couldn't really say no."

"Of course not. Well, maybe I'll drop by later tonight."

"I'm not sure when we'll get back," Valkyrie said, feeling terrible all over again. "How about, if I'm back at a reasonable hour, I let you know, OK?"

"Sure, that's fine. Are you having a good day so far?"

She swallowed. "It's great. Everything's great."

"Even your cousins?"

"Surprisingly, yes. I really have to go."

"All right then. Merry Christmas."

"Skulduggery?"

"Yes?"

Valkyrie hesitated, a jumble of words on her tongue. "I'm really glad we're friends," she ended up saying.

"Me too, Valkyrie."

"Bye."

She called Fletcher, and told him she couldn't see him. He wanted to know why he couldn't just pop over, present her with her gift, and vanish. She didn't tell him she didn't want to see him. She could lie about this on the phone – not face to face.

"Fine," he said, sounding annoyed. "I won't come over."

"But tomorrow," she said. "I want to go out on a date."

"You what?"

"A date. I think we should go out."

"Go out where?"

"I want to go dancing."

His voice turned sceptical. "Seriously?"

"There's a nightclub in Skerries that has a disco thing every

Christmas for under-eighteens. I just want to have a good time with you. We never get to do normal things, and we're not going to live forever, you know? I think we should cram the normal stuff into our lives now, while we have the chance."

"You OK, Val? You're sounding pretty... morbid."

"Will you take me dancing or not?"

He gave an exaggerated sigh. "Fine."

"Also..."

"Yes?"

"Tomorrow, I think you should meet my parents."

For the first time since she'd known him, Fletcher Renn was too stunned to speak.

Valkyrie put the phone down, undressed and touched the mirror. Her reflection stepped out, started putting on the clothes Valkyrie had just taken off, while Valkyrie donned her black outfit.

"You're going to die," the reflection said as it dressed.

"I know," Valkyrie replied, irritated.

"You might never come back."

"You know what to do if that happens."

The reflection nodded. "Take over your life. Be a good daughter. Make sure our parents are happy."

Valkyrie looked up. "What did you say?"

"I'm sorry?"

"You said make sure our parents are happy."

"I said make sure *your* parents are happy."

"You said *our*."

"Oh. It must be another glitch. I was never meant to be used this much, as you know. Do you have any more instructions for me?"

Valkyrie looked at it. It would be an absolutely perfect copy except for the fact that she doubted her own face had ever looked quite so innocent. She put on her jacket, and went over to open the window. "Just stay up here for half an hour."

"OK. Merry Christmas."

Valkyrie slid out of the window and let herself fall. She landed gently and hurried away from the house.

She went down to the pier, checked the time on her phone, and looked around for whoever it was who was picking her up.

Valkyrie didn't like the fact that the banshee apparently knew where she lived. Haggard was her safe place, her haven, and the times when her other life had encroached upon it disturbed her more than anything. Dusk had led a small army of the Infected here – it was on this exact spot that she'd finally managed to lose them. Remus Crux had visited Haggard twice

– the first time to arrest her, the second to try to kill her. Such invasions were unforgivable in her eyes.

She heard hoofbeats and turned as the great black Coach-a-Bowers materialised in front of her.

"Oh, hell," she said.

The headless horses swung around as they slowed. The driver, the Dullahan, gave a last tug of the reins and the horses settled. Their bodies were sleek and muscled and beautiful. They were huge – their backs level with Valkyrie's eyes – and steam rose from them into the cold air. Their heads had been severed halfway up the neck, and now that she was close enough Valkyrie could see that it hadn't been a clean cut. She saw nicks and tears and false starts, evidence of uneven sawing. The wounds hadn't healed over, but neither were they leaking blood.

The Dullahan didn't climb down. He didn't even give any indication that he knew she was there. Could he see her? Could people without heads see?

And then the carriage door opened and a single pale arm drifted out of the darkness within. The hand beckoned to her, the finger curling slowly.

Valkyrie stepped forward on unsteady legs, and reached up to take it.

21

NYE

The hand was cold to her touch. Another reached out, taking gentle hold of her wrist. Another hand then, closing around her sleeve, and another, and with every hand that held her, Valkyrie was pulled just a little closer to the open door. She put a foot on the step and rose up off the ground, and there was a sound, like a sigh, as the hands guided her inside.

Valkyrie's breath left her. Her lungs filled with cold. Her blood slowed in her veins as her heart stopped beating. She no longer felt the weight of her clothes against her skin. She sat back in the seat, a dead thing now, feeling nothing, and her mind became dull.

There was no warmth in the carriage. Three people sat opposite, looking at her with blank eyes. A part of her wondered briefly where all the others had gone. She had expected, after all, a carriage filled with the dead. But no, there were just these three, and that idle curiosity faded from her mind before she could ask them any questions.

She looked away. She didn't care what they were wearing, or what they looked like. A man and two women, that's all she saw before she lost interest. The carriage trundled along uneven ground. The seats were red leather, but the colour was muted. She parted the black curtain with a hand so pale it was turning blue, and she looked at her reflection in the window and saw the face of a corpse, framed by dark hair.

She took her hand away, the curtain falling back into place. She sat on the red leather seat, opposite the three dead people, and the dullness in her mind became a thick and heavy blanket that suffocated her thoughts in their infancy.

And time did what time did – it passed.

*   *   *

Valkyrie was gazing blankly at the shoe of a fellow passenger when she became aware of the carriage slowing to a stop. She dragged her gaze upwards, to the window, but the curtains were still drawn and she felt no urge to part them now. The door to her right opened, and the three dead people left without speaking. Moving without energy, she followed them.

They were in a warehouse of some sort. It was as cold here as it had been in the carriage. The Dullahan was waiting for her, and she followed him away from the others, into a room of tables. The head of a woman blinked at her from where it lay, on its side, beside a body separated from its limbs. Dead people, in various stages of dissection, hung from the walls on hooks and large iron nails. They looked at her as she passed, but made no sound.

The Dullahan stopped before a creature wearing a grubby smock, its arms and legs impossibly long, hunched over a corpse on a table. It swivelled its head as Valkyrie approached. In the gap above the surgical mask and beneath the cap, she could see the oily pallor of its skin. Its eyelids were punctured with broken bits of black thread, and its pupils were small and yellow.

It put away the knife it had been using to poke around inside the corpse, and pulled the mask down to its chin. It had a large scab where the nose ought to have been, and a mouth, like the eyes, that had once been sewn shut, but which now gaped at her with a smile like an open wound.

"I've been looking forward to this," it said, its voice high-pitched and breathless. It was impossible to tell whether this creature was male or female. "Do you know who I am?"

Valkyrie nodded. "Your name is Nye." Her voice sounded odd to her.

"Indeed it is. I'm the only living thing in this place. Do you know what that makes me?" It didn't wait for an answer. "It makes me *better* than you."

Valkyrie didn't say anything. None of this mattered.

Nye looked at the Dullahan, and annoyance flashed across its face.

"I know, damn it. I will. Well, I'm not *going* to deviate, am I? I learned my lesson!"

Seemingly satisfied, the Dullahan turned and walked out.

"But just to be sure," Nye called after him, "if she doesn't make it, I get to keep what's left, yes?"

The Dullahan didn't slow down.

Once he was gone, Nye stood up straight, its head nearly brushing against the lights hanging from the ceiling. It looked at her. "You're here to get your true name sealed," it said. "It isn't easy, you know. Not many people ever find out what their true name *is*, so people like me don't get a lot of practice doing what we have to do. What did the banshee tell you?"

"She said I'd have to die," Valkyrie answered.

"Which you have already done," Nye nodded. "You died in the Coach-a-Bowers, and you'll be dead until you leave this place and life returns to you. Did she say anything else?"

"You'd need to operate."

That open-wound smile again. "Yes. It's a delicate procedure, requiring me to carve three symbols on to your heart in an impossibly precise fashion. I would ask you if you are prepared to accept this risk, but I honestly don't care. The fact is, you're dead, and you're here, so your free will is a little compromised, isn't it? You're not thinking too clearly. Even if you changed your mind right now, I'd still go ahead with the operation and you wouldn't be able to stop me. I haven't done this in years, so I'm mildly curious to find out if I can do it without killing you forever. Undress now, please."

No argument occurred to her, so Valkyrie did as she was told while Nye wiped its instruments on old rags and laid them out on a small tray. When she was done, she lay on a table and Nye strapped her wrists and ankles tight. It spat on the blade of its scalpel, and looked down at her.

"The truly tragic thing about all of this," it said, "is that you won't feel any of the great pain I'm about to put you through."

Nye pressed the tip of the scalpel to Valkyrie's shoulder and slit her skin all the way to the breastbone. Blood, with no functioning engine to pump it, trickled lazily.

"This ought to be excruciating," Nye said, its voice straining with effort as it continued to cut down to her belly. "If you were alive right now, you'd be screaming. Begging me to stop. I'm going to be cracking open your ribcage in a minute, so that would *definitely* be sore."

Nye stood back, putting down the scalpel and shaking its hand loosely, like it was getting rid of a cramp. "That wasn't easy," it told her. "You've got an impressive amount of muscle around the abdomen."

Valkyrie didn't want to see this – didn't want to see what Nye was doing to her. She tried telling it, but she possessed no energy to speak. Nye looked into her eyes and its own eyes widened, as if it understood.

"Oh, my!" it said suddenly. "Oh, you're quite right! I am being *very* unprofessional!" Nye took a moment to fix its surgical mask back over the lower half of its face. "Hygiene is most important in the operating theatre. I'm terribly sorry."

Nye peeled the flaps of skin away from the chest wall, and

Valkyrie looked down at herself as her flesh came apart as easily as a zipper being undone.

"Some people use an electric saw to get through the ribs," Nye continued, "but I find it somewhat unsatisfying." It held up large pruning shears, the kind Valkyrie would have found in the garden shed at home. "And these are much more effective."

Valkyrie closed her eyes as Nye bent over her again. She heard a loud crack, and looked around, craning her head, seeing all the dead people on the walls around her. None of them seemed to care about what was going on. There was another crack, and when she looked back at herself, Nye was lifting her sternum away from her body.

"Almost at the heart," Nye told her. "Now, I *am* going to have to remove it so that I can carve in some symbols, which will take a little time, but I'm fairly confident that I can reattach all the necessary arteries and such afterwards. Heart surgery isn't *brain* surgery, after all," it added with a chuckle. "Little medical humour for you there."

It went back to work and Valkyrie lay there, knowing she should be filled with pain, yet unable to escape the dullness that had settled over her mind.

Nye lifted her heart from her chest and showed it to her.

"You'll forgive me if I don't make any jokes about how I've

stolen your heart," it said. "I've used them all up on previous patients, I'm afraid. Rest assured, every last one of those jokes was suitably morbid and witty."

Valkyrie watched her heart being placed on a tray beside the pruning shears. Nye's yellow eyes narrowed as it smiled beneath its mask.

"There," it said. "That wasn't so bad now, was it? I didn't drop anything. I didn't nick the kidneys or put my thumb through a lung. The first part of this operation, I think you'll agree, has been a resounding success. And now it's time for supper."

Nye turned and walked away on its impossibly long legs, leaving Valkyrie strapped to the table.

22

SOUL SEARCHING

ye returned an hour later and put Valkyrie's heart in a vice. She watched the vice being tightened, and a part of her mind started to scream, fearing the heart would burst. Nye's hand came away from the vice and she relaxed, settling back into the dullness that death brought. Nye spoke to her while it held a scalpel over a flame, telling her about past glories, about the life it had had outside these rooms. The words meant nothing to Valkyrie, forgotten as soon as they reached her ears.

Nye hunched over the vice and gently pressed the red-hot

scalpel against her heart. A book lay open beside it, and before every stroke of the scalpel, Nye would consult the pages, measuring the length and breadth of the symbols detailed within, calculating depth. The scalpel went from her heart back to the flame, then to her heart. Again and again, this process was repeated. Slight trails of smoke rose from the lines being carved. Valkyrie could hear the soft sizzle of the meat.

An hour, it took Nye, to complete the first symbol. The second one, a simpler pattern, took half that time, but the third one took twice as long.

"Once this heart is back inside you," Nye said, yellow eyes fixed on its work, "and once it begins beating again, these symbols will inhabit you. Do you understand me? Do you understand anything I'm saying? The dead here are so dim-witted."

Valkyrie grunted.

"Oh, good, you *can* understand me. When you walk out of here, you will *own* your true name, instead of your true name owning you. Armed with this knowledge, you can do great things. You could be the greatest sorcerer this world has ever seen." Nye glanced at her. "Or you could be the most terrible."

The door opened, and Nye's eyes returned to the heart as the Dullahan strode in.

"Almost finished!" Nye called. "I can't be rushed on things like this, you know! One wrong stroke, one part of a symbol too thin or too thick or too deep or too shallow, and it's not going to work! I am a professional and I must not be hurried!"

The Dullahan stood still, and Nye straightened up, uncoiling its long body. "Oh," it said, in response to whatever the Dullahan was silently saying. "Of course. No, no, I completely understand. Your duties take you elsewhere. You are a busy man, after all. Have no fear, when the operation is complete, I shall send this girl on her way, back to the land of the living. Of course not. I wouldn't dream of such a... Now, listen, as I've said before, those experiments are over, and you *know* that. That part of my life is behind me. I realise now that I was misguided and... I learned my lesson. Yes. Well, if you can't trust a surgeon, who *can* you trust?"

Nye listened for another moment, then nodded gravely, and the Dullahan turned and strode out. The door closed behind him.

Nye returned its attention to the heart, and didn't speak for fifteen minutes.

Finally, it straightened up again. "Done," it said. "And a splendid piece of work it is too, if I do say so."

It took the heart from the vice, and showed it to Valkyrie.

"You see the precision?" it said. "See the craftsmanship? China Sorrows herself could not have constructed these symbols any better. A work of art, don't you agree?"

Nye pulled the surgical mask down off its face. "But I'm afraid I have a bit of bad news. The Dullahan has been called away. You may have heard me agreeing to look after you, to deliver you back to the living. But the bad news, the truly unfortunate and tragic news, is that I was lying the whole time."

Nye dropped the heart on to the tray beside the table, disturbing the instruments, making them jangle.

"No one will know you never left. I can hide you among the corpses here. You'll never be found. I'll tell the Dullahan, and I'll even tell the banshee if she comes to investigate, that I waved goodbye and watched you leave. Who knows what could have happened to you after that? You could be lying in a ditch for all we know."

Nye leaned down over Valkyrie, its face centimetres from her own. "You're mine now," it said. "You've been delivered to me to help with my research. I know you have. All these corpses around you? All these dead people, and many more besides? They've all helped me. They've all *tried*, at least. But you... I have a good feeling about you."

It stalked off, with great loping strides. Valkyrie turned her head to watch it.

"What do you know about the soul?" it asked from the other side of the room, as it pulled a sheet off a large instrument cart. "Not much, I'd wager, but you've undoubtedly seen it in different forms."

Nye pushed the cart over. Its wheels creaked and the blades and saws and clips clattered. "Ghosts, Remnants, even gists, are forms the soul can take. But none of them are its *pure* form."

The cart banged into the table. The blades were caked with old blood.

"The pure soul resides somewhere in the body, somewhere it can't be disturbed. I've narrowed it down to the likeliest places, but as yet I haven't found it. I do, however, feel like I am on the cusp of a breakthrough." It picked up a long breadknife. "I'm going to do you a favour. I'm going to dissect your brain last. That way, if I find your soul among your innards or inside your organs, you can at least partially share in my moment of glory."

Nye pulled the mask up over the scab of its nose. "This is going to get messy."

23

THE GRAVE

The country roads started out plump and healthy, before narrowing as they came closer to Roarhaven, finally becoming little more than starving veins that twisted through a dead and frozen landscape. The town squatted between a stagnant lake of foul water, a few desiccated trees bordering its banks, and a hillside of frosted yellowed grasses and gorse brush. The main street, if that's what it was, possessed a gnarled handful of shops and businesses necessary for survival, but this was not a town that attracted visitors. Roarhaven was the town where sorcerers lived.

Tesseract parked his truck and moved through into the trailer. His whole life was in this trailer, firmly secured against the rigours of the road. Everything was held down by straps and buckles and bolts. The wall above the desk was lined with his metal masks. He took one down, one that had a frown over the eyes and a snarl carved below the nose. Sometimes he preferred the blank ones, but today he was feeling like he wanted some expression.

He checked the needles around the edges, and when he was sure nothing was clogged, his hands went to the mask he was already wearing. There was a slight *hiss* as the needles retracted and the mask detached. He took it away and looked at his lumpy face in the small mirror. Every day, the lumps were different. Sometimes his cheeks would bulge, and his forehead swelled. Other times it would be his nose that would swell up and his chin that would jut out. Whatever way the lumps arranged themselves, he was always ugly. The masks made his skin pale and greasy, and the angry red wounds where the needles slid in, arranged in a border around his face, would weep with pus.

Even as he was looking at himself, he saw his flesh begin to rot. He quickly pressed the new mask to his face, hearing the needles hiss as they slid into the wounds. He felt the rot stop, and recede, as the liquid contained in those needles did its job. Saving his life for yet another day. He made slight adjustments to the straps, and left the trailer.

A woman was waiting for him outside – Ceryen. She led him up the hill on the east side of the town, to where the Torment was peering into a large hole that was being dug by a man named Graft.

Tesseract gave the Torment his report, keeping it short and succinct. The Torment nodded.

"If you want me to continue," Tesseract said, once he'd finished, "I'm sure we could come to an arrangement. A group rate, perhaps. Skulduggery Pleasant, Valkyrie Cain, Erskine Ravel, Tanith Low, Ghastly Bespoke. And the Teleporter, if you wish."

"We have plans to take care of them," the Torment said with a wave of a hand. "Our contract with you is now complete."

Tesseract was disappointed, but didn't press the point. He was a professional after all. "In that case, all that remains is my fee."

"Of course," the Torment said, but he made no move to pay him.

Something pricked Tesseract's skin, and he turned his hand

as a tiny white spider scuttled into his sleeve. One of Madam Mist's, if his files were correct. Tesseract felt hot, and his tongue felt heavy.

"You were in a bar fight," the Torment said. "There is nothing wrong with this, and you got the information you needed to complete your assignment. Unfortunately, the men you killed were citizens of Roarhaven."

Tesseract tried to reach for him, but his arm wouldn't move. He swayed on his feet, unsteady.

"I personally did not care for these men. They were irritants and braggards. But if we are to control this town, we need to follow its rules. You took the lives of Roarhaven mages. So we take yours."

The Torment walked away. Tesseract saw Ceryen out of the corner of his eye. He couldn't even move his head any more. He felt her hand on his shoulder, and she gave a push. He toppled forward, into the hole, into the grave, landing in a twisted position with his right ear pressed into the cold, wet earth.

"OK," Ceryen's voice came from above him, "fill it in."

"There are two shovels," he heard Graft mutter. A rain of dirt pattered across Tesseract's back.

"I'm the brains," Ceryen responded. "You're the brawn."

"The brains of what, exactly? Digging a hole? They really entrusted you with a lot of responsibility, didn't they?"

Another shovelful of dirt came down, heavier than the last.

"They did, actually," Ceryen said. "You think this is just digging a hole? Filling it in? It's not. This is disposing of evidence. If it was a simple hole-digging job, you'd have been able to take care of that yourself now, wouldn't you? You wouldn't need supervision."

"I *don't* need supervision," Graft said. "I need someone using that second shovel."

Every last ounce of feeling was leaving Tesseract's body. It took all of his remaining strength to turn his head even the slightest fraction, but turn it he did, until he was looking straight down, his chin tucked into his chest. Then he could move no more.

"You know your problem?" Ceryen was saying. "You complain too much."

The dirt came tumbling down on the back of Tesseract's head.

"No, I don't," said Graft.

"You do. You think you should be leading. You think the direct way is the only way. You have no idea about tactics, or strategy."

"It's a hole, Ceryen. What strategy is there, other than dig it?"

Ceryen's voice turned smug. "Get someone else to dig it."

A few moments passed, and Graft said, "I hate you."

Another shovelful of earth came down, and another, and their voices grew dull as they buried Tesseract alive.

24

THE DEAD GIRL

Valkyrie lay in the semi-darkness.

Nye wasn't there. Nye had left to go to bed. Valkyrie didn't care. She lay there in the semi-darkness with her heart outside her body.

Her gaze drifted from the ceiling. The main lights were out, and only patches of the room were visible. The bodies on the walls were nothing but shapes. Her eyes took in their forms, took in the geometry of the room, took in the tables and carts. Then she closed her eyes, and when she opened them, Skulduggery was standing over her.

"I'm here to rescue you," he said. He was dressed all in black. Even his shirt was black. "Can you understand me?"

Valkyrie nodded. Hope blossomed, flowered.

"Good," he said. "Remember when you rescued me from the Faceless Ones? You came in and dragged me out? I'm returning the favour, because that's what partners do." She waited for him to start unbuckling the straps holding her down. Instead, his head tilted. "Why are you here, by the way? This is an odd place to be."

They didn't have time for this. Nye would be back soon.

"Are you here for an operation?" Skulduggery asked. "Why would you need an operation? What's wrong with you? Why are you folded open like this? Why is your heart over there?"

"Please..." she whispered.

"Please? Please what? Please help you? Why would I help you? You're going to kill me."

Valkyrie shook her head. This wasn't right. "No..."

"Yes, you are. You're going to kill me, Valkyrie. You're going to kill *everyone*. Why should I help you? Can either of *you* give me a reason?"

Her parents were standing on the other side of the bed. She didn't know how they'd got there.

"My Stephanie wouldn't kill anyone," her mum told Skulduggery.

"*My* Stephanie would," her dad said sadly.

Valkyrie's mouth was dry. "I'm stopping that from happening."

"Can we take that chance?" her mum said. She patted her belly, which was huge. "I've got another child on the way. A better child. Better than you. We can't risk you hurting it."

"I think we should shoot her," Valkyrie heard her own voice say. Her reflection was standing beside Skulduggery, dressed in the clothes Ghastly had made for Valkyrie, but they were all in pink. "Why do we need her? I can take her place."

This was wrong. This wasn't real. This didn't make sense.

"But you can't do magic," Valkyrie's dad said.

"I think that's a good thing," her reflection responded. "Valkyrie can do magic, and she's going to kill the world if Skulduggery doesn't shoot her."

"Who's Valkyrie?" asked her dad.

"Stephanie," said the reflection.

"Oh," said her dad.

"She's right," Skulduggery said, and took out his gun. "I'm going to have to shoot you, Valkyrie."

"Not real," Valkyrie mumbled.

"I'm sorry?"

Valkyrie focused on a single spot on the ceiling above her. The harder she stared, the less defined the figures around her became. Her mother and father faded away. Her reflection slowly disappeared. Only Skulduggery remained.

This was all in her head.

"You're right," Skulduggery nodded.

She ignored him, and the gun he was holding.

"You can't ignore me forever," he pointed out. "And I'm not going to shoot you. Imaginary bullets are surprisingly ineffective against... everything, really. I'm not going to come for you, you know. There is no one coming to rescue you. You got yourself into this mess, and it's up to you to get yourself out."

Skulduggery holstered the gun, and faded away, leaving Valkyrie alone again.

No.

She held on to it, that momentary hope that had spread through her. She caught it before it flitted away and her mind returned to the dull state of non-being. How long had she lain here like this, without a thought entering her head? Even now it was a struggle to keep her mind remotely sharp. She needed to get free. She needed to escape.

Her body was numb. She couldn't feel the air around her, or how the spaces connected. She clicked her fingers and couldn't feel the spark – couldn't focus enough to turn it into a flame. The Necromancer ring was in her jacket, in the pile of clothes on the next table over. Magic wasn't going to save her. Not here.

Nye had left its serrated breadknife on the table beside Valkyrie's knee, but it was too far to reach. The cart, on the other hand, was still in place beside her, and on it were all the instruments that had been used to cut her open and poke about inside.

She strained against the strap that secured her left wrist, and her fingers stretched for the tip of the scalpel. She tapped it, lightly, and it moved, and she tapped it again and suddenly it was within reach. She closed two fingertips around it, and slowly pulled it off the cart. But her numb fingers didn't have a good enough grip, and the scalpel fell to the floor.

Anger flashed into her mind and she kept it there, refusing to let it go, to allow the apathy to return.

She reached for the cart itself and shook it as best she could, trying to move some other blade closer. But the instruments only rattled and moved further away. She got a good grip on the edge of the cart and pulled it, in an effort to tip it over. The cart tilted for a moment, then slipped from her grasp, clattering back to its four wheels and knocking against the big lamp Nye had been using as an overhead light. The lamp toppled, hitting the table and sliding along it on its way to the floor. Valkyrie made a grab for it. The lamp hit the ground, and Valkyrie looked down and realised she was holding the lamp's electrical cord.

She had something. Now she needed to think clearly enough to figure out if it could be of any use.

She pulled on the cord, then carefully inched her fingers back along it, and pulled again. She repeated the exercise slowly, until there was a loop of cord moving across her belly. The loop found her other hand, and her movements became more confident. She pulled on that cord until it became taut, and then she pulled harder.

She heard the plug being yanked from its socket, then she pulled it across the floor. It got caught twice, probably on the legs of tables, but Valkyrie managed to loosen it, and kept pulling. She didn't know how long it took, how many seconds or minutes – all she concentrated on was the task. And then the plug was in her hand. She let it go, let it hang on a long piece of cord, down by the table. She started to rotate her wrist.

The plug swung in a wide circle. Before she released it, she made sure that the slack was wrapped around her other hand. Then she let go, and the plug rose through the air and hit her leg. She pulled it back. It touched against the breadknife, then fell off the edge of the table.

Valkyrie gathered it back in her hand, swung it again, and released it a second time. The plug landed behind the breadknife, and when she pulled it, the breadknife moved a little before the plug slipped over it.

She tried a third time, and missed completely.

The fourth time, the breadknife moved closer to her hand.

It took eight swings until the breadknife was in her hand. She held the handle so that the blade was pressing into the strap on her wrist. She started sawing. At first, the serrated edge caught on the strap and every movement was an uncoordinated jerk. But then the blade found purchase, and Valkyrie found her rhythm, and she started to cut through the strap.

Her eyes wandered as she cut, her gaze drifting from the walls to the ceiling, becoming transfixed by a low-wattage bulb at the far end of the room. In the gloom, it was as bright as the sun.

She looked at the bulb.

The bulb flickered and Valkyrie frowned, unable to remember how long she'd spent looking at it. She dragged her eyes away and looked down at her hand. She still held the breadknife, but she was no longer cutting.

She snarled, the anger flaring and driving back the dullness. She focused on the blade and the strap. Nothing else mattered. There was nothing else in the world, only this blade and this strap.

And then the blade cut through the strap, and her hand was free.

Valkyrie dropped the breadknife and reached across to undo the strap on her right hand. Both hands loose, she pushed herself into a sitting position, and reached down to undo the ankle restraints. And then she was free.

Moving slowly, she swung her legs off the table, and stood. There was a table nearby, stacked full of bandages. She took a roll and wrapped it around her torso, around and around, then walked unsteadily to her pile of clothes. She dressed slowly, feeling no sense of comfort or relief. She took out her phone but could get no signal.

Valkyrie went to the door and opened it, moving into the corridor beyond. This wasn't how she had come in, but she walked on nonetheless. All she wanted was to get out. She didn't care how.

She passed a room where every blade ever forged hung on rusty nails, and another room containing nothing but heads in jars that gaped at her as she passed. A third room was empty, the walls splashed with blood.

She got to a large hall, reached the door on the other side, then stopped. Her heart. She'd forgotten her heart, and all the other things Nye had removed from her. Valkyrie turned, and something caught her eye and she looked up. Nye lay sleeping in a hammock high above her, its arms and legs dangling down. She looked at all the pulleys and ropes and levers, but didn't wonder about the process Nye went through to raise itself off the ground every night. She heard the surgeon snore.

Moving quietly, she retraced her steps, passing the rooms with the blood and the heads and the blades, and stepped back into the operating theatre. She took her heart and her sternum and put them in a bag she found in the corner, and then she left by the other door.

She emerged into the warehouse where she had first stepped down from the carriage. The dead stood around, barely looking at her as she passed between them.

"Where do you think you're going?"

Valkyrie turned as Nye ducked through the doorway.

"You think you're going to escape?" it asked, walking over.

It was still wearing the smock, but not the mask or the cap. Thick veins pulsed against the pale skin at its temples. "You can't escape, you stupid girl. You're dead. In here, as in the Dullahan's carriage, you enjoy an untroubled existence. You're one of the dead things. But outside of these walls is *life*. You set one foot outside, you collapse. Blood spurts and your body caves in. You're carrying your heart around in a *refuse bag*, for God's sake. What did you think was going to happen?"

"Let me go," Valkyrie said, her tongue thick in her mouth.

"No," Nye said. "Get back on the table. I'm not finished with you."

"Fix me then," she said.

Nye's ruined mouth jerked into a surprised smile. "I'm sorry? What? You're giving me orders, is that it? Is that what you're doing?"

She nodded.

"You don't give me orders!" Nye screeched, and it was in front of her before she even realised it had moved. The back of its hand swooped down and caught the side of her face. The force of the impact sent her stumbling, but she felt no pain.

"I'm in charge here!" Nye yelled, and kicked her. Valkyrie rolled across the ground, and the bag was snatched from her grasp.

"We'll see how many orders you give once your heart has been incinerated!" the surgeon spat, and turned to stalk back to the door.

Valkyrie pushed herself up and reached out, but Elemental magic was still closed off to her. A thought flashed into her mind, and she plunged her hand into her jacket pocket, sliding the ring on to her finger.

Shadows coiled around her, and a great wave of darkness smashed into Nye and took it off its feet. The surgeon squealed in fear and Valkyrie slammed the wave to the floor. Nye struck the hard ground and bounced slightly.

Valkyrie went to walk towards him, but, like an eager servant, the shadows swept her up. She touched down beside Nye and it scrambled up, tried to run. She was vaguely aware of an intent, to simply stop him from fleeing, and then suddenly the shadows wrapped themselves around Nye's right leg, its long right leg, and wrenched.

Nye screamed as its leg snapped in a dozen places, and it fell to the ground.

"Please!" it called. "You don't know what you're doing!"

The shadows played with Valkyrie's hair.

"That's Necromancy!" Nye yelled. "But you're dead! It's death magic wielded by a dead person – you don't know what you're doing! You can't control it – you're not strong enough! Please don't kill me!"

"Fix me," Valkyrie said.

"I will!" Nye cried, tears streaming down its face. "But my leg is broken! Let me mend it and then I'll—"

"Fix me now," Valkyrie said without emotion, "or I'll let the shadows kill you."

Nye nodded quickly. "Yes, yes, of course. Just get you back to the table and—"

"No straps," said Valkyrie. "Nothing tying me down. You do this or you die."

25

DIRT

urviving the poisoning wasn't the hard part. Tesseract had survived poisonings before. The fluids that his mask injected into his skin were designed to bolster his immunity and his natural, and unnatural, defences – mainly against the rotting disease that cursed him, but also, as a happy side effect, any other diseases, afflictions and poisons he happened to encounter on his travels. So the poisoning hadn't really troubled him for more than a few minutes.

The being buried alive part, however, was more of a reason to worry.

He had made a small air pocket for himself, giving him a little more time to shake off the poison's effects. When the feeling returned to his limbs, he tried to heave himself up, but the weight of the earth was just too much. The hole was, at the most, one and a half metres deep. That meant that all he had to do was stand up and he'd be out.

Standing up, however, was not as easy as it had once been.

His fingers scrabbled at the dirt, digging upwards slowly. He managed to get them reasonably far up, before realising that all he had achieved was to put himself in an even more uncomfortable position.

He lifted his body, straining against the weight, and kicked his legs. Loose earth shifted beneath him as he moved his right knee slowly. Moving the second one was more difficult, but he managed it. Now both knees were beneath him, his face was still pressed to the bottom of the grave, and his arms were somewhere above. If he died down here and was dug up in hundreds of years' time, he had a feeling the archaeologists would be puzzling over what exactly he had been doing upon his ridiculous death.

Tesseract took a deep breath, the last of the oxygen, and raised his head. His legs were burning, his back muscles screaming at him, and he felt like every tendon in his neck was about to snap. He pushed upwards, forcing his body straighter, his hands clawing at the freezing dirt. The fingers of his left hand suddenly felt no resistance. He pulled himself up, his right hand breaking through now, and then he felt air on his scalp, and all at once his head was free.

He gasped, sucking in air through his mask and blinking the dirt away from his eyes. His vision was blurry, but he was relatively sure he was alone. The way his luck had been going lately, he wouldn't have been at all surprised to find Ceryen and Graft standing here, still arguing.

A little more effort was required to climb out of the grave, and then Tesseract sprawled on the sodden grass, his vision clearing as he looked up at a sky so grey it could have been made from slate. He was just thankful to be looking up at any kind of sky at all. Slate grey, he decided, was a particularly beautiful shade of grey.

He got to his feet. There was cold clay in his clothes, down his back, down his trousers, in his mask. He brushed off what he could, shook out what he was able, but there was no denying the fact that it still felt like he had just crawled out of his own grave.

He looked down the hill, at the town and the lake and the Sanctuary. He didn't take it personally. He was a hired killer, after all. It would be pretty hypocritical to take a murder attempt personally, after everything he'd done. But that was no reason to let them live.

Graft, from what he could remember from his files, lived just off Roarhaven's main street. Tesseract found him in a small house, freshly emerged from the shower, and killed him while he begged for his life.

Ceryen worked directly for the Torment, though, so she would have returned to the Sanctuary. Tesseract entered without being seen. Everyone was too busy setting it up for business to bother guarding the entrance. After fifteen minutes of sneaking around, he heard the Torment's voice, and followed it through the long corridors.

He peered round a corner, saw the Torment and three other Children of the Spider – Madam Mist, a young woman called Portia and a young man called Syc. Ceryen trailed behind at a respectful distance. The Spider people were talking among themselves.

Tesseract had encountered Portia before, but had only heard stories about Mist, and had only ever seen a blurred photograph of Syc. He didn't know much about them though, and that made him uneasy.

The Torment led his brethren through a heavy set of double

doors, and gestured at Ceryen, dismissing her. She bowed, waited until the doors were shut, and walked towards Tesseract. He stepped back into the shadows to watch her pass, then followed. When they were far enough out of earshot, he made himself known by reaching down and tapping her leg. She screeched as it bent back on itself and she crumpled to the ground.

"Hello, Ceryen," Tesseract said, walking around so she could see him.

"My leg!" she cried. He had never worked out why some people liked to name the parts of them that had broken. "Please don't kill me!" He knew what was coming next. Tales of woe and then begging, interspersed with logic and reason. "The Torment ordered it! I was following orders! Please don't kill me! I have a family!"

"And yet I'm going to kill you anyway."

She lunged at him, but he reached down, and caved in her head with a touch.

"You are not an easy man to kill."

Slowly, Tesseract turned to face the Torment, who stood with Madam Mist at his side. He heard movement behind him, and didn't have to glance back to know that Portia and Syc were closing in to trap him.

"You shouldn't have tried to cheat me," Tesseract said. "I would have returned home and we would never have crossed paths again. Instead, we are where we are. You understand, I cannot let you live."

"You speak as though you hold the upper hand. There are four of us."

"Being outnumbered means very little to me. You will still die one by one."

The Torment vomited blackness that splashed to the ground and became spiders, as big as rats. Tesseract kicked one away from him, stomped on another, and backed away as thousands of smaller spiders, tiny spiders, spilled towards him like water. They flowed from the folds of Madam Mist's long dress, scrambling over her body, in and out of her clothes, crawling up her neck and disappearing behind her veil.

He heard blades being unsheathed, and spun to dodge the first swipe of Syc's twin daggers. He tried to grab him, but Syc was fast, faster than anyone Tesseract had ever seen. The blades flashed again and Tesseract stumbled. He stepped on a mass of spiders and they crunched beneath him.

One of the big spiders scuttled up his leg, digging its talons in as it came. Tesseract snarled and looked down. Syc was young and inexperienced and unimaginative, and he took the bait. When he sprang, Tesseract caught him and hurled him into the wall. Syc kept him at bay by vomiting, like the Torment had. The inky blackness coalesced, formed spiders, not as big as the Torment's, but definitely getting there. Tesseract backed away again. Too many damn spiders.

Portia came for him. Like Syc, she had a way to go in her studies, but the fact that she wasn't able to complete the full transformation to spider made her look even more fearsome. She had grown to twice her size, with black armour covering her chest and back. Four extra arms sprouted from her elongated torso, each tipped with claws, but it was Portia's face that was the most terrifying. Her fine-boned features had disappeared, replaced by a mouth that was a gaping hole, filled with fangs that dripped venom. Eight black eyes were grouped around her head.

Tesseract dodged as she attacked. Spiders were crawling all over him. Their poison was in his system and making him clumsy. He should have run when he'd had the chance. He looked up to see Syc plunging a dagger at his chest.

He blocked, fingers closing around Syc's wrist. The bones there broke and Tesseract took the dagger and slammed an elbow into Syc's face. He kicked him and the younger man went down, falling on thousands of spiders. Tesseract used him as a springboard to leap on to Portia. He held on as she tried to dislodge him, then slipped the dagger between her armour plates. He dropped to the ground as she reared back, shrieking.

Something flitted to her face, and clung there. Something black. Tesseract turned, saw Anton Shudder striding through the corridor, Remnants swirling around him.

One of those foul black things crawled into Syc's mouth, and the young man gagged and choked. Barely aware of the Torment and Mist already fleeing, Tesseract knew it was too late for him to make his escape. So he leaped forward, to Shudder, kicking him to drive him back. Shudder smiled, and reached for him, and Tesseract seized his arm and broke the bones.

Shudder hissed in pain and stepped back. "You've damaged me," he said.

Then the Remnant darted out of his mouth, to Tesseract's mask, and for a moment Tesseract couldn't see anything. It squirmed in through the eyeholes and he felt it cold on his face, sliding down. He glimpsed another Remnant attaching itself to Shudder's unconscious form – waste not, want not – and then he fell to his knees. The Remnant found his mouth, and Tesseract gagged as it forced its way in.

26

THE TRUTH

Valkyrie stepped into the sunlight and she was alive again.

She rubbed her eyes, as if she was awakening from a long sleep. Feeling flooded through her. Emotion. Sensation. The cold air forced the grogginess from her mind, which began to sharpen as the world came into focus around her. She was in the docklands. The weak sun was directly overhead. It was midday.

"You haven't fallen apart," Nye said.

Valkyrie turned. Nye stood inside the warehouse, where

everything was grey and lethargic. She looked at the line she'd crossed as she'd moved from dead to living – a line where the gloom of the warehouse was beaten back by the vivid clarity of life.

"I've done a good job," Nye nodded, more to itself than to her. "And it wasn't easy, what with the pressure I was under. But I did it. I'm one of the few who could."

"How many more like me do you have in there?" Valkyrie asked.

"Like you?"

"People who aren't supposed to be there."

"None," it said, shaking its head. "Everyone else was delivered by the Dullahan according to the rules. The Dullahan always follows the rules. He makes sure I do too."

"Sometimes he messes up. You were going to keep me."

Nye smiled. "Can't blame me for trying, eh? But all's well. You're walking, talking, living, breathing – and not falling apart. And your true name is sealed. It wasn't easy, but I knew, if anyone could do it, I could."

Valkyrie reckoned she ought to do something, but she couldn't think what. Arrest it? Punch it? Threaten it? She decided to go with threatening. "I'll be keeping an eye on you," she said. "If I ever hear of you trying anything like that again, I'll come back and drag you out of there."

Nye nodded. "Yes, yes, you're very frightening. Better run along and play now. Grown-ups have work to do."

It smiled, and the warehouse door slid closed. Valkyrie glowered. She should have gone with option two.

She hailed a taxi. She was halfway home before she thought to check that she had any money, but thankfully she found some cash in her back pocket. The driver listened to the radio all the way to Haggard, and Valkyrie watched the world pass. She got out at the pier, hurried to her house, and rose to her window. She slipped her fingers through the crack, opened it and climbed in.

Her room was empty, the reflection elsewhere. Valkyrie was glad. She looked around and realised she was smiling. It was good to be home. It was good to be alive, and safe, and home, and it was good to know that she wasn't going to become a monster who would murder the world. That was particularly comforting.

She heard someone coming up the stairs, and recognised her own footsteps. The reflection opened the door, not looking the least bit startled to see her.

"Your parents have gone out," it said, and Valkyrie

wondered if it had said 'your' simply to reassure her that its earlier mistake would not be repeated. "Do you want to resume your life?"

Valkyrie shook her head. "I just want to take a shower and eat something, then I'll be heading out again."

"I'll stay up here then, shall I?"

Valkyrie remembered, in her hallucination, the reflection encouraging Skulduggery to shoot her. "Yeah, you do that."

She went downstairs, grabbed a plate of leftover turkey and a glass of milk while she turned on her phone. Messages popped up – three missed calls. She cringed, and called Skulduggery to apologise for sleeping in. He sounded bemused, but told her he was on his way, and he'd be there in half an hour.

Valkyrie ate more turkey and drank more milk, then took a shower. As she stood under the spray, she ran her hand along her chest, not detecting the faintest trace of any scar. Nye was good – its skills might even be comparable to Kenspeckle's. And she reckoned their bedside manners were roughly the same, too.

She dressed, grabbed the present she'd wrapped for Skulduggery, and climbed out of the window without even glancing back at her reflection. She walked to the pier, wondering if she should tell Skulduggery what she'd done. Now that the danger was over, now that the future was changed, could she share this secret she'd had to keep for three months? He'd understand why she hadn't said anything. If anyone would understand, he would.

She reached the pier. The Bentley was already parked, and Skulduggery stood beside it, looking out at the sea that thundered against concrete and rock. He had brown eyes today, and thin lips. Same cheekbones and jaw, and the same waxy skin. His hat was cocked at its usual angle. Valkyrie marvelled at the way it tended to stay on, no matter how hard the wind was blowing. Then she realised he was probably manipulating the air around his head. Sneaky and stylish, the perfect combination.

She held out her hands. "Present."

He looked at her. "You're not getting your present."

Valkyrie frowned. "What? Why not?"

"Because it was a *Christmas* present. It's not Christmas any more."

"Of course it is. There's twelve whole *days* of Christmas."

"They don't count."

"Yes they do."

"The twelve days are merely to let people know when it's

time to take down their tasteless decorations. It's St Stephen's Day today, and I didn't get you a St Stephen's Day present."

The wind whipped her hair in front of her face. "But... But that's not fair! I have *your* present!"

"Can I have it?"

"No you can't!"

"Why not?"

"Why do you think? Because you won't give me *mine*."

"Ah, that's just mean."

"How can you consider *that* mean when you started it?"

"I'm not giving you *your* present because I just don't give Christmas presents after Christmas. I don't see the point. But you have no such policy, and so no such excuse. The only reason, that I can see, that you won't give me my present is because of sheer bitterness. You're just being mean."

Valkyrie glared. "Fine. Here's your present."

She took it from her jacket and threw it to him. He examined the wrapping. "It's a fairly distinctive shape."

She grunted.

"I'm not entirely sure I need to unwrap it. I think I can guess what it is."

"Good for you."

"Valkyrie, is it a hairbrush?"

She jabbed a finger at him. "Yes! See? That's a thoughtful gift! You haven't needed a hairbrush in hundreds of years, but you do now! Sometimes, anyway."

"Yes, but you got me a *hairbrush* for Christmas."

"It works on two levels! It's thoughtful *and* amusing! The present you gave me works on *no* levels, because you didn't *give* me a present. Don't you dare complain."

Skulduggery hesitated, then put the gift in his pocket. "It's a very thoughtful and amusing present, Valkyrie. Thank you."

"You're welcome. Can we get in the car now? It's really cold."

"Did you have a nice Christmas?"

"Sure."

"How did your family event last night go?"

"Fine."

"Do you think it will become an annual tradition?"

"Nope."

"OK then," Skulduggery said.

Valkyrie nodded. "Let's go."

She moved to the Bentley, then looked back at him. His arms were folded. "You're not moving."

"We are hurtling through space at a rate of 390 kilometres per second, Valkyrie. I would hardly call that not moving."

"Then we are not moving to the *car*," she sighed.

"This is true."

"And why are we not moving to the car, Skulduggery?"

"Because," he said.

"Because what?"

He looked around to make sure there was no one watching, and let his face flow away. Once he was back to his usual skeleton self, he continued. "Because I am waiting for you to tell me what is going on. You've been keeping something from me – and that ends now."

"Oh."

"Ordinarily, of course, I would respect your privacy, but—"

"No you wouldn't."

"Sorry?"

"You wouldn't respect my privacy."

"Yes I would."

"Skulduggery, you never respect my privacy."

"I do so all the time. Just last week, I respected your privacy."

"What was I doing?"

"Well, you weren't around."

"That makes almost no sense."

"But it does make a *bit* of sense, which is all I need. As I was saying, ordinarily, I wouldn't ask, but whatever you're keeping from me is interfering with your work. You are my partner, after all."

"OK," she said, "I'll tell you. I was going to tell you anyway, eventually. But before I do, I've already sorted everything out. I solved the problem. So keep that in mind when I tell you this. Promise?"

"I promise."

"OK." Valkyrie took a deep breath. "Are you ready?"

"I am."

"You're sure?"

"Quite sure."

"OK. So I'll tell you. Here I go. Skulduggery..."

"Yes, Valkyrie?"

"I'm... I don't know how to say this. I..." She swallowed. "I'm Darquesse."

Immediately, she felt better. Immediately, she felt cleaner, and lighter, and back to her old self. She found herself smiling.

"Right," Skulduggery said.

"Yep."

"You're Darquesse."

"That's it."

"In what way?"

"In a... what do you mean, what way?"

"You're Darquesse in a metaphorical way? *We all have evil in our hearts, we're all Darquesse* sort of way?"

"No," Valkyrie said slowly. "I mean I'm Darquesse. In a literal, *I'm Darquesse* sort of way."

His head tilted. "So you're Darquesse?"

"Yes."

"The same Darquesse who's going to kill everyone?"

"That's me."

"The same Darquesse who kills your parents?"

"Apparently so."

"And how have you reached this conclusion?"

"Remember years ago, when you were fighting Serpine, and the Book of Names fell? I caught a glimpse of my true name, so quick it didn't even register. But when I heard the name Darquesse a few months ago, I knew I'd heard it somewhere before, and that's where. It's mine."

"I see," Skulduggery said. "How long have you known?"

"Roughly since we first heard about her. After the Sanctuary was destroyed."

"And you've kept it to yourself?"

"Until now."

"Why didn't you tell me this before?"

"I wanted to take care of it."

"Have you?"

"I wouldn't be telling you all this if I hadn't. Darquesse will not be making an appearance for the foreseeable ever. The world is safe."

"How did you manage that?"

"I'll tell you," Valkyrie said. "But first you tell *me* what you think happens. Why do I kill everyone? Or why *would I* have if I hadn't just, you know, stopped me?"

"The likeliest scenario would be that someone learns who you are and uses your true name to control you."

"Exactly. So that's taken care of."

"How?"

"I sealed my name. I spoke to a few people, tracked down some other people, figured it out and implemented my plan all on my own. Are you proud of me?"

"Who did it?"

"Did what?"

Skulduggery cocked his head. "Who sealed your name?"

"It doesn't matter."

"Kenspeckle couldn't have done it. Something like that would take years of research and trial and error, even for him."

"It doesn't matter, OK? It's done. My heart was taken out,

the little symbols were drawn on, and I was stitched back together."

"By whom?"

"I don't want to talk about it."

"You said you'd tell me."

"I said I'd tell you what I've been up to lately. I didn't say I'd give you this person's name."

"There's only a handful of possibilities..."

"Skulduggery, drop it."

"You should have told me," he said. "I could have made sure it was safe."

"Don't worry about it."

"You had your heart removed from your body," he said sternly. "You were *dead*."

"You're dead all the time, and you're fine."

"Who did it?"

"I don't want to talk about this. I don't want to talk about the person who did it. I just—"

"*Person*," Skulduggery said. "You keep saying *person*. Not *he*, or *she*. Is it in an effort to further protect the identity, or is it... Is it an *it*?"

"I don't know what you're—"

His voice turned hard. "Doctor Nye."

"What does it matter?" she blurted. "OK, fine, it was Nye! So what? It did its job, and now I'm back home and everything's grand."

"Nye's a sick, twisted, evil freak, Valkyrie. You're lucky you came back. You're very, *very* lucky."

"I know," she said quietly, and looked away.

"You should have told me. You should have trusted me. You should have..." He stopped, and went silent. And then he said, "Never mind."

She looked up. "What?"

"You were scared. I understand. You didn't know how I'd react."

"Well... yeah."

He stepped towards her, and his hand went to her shoulder. "That was a mistake," he said gently. "I'm not going to judge you, Valkyrie. I'd never judge you."

Suddenly she felt like crying. "I'm sorry I didn't tell you."

"What a burden it must have been. You're very brave for facing it alone."

"Thank you," she mumbled.

"Amazingly, astonishingly *stupid*, but brave."

She cracked a smile. "Yeah."

"Very foolish, is what I'm getting at."

"I can see that."

"Thick, basically. Just thick. Dumb as a bag of hammers. Not too bright there, Valkyrie."

"You can really stop complimenting me now."

Skulduggery pulled her gently into a hug, and patted her back. "You brainless moron. You simple-minded cretin. You're a half-wit. A dimwit. An imbecile. You're as sharp as a marble. Thick as a ditch. Not the sharpest knife, nor the brightest crayon, and not the brightest bulb. You just fell off the turnip truck. The wheel is turning, but the hamster is dead."

She laughed into his chest. "Please stop talking."

He pulled away from her. "In future, you tell me if you think there's even the *slightest* chance you might be responsible for Armageddon, agreed?"

"Agreed."

He hesitated. "And you know, of course, that you might be wrong."

"About what?"

"About what makes you become Darquesse. We don't *know* what triggers it, we're only guessing someone tries to control you."

"So basically, even though I've just sealed my true name, that doesn't mean I won't turn? Yeah, I've thought of that. I don't believe it, but I've thought of it."

"OK," he said, and nodded. "Just wanted to make sure." He turned back to the Bentley, and opened the door. "I knew you were keeping *something* from me," he said. "I didn't think it was quite so *big,* though."

Valkyrie smiled. "What did you think it was?"

"It seems laughably insignificant now."

"Let's hear it."

"I... OK, I thought you were going to tell me that there was something going on between you and Caelan. You know what? I actually think I'm relieved."

Skulduggery chuckled, and got in behind the wheel. Valkyrie turned away so he wouldn't see her smile drop, and got in the other side.

"Where to?" she asked as she buckled her seatbelt.

"Someone told Tesseract where I lived. I spent all of yesterday asking questions, and I finally found who the culprit is."

"Do I know him?"

"Yes you do."

"Are we going to track him down?"

"Yes we are."

"Am I going to enjoy it?"

"Immensely."

27

BACK WITH FINBAR

Finbar Wrong was curled up in the corner, with the wooden shutters on the windows closed. It was dark, and the place was quiet. Wreath had been forced to break the lock to get into the tattoo parlour. He'd moved quietly through the ground floor, then came upstairs, cane in hand. He didn't know what use Necromancy would be against a Remnant in its true form, but it was better than nothing.

He'd spotted Finbar the moment he'd stepped in, and he'd been watching the psychic rock back and forward with his head down for three minutes. Every now and then, Finbar would mutter something. Wreath was now using his cane only to lean on. The Remnant wasn't here any more.

"Finbar," Wreath said. He got a mumble in reply. He repeated himself, louder this time, and Finbar looked up.

"Who's that?" Finbar asked.

"Solomon Wreath. You know me."

Finbar nodded. "I know you. Yes. You're a Necromancer."

"That's right."

"What do you want? I'm very..." Finbar stood up and straightened his T-shirt. "I'm very busy."

"The sign on the door said closed."

Finbar shook his head. "Never trust a door; they'll always lie to you. Mr Wreath, I don't want to be rude to someone as scary as you, but I don't tattoo Necromancers. It's a policy I have, that I came up with just there."

"Finbar, what do you remember about the last few days?"

Finbar frowned. "Why d'you ask? The fact that you asked means there's something I obviously don't remember. What is it?"

"What *do* you remember?"

"I remember... I had a vision of something. A person. Dressed all in black."

"Yes. Do you remember their face?"

"It's... It's hazy... Yes. I do."

"Who was it?" asked Wreath. "Who did you see?"

Finbar's eyes widened. "I saw *you*."

"What?"

"I saw you, coming in here and threatening me and... and doing something..."

Wreath sighed. "That was two days ago."

"It was?"

"You had that vision two days ago, so you sent your wife and child away and waited around to see if I'd turn up."

"And here you are," Finbar said dramatically.

"Actually, this is my second visit. I was here two days ago, and I'm here again."

Finbar frowned. "Did I hit you with a cushion?"

"So you *do* remember. Do you remember anything about what you did afterwards?"

"Why should I tell you?"

"Believe it or not, Finbar, I'm here to help. I think Valkyrie Cain is in danger, and if you can remember what happened to you over the past two days, I hope to be able to stop something bad from happening to her."

Finbar looked at him, like he was trying to make up his

mind whether to trust him or not. Surprisingly, he decided to give it a go. "I remember this morning," he said. "Or maybe it was yesterday. I locked the door and came up here. I think I've been to the toilet a few times. And had some tea."

"And before that?"

"I... I, uh... I don't know, it's hazy... I think I was in a forest. I woke up, and there were all these trees, and I started walking. I'm not sure. I've been having these awful, awful headaches."

"What forest?"

"Don't know. I walked out, and someone stopped to give me a lift. I couldn't see straight. The headaches, you know? I'm seeing... stuff."

"Visions?"

"Or nightmares. Can't tell. I think something went wrong. With me. In my head, like."

Wreath had no way of knowing if the damage the Remnant had done was permanent. Some doors, once opened, can never truly be closed. He looked at this skinny man with the tattoos and the crumpled T-shirt and felt sorry for him.

"What are you seeing?" he asked.

"I really don't know. It's too confused. It's not nice, I'll tell you that much. What kind of danger?"

"I'm sorry?"

"What kind of danger is Valkyrie in?"

"I don't know yet. I want to find out more before I tell her, though."

"You should talk to the Skul-man about it," said Finbar.

"Yes," Wreath said. "Maybe I will. Finbar, thanks for your help. And I'm sorry about the headaches."

"Me too."

Wreath left him and walked down the stairs, but when he opened the door there was something waiting for him.

28

THE Z-WORD

Nobody likes zombies.

That was the lesson Valkyrie was learning. They'd been scouring the city, looking for Scapegrace and Thrasher, and everyone they talked to made a face whenever the Z-word was mentioned. Noses were wrinkled in disgust, like the word brought with it a bad smell. Those who knew anything, anything in the slightest, were more than happy to share that information. Nobody clammed up, nobody refused to answer questions, and nobody demanded anything in return. Zombies, it seemed, were not afforded the same street code as other criminals and killers.

"I know them," a notoriously tight-lipped sorcerer named Tarr had said. "One of them talks big and the other one agrees with everything he says. They the two you're looking for? Yeah, I know them. They're living out of a refrigerated truck that's got two flat tyres. It's parked a couple of streets over."

They found the truck where Tarr said it would be. As they approached, they saw two men walking towards them from the other direction. When the men saw them, they stopped, spun, and proceeded to slip and slide on the icy pavement in a manic effort to get away. Skulduggery and Valkyrie strolled up to them.

"Hello, Vaurien," Skulduggery said.

Spinning around again, and barely managing to stay on his feet, Scapegrace glared. "Why are you after us? We haven't done anything wrong."

"You're zombies."

"But we haven't killed anyone."

"Yes you have."

"*Recently*. We haven't killed anyone *recently*."

"You told Tesseract where Skulduggery's house was," Valkyrie said.

Scapegrace shook his head. "No we didn't."

"Six sorcerers were killed in a Dublin bar," said Skulduggery, "three nights ago. The one witness we found who would talk said that a big man in a metal mask took them apart, and afterwards he spoke with a pathetic little zombie who cowered and wailed. That was you, am I right?"

"No," Scapegrace said. He pointed at Thrasher, who was grabbing a lamp post and pulling himself up off the ground. "It was him."

"Oh," Thrasher said.

"We've let you wander around," Skulduggery said, "because we reasoned you're not that big a threat. We didn't think you'd be too eager to recruit more members, not after your little horde went crazy the last time. But now you have proven yourselves to be a nuisance the world could do without."

"Spare my master!" Thrasher wailed. "End my life, but leave my master alone! I beg of you!"

"I agree with him," Scapegrace said.

Thrasher jumped between Skulduggery and Scapegrace. "Master, run! I'll hold them off!"

"You couldn't hold off a sneeze," Scapegrace muttered.

"But I'll die trying!"

Thrasher lunged at Skulduggery, who pushed him towards Valkyrie, who stepped sideways and tripped him as he passed.

"OK," Scapegrace said nervously, "how about a deal?"

Skulduggery took out his gun. "What could you possibly offer us?"

"Information."

"About what?"

"About things. Things on the street. Secret things. Dark things."

"Such as?"

"Well, I... I don't know any right *now*. I mean, we'd have to go undercover for you. We'd be your spies, going places you could never go."

"I don't really think you'd be very good at that," said Skulduggery.

"OK, OK then, how about you making us your back-up? You could have a secret army of zombies—"

"There are only two of you."

"You could have a secret zombie duo as your back-up, ready at any moment to respond to your call. We could be part of your team, saving the world, beating the bad guys..."

"I think you'd probably betray us. Or just be useless."

"We wouldn't be, I promise." Scapegrace looked like he was going to start crying. "Please. You can't kill me."

Skulduggery raised the gun. "You're already dead."

"Not really. Not properly dead. I can still do things. I can still think."

"You won't even know what's happened."

"But... but I want to stay. I'm sorry, all right? I'm sorry for all the bad things I've done. Valkyrie, I'm sorry for trying to kill you all those times. Please, don't let him... don't let him do this."

He looked at her with his dull eyes, his burnt face slack and rotting, and for a moment he reminded her of a dead dog by the side of the road. "Skulduggery," she said, "we can't kill him."

Skulduggery's gun-hand didn't waver. "And why not?"

"Look at him. It would be different if he was attacking us, but... he's not."

Scapegrace held up his hands. "See? I'm not attacking anyone. And neither is Thrasher. Are you, Thrasher?"

Thrasher sat up. "I think I bit off a piece of my tongue."

"We don't want to hurt anyone," Scapegrace said. "We just want to be normal again. I want to live. I want be alive."

Skulduggery lowered the gun, but didn't put it away. "Impossible."

"No, not impossible. There's a doctor who can help us. Kenspeckle Grouse."

"And why do you think Kenspeckle can help you?"

"Dreylan Scarab talked about him. He said he was the best in the world. If anyone can help us, he can. Do you know him? Do you think he would help us? Could you set up an appointment?"

"You really want to change?"

"Yes. God, yes. I hate being like this. I just want another chance."

"Please," Thrasher said. "It's Christmas."

"He has a point," said Valkyrie.

Skulduggery looked at her. "'*It's Christmas*' is not an argument. It's not a reason. It's just a statement of the obvious."

"But this *is* the season of forgiveness."

Skulduggery holstered his gun. "Fine. You want us to take these two to Professor Grouse, we'll take them. If he can't do anything for them, we destroy their brains. Agreed?"

"Agreed."

"I'm not sure I like that," Scapegrace murmured.

Valkyrie smiled. "I don't care."

* * *

Thrasher yelped in anguish as a piece of his ear was cut off. Kenspeckle muttered something, probably telling him not to be a baby, as he carefully laid the piece of ear on a Petri dish. Valkyrie stood outside, looking in through the transparent door.

Kenspeckle turned to Scapegrace. "Sit up on the bed," he ordered, his voice coming through the speaker on the corridor wall. Scapegrace did what he was told, but as the scalpel moved towards his left ear, the ear fell off. Scapegrace looked embarrassed. Kenspeckle examined the ear.

"Is this glue?"

Scapegrace nodded, a little sheepishly.

"And these small holes here – piercings?"

"Staples."

Kenspeckle sighed, put the ear on a second Petri dish, and left the room. The door slid shut behind him. He joined Valkyrie.

"Well?" she asked. "Can you cure them?"

"I don't know yet. Theoretically, yes. Zombies were an accident – much like champagne and penicillin, but much less welcome. Necromancers weren't working on a way to turn people into shambling pieces of unintelligent rot—"

"Hey," said Scapegrace from the other room.

"—they were trying to return the dead to full life. This is as far as they got. Not complete and utter failure, but look at them – they're not exactly a roaring success either."

"I resent that," Scapegrace said.

"The question is, can I take what the Necromancers have done and go further? Can I complete the resurrection with my own brand of science-magic? That's what intrigues me. Then there are all the variables. Can I reverse the decomposition? Can I return the body to its natural state? Can I reverse brain death?"

"My brain isn't dead," Scapegrace said angrily. "It's sleeping."

"All together, a fascinating proposition. Thank you for bringing it to my attention, Valkyrie."

"My pleasure. I'd keep this door locked, though, if I were you."

"I intend to."

Scapegrace jumped off the bed, looking startled. "What? What was that? I've got to stay in the same room as *him?*"

Thrasher did his best not to look wounded.

"This will not do," Scapegrace insisted. "We are not prisoners, we are guests. And as such, I demand separate rooms."

"You are my patients," Kenspeckle said, "and you will do

what I tell you. Mr Scapegrace, how much time had passed from the moment you were brought back as a zombie to the moment you infected Gerald here?"

"His name is Thrasher."

"I refuse to call him that. How long, Mr Scapegrace?"

"I don't know," Scapegrace scowled. "Two hours, maybe three." He jabbed a finger at Thrasher. "And you – don't get used to being called that ridiculous name."

Thrasher hung his head.

"Three hours," Kenspeckle murmured.

"Why is that important?" Valkyrie asked.

"It very possibly isn't important in the slightest, but as usual I have my theories, and now seems to be an excellent time to test them."

Scapegrace stalked up to the door. "Concentrate on curing me, OK? That's the only reason we came to you. That's your only purpose. Drop everything and focus on bringing me back to life."

Valkyrie raised an eyebrow at him. "Before anything important falls off?"

Scapegrace glared, and Thrasher cleared his throat and looked down at his shoes.

"And what about you?" Kenspeckle asked, glancing at

Valkyrie. "How are you going to spend the rest of the day, while I conduct tests on dead people? Are you going to be fighting? Running? Chasing?"

"Dancing," she said with a smile. "I'm going to be dancing."

29

HER GUARDIAN ANGEL

He could still taste her blood. He ran his tongue over his lips, liking the way it electrified his whole body. It was as if he had a pulse again, a working heart that beat in his chest. It was as if he was alive.

Caelan watched Valkyrie with her family, through the window of their kitchen. He watched her talk and smile and laugh. He was in love with that part of her, the part she didn't allow him to see. When they were together, her guard was up, she was always careful around him, always wary. But here, at home, she could relax. She could drop the act. She could be herself. He doubted even Skulduggery Pleasant got to see this side of Valkyrie Cain. He doubted even the great Skeleton Detective knew this part of her.

Caelan sat back against the wooden fence of the garden. Finding her had been easy. Now that he had tasted her blood, there was nowhere she could go that he couldn't follow. There were many aspects to being a vampire that he hated, but even he had to admit, sometimes his predatory abilities came in useful. Because of them, Valkyrie would never again be alone during the day. While the sun was up, she would always be protected, always watched over.

She didn't know it yet, but he was her new guardian angel. The only thing left for him to do was to find a way to be around her at night, when the monster within showed its face.

Even his love wasn't strong enough to protect her from that. Since he had tasted her blood, in fact, the monster had got stronger, more ferocious. In a frenzy, it had torn apart his room in the Midnight Hotel, which was undoubtedly why Anton Shudder had abandoned him.

The day before, he had returned to find that the hotel had already moved on without him. He didn't blame Shudder. The only part which surprised him was the fact that it had taken so long. Caelan had barely made it to his emergency cage by nightfall, and he'd shackled himself up just as he felt the monster emerging. Just in time.

He didn't like to think what would have happened if he'd been too slow. His mind, robbed of its reason and superficial humanity, would have focused on Valkyrie, and Valkyrie alone. Caelan knew he would never forgive himself if he harmed her in any way.

It was getting late. The sun would be down soon, and night would swoop in. His insides tearing, he forced himself to his feet. He took one last look at Valkyrie through the window, and jumped the fence.

30

MEET THE PARENTS

Valkyrie smudged her mascara and stormed away from the mirror, cursing. She hated make-up. She hated the fact that she had to *wear* make-up. Her dress was fantastic, her hair was glossy, her shoes had actual heels. So why did she need make-up? She was going for the bare minimum, but she had still managed to almost poke herself in the eye three times already. Growling, she returned to the mirror to finish the job.

Finally, she was done. Her phone rang.

"Hey," said Fletcher. "You ready?"

Valkyrie looked at herself in the mirror. Presentable. "Yes," she said.

"Cool, I'll be there now."

"Don't teleport."

He paused. "What?"

"Fletch, you can't teleport into my *room*. This is a *date*. You knock on the front door. You meet my parents."

"You were serious about that?"

"Oh yes. I've told them about you. You are my boyfriend, we've been going out for three weeks, you used to go to my school, where you were two years ahead of me. You've just started college. You're studying economics."

"Economics? Val, I know nothing *about* economics."

"Neither do my parents. It'll be fine. Your folks are separated and you live with your dad, somewhere not too close to here. You're taking me to an under-eighteens' disco. Say no more about it than that."

"I really don't know about this. Val, parents don't like me when they first meet me."

"Fletch, *nobody* likes you when they first meet you. You're incredibly annoying, remember?"

"Oh, yeah."

"Knock on the front door in a few minutes."

"How many minutes?"

Valkyrie sighed. "I don't know. Surprise me."

She hung up, put her phone in her purse, hung the purse off her shoulder, and went downstairs. Her parents were in the living room, watching TV. The Christmas tree was all lit up, the fire was roaring, and the mantelpiece was filled with cards. Her dad frowned at what she was wearing.

"It's a little black dress," she told him.

"It's a little *too* little," he frowned back. "And where's the rest of it? I can see your knees."

"Don't be a prude," his wife said from where she was sitting. She was far too comfortable, and pregnant, to get up. "Steph, you look lovely. Tell her she looks lovely, Des."

"Stephanie, you look lovely. I do think the knees are a bit much though."

"Dad."

"Des."

"I'm just expressing an opinion, that's all. Personally, I think knees should be kept for the eighth or ninth date, or the wedding day. As a nice surprise, you know? '*Oh, my darling, you have knees! I never would have thought!*'"

The doorbell rang, and Valkyrie's dad barred the way out of the room.

300

"Sorry, Stephanie," he said, hiking up his trousers, "but it is a father's duty to open the door to the first boyfriend. You stay here with your mother and talk about knitting patterns. If I approve of him, and like the cut of his jib, we may even adjourn to my study for brandy and cigars."

"You don't have a study."

"I mean, obviously, the downstairs toilet."

"And do you even know what a jib is?"

"Of course I do," he said defensively. "It's a hairstyle of some description."

"No, it's one of the sails on a ship."

"And how do *you* know that?"

Valkyrie shrugged. "It's just one of the things I know."

"Well, just for that piece of showing off, young lady, you get to wait here while I interrogate your gentleman caller."

And he was gone. Valkyrie looked back at her mum, who smiled and shrugged. "Let him have his fun," she said.

Valkyrie strained to hear what was being said out in the hall, but all she could pick up were mumbles. She had a terrifying image of her father and Fletcher, standing there mumbling and looking down at their shoes. But then she heard the front door close, and footsteps approached. Her father led the way in.

"His hair is huge!" he exclaimed.

Fletcher followed him in, looking sheepish but cute in dark jeans and a black shirt.

"Look!" her dad continued, pointing. "It's just sticking up at odd angles! Like a demented porcupine!"

"Stop teasing," Valkyrie's mum said, clambering to her feet. She shook Fletcher's hand. "Your hair looks wonderful, Fletcher. I'm Melissa, and this is Desmond."

Her dad glared. "I told him he should call me Mr Edgley."

"Don't mind him, Fletcher. You can call him Des."

"Stop undermining my authority."

"Sorry, dear. You say something now."

"Thank you." Her father peered at Fletcher through narrowed eyes. "What are your intentions towards my daughter then? I hope you don't think you're going to be holding her hand or anything. Just because her knees are visible does not mean she is the kind of girl to hold the hand of a strange-haired boy on their first date."

"No, sir," Fletcher said, "not at all."

"Where are you planning to take her?"

"A dance, sir."

"And yet you brought no flowers, no heart-shaped box of

chocolates. It's been a few years since I was on a date, Fletcher, as you can see by my wife..."

"Oi."

"...but I still remember the rules. A bouquet of flowers and a box of chocolates. Every girl loves them."

"I don't like bouquets of flowers," Valkyrie said.

"Every girl apart from my daughter, naturally."

"I wouldn't have minded the chocolates, though."

"Hear that, Fletcher?"

"Des," Valkyrie's mother sighed, "would you please leave the poor boy alone? Fletcher, Stephanie tells us you're in college. How's that going?"

"Really well," Fletcher said, trying to smile. "I'm doing economics. That's the study of the economy. I love it."

"Which college?"

"Hmm?"

"Which college do you go to?"

Fletcher nodded. "Yes."

"I'm sorry?"

"Oh," Fletcher said, and laughed.

Valkyrie's parents looked at Fletcher in near bewilderment. Fletcher looked back at them in total bewilderment. Valkyrie shook her head.

"He's not good with first impressions," she said sadly. "He doesn't know what he's saying. We should go, before he starts to dribble. Fletcher, I expect you have the taxi waiting outside?"

"Um. Yes?"

"Perfect. Mother. Father. He's not a total idiot. Please believe that. Fletcher, let's go."

She led the way out and Fletcher followed.

"You're going to need a jacket!" her dad called after them.

"I'll be fine!" she called back, and then stepped outside and gasped at the cold, but kept walking. Fletcher hurried to keep up.

"That went well," he said.

"The moment we're out of sight," said Valkyrie, "teleport."

A gust of freezing wind tore in across the sea and Valkyrie fought to keep her dress from flying up around her waist. She wasn't used to dresses.

She stepped out of the queue to see how much further they had to go, and groaned. There were a lot of people waiting to get into Shenanigans, the number one nightspot in Haggard's neighbouring coastal town. Valkyrie wasn't sure, but she had a suspicion it was also the *only* nightspot in

Haggard's neighbouring coastal town, which wasn't much to brag about.

According to her mother, it had once been an amusement arcade, out here on the tip of the peninsula, practically on the stony beach itself, back before the advent of home computers and games consoles. It had closed down, been extensively remodelled, and reopened as a pub, then a nightclub, then both. Now, finally, it was a nightclub again – a two-storey den of loud music, smoke machines and flashing lights. The place had changed owners more times than it had changed names.

Valkyrie's parents used to take her here as a child. She played on the rocks, with the smell of the fishing boats coming in with their haul. Tonight, however, the tide was in and the fishing boats bobbed on the waves, and all she could smell was the sea.

She glanced at Fletcher, saw him visibly straining against his own irritation. He hated queues. Getting where he wanted to be instantly was as much a part of his life these days as breathing, and he really resented having to wait in line with other people.

The wind was getting stronger, threatening to mess her hair. She moved her hand discreetly, diverting the gusts around her. Standing in a bubble of calm, Valkyrie hoped nobody would notice that her hair was now still and her dress was staying down. Thankfully, they all seemed to be far too busy shivering.

They reached the front of the queue and passed in through the doors, into the warmth, just before the doormen announced that the club was full. Fletcher turned to her and she grinned, kissed him, then took his hand and led the way to the dance floor.

31

THE FIRST WAVE

hastly parted the blinds and looked out on to the quiet street. Still dark. Still empty. Still glistening.

"You look like you're waiting for someone," Ravel said from behind him. "Anyone I know?"

"I'm just looking, Erskine."

Ravel took a sip from his mug of tea. "You know who I'd like to meet again? Tesseract. And this time we'd be ready for him."

Skulduggery, not bothering to lift his gaze from his

newspaper, said, "I wouldn't be too eager for a rematch, if I were you."

Ghastly lifted a swatch of material to a small table, and sat at the sewing machine. "It's been a while since I faced anyone that good. It was only a few seconds, but it was enough."

Ravel smiled. "You boys have lost your sense of adventure. There was a time when we'd have raced headlong into something like this."

"We're not young men any more."

"Be honest, though – doesn't the thought of the Dead Men getting back together fill you with a dangerous kind of glee?"

"The Dead Men aren't getting back together," Skulduggery said. "It's just *us*, sitting around at Christmas because we've got nothing else to do."

Ghastly pressed his foot to the pedal. The low *whir* of the machine caught his thoughts and settled them. He was always calmer when working. "Besides, I don't go looking for fights any more, especially against people like Tesseract. I have responsibilities now. I have this shop. And you two are going to have to grow up sooner or later, you know. People expect a certain level of maturity from Elders."

There was the sound of fingers digging into newspaper. "Do not joke about that, Bespoke," Skulduggery said.

Ghastly smiled as he fed the sleeve of the jacket through the machine, making minute adjustments as it went. "You haven't changed your mind about taking it on?"

"I think I would be a horrifically bad choice. Maybe Corrival can be convinced to ask someone who is less controversial than I am – China, perhaps."

"Oh, everyone would love that," Ravel laughed. "A founding member of the Diablerie and a devout follower of the Faceless Ones."

"Ex-follower."

"That will make such a difference to the people with long memories." Ravel sat back. Then he said, "Your friend Tanith is an interesting girl."

Ghastly hissed as the sleeve bunched up under the needle. He corrected the mistake and nodded. "That she is."

"How long have you known her?"

"A few years," Skulduggery said. "Not long. Bliss brought her in to help out against Serpine. She's been a good friend to Valkyrie, and a good ally to the rest of us. And you, Erskine, are to stay away from her."

Ravel laughed. "And why is that?"

He looked at Skulduggery and Skulduggery tilted his head, but said nothing. Ravel's smile died away, and he glanced over at Ghastly. "Oh," he said. "Right. Sorry."

Ghastly raised an eyebrow. "Sorry about what?"

"Nothing. Nothing at all. Tanith's great, but she's not my type. I mean, I'm not saying there's anything *wrong* with her. She's amazing. But, you know, not for... not for me, basically. For someone else, though, I'd say she'd be, uh, perfect. If, you know, if someone else liked her."

Ghastly concentrated on sewing, and Ravel changed the subject pretty fast.

"I was thinking, actually, about this Council thing. Maybe it won't be so bad. It could be a new start for everyone. New Council, new Sanctuary... The slate wiped clean. I think it's time you had a clean slate, Skulduggery."

Skulduggery folded the newspaper and put it down. "Meaning what?"

Ravel hesitated. "Whatever burden it is you're carrying around, whatever you did during the war that was so terrible, maybe it's time you let it go. It might be good for you, to reclaim your family crest. Sooner or later, you'll have to forgive yourself and move on."

Skulduggery was silent for a moment. "Is that so?"

Ghastly stopped sewing. "I agree with Erskine. The fact is, I think Valkyrie might be your way to do just that. I think she's a good influence on you, to be honest. She makes you a better person."

"You didn't always see it that way. She told me about the vision your mother had – about Valkyrie and myself fighting side by side, and falling."

"And the world falls with you," Ghastly said. "I think my mother was the first Sensitive to foresee the arrival of Darquesse, but I don't think that future will happen. Not any more. The two of you, together, are strong enough to change what's to come."

"You sound uncharacteristically optimistic, Ghastly."

"It's Christmas. I'm allowed my optimism."

Someone knocked on the door, and Ghastly got up to answer it.

Ravel smiled. "Who could that be, I wonder? Who would venture out on such a cold, unforgiving night as this? A certain young Englishwoman, perhaps?"

Ghastly glared at him. "Do not say anything."

"Not a word."

Ghastly opened the door, but instead of the shapely figure of Tanith Low, he was greeted with the portly figure of

Corrival Deuce. "Grand Mage," Ghastly said, slightly dismayed.

"Don't sound so bloody enthusiastic," Corrival sighed, shuffling by him. "Oh, it's nice and warm in here. Hello, lads."

Skulduggery and Ravel stood.

"What's wrong?" Skulduggery asked.

Corrival laughed. "Why must something be wrong? Can I not visit old colleagues without some dastardly ulterior motive? It's the holiday season, for God's sake."

Ravel frowned. "So... there's nothing wrong?"

"Nothing. You can relax now. That's an order." Corrival picked up a wooden chair, brought it closer to the others. "So what's going on? Three old friends sharing war stories, is that it? No ladies? No other company?"

"Just us," Ghastly said.

"Not ideal," said Corrival, "but it'll do."

Corrival slammed the chair into Ghastly's back. The skylight exploded in a shower of broken glass, and Solomon Wreath dropped down into the shop at the same time as the door crashed open and Anton Shudder strode in. Ravel charged at Wreath and Skulduggery went for Shudder.

Corrival's lips were black and dark veins spread beneath his skin. He pushed at the air and Ghastly was lifted off his feet. He hit the wall, breaking shelves.

Shudder was holding his right arm like it was broken, but his gist was darker and more furious than ever. It flew at Skulduggery and he barely had time to dive out of its path. Tackling the gist itself was futile – the only way to fight Shudder was to take the fight directly to him. Skulduggery clicked his fingers and hurled a fireball, but the gist swooped down to intercept.

At the other end of the shop, Ravel was doing his best to avoid the sharpened shadows that Wreath was firing at him. He sent the Necromancer stumbling with a wave of air, then lunged, trying to wrestle the cane from his grip.

Ghastly dived and rolled to avoid another wall of air, and he came up beside Corrival and swung a punch that would have felled someone twice his size. But Corrival merely grunted, and Ghastly was reminded of his mercifully short fight against Tesseract – an enemy who did not seem to feel pain. Corrival hit him and the world spun. Ghastly fell back.

The gist screeched as Skulduggery reached for one of the massive rolls of fabric that Ghastly kept along the wall and yanked it out. The fabric, a very expensive deep red, unspooled with a rumble, and the gist flew straight into it and became tangled. Before it could shred its way clear,

Skulduggery used the air to fling himself at Shudder. He got behind him, wrapped an arm around his throat, and tightened. The gist shrieked as it was pulled back into Shudder's chest.

Ghastly snapped his palm at the air and Corrival hurtled backwards. He looked over at Ravel, who had taken Wreath's cane and was using it to beat the Necromancer senseless. There was movement at the broken skylight, and a Remnant flitted down, attaching itself to Ravel's face. Ravel jerked away and fell to his knees. Ghastly ran to help but it was too late – black veins were already spreading across Ravel's skin.

"Skulduggery!" Ghastly shouted. "We have to go!"

He turned to the door as Tesseract walked through.

Skulduggery grabbed Ghastly. "Hold on," he said, and they flew upwards, up through the skylight and into the cold night air.

32

SHENANIGANS

Shenanigans was packed. Valkyrie and Fletcher went up to the second floor, where there were huge mirrors on one side, perhaps in an effort to convince the dancers that the dance floor was bigger than it was. The mirrors were a distraction. Fletcher kept glancing at his reflection as he danced, checking his hair. Valkyrie didn't laugh at his vanity, though – she took a few glances at the mirrors herself, just to make sure she looked as good as she reckoned she did.

There were two steps leading down to the dance floor. No

alcohol was being served, but even so, three people had already stepped off them without realising they were there, and fallen flat on their faces. Valkyrie remained amused by the whole thing.

They danced, and laughed, and talked loudly over the music, and then Fletcher went to the bar to get her a Coke. Valkyrie stood by the edge of the dance floor, and a boy approached. He was Fletcher's age, with brown hair cut short, and a nice smile.

"Hi," he said.

Valkyrie gave him a polite smile back. "Hi."

He leaned in so he could be heard. "Can I buy you a drink?"

She shook her head. "My boyfriend's getting me one."

"That's your boyfriend?"

She nodded.

"He's a lucky guy."

She smiled again.

"Name's Owen. What's yours?"

"Valkyrie," she answered.

"Sorry?"

She blinked. "Stephanie," she said loudly. "My name is Stephanie. Hi, Owen, how are you?"

"Oh, I'm good," Owen said. "I've been watching you all night."

Valkyrie nodded again and leaned in. "Yeah, that's a little creepy."

He laughed. "I was wondering if I could have your phone number."

"I've got a boyfriend, Owen."

"I've got a girlfriend, Stephanie. That doesn't mean you can't give me your number."

"Very true," she said, patting his arm. "It just means I won't."

Valkyrie slipped by him and didn't look back. She pushed her way into the crowd, eventually breaking through. She went straight to the ladies' toilets. For once, there wasn't a line of girls waiting to get in, but Valkyrie still had to wait a minute for a cubicle to become empty. She stepped in and locked the door behind her.

The music was muted in here, enough to hear the chatter of the girls around her. When she finished, she undid the latch on the door, and went to the sinks to wash her hands and check her make-up. Not one smudge. Whenever she felt like the dancing was about to result in perspiration, Valkyrie and those around her would suddenly be caught in a mysterious but welcome blast of cool air. Magic was astoundingly handy at times.

A crowd of girls came in behind her and she turned to leave, but they blocked her path.

"That's my fella you're chatting up," the first one said, a pretty blonde with an ugly sneer and too much make-up.

Valkyrie stepped back. "I'm not chatting up anyone," she said. "I'm here with my boyfriend."

The blonde's three friends closed in around her, girls in low tops and short skirts and high heels. Valkyrie recognised one of them from school, but didn't know her name.

"Looked like you were chatting him up to me," the blonde said, her head tilting with the attitude of someone who's starting a fight.

"You're talking about Owen?" Valkyrie asked. "We had a very short chat, that's all. I have no interest in him, if that's what you're worried about."

The blonde jabbed a finger into Valkyrie's chest. "Do I look like I'm worried? You think I'm scared he'll go with you, do you?"

Valkyrie smiled patiently. "I like how you do your make-up. Do you use a brush, or just dip your head in the bucket?"

The blonde's head shot forward. Valkyrie managed to turn

her face just in time, and got a *whack* into her cheekbone instead of a broken nose. She stumbled back against the sinks as all four girls came at her. Two of them grabbed her hair and she cried out as she was pulled forward. She fell to her knees and the blonde, she was pretty sure it was the blonde, slammed a kick into her ribs. The breath left her body. They were all around her, cursing her, kicking her, not letting her get up.

The blonde kicked again and Valkyrie blocked it, held it, and with her other hand she scooped the blonde's supporting leg from under her. The blonde screeched as she fell, taking one of her friends with her. Valkyrie reared back, driving the point of her elbow into the muscle of another girl's thigh. The fourth girl, now temporarily alone, stood back as Valkyrie got up. Valkyrie punched her, hard, across the jaw, and she went down.

Valkyrie held her ribs, struggling to breathe. Kicks like that would have been easily absorbed by Ghastly's clothes if she'd been wearing them – but she *wasn't* wearing them. She was in a nightclub toilet, fighting in a dress that was too damn short.

The girl Valkyrie had hit in the thigh flung herself at her. Valkyrie deflected the fingernails that were aimed at her face and gave her a shove, and the girl's head cracked into the wall.

The blonde and her one remaining friend were on their feet

now. Valkyrie ducked under a swipe and her fist sank into the friend's soft belly. She wrapped an arm around the girl's waist and flipped her over her hip. The blonde was struck by her mate's flailing legs, and staggered back against the closed door of a cubicle.

Valkyrie faced the blonde, surrounded by the sobbing, groaning forms of her other attackers. She slipped off her right shoe. Fury distorting her face, the blonde launched herself forward, and Valkyrie's bare foot hit her square in the chest and drove her back. The cubicle door crashed open, the blonde landing on the terrified girl within.

"Sorry," Valkyrie called. She put her shoe back on and grimaced as pain shot through her ribs. The light flickered weirdly and threw shadows across the walls. She turned to go, and was just leaving when she heard one of the girls gagging. She stopped. If anything she'd done resulted in serious injury for anyone in the bathroom, as detestable as they may be, she knew she wouldn't be able to sleep for a month. So she turned, walked back in, and froze. All four girls she'd fought, plus the other girl who'd been in the cubicle, were now standing, and they looked at her and smiled with black lips.

"No," Valkyrie whispered.

"You can't get away," the blonde said. Black veins spread

over her face. Valkyrie had seen that happen before, back when Kenspeckle had been possessed, back when he'd tortured Tanith.

"We're all out of that little room," the blonde continued. "Every single one of us. And one of us has seen the future. We know you're going to kill the world, Darquesse."

Valkyrie paled. "That's a lie. That's wrong. That isn't the future any more. I changed it."

"Then we're going to change it back. We're not here to fight you. We're here to join you. We want to help."

"Don't come any closer."

"You're frightened. You're confused. We understand. That's why we're here. We're here to guide you and to serve you. We love you, Darquesse."

Valkyrie spun and bolted.

She ran for the first set of stairs, barging through a crowd of the young and the beautiful. Someone screamed, and then someone else screamed, and Valkyrie looked up to see a cloud of black streaming down over the bar. Remnants, hundreds of them, diving at the people as they panicked below. She watched the shadow creatures crawl up to screaming mouths, impervious to the desperate attempts to keep them out. Throats bulged as the creatures forced their way inside.

Valkyrie looked around for Fletcher, saw him across the room, shouting for her. The crowd surged, knocked him over, and he was lost to sight. She forgot about the stairs and ran for the edge of the terrace. She vaulted over the railing and fell, the Remnants swirling all around her as they attacked the people on the dance floor beneath.

She used the air to slow her descent, but still landed heavily on top of a young couple who were trying to get away. All three of them collapsed, and immediately half a dozen Remnants attached themselves to the young man's back and shoulders. Valkyrie had to leave the girl to scream as her boyfriend was taken over, and then the music was cut off and all she could hear was screaming.

She ran past terrified dancers, avoiding the grabs of those the Remnants had already overcome. She dodged into a Staff Only area and ran the length of it, out through the open door, finding herself at the rear of the club. Seawater sprayed over the edge of the concrete barriers, making the ground dark and wet. Valkyrie took out her phone to call Skulduggery, and saw she had three missed calls from him. She heard footsteps and looked up. A Guard was hurrying over.

"What's going on in there?" he asked. "What's happening?"

"There's a fight," Valkyrie said, struggling to think of something. "I wouldn't go in there if I were you."

The cop didn't answer; he just slapped the phone from her hand and charged, and they hit the low wall and tumbled over into the cold, heaving water.

There was a moment of shock that Valkyrie pushed back as quickly as she could, and then she swam for the slipway. The Guard rose up from beneath her and pulled her down. They grappled in the freezing dark. Her fingernails raked across his face and he let go. She broke free and swam. The cop was right behind her. She changed course, forgetting about the slipway now and just swimming back to the wall.

She gripped the water and it churned, lifting her from its depths, throwing her to the barrier. She crashed against it and held on, gasping, then threw a leg over and fell to the road on the other side. She'd lost her shoes somewhere in the sea.

There was water in her ears, so she didn't hear the cop behind her until his arms encircled her waist. He threw her into the side of a parked van and she fell. He grabbed her ankles and hauled her back. She cried out, her dress bunched up and her shoes gone and her wet hair in her eyes. The cop dragged her some more and laughed.

Valkyrie swept her hand behind her, and a gust of wind hit

the cop hard enough to make him release her. She got up as he pulled a long baton from a deep pocket and grinned at her. A sliver of streetlight caught the side of his face – Valkyrie could see the dark veins beneath his pale skin.

She snapped her palm against the air. The space shimmered, but the cop was already moving, dodging the strike. She clicked her fingers in his face and a flame flared. He cursed and staggered back, hands at his eyes. She kicked him square between the legs and he buckled, but he blocked the knee that came for his face and lunged at her. Valkyrie sidestepped and he went past, tripping over her foot. His face hit the side of the van with a sickening *thud*. He lurched unsteadily to his feet. She kicked his leg, deadening the muscle. He toppled sideways against the van, blood streaming from his shattered nose. She clicked her fingers and hurled a fireball. It hit his arm. He howled and dropped the baton, and she kicked it away.

"No way," said a disbelieving voice behind her, and she turned, snarling at whoever it was who dared interrupt. Then she froze.

"Stephanie," her cousin Carol said in astonishment, "why are you beating up that policeman?"

33

THE TWINS

The cop seized the opportunity offered by Valkyrie's distraction, and dived on her. She fell back, his hands on her throat, his face twisted.

"Let go of her!" Crystal roared, trying to drag him off.

Carol started whacking her handbag into his head. When that had no effect, she tried clawing his eyes out. The cop cursed, but didn't take his hands from Valkyrie, and then Fletcher was there, barging between Carol and Crystal. He wrapped an arm around the cop's throat, and all three of them managed to haul him away. Carol and Crystal let go, and Fletcher and the cop vanished.

The twins stared.

"*Whu?*" said Carol.

Fletcher arrived back, without the cop. "They're everywhere," he said. "The entire club..."

Managing to get her breathing under control, Valkyrie listened. "No more screams," she said. "Oh my God, they got everyone."

"Where did you go?" Crystal asked Fletcher.

Valkyrie picked her phone up off the ground. "Everyone hold hands. Fletcher, the pier beside my house. Go."

They teleported to the pier, just four miles up the coast. Carol and Crystal staggered away from them, eyes wide at their new surroundings, and in unison, they doubled over and threw up on their own shoes.

"What's happening?" Carol wailed.

"You're safe now," said Fletcher.

"We were outside Shenanigans!" Crystal screeched. "How are we here?"

"I teleported you," he said, doing his best to sound reassuring.

Carol blinked. "Like in *Star Trek*?"

"Exactly like in *Star Trek*," he smiled, "without the machines."

Carol swung her gaze to Valkyrie. "And you. You. You set fire to that Guard. You set fire to a policeman!"

"No," Crystal said. "She *threw* fire. Stephanie, you *threw* fire at him. And then you pushed him away, but you didn't even *touch* him. How did you do that?"

"It's complicated," Valkyrie said, suddenly feeling very wet and very cold.

Crystal stepped back, wary. "Are you a mutant?"

"I'm sorry?"

Carol's eyes widened. "Do you have super powers?"

"No, I don't. It wasn't super powers, it was... well, magic."

Carol laughed suddenly, and a little crazily. "You expect us to believe that?"

"You'd be willing to believe that Valkyrie is a super-powered mutant," Fletcher said, "but not that she's magic?"

"Who's Valkyrie?" Crystal asked.

"I am," Valkyrie answered. "It's like a code name, or something. You can still call me Stephanie, though. In fact, I'd really rather you still called me Stephanie. I'll answer your questions in a second, OK? I have to make a call."

She turned away, and speed-dialled Skulduggery. "Remnants," she said when he answered.

"I know," he said. "What happened?"

"They came after me in the nightclub. Hundreds of them. They've taken over everyone inside."

"Are you OK?"

"Yeah," she said. "I'm sore, and freezing, but we got out."

"Get to Kenspeckle's. Ghastly's already there."

"We have to warn the others."

Skulduggery hesitated. "You let me worry about that."

"What do you mean? They're all in danger."

"For all we know, the Remnants have already got to them. Valkyrie, I'll check it out. I'll do my best to gauge if they're still who they are, but you have got to get *yourself* to safety."

"What about my parents? If the Remnants possess someone who knows where I live..."

"Your reflection isn't alive – they can't possess it. Tell it to alert you if anything happens. That's the best you can do."

"I don't like this..."

"Just get to Kenspeckle. He's already locking down the building. You and Fletcher stay there with Ghastly and wait for me. Do not answer your phone to anyone. Understand?"

"Yes."

"Be careful. I'll see you soon."

He hung up.

"OK," Carol said. "Just what is going on? Explain it to us.

Right now. Or we will... We will tell our parents. And they'll tell your parents, and you'll be in serious trouble."

"Don't tell your parents," Valkyrie said, her eyes narrowing. She forced herself to be nice. "Guys, we don't have a lot of time here, but you know all those things Uncle Gordon wrote about?"

"In his books?" asked Carol. "We were never allowed to read his books. Mum said there were dirty bits."

"I read them," Crystal said, somewhat meekly.

Carol looked astonished. "When did you read a book?"

"I read a few of them," Crystal said defensively. "They're all about magicians and wizards and monsters. There are some dirty bits, but they're not that bad."

"It's all true," Valkyrie interrupted, "except they're not called magicians and wizards, they're called sorcerers and mages. Everything Gordon wrote about was true."

"Even the dirty bits?" Crystal asked.

"Well... maybe not the dirty bits."

Carol put her hands on her hips. "How did *you* become magic?"

"Some people are born with magic inside them. All it takes is the proper training to let it come out."

"We're your cousins," Carol said. "Are we magic? Does it run in the family? Is there a test we can take to find out?"

"There's no actual test," Valkyrie said slowly, desperately searching for a believable lie, "but the fact is, you're not tall enough to be magic."

Crystal looked disappointed. "Really?"

"That's true," Fletcher said. "There is a height requirement, and you guys are just a little under it."

"We could wear higher heels," Crystal tried.

"Not going to work," he said with a sad shake of his head.

"That man," Carol said. "The thin man at Gordon's will reading, with the ridiculous name. He's involved in this, isn't he?"

"Skulduggery Pleasant," Valkyrie nodded. "And yes, he is."

"I knew there was something wrong about him. I knew it the moment Mum said there was something wrong about him. I'm a very good judge of character. So, OK, you're witches and wizards and whatever else..."

"Sorcerers," Valkyrie insisted.

"...but why were you fighting with the cop?" Carol continued. "What's that all about? And what was going on in there? The bouncers said it was full, so we were trying to sneak round the back, and then we heard all this screaming."

"The cop wasn't a cop. He was a Remnant – like an evil ghost. They crawl inside your mouth and absorb your personality and possess you. If you don't get rid of them within four days, they're inside you forever."

"Gross," Carol muttered.

"Listen, I have to dry off and get changed. Fletcher can fill you in on everything else while I'm gone, and then we'll take you home. Fletcher, my room."

"Wait," Carol said, "you're going to leave us here alone?"

"Two seconds," Fletcher smiled. He took Valkyrie's hand, and they appeared in her bedroom.

"Keep them calm," she told him. He nodded, and vanished. She crept to the bathroom, stripped off her clothes and jumped in under the hot shower. She hugged herself until the goose pimples went away, then got out and found a towel. She scooped up her wet clothes and hurried across the landing, just as her mother reached the top of the stairs.

"You're back early, I see."

Valkyrie forced a smile on to her face. "Yep."

"I didn't hear you come in."

"I'm ninja quiet," Valkyrie nodded. "Just got home there now."

"Did you have a good time?"

"It was OK. The music was rubbish and the people were annoying. Apart from that it was fine."

"And did Fletcher enjoy himself?"

"I suppose. I was really tired, though, so I just wanted to go to bed."

"Do you think you'll be seeing him again?"

"Fletcher? Yes. He's great, actually. He just *seems* stupid."

"Well, I thought he was lovely," her mum said, then frowned. "Are your clothes wet?"

"I left the shower door open," Valkyrie replied, as sheepishly as she could.

Her mother rolled her eyes, then kissed her cheek. "Goodnight, sweetheart."

"Night, Mum."

Valkyrie went to her room and closed the door quietly behind her. She touched the mirror and her reflection blinked, and stepped out.

"Let me know," Valkyrie said, "the moment anything goes wrong. Now get into bed." She took out her black clothes and began to dress.

"What are you going to do?" the reflection asked.

Valkyrie looked around. "I told you to get into bed."

"I will," the reflection said. "But you need someone to talk to."

Valkyrie laughed. "You? I'd be better off talking to *myself*."

"The Remnants know you're Darquesse."

"None of that's going to happen any more. Why are you asking questions? Every time you're activated you have all of my thoughts and memories. You know everything I know."

"Actually, I know more."

Valkyrie narrowed her eyes. "What?"

"I know the things that you don't want to face. The Remnants know that you are Darquesse, so that means they have a Sensitive. It makes sense that they'd take over one, if not both, of the most powerful Sensitives in the country."

"Finbar Wrong," Valkyrie said, "or Cassandra Pharos."

"And if they have control over one or both of *them*, who else do they have control over? China, maybe? Tanith? Fletcher?"

"What are you talking about? Fletcher helped me escape just five minutes ago."

"And in the four minutes since he's been out of your sight, anything could have happened."

Valkyrie wanted to tell the reflection to shut up, but it was speaking the truth and she knew it.

"You can't trust your friends," the reflection said.

"I can trust Skulduggery. Remnants can't inhabit anything dead."

"And yet you *don't* trust Skulduggery," the reflection said casually. "If you did, you would have told him that you were Darquesse months ago."

"You *know* why I didn't tell him that," Valkyrie said angrily.

"Yes I do, but you don't."

"I'm getting kind of sick of this snarky new attitude of yours."

"You were telling yourself that you didn't want Skulduggery to look at you any differently, but that's not the reason at all."

"That's enough," Valkyrie growled. "Just go to sleep, would you?"

"The reason you didn't tell him..."

"I said, *go to sleep.*"

"Is because you're scared of him."

Valkyrie laughed. "I'm scared of him? That's it? That's your big insight? I'm not scared of Skulduggery, you idiot."

"You were afraid of what he'd do to you if he found out. When you were strapped to that table and you hallucinated, when you saw him take out his gun to shoot you... *That's* what you're afraid of."

"He would never hurt me," said Valkyrie.

"You don't believe that."

"Actually, yes, I do."

"Actually, no, you don't. Ask yourself, what if the visions don't stop?"

"What?"

"If the Sensitives keep having visions of Darquesse – if sealing your name didn't change the future. What do you think Skulduggery will do if you're still a threat?"

"Shut your mouth," Valkyrie snarled, "and go to sleep."

"Of course," the reflection said, and did what it was told.

Valkyrie fumed as she pulled on her jacket over her T-shirt. She called Fletcher's phone. "I'm ready," she said when he answered.

In the three seconds in which she waited for him to teleport over, she was seized by a panic. Maybe the Remnants *had* got to him. Maybe he was going to teleport her right into the clutches of her enemy. Fletcher appeared in front of her, and held out his hand.

She hesitated.

"How are the twins?" she asked.

"I think I've managed to calm them down."

Valkyrie took his hand with her left hand, leaving her right hand free to fight if she needed to. Her heart pounded, and then they were outside again, by the pier – *not* surrounded by Remnants. She did her best not to make her sigh of relief too audible.

"Carol's having a panic attack," Crystal said, jerking a thumb at her sister, who was walking in circles and hyperventilating.

"I just got her to stop that," Fletcher muttered, and hurried over to her.

"Is he your boyfriend?" Crystal asked, once he was out of earshot.

"He is," Valkyrie answered.

"He's older than you, though. He might prefer someone like me. I'm closer to his age."

"Yeah, no. Don't see that happening."

"Does he have a brother?"

"Nope."

"He's gorgeous."

"He thinks so."

"His hair is amazing."

"It defies both gravity and reason."

"Where did you meet him?"

"I helped save his life."

"Oh," Crystal said, nodding like suddenly the whole thing made sense. "So he's your boyfriend out of gratitude."

Valkyrie sighed.

34

REMNANTS
UNLEASHED

Eamon Campbell was a hail, rain, sleet or snow kind of milkman. He took his job seriously, applying the same level of dedication to his work as his father had, and *his* father before him. There once was a time when Eamon had hoped that the tradition might carry on after he was gone, but unless his son lost his enthusiasm for accounting sometime soon, Eamon feared the days of the Campbell milkmen were drawing to a close. Eamon had no time for accounting. It was all numbers and digits and complicated pieces of paper. He didn't like it and he didn't trust it.

He liked milk, though. Milk was simple. The best things in life, Eamon had often thought, were simple. His job. His wife. The best things.

He didn't mind the early starts. In fact, he liked being up before anyone else, working in the dark, bringing the milk to people's doorsteps. He was the last of a dying breed, as he was fond of telling anyone who'd listen. These days, everyone got their milk in great big shops. Where was the personal touch? he often asked. Where was the effort?

Eamon slowed his milk truck, careful on the icy roads. A lot of people were complaining about the weather. Eamon wasn't. He was used to it. When you started work at three o'clock in the morning, you could get used to anything. He turned off the radio, tutting at reports of fights breaking out in a nightclub. Things were a lot different when *he'd* been young, and no mistake.

He got out, opened the side panel of the truck, gathered three cartons in his hands, and left them at the doorstop of Number 11. Number 12 bought their milk in a supermarket, so all he gave them was a scowl. He left two cartons at Number 13, and the same at Number 14. He missed the clink of milk bottles as he worked. Some of his fondest childhood memories were of the clink of milk bottles in his father's big hands.

He saw the jogger heading his way, keeping to the grass verge along the pavements, and muttered under his breath. The jogger had appeared a few months ago, passing Eamon at the same time every morning, giving him a nod and a smile as he went by. He wore reflective armbands and belts and flashing lights on his wrists. He looked ridiculous, but that wasn't why Eamon hated him. Eamon hated him for the simple reason that he had stolen Eamon's alone time.

This time of the morning, from 3 am to 5:30 am, was Eamon's. He was the only one up, the only one awake, the only one active. And then this eejit, lit up like a lanky Christmas tree, started interrupting his routine. A nod and a smile. Eamon didn't want *anyone* nodding and smiling to him, especially not some bloody gobsheen they could probably see from space.

Eamon's reaction was to simply ignore the man. For the first few weeks, this worked fine. The jogger jogged by, nodded and smiled, and Eamon looked down at his milk, or looked up at the stars, or looked across at a hedge. The jogger must have realised he was being ignored, because he started to run as near to Eamon as he could, and when that didn't work, he added a wave to his repertoire, and then a "Howyeh". It was getting harder and harder to ignore him, but Eamon was determined that this blow-in would not beat him.

Eamon filled his arms with milk cartons and glanced up, noting that the jogger wasn't doing his usual prancing gazelle run. He was sprinting. Eamon could understand sprinting. You ran fast because you had somewhere to get to. He didn't understand this jogging lark. It was a run, only slower, so obviously you were in no hurry to get where you were going. So why not walk?

Still muttering to himself, Eamon crossed the road, heading for Number 9. He happened to glance at the jogger again, whose quick feet crunched over the frost-covered grass. Sprinting. Not like a gazelle, but like a lion. Like a lion, closing in on its prey.

The jogger left the grass and ran on to the road. He ran straight into Eamon and took him off his feet. The cartons flew through the cold air, hitting the ground and bursting. Spilt milk. Eamon almost cried.

"What do you think you're doing?" he yelled, shoving the jogger off him. "You could have killed me!"

He picked himself up off the road, fuming. The jogger

was already on his feet. There was something wrong with his face.

The jogger's hands closed around Eamon's throat, tightening to a choke that instantly made the blood pound in Eamon's head. He squawked and slipped backwards, taking the jogger with him. They slipped and slid, but the choke stayed on, the grip impossibly strong. The jogger's face was mottled with dark veins and his lips were black.

"I never liked you, old man," the jogger said with a grin.

Eamon hit the side of his truck and felt around for a weapon. Smashing a milk bottle into his attacker's head would have stopped him. Smashing a milk *carton* wasn't going to have the same effect.

Eamon pushed back, propping himself against the truck to gain whatever purchase he could. The jogger's running shoes, the heels of which flashed with pretty lights, slipped on the ice, and once Eamon had a bit of momentum going, he piled on the pressure, steering his attacker towards the puddle of milk. The jogger's legs went from under him, and the choke was lost. The jogger hit the ground and Eamon reeled back, gasping for breath. The jogger laughed, and opened his mouth wide.

Eamon watched as a black shadow pulled itself out of the

jogger's mouth and flitted through the air, to the door of Number 9. It opened the letter box and disappeared through.

Eamon stared. Never, in all his years' delivering milk, had he seen anything like *that* before.

He looked back at the jogger, who seemed to have fallen asleep. He lay there, all those stupid lights still flashing, the dark veins gone, no more a threat to Eamon than a baby duck. But that thing, the shadow thing, was in Number 9, and Eamon had a responsibility to help the people he delivered milk to. He started across the road, hands balled into fists.

Before he was halfway over, the hall light turned on, and a moment later, the door to Number 9 opened. A bare-footed girl, maybe twenty-five years old, stood there in her pyjamas. Eamon took off his hat, and was about to speak when the girl bolted out of her house, straight at him.

He had time to see those same dark veins on her face as he turned to run, but she leaped on to his back. He tried to throw her off, but she was strong, stronger than him, and she nothing but a slip of a girl. She laughed as he struggled, her hands gripping his head, so tight he felt his skull might burst. He knew if he fell, he was finished. He had to stay on his feet. So long as he stayed on his feet, he had a chance of dislodging her and getting out of there.

He stepped into the puddle of milk beside the unconscious jogger and slid on the wet ice. Eamon fell to the road, the girl laughing all the way down.

35

SCRUTINOUS

eoffrey Scrutinous looked into the eyes of the hysterical woman and said, "No, you didn't."

She grabbed his arm, tears running down her face. "I did, I swear! I know it sounds insane, but I saw these... these *things*, these *shadow things*, climb inside people's *mouths*!"

"You didn't see that," Scrutinous said, speaking calmly and maintaining eye contact. His hair was especially wild and frizzy tonight, but he was hoping she'd ignore that and keep looking into his eyes. "And you're not panicking right now. You're feeling much calmer."

She nodded, and took a deep breath. "I am, actually. But I still saw—"

"You saw people turn violent," Scrutinous interrupted, "and then you got out of there. That was quite shocking to see, wasn't it?"

"Oh, it was."

"You're glad you left when you did."

"You have no idea how glad I am," she told him.

"You're going to go home now, get into bed, and in the morning you won't remember any of the bad stuff that happened tonight."

She released his arm and gave him a shaky smile. "I really have to go. Thank you for your help, but I..."

"Not at all, not at all. Safe home now."

The woman smiled, pulled her coat tighter around her, and hurried away. Immediately, Scrutinous started walking for his car. He pulled out his phone and dialled.

"This is bad," Philomena Random said upon answering the call.

"It sounds like Remnants," Scrutinous said. "Break it off.

We're not going to be able to contain this and it's too dangerous out here. Get back to the Great Chamber. I'll meet you there."

He hung up and heard a cry. Cursing under his breath, he moved to the corner and peeked around, as a fat man threw a Guard against a shop window. The window cracked and the cop rebounded off. He was battered and bloody, and could barely stand.

"I hate people," the fat man told him. "Bags of meat, that's all you are. Disgusting bags of meat."

Not for the first time, Scrutinous really wished his chosen Adept discipline had been combat-based – then situations like these would not be as daunting as they were now. The plain fact of the matter was, he hated violence, he always had, but that was mainly because he was so rubbish at it.

The cop did his best to throw a punch. It hit the fat man, but failed to do any damage.

"Look at what I'm wearing," the fat man said, and hit him back. The cop folded, gasping. "It smells. Can you smell it? It stinks. You stink. You all stink."

But what was Scrutinous going to do? Stand here at this corner and watch a Remnant kill a mortal – just because he didn't want to get into a fight? That was against his code, wasn't it? Well, it would have been, if he'd had a code. He really wished that he'd bothered to come up with a code, then situations like this would be much easier to resolve.

The fat man closed one chubby, meaty, sweaty hand around the Guard's throat, and pinned him to the wall. The Guard struggled and kicked, but his face was already turning purple.

Scrutinous scowled, and sprang into action.

"Excuse me?" he said.

The fat man turned his fat head. "What? Who's there?"

Scrutinous peeked out from behind the corner, and gave a little wave. "Uh, me. I'm going, um, I'm going to have to ask you to put down that mortal."

"Is that so?" the fat man sneered.

"I'm... I'm sorry, but I have to insist."

The fat man laughed and tightened his grip on the Guard. Scrutinous took a few quick breaths to get the blood pumping, and then he leaped out and sprinted towards them. But his sandals had no grip, and so he slipped on the icy road and fell, skinning his knee and cracking his elbow.

As he rolled around on the road in pain, the fat man shook his head. "You're rubbish."

"That's just what I was thinking," Scrutinous said through gritted teeth.

The fat man let the now unconscious Guard drop, and walked over. "You're a sorcerer, then? What can you do?"

Scrutinous forced himself up. "I'm a trained fighter," he lied. "Come one step closer and I'll tear out your larynx with my Tiger Paw Technique."

The fat man smirked, and Scrutinous stopped hobbling long enough to fall back into a t'ai chi pose he had seen once. A fat fist crunched into his nose and he reeled, staggering towards a bright light. Was that it? Had that single punch killed him? Was he leaving this world behind, travelling into the Great Unknown? And then he heard the engine, and a car door open, and knew he was stumbling towards a set of headlights.

"More bags of meat?" the fat man said. "Fine with me."

"No meat here," Skulduggery Pleasant said, stepping between Scrutinous and the fat man, "but plenty of bone." He had his gun out, aimed directly at the fat man's head.

The fat man smiled. "You wouldn't shoot."

"No?"

"I'm innocent. I'm mortal."

"The man before me is innocent," Skulduggery said, "and mortal, but the Remnant inside him is twisted and evil. And it has ten seconds to vacate."

"Why bother? I'll just find someone else to possess."

"You do that. Find someone in better shape. You're about to give that man a heart attack."

The fat man looked down at Scrutinous. "You're lucky."

He threw back his head and the Remnant crawled out of his mouth, flying into the air, disappearing in the darkness. The fat man collapsed to the road, unconscious.

Skulduggery helped Scrutinous to his feet. "You OK?"

"I skinned my knee and hurt my elbow."

"Poor you. Get in the car – we have to get to the Great Chamber."

Scrutinous limped to the passenger side as Skulduggery got back behind the wheel. It was a nice car, the Bentley. It moved fast.

"How did it start?" Scrutinous asked.

"I don't know yet," Skulduggery replied. "Shudder, Ravel, Corrival Deuce – they've all been possessed. I'm quarantining the people who I *know* are unaffected until I have a better idea of what we're up against."

Scrutinous looked at him. "They got Deuce? Already? But... why? He's not the most powerful sorcerer around, he's just..."

"He's our Grand Mage. This isn't like the outbreaks we've had before, Geoffrey. This time, the Remnants seem to have a plan."

Scrutinous paled. "If that's the case, then... then one of their first ports of call would be the Great Chamber, to stop us organising the fight back."

Skulduggery nodded. "No one at the Chamber is answering their phone."

"Then why are *we* headed there?"

"Because every single sorcerer in the city will be on their way to help, and that's where they'll be going."

"Into a trap."

Skulduggery looked at him. "Aren't you glad you got out of bed this morning?"

36

QUIET, PLEASE

China's library never closed. No matter what time of the day or night, no matter what season, no matter the weather, the library stayed open. Knowledge did not take holidays, after all, and neither did China. There were no windows in the library – she hated the thought of the sun fading the spines of her books – but the windows of her apartment showed a Dublin that glistened with frost. It was cold and silver out there. It was warm and tastefully lit in her apartment. There were moments when China could not understand why anyone would ever want to go outside.

The man on the radio told her of police being called to a riot in North County Dublin. The man's voice was too thin, too weedy for his chosen profession, but she forced herself to listen as he offered up the few meagre scraps of information he possessed. He mentioned the name of the nightclub, repeated the same eyewitness accounts, and generally got overexcited at the first real piece of news ever to come his way at this hour of the night.

China turned off the radio, then crossed the hall from her apartment and walked through the library, taking into account the shifting stacks that arranged themselves according to necessity.

It was an old trick, showy and gauche, and somewhat misleading. The stacks actually shifted in response to the mood of the room. If the mood was hostile, the books on combat would move to the front; if it was paranoid, the books on secrets and how to keep them would be foremost. It wasn't a sophisticated trick, but China kept it because it reminded her of the library she'd had in her old family home.

She used to get lost in those stacks for hours, surrounded by books on the Faceless Ones. It had been a happy childhood. Completely insane, but happy. When she looked back on it now, she could see what a hollow comfort her faith in the old gods had been. From the day the first cracks in that faith had appeared, it had taken decades for her to break through.

Every disciple of the Faceless Ones knew that if the old gods returned, they would bring hell with them. And yet every single one of them hoped that they would be among the few to be spared, to be elevated to godhood alongside their masters. A ridiculous expectation, but one that was reinforced by centuries of brainwashing.

As intelligent as sorcerers like Serpine and Vengeous were, as intelligent even as Mevolent himself was, they could not break free of a dozen lifetimes worth of conditioning. Bliss had managed it, and China had followed, but it hadn't been easy.

But it *had* been worth it. True, she had generally had more fun in the old days, but at least she was alive, and independent, and she didn't have to spend half her day praying. She'd never liked the praying part. She'd never been able to understand why the Faceless Ones weren't praying to *her*.

She slid a book from its place, catching sight of Flaring in the next aisle over. Flaring was an ideal patron of the library. She didn't talk loudly, she didn't leave books scattered around, and if she did have to borrow a work, she made sure to have it back within a reasonable amount of time. If only every library patron was as satisfactory as Flaring.

China opened the book in her hand, scanning the index, and something caught her eye. She looked back to the gap on the shelf. Flaring was out of sight now, but China knew she had seen a shadow move. She was not one to dismiss *anything* as her imagination playing tricks. China's imagination was a wondrous thing, as every mage's imagination needed to be, but it was also a disciplined, *ordered* thing. It was in many ways like a well-trained pet, and it did not, under any circumstances, *trick* her.

She became aware of a sound from the next aisle. It was Flaring. She sounded like she was retching. And then the sound suddenly stopped.

China was a logical woman, one not prone to jumping to conclusions, but two facts immediately surfaced in her thoughts. The first was that the Necromancers had a Remnant they'd been examining, and the second was a rumour she'd heard, just a few hours earlier, of an argument between Solomon Wreath and his High Priest.

Her mind flowed over the facts and the possibilities, and she replaced the book on the shelf and stepped slowly backwards. There was a Remnant loose. In fact, taking into account the nightclub riot so close to Haggard, there was probably more than one. A lot more.

China turned, walking smoothly and without unnecessary

haste. If she could silently alert the other patrons and evacuate them all, then she could seal the library and trap Flaring, and the Remnant, within. If she couldn't, or if she felt the odds were leaning even slightly out of her favour, she would abandon everyone and seal the library anyway. Skulduggery could be here within minutes, take care of the problem, and the library would reopen without the loss of too much goodwill. A solution elegant in its cold simplicity.

But when she passed Jago Balance, and saw him struggling with a Remnant that was forcing itself down his throat, she knew her solution was no longer feasible.

She stepped back before he turned, taking a different route. She almost jumped when Hidalgo emerged from an aisle in front of her. He had that distracted look in his eye he always did, that seemingly only went away when he saw her. True to form, as soon as his gaze fell upon her, he straightened up and sucked in his belly.

"Hello, China," he said quietly, a happy smile breaking out.

She put a finger to her lips, and he blushed.

"Sorry," he whispered, and hurried down another aisle like a chastised schoolboy. He was acting completely normally. He wasn't acting like he was possessed.

She started down the aisle after him, and froze. His back

was to her, his hands were at his face and he was gagging. Then he straightened up.

China walked on, forcing herself not to break into a panicked and undignified run. The door was close by. All she had to do was reach it and then she was out. Down the steps and into the car. Call Skulduggery as she was driving away. Once she knew she was safe.

But there were people by the door. China could see them through the narrow gaps between the books and the shelves. At least four of them, standing there, not talking. She heard someone behind her, but didn't look round. Instead, she took a book from its place and moved onwards, flicking through the pages as she walked, pretending to read.

The material of her gorgeous skirt was soft and tight. Completely impractical for fighting. The heels of her gorgeous shoes were high and thin. Completely impractical for fleeing. For one dizzying moment, China found herself envying the rather vulgar style of Tanith Low, constantly attired as she was in the clothes of a common brawler – leather and boots and straps and buckles.

Then China came to her senses. All that leather may prove useful once in a while, but class was a gift that gave eternally.

She approached the back wall of the library without

encountering anyone, friend or foe. A secret door there led to a platform, just big enough for one. The platform lowered the passenger to the basement. All very secret, all very private. Nobody knew about it except for China. Well, except for China and her *assistant*...

Who was standing there now, hands clasped before him. She ducked back before he saw her.

This was what she got for trusting someone. Back in her Diablerie days, she'd have killed anyone who knew about her secret escape route. Footsteps behind her and she dodged left, scowling as she did so. Forced to scurry in her own library. She hurried through the stacks and ducked down, and listened to them talking.

"Have you seen China?" her assistant asked quietly.

"Glimpsed her," came the reply. Flaring.

"Think she knows?" asked another voice, a man's this time.

"Possibly," her assistant said. "Do we have everyone?"

"I think so."

"Then there is nothing to be gained from stealth."

China saw movement, and pressed herself back into the shadows.

"China," her assistant called loudly. "We know you know. Why don't you come out?"

"It's really not that bad," called Flaring.

"Be quiet," the assistant said. "Whatever chance we have of her surrendering to me, we have none at all of her surrendering to the likes of *you*." His voice grew louder again. "This is most undignified, I hope you realise. You're hiding, for goodness' sake. China Sorrows is *hiding*. I have to say, cowering does not become you."

No matter how much she wanted to gouge out his eyes at that moment, she was forced to agree with him there.

"We'll find you!" the man shouted. "If you fight us, we'll hurt you!"

"Will you shut up?" the assistant barked. "China, we have known each other for a long time. I have been your faithful assistant for centuries. I don't want to see you scrambling around in the dark, like a scared mouse with the cats closing in. If you're worried about what will happen, please don't be. You don't lose who you are. I am still me. You will still be you. Once the Remnant is inside you, you become *more*, not less."

Moving quietly, China took off her shoes. She closed her eyes. The other reason why she kept the old trick of the moving stacks was far less sentimental than reminding her of her childhood. Sometimes, very occasionally, old tricks became very useful, such as when the library was attuned to *her* moods much more than anyone else's. China told the library what she needed, and the library obeyed.

The stacks moved suddenly, slamming up against the possessed sorcerers, forcing them apart, making them stumble and stagger and cry out in shock. China leaped up and ran, bookcases creating walls on either side of her, forming a straight line to the door. But there was someone in her path. Hidalgo had managed to avoid being shunted aside. He turned and saw her, and started to smile just as the bookcase to his left shot into him, squashing him against the bookcase on his right.

China sprinted by. She plunged out into the corridor and slammed the door shut, tapping the symbol over the lock. The seal wouldn't hold them for long, but it would be enough for her to make her escape.

She turned for the stairs, but two mages were just reaching the top. They smiled when they saw her. She didn't wait to find out if the smiles were genuine, and she didn't bother to warn them of the danger. She ran into her apartment, headed to her bedroom and grabbed the bag she kept for emergencies. She tapped the symbols tattooed onto her legs and felt the energy charge through her muscles.

At a gesture, the window flew open and China vaulted out. The cold hit her, the wind gushed around her, and she fell three storeys to land in a crouch on the pavement. Nobody was around to stare. Headlights approached. She waved, and a taxi braked, skidding slightly on the icy road, and she jumped in the back.

"Drive now," she commanded, "and drive quickly."

The driver laughed, then glanced back at her, and fell in love.

"Drive!" she snapped.

Whimpering, he stomped on the accelerator and the car fishtailed as it leaped forward.

"Watch the road!"

He fixed his eyes ahead.

"Head for the city centre," she said, unzipping her bag. "I'll tell you where exactly we're going once I make a phone call."

She saw his eyes flicker to her in the rear-view mirror. "I love you," he said.

China didn't bother to respond. She took a pair of expensive boots from the bag, put them on the seat beside her, and took out the rest of the clothes. They were dark, tight-fitting, and stylishly practical.

"You don't mind if I get changed back here, do you?" she asked.

She heard him whimper again.

37

ENEMY HANDS

"Philomena," Scrutinous hissed. "Philomena! Get over here!"

Caught sneaking across the quiet street, Philomena Random jerked around, fists clenched, ready to fight. She saw Scrutinous waving frantically and hesitated, then jogged over. The moment she was close enough, Skulduggery stepped out and levelled his gun at Random's face.

Random held up her hands. "Don't shoot. I'm me."

Skulduggery shrugged. "Unfortunately, Phil, if you were possessed, that's exactly what you'd say."

"Don't call me Phil. My name is Philomena."

"If you were possessed, you'd say that, too."

"Geoffrey," Random growled, "tell him to put his gun down. The Remnants didn't get me. I've spent the last half-hour running from cover to cover to get here. I haven't been seen by anyone or anything."

"We'd like to believe you, Philomena," Scrutinous said.

"Ask me then," Random said. "Go on. Use your mojo on me."

"I don't know if it'd work on a Remnant."

"Why wouldn't it? It works on mortals, it works on mages. Why wouldn't it work on a Remnant?"

"Do it," Skulduggery said. The gun in his hand was scarily steady.

Scrutinous looked into Random's eyes. "You're going to tell me the truth," he said.

"Yes, I am," Random answered.

"You're not going to lie to me."

"No, I'm not."

"Who are you?"

"I'm me, you moron."

"No need to be snarky."

"Then get to the point."

"Do you have a Remnant inside you?"

"No, I most certainly do not. Satisfied?"

Scrutinous looked at Skulduggery. "I didn't feel anything odd. I think it's her."

Skulduggery put the gun away. "Philomena, we have reason to believe the Great Chamber is already infested. I think the Remnants are having a race to get to the most powerful vessels they can. This would be one of the first places they'd go."

"So what are we going to do?" Random asked.

"We have to make sure. If we're lucky, the sorcerers inside figured out what's been going on in time, and they've sealed themselves away. If they have, we just have to reach them and get them out of there."

"But you don't think that's what happened?"

"No, I do not – but we have to be sure."

"So we're going in," Scrutinous said.

Random laughed. "No, we're not."

"Yes, we are."

Random's laugh dissolved. "No, we are not. Are you crazy? Skulduggery, you're used to this kind of thing, but Geoffrey and I are in public relations. We don't fight, or shoot guns. We convince mortal witnesses that they didn't see what they actually saw. We can't storm a building that's fallen into enemy hands. We couldn't storm a *closet*."

"You're going to have to learn," Skulduggery said, "because you two are the only way I have of making sure people are who they say they are."

"But it's *scary*," Random whined.

Scrutinous laid a hand on Random's shoulder. "I was in a life or death struggle earlier tonight, Philomena. I was almost killed. But I got through it. Was I injured? Yes. Was it serious? My knee still stings. But I'm alive. I did it. You can too."

Random took a breath. "OK. OK, let's do it. But you're going first."

"Actually," Scrutinous said, "Skulduggery's going first. He's got the gun."

"Well, I'm not going *last*," said Random. "I'll go in the middle."

Scrutinous glowered. "*I'm* going in the middle. I'm injured."

"You skinned your *knee*."

"Skinning your knee is one of the most painful non-lethal injuries there is."

"It's not worse than a paper cut."

"I said *one* of the most painful," Scrutinous pointed out.

"The pair of you," Skulduggery said, "shut up. I'll lead the way. You two can walk side by side behind me. Happy?"

"Not really," said Random, but Skulduggery was already walking across the street. Scrutinous grabbed Random's arm and dragged her across. They followed Skulduggery down the steps and through the iron door. It closed behind them as they passed into the corridor with the carved walls.

"If a Remnant takes control of me," Scrutinous whispered to Random as they crept along, "I... I would rather you kill me than allow me to hurt anyone."

Random looked at him, and nodded solemnly. "You have my word. And if one of those *things* takes control of *me*, I... I want you to leave me alone and let me go about my business."

"You're hysterical," Scrutinous said. "You don't really mean that."

"I am *not* hysterical and yes, I *do* mean that. If I'm possessed, you are not allowed to let *him* shoot me."

"But you'll be evil."

"At least I'll be walking around. Do I have your word?"

"No," said Scrutinous crossly, "you do *not* have my word."

"Fine," Random snapped. "Then you don't have my word either."

A door opened, somewhere beyond the Great Chamber, and they heard shouting, and cries of alarm. Crashes and bangs and the sound of things breaking. A battle being fought.

They hurried to the door ahead, looked into the Chamber just as figures sprinted through. A fireball exploded and the air rippled. It was the ridiculously named Four Elementals, all five of them, and it was three against two. Black veins stood out clearly on the faces of the three attackers. The two defenders backed away.

Skulduggery strode in, Scrutinous and Random hurrying to keep up. "How about we even up the odds in here?" he said, at which point all of the Four Elementals looked around. Skulduggery stopped walking immediately, and said, "Oh, hell."

The two defenders were black-lipped, vein-ridden Remnants too. This wasn't a battle between good and evil, it was more a squabble between siblings.

The Four Elementals pushed at the air as one, and a wave of air hit Scrutinous and Skulduggery and Random, and tossed them back off their feet. Random hit the wall beside the door and dropped to the ground, while Scrutinous and Skulduggery sprawled out into the corridor. Scrutinous looked up, dazed, in time to see a Remnant flit towards Random, and then Skulduggery was pulling him to his feet, and they were running.

There were more shouts and Scrutinous glanced back, saw Shakra joining the Four Elementals as they sprinted in pursuit, saw even more sorcerers emerging behind them. And above them, darting from point to point, Remnants, closing in. Scrutinous piled on the speed, his sandals slapping the hard floor, the beads around his neck leaping up to hit his goatee. Skulduggery was fast, and was already close to the exit. Scrutinous was not.

Something cold latched on to the back of his neck, and slithered around before he could even get his hands up. He stumbled, tried to call for help, but the moment his mouth opened the Remnant slipped inside. Ahead of him, Skulduggery had the door open and was looking back. Scrutinous tried to scream as the black-lipped sorcerers caught up to him and the cold feeling spread down into his throat. When he looked back at the door, Skulduggery was gone.

38

FIGHTING

The early morning sun did nothing to beat back the freezing cold. Few cars ventured out, but Tanith's bike hugged the treacherous roads like it was a warm summer's day. She pulled into a garage where the only other vehicle was an SUV, set the bike down on its kickstand, and took off her helmet. Her hands were numb as she slipped the petrol nozzle into the tank. The gauge on the pump clicked steadily upwards, her own chattering teeth adding to the symphony.

Even though Kenspeckle had healed the injuries sustained

when Tesseract had thrown that *stereo* into her *head* – the very thought of it stirred her anger – the cold was making her face ache. Standing there, freezing, she decided to finally ask Ghastly to make her some warmer clothes. She'd always liked the clothes he'd made Valkyrie, and the fact that they acted like body armour was a bonus she could probably do with. Those kinds of clothes were expensive, though – but she figured if she asked him nicely...

She returned the nozzle to the petrol pump and hurried in to pay. The warmth embraced her the moment she set foot in the door, and she shivered in appreciation.

"Cold out," said the guy behind the counter.

If it had been Valkyrie standing there instead of Tanith, the guy would have been fixed with a withering stare for stating the bloody obvious. As it was, Tanith smiled as she approached.

"It is indeed," she said.

The guy, no more than eighteen, smiled as he brought up what she owed. "Nice bike," he said. His nametag identified him as Ged. "I want to get a bike, but the insurance is way high."

Tanith handed over cash. "Well, they're not the safest way to travel, I have to admit."

He nodded, still smiling. "I like your coat."

"Thank you."

"I like your boots."

He was still smiling. Not in an endearing way, and not, bless his heart, in a flirtatious way. Just smiling. Just standing there smiling, making random comments.

"Thanks," Tanith said again. The door opened behind her and a gust of cold air swept in. "Well, be seeing you."

A middle-aged woman stood between her and the door. She was plump, her hair a little too red to be entirely natural. She wasn't moving, wasn't shivering, wasn't shopping, wasn't looking through her handbag. She was just standing there, looking straight at Tanith, a faint smile on her face.

Ged grabbed Tanith's hair and yanked her backwards, halfway over the counter. The middle-aged woman ran forward, fist plunging into Tanith's belly. The air left Tanith's lungs and she wanted to fold up, but Ged still had her hair. She tried to break his grip, but he was stronger than he looked. The woman hit her again, and again, then leaned in, hands on Tanith's face.

"This won't take a minute," the woman said, and opened her mouth wide. Something stirred within her throat, something black, writhing and wriggling its way up her gullet. Tanith saw eyes, slits of white. She stopped trying to break

Ged's hold, and instead slapped both hands against the woman's ears. The woman sagged, dazed, her mouth closing, forcing the darkness back down inside her. A Remnant. It had to be. The woman took a step back and Tanith kicked her in the face.

Ged growled, and Tanith cried out as she was hauled all the way over the counter. Ged dropped her on the floor on the other side and knelt on her, firing punches. She covered up as best she could, but the punches were getting through and rattling her skull.

In desperation, she heaved herself sideways, letting her legs swing up wildly. She caught him on the shoulder and he grunted. She scrambled up, but he was on her already, forcing her back. Her hip slid along the wall and she twisted, flinging him against a rack of car-cleaning products.

Tanith sprang over the counter, ignoring the middle-aged woman who was trying to get to her feet, going right for the door.

A little boy, aged around eight or nine, stood there.

"Why did you hurt my mammy?" he asked.

Ged charged into her, and they crashed into a row of shelves. The shelves toppled. Jam jars smashed and bags of sugar exploded and a dozen other household goods spilled out across the floor. Tanith rolled on top and rammed her elbow into Ged's grinning mouth. As she hit him, he actually started laughing. She drove her knee up into him and he grunted, and the laugh was reduced to a pained chuckle.

She pushed herself up. The middle-aged woman was on her feet, but shaking her head, like her equilibrium was lost and she was trying to get it back.

"Mammy!" the little boy cried, hurrying to her. He passed Tanith and suddenly swung around, his little fist crunching against her ribs. Sharp pain stabbed through her side, and she doubled over as he hit her again.

The little boy looked at his hands, eyes bright. "This is new," he murmured. He took hold of her, stepped back and launched her across the floor.

"I'm fairly certain that I just broke my little hand," the boy said, sauntering over. "Not that it matters. I'm about to get an upgrade."

Tanith raised herself to her hands and knees, but the little boy lunged, his foot smacking into her cheek. She sprawled on to her back.

"We had a deal, you see," the little boy continued as he stood over her. "The three of us. We all want a sorcerer's body, so we decided that the one who beats you, gets you. They both went for the older and stronger vessels. But me? I had a feeling you wouldn't be too eager to hit a child."

The Remnant made him stronger, but it didn't make him any heavier. She swung her leg into his ankle and he toppled into the magazine rack, which collapsed on top of him. Tanith sprang up. Ged and the woman were closing in.

"You can't kill us," Ged said, blood pouring from his ruined mouth. "These are innocent people we're using."

"Good people," the woman nodded.

"If you give yourself to me," Ged promised, "I promise I'll take good care of you."

"You'll be happier with me," the woman said. "I'm getting used to a female body, and us girls have to stick together, don't we?"

"I don't care if you're good people," Tanith snarled. "Kenspeckle Grouse was a good person, but he still hammered nails through my hands and legs. If either of you takes one more step, I'll hurt you."

Ged and the woman looked at each other, laughed, and came closer.

Tanith took three quick steps and jumped, twisting her hips slightly and snapping out both legs. The toe of her left boot hit Ged's cheek, and the heel of her right boot crunched into the woman's nose. They went sprawling on either side of her as she landed.

She ran out into the cold and hopped on her bike. Pulling on her helmet, she moved the bike off its kickstand and fired up the engine. She looked back to see the boy sprinting after her, screaming in fury as she roared out on to the road.

39

MURIEL

Muriel Hubbard came in, left her car keys on the hall table and draped her coat over the banister. She went looking for her husband, found him in the living room on the phone, talking about a riot. Today was his day off, but they still came running to their Chief Superintendent whenever anything bad happened. Her own phone rang, and James looked around, gave her a tight smile. She smiled back and left the room, bringing the phone to her ear.

"Mum." It was Ashley. She was whispering. "I need help."

Muriel adjusted the thermostat in the hall, it was much too warm in the house, and walked into the kitchen. "What's wrong, sweetie?"

"They're after me."

"Who is after you?"

"The others."

"Your friends?"

"They're not my friends."

Muriel brought the kettle to the sink and filled it. "Are you arguing with Imogen again? Sweetie, you know what she's like. Give her a few hours and she'll be all apologies."

"Imogen's dead."

"Oh, don't be so dramatic. You'll forgive her, you always do."

"Mum. Imogen is dead. They killed her."

"Who killed her?" asked Muriel.

"The others. Dan and Aoife and the others." Her daughter's voice shook. "They... they tore her apart."

Muriel nodded. "And why did they do that?"

"I don't bloody know!"

"There's no need to curse, Ashley. We've all had arguments, we've all had fights, we've all torn strips off each other. True friends work it out."

"Mum, you're not listening to me. I don't mean they tore her apart with *words*. They tore her apart with their *hands*. She's not dead to *me*, Mum, she's just *dead*. Are you understanding me now? They physically attacked her and physically *killed* her."

Muriel sighed. "Then why don't you come home?"

"I'm hiding."

"Where?"

"I'm in the playground, in the little hut thing."

"Where the little kids play? You can fit into that?"

"They're looking for me. They want Dad."

Muriel poured boiling water into a cup and dipped a tea bag in. "Why do they want your father?"

"I don't know. They said he has influence."

"Of course he has influence, he's the Garda Superintendent."

Ashley's whisper rose again. "I know who he is, Mum! I'm just telling you what they said! They said they could use him, and they wanted to get to him through me!"

"Oh, right." Muriel took a sip of tea.

"They're here," Ashley said, much quieter.

"Your friends?"

Ashley didn't answer. Muriel took another sip as she waited

for her daughter to speak again. She heard a distant shout, and the sound of movement, the phone being jostled, and then rushing wind in the receiver.

"Mum!" Ashley cried, loud enough so that Muriel had to hold the phone away from her. "Get Dad! They're after me! I'm heading home, but they're right behind me! They're faster!"

Jostling. The rush of wind. Ashley's panicked breathing. Muriel shook her head, and looked up as her husband walked in.

"There's something happening in town," James said, picking up his car keys. "Bunch of people going crazy, apparently. Riots in the streets. Have you seen my coat?"

"I think it's on the bed," Muriel told him. He nodded, went upstairs. "Sorry sweetie," she said into the phone, "what were you saying?"

"Get Dad!" Ashley screamed. The sound of movement abruptly ended with a loud *thud*.

Muriel heard Ashley crying, but she sounded far away, like she'd dropped the phone.

James came back in, his coat on. "Maybe you should stay indoors," he said. "It mightn't be safe out. Where's Ashley?"

"I'm just talking to her now," Muriel said.

He nodded. "Tell her to come home."

"Oh, she won't like that."

"Tell her she can give me one of her teenage tantrums later and I'll sit through the whole thing, I promise. But it's not safe out."

"It's not even safe *in*," Muriel said with a chuckle.

James laughed, then stopped. "I don't get it."

Muriel hit him and he flew back against the kitchen counter and collapsed on to the tiled floor. The first time in thirty-two years of marriage that one of them had raised a hand to the other. Sad, really.

Another voice came over the phone. Low. Mocking. "Is that Ashley's mammy?"

"Hello, Dan," Muriel said. "You're too late, I'm afraid. You should have gone after him through the *wife*, not the daughter." She heard Dan curse, and it made her smile. She opened her mouth wide and the Remnant struggled out. Her body dropped, and it flitted to her husband and climbed down his throat. James's eyes flickered open. He groaned softly as he sat up, really wishing he hadn't hit himself so hard. He reached for the fallen phone as he stood.

"Still there, Dan? Now I'm the one in control of all those nice policemen and women, and you're *what*, exactly? A spotty teenager?"

"No," Dan said defensively. "I have a Plan B."

"Oh, I'd love to hear it."

"Well, first I'm going to kill your daughter here. Then I'm..." James heard other voices, and after a moment Dan came back on. "OK," he said, "apparently, I'm not going to kill your daughter. Aoife got a bit carried away, the little psycho. But I'm still going to have fun. You're the Superintendent? Then I'm going to be the *Taoiseach*."

James laughed. "From spotty teenager to prime minister – not a bad promotion. Providing someone doesn't get there before you. You'd better hurry, Dan. If you keep wasting time like this, all the super-powered sorcerers and the very important mortals will be taken."

Dan didn't answer; he just hung up. James laughed, got to his feet, and stepped over his unconscious wife. Then he left the house, going in to work on his day off.

No rest for the wicked, he thought to himself, and laughed.

40

THE PLAN

The Hibernian Cinema was in lockdown. The doors were barred and the windows covered. Every non-essential wing of the science-magic facility was sealed off. Kenspeckle was taking no chances.

Valkyrie sat in the Medical Bay. She'd been here for hours, had spent the morning inhaling a bowl of steam that Kenspeckle had shoved into her hands. "So you won't catch cold," he'd gruffly said as he busied himself with something else.

Fletcher was beside her, watching the news on TV, and

Tanith and Ghastly were across from them, sitting side by side on one of the beds. China sat in the corner, making phone calls that weren't answered, doing her best to stay away from Clarabelle, who seemed to be fascinated by her. Skulduggery walked in, hat pushed back off his brow, the only sign that he was concerned.

"China?" he asked.

"Nothing," China said. "Everyone's gone straight to panic stations."

"Don't make any more calls," Skulduggery said. "If they haven't answered by now, we can assume they've been compromised. From this moment out, we trust no one."

"How many?" Tanith asked. "If they've all escaped from the Midnight Hotel, and we have to assume they have, how many of them are we talking about?"

"We don't know," Ghastly said. "A thousand. Maybe two. No one's ever been able to accurately count."

"Two thousand Remnants," she breathed. "What do they want? What are they after?"

Valkyrie went pale.

"They're after Darquesse," Skulduggery said, before she could even consider confessing. "That's what they told Valkyrie. One of them must have hijacked a Sensitive and seen that version of the future. Now they have someone to worship."

Tanith frowned. "So you're saying they have a purpose? Remnants have a *purpose*? A reason to *organise*? That's unheard of. That's... bloody terrifying."

"They're all over the news," Fletcher said. "Reports of a riot in the nightclub, disturbances all over the city, and another riot in Galway."

"No," Kenspeckle said, walking in, "the Galway thing wasn't the Remnants. That was me."

Valkyrie frowned. "What?"

He smoothed down his lab coat. "Ever since my experience with the Remnants three months ago, I've been working on a carefully controlled virus. It heightens aggression and anti-social behaviour, lasts a few minutes, and then vanishes, leaving the infected people unconscious, with no memory of what happened. We placed canisters full of this virus around the country where they've lain dormant, until tonight."

Fletcher stared at him. "Why? I mean... for God's sake, *why*?"

"It's our cover story," Skulduggery said. "It gets the civilian population believing that there is a somewhat rational explanation to all this madness, while at the same time scaring them into staying off the streets and locking the doors. Leaving us to operate unhindered."

"I thought we might need it," Kenspeckle nodded. "Granted, I thought it would be a few *decades* before we'd need it, so it's a good thing I work fast."

"But the Professor says it won't hurt anyone," Clarabelle said happily.

"It's a thought virus as much as anything else," he said. "If the infected person is in danger of harming himself or anyone else, he falls asleep ahead of time. I've done what I can to reduce the risk of injury, but the point is the real Remnant attacks will be mixed up with our fake ones, so it'll look like the same outbreak. When we have the real problem solved, and all those dreadful things are locked away, I'll pass the secrets to the antidote to some struggling young doctors who just want to make the world a better place. They'll save us all, be heroes, and whatever wonderful projects they're working on will have ten years' worth of funding overnight. Everyone, as they say, wins."

"Now all we have to do is solve the real problem," Skulduggery said.

Valkyrie put the steaming bowl down. "This happened before," she said. "You told me about it. Years ago, in Kerry."

"Eighteen ninety-two," Skulduggery nodded. "They took over an entire town. A giant Soul Catcher was built in the MacGillycuddy's Reeks to trap them."

"Who reeks?" Fletcher asked.

"It's a mountain range on the other side of the country. And that machine, the Receptacle, is our only chance to stop them."

"OK then," Tanith said, "so we lure the possessed there, turn it on, the Remnants get sucked out of the bodies they're in, and the problem's over."

"As usual," China said, "it's a little more complicated than that. For one thing, we're hardly going to be able to lure them back to the only place in the world where they *know* they can be hurt. They fell for it once, they're not going to fall for it again. And for another thing, I'm fairly certain that nobody knows how to even turn this giant Soul Catcher *on*."

"Nobody alive," Skulduggery agreed. "Gordon Edgley was the only person I knew who had that knowledge."

"I can find it," Valkyrie said, stepping forward. "It'll be in his study. He kept all his research there."

Skulduggery shook his head. "It's far too dangerous."

"Fletcher can teleport me over, I'll find out what we need to know, and we'll be back in three minutes."

"We'll all teleport over," Skulduggery said.

"Uh, I tend to find things quicker when I'm alone."

"This isn't open for discussion."

"China's right, though," Ghastly said. "Activating the Receptacle is one thing, but how are we going to lead the possessed there?"

Skulduggery looked at Fletcher. "How many people do you think you can teleport at one time?"

"Uh," said Fletcher. "Don't know. Ten?"

"You're going to need to teleport a lot more than that. If we lure the possessed into one spot, if we have them all touching, or connected, maybe standing on the same surface, do you think you'd be able to teleport them to Kerry?"

Fletcher stared. "Two thousand people? Two thousand *evil* people?"

"Do you think you could do it?"

"No. Not a chance."

"But it's possible," Skulduggery said. "I saw Cameron Light teleport a ballroom full of people halfway around the world without batting an eyelid."

"Well, that was Cameron Light," said Fletcher. "I've only been doing this a few years. I still haven't a clue what I'm doing half the time. Plus, I've never been to Kerry, and I can't teleport somewhere I've never been."

"First things first. We need to know if we can turn it on. Fletcher, you're going to teleport all eight of us to Gordon's house."

Kenspeckle looked around. "What's this? I'm going too?"

"We have to stay together," said Skulduggery.

"But I don't want to go," Kenspeckle frowned. "I object to the very idea of teleportation."

"Sorry, Professor, I'm really not giving you a choice. We'll only be there a minute."

"I want to teleport!" Clarabelle announced, smiling excitedly. "Will I change my shoes? I have wellington boots with cows on them."

"Your shoes are fine," Skulduggery said. "Everyone step in and link arms. Fletcher?"

Fletcher waited until everyone was linked, and the bright Medical Bay changed instantly into the darkening living room of Gordon Edgley's house.

"Ooh," Kenspeckle murmured, "I don't feel well."

"I'm going to be sick!" Clarabelle laughed.

"Everyone stay here," Valkyrie said. "I'll take a look in his study."

"I'll come with you," said China.

Skulduggery held up his hand. "There's nothing up there

that you can add to your collection, China. Valkyrie will be quicker alone."

China rolled her eyes. "You're all so suspicious of me." But she stayed where she was.

Valkyrie turned on a few lights as she hurried to the stairs. It was late afternoon and already dark. She reached the landing and closed the door of Gordon's study behind her. Moving quickly, she passed through into the hidden room, and pressed her finger to her lips as Gordon's image shimmered up before her.

He raised an eyebrow. "We have company?" he whispered.

"They're downstairs," she whispered back. "Gordon, we have a serious problem. The Remnants are loose, and you're the only one who knows how to activate that big Soul Catcher in the MacGillycuddy's Reeks."

"The Remnants are loose? What, all of them?"

"It seems that way. *Do* you know how to activate it?"

"The Receptacle? Yes, it's fairly straightforward. All you need is the key, and I know where that is. How do you plan to lure them there?"

"We're still working on that. Skulduggery wants Fletcher to teleport them over, but Fletcher says he can't teleport that many people."

"Of course he can. You need to read *Into Thin Air* again. Not only is it one of my best books, full of danger and intrigue, and the winner of the Bram Stoker Award, a Hugo *and* a Nebula, but as research I conducted many interviews with Teleporters. There are quite a few chapters which could help Fletcher reach his potential."

"We don't really have time to read, Gordon."

He shook his head sadly. "That's the problem with the world today – no one takes the time to sit down with a good book."

"Actually, the problem with the world today is that the Remnants are loose and trying to kill everyone."

"I don't know, I still say it's that no one likes to read any more."

"Gordon, I need you to do me a favour."

"Anything."

Valkyrie hesitated. "I need you to talk to Skulduggery and the others."

"Anything but that."

"It's time for you to make your grand return."

"No it's not," said Gordon.

"We need you."

"I can tell you what you need to know, and you can tell

them. Wouldn't that be so much better? That way, you get to save the day."

"I've saved the day plenty, Gordon. We don't have the time to do this our usual way – you know everything we need to know. Why are you afraid?"

"Because I am not *me*, Valkyrie. I am not Gordon, no matter how much I pretend to be. I am little more than a recording."

"You think they'll be disappointed?"

"It's not that, it's... You treat me like you have always treated me, and I appreciate that. But to everyone else, to all my old friends, I will appear... diminished. And my ego, while furious and grand, could not take that kind of attack."

"You won't help us because of your ego?"

"My dear niece, a great portion of who I *am* is ego. Confidence bleeds to arrogance, and arrogance props me up when my limbs are too weak."

"Gordon, you have to do this. You have to make the sacrifice."

"I've never been good with sacrifice. I'm better with small donations."

"I'm pretty sure the Remnants intend to worship me."

He raised an eyebrow. "Really?"

"What if this is how I become Darquesse? What if sealing

my name didn't change *anything*? What if I'm driven to do what I do because I have two thousand insane shadows *telling* me to? I don't want to kill anyone, Gordon. I don't want to hurt my parents. Please. Help us."

Gordon softened. "Very well, Stephanie. Take me to them."

She picked up the Echo Stone in its cradle. "Thank you."

He nodded. She tapped the Stone and his image faded away, and she went downstairs. The others were talking in the living room, arguing over plans and possibilities. They stopped when Valkyrie walked in and watched her place the cradle on the table.

"There's someone I want you to meet," she said, a little nervously. "Before you do, I just want you to know that I didn't like keeping this a secret." She tapped the Stone again, and Gordon appeared.

"Hello," he said.

Eyes widened. Mouths dropped open. Skulduggery remained still.

Gordon quickly continued. "Do not blame Valkyrie for this. I insisted that she not tell any of you that I was... around. She tried to get me, on many occasions, to change my mind, but I was resolute. I suppose I was somewhat embarrassed, or ashamed of my current incarnation. And while I do not pretend to be the man you once knew, I believe that I can be of some assistance in this hour of need. Treat me the same way as you would a book, or similar font of knowledge." Gordon cleared his throat and waited for the rebuke.

"It's about time," Skulduggery said.

Now it was Gordon's turn to look surprised. "You knew?"

"Of course."

Valkyrie frowned. "You knew? How could you know?"

"Whenever we needed to find information that only Gordon would have," Skulduggery said, "you'd come here, alone, take a few minutes, and arrive back with precisely the answer we were looking for."

"So you never believed me when I told you I'd been researching?"

"No."

"You thought I was *cheating*?"

"You *were* cheating."

"But you *thought* I was cheating! That's *worse* than me cheating, the fact that you *doubted* me!"

"Your logic is astoundingly confusing."

"Why didn't you say anything?" Gordon asked.

"If I was right," Skulduggery said, "and if Gordon had copied his consciousness on to an Echo Stone, I imagined that version of Gordon would be a tad sensitive about his situation. When you were ready to tell me, you'd tell me. I was prepared to wait. It's good to see you, old friend."

Gordon blinked. "I... yes. It's, it's very good to see you too."

Ghastly smiled from across the room. "Welcome back. I'd shake your hand if I could."

"Ghastly, it truly is wonderful to see you," Gordon responded. "I heard you were a statue for a time. You're looking much better. And China... you're even more beautiful than ever."

China's own smile was warm. "Hello, my darling dear."

Tanith made her way forward. She licked her lips, and when she spoke, her voice shook. "I am," she said, "such a big fan."

"Oh," Gordon responded, obviously delighted. "Thank you."

"I have read all your books. All of them. *And The Darkness Rained Upon Them* was brilliant. It's probably my favourite, after *The Coward Colonel Fleece* and *Brain Muncher*."

"Fleece has always been my best character. You must be Tanith, then. Valkyrie has told me so much about you, but I'd heard tales of your exploits even when I was alive. Did you know that one of my short stories is based on a tale I heard about you?"

Tanith's smile grew so wide Valkyrie thought she might swallow her own head.

"Enough fawning," Kenspeckle said. Tanith nodded self-consciously and stepped back. "Gordon, it's good to see you, but we don't have time for idle chatter."

"We were talking about my work," Gordon replied. "There is nothing idle about that."

Kenspeckle sighed. "Nevertheless, can we move on to something that could help our situation? The more time we spend discussing how brilliant, or otherwise, your books may be, the more people get hurt."

"Of course," Gordon said. "So long as we all agree that my books are indeed brilliant."

"Fine," Kenspeckle growled. "Now can we talk about something that matters?"

"By all means. Valkyrie told me your plan, and of Fletcher's uncertainty. I spent four weeks interviewing Teleporters, and I am positive that I can impart what I learned quickly and easily. Uh, hello."

Clarabelle had walked up while he had been speaking, and now she stood in front of him with a faintly quizzical look on her face. She chewed lightly on her lower lip, like she was trying to solve a particularly difficult equation, and slowly bent forward, so that her head passed through Gordon's chin.

"Ah," said Gordon.

"Oh, for heaven's sake," Kenspeckle muttered. "Clarabelle, stop that."

She straightened up, and started to circle Gordon, examining how real and solid he looked. Gordon, for his part, smiled and did his best to ignore her.

"So you can tell Fletcher how to teleport two thousand people?" Skulduggery asked him.

Gordon nodded. "Oh, yes. It's not a technique, you see. It's a state of mind. It's an idea that must be understood and accepted. I feel certain that if I explain it as it was explained to me, Fletcher will grasp the intricacies and be able to perform what is expected of him before the day is out."

"Perfect. It's a good thing you're still around, Gordon."

Gordon smiled, was about to say something modest, when two slender fingers emerged from his forehead and wriggled about.

"Clarabelle," Kenspeckle said crossly, "get your hand out of Mr Edgley's head."

Clarabelle withdrew her hand sulkily.

"There is another matter," Skulduggery said. "The Receptacle."

"Yes, of course. Activated by a key that was broken into two pieces and hidden. It's not a key as we know it, in fact; it's just a flat piece of gold, the length and width of your hand. Whatever imperfections there are in the gold, however, activate the machine."

"Do you know where the pieces are?" Skulduggery asked.

"One piece is in Drogheda," Gordon said, "in St Peter's Church. It was attached to Plunkett's case, that's all I know about it. The other piece was hidden in Newgrange, until it was stolen by a man named Burgundy Dalrymple. He lives in the outskirts of Meath."

"Dalrymple," said China. "I've heard of him. He fought for Mevolent during the war. Good with a sword."

"Better than good," Gordon said. "A master swordsman, he was. When the war ended and his side lost, he adjusted better than most, and he did OK, all things considered. But he was one of the people possessed the last time the Remnants were loose. The Remnant was torn out of him at MacGillycuddy's Reeks, along with all the others, but Dalrymple... Dalrymple had difficulties after that."

"What kind of difficulties?" Skulduggery asked.

"Once a Remnant abandons somebody, and then that person reawakens, they can't remember anything of the experience. But occasionally, they do remember *sensations*. Dalrymple remembers the *sensation* of not being alone, of being part of something greater than he, and he's been trying to recapture that feeling ever since. He's been waiting for the Remnants to return, and he probably stole that half of the key so that when he *is* possessed once again, no one will be able to activate the Receptacle to tear them apart."

"What about the machine itself?" China asked. "Have you seen it?"

Gordon shook his head. "It's in a hidden cavern. I don't know how to find it, and I don't know how to get to it. It's supposed to be amazing though. I spoke with some of the sorcerers who built it and they told me enough to get my imagination working."

"Why didn't they tell you how to find it?" Fletcher asked.

"The Receptacle saved the world," Gordon told him. "It was their last-ditch effort against the Remnants. Once it was used, they vowed to seal it up so no one could tamper with it, or take it apart, or corrupt it. One of them said to me that when you're dealing with magic, you can never trust your enemies to stay beaten, or to stay dead. If we ever had to face those things again, they ensured that at least we'd have a weapon."

"And we have no time to waste," Skulduggery said. "Fletcher, take us back to the Hibernian."

Valkyrie picked up the Echo Stone in its cradle and they all linked arms. In an eye blink, they were back in the Medical Bay.

"That was much better," Clarabelle beamed. "I only threw up a little bit in my mouth."

Skulduggery turned to Gordon. "Are you sure you can teach Fletcher what he needs to learn?"

Gordon smiled, and nodded. "It shouldn't be a problem."

"Then you're going to get started almost immediately," Skulduggery said. "But first, Fletcher is going to teleport Valkyrie and Tanith to Drogheda, to search that church and find the first half of the key. China, you'll accompany me to track down this Dalrymple fellow."

"I love it when you get all commanding," China said, without any significant trace of sarcasm.

"Ghastly," Skulduggery continued, "you're going to drive Fletcher to MacGillycuddy's Reeks. Gordon, I'd like you to accompany them to Kerry, if that's OK with you?"

Gordon blinked a few times, and when he spoke, his voice was oddly strangled. "Of course. Glad to be of assistance."

Valkyrie didn't say anything, but she knew Skulduggery had

just paid Gordon the highest possible compliment – he'd treated him like a real person.

"You'd better hope you can educate this boy in a few hours," Skulduggery said.

"All he needs is to realise the fundamental truth behind teleporting," said Gordon, "and then he'll be able to do what he needs to. Shouldn't be a problem."

"Kenspeckle, I'm afraid we're going to have to use this as our base of operations," Skulduggery said. "When Ghastly and Fletcher reach the MacGillycuddy's Reeks, they'll teleport back to us, we'll lure the possessed here until they're all in one place, and then Fletcher will teleport *everyone* to the Receptacle."

"How are we going to lure them in?" asked Ghastly. "It's chaos out there."

Skulduggery shook his head. "It's not as disorganised as you might think. Look at it this way – the Remnants have been locked away without bodies for years. Their first night out, some of them are going to go a little crazy. But they do have purpose, and that purpose is Darquesse. They're going to start to group together. The Remnants might not have leaders, but their human hosts do. Once we get the leaders chasing us, the others will fall in behind. And the fact is, sooner or later,

Erskine or Shudder *are* going to figure out where we are. They *will* be coming for us."

"Happy happy," Tanith said, "joy joy."

"We're going to need some way to physically connect the possessed," Fletcher said.

"I can do that," said Valkyrie. Everyone looked at her, and she reached out to the shadows in the room, and they rose up like mist around them. "It's one of the training exercises in Necromancy," she said. "When they're this spread out, the shadows can't hurt anyone, but it'd still work as a bond. All Fletcher would have to do is teleport me, and everyone these shadows are touching would come with us."

"That's fine here in this room," China said, "but would you be able to connect all those Remnants?"

Valkyrie hesitated only a moment. "Yes," she said. "I would."

"Excellent," said Skulduggery. "Ghastly, you'd better set off as soon as Fletcher's teleported Valkyrie and Tanith. It should take four or five hours in this weather to get to Kerry, even with the Bentley's tyres."

Ghastly blinked. "You're letting me take the Bentley?"

"It's faster than your van. Just... take good care of her, OK?"

"I will."

Skulduggery went silent. When he spoke again, it was with great reluctance. "Not one scratch."

"OK."

"Not *one*, Bespoke."

"You concentrate on getting the keys. Let me worry about your car."

"I'm multi-talented, I can do both. OK, that's everything. Unless anyone has any other questions, let's get to it."

Fletcher took the Echo Stone from Valkyrie. "Don't get into any trouble while I'm gone," he said to her. "I know you're not going to be able to resist the temptation, but you have to remember that I won't be able to rescue you."

Valkyrie smirked. "I think I can manage without you for a few hours."

He nodded, and leaned in, and they kissed. "Please stay safe," he whispered. His kisses were much nicer than Caelan's. Softer. Sweeter. Warmer. She banished thoughts of Caelan from her mind, and kissed her boyfriend again.

"I will," she whispered back.

They looked around when Ghastly cleared his throat, and watched him touch the tattoos on his collarbones. Clear skin flowed over his scars, and he walked awkwardly up to Tanith. "Um," he said to her. "Don't die."

"OK," Tanith said.

"When this is over," he continued, "I'm going to make you dinner. You don't have to like it, and you don't have to eat it, and I suppose you don't even have to be there, but... But that's what I'm going to do."

Tanith frowned. "Are you asking me on a date?"

"I think so, yes. Will you have dinner with me?"

Tanith smiled the most beautiful smile. "I'd love to," she said. She laid a hand on his chest, tapped her fingers on his collarbones, and the clear skin retracted. Once his scars were revealed, Tanith kissed him, once, on the lips. "I like steak," she said. "Can't go wrong with steak."

"Steak it is," he murmured.

He stepped away, and Valkyrie grinned at Tanith.

"Oh, good God," China said, rolling her eyes. "I do hope the Remnants kill *me* first."

41

THE HEAD IN THE BOX

Drogheda town centre was lit up against the dark, but there was no one around to appreciate the Christmas lights. It was far too cold for people to be walking the streets, and the roads were far too icy for driving. Fletcher left Valkyrie and Tanith on the main street, gave Valkyrie a quick kiss, and offered another to Tanith. Valkyrie punched his shoulder and he vanished with a pained expression on his face.

"My eyeballs are cold," Tanith said. "That's not a good sign."

They walked quickly, in an effort to warm themselves up.

"They're saying this is the coldest winter in sixty years," Valkyrie muttered. "I need a woolly hat and mittens."

"Mittens," Tanith echoed wistfully. "Maybe tied to my sleeves..."

"I need earmuffs too," Valkyrie decided. "Fluffy ones. My ears are red, aren't they?"

Tanith took a glance. "Yep. But not as red as your nose. I'm going to ask Ghastly to make me clothes like yours. Then only my hands and face will get frostbite."

"Have you thought, maybe, that the reason you're freezing your bits off is because you don't wear *enough* clothes? How about wearing something under that waistcoat?"

Tanith pulled her coat tighter around her. "My waistcoat is not designed to have anything under it but me, Valkyrie."

"And you wonder why you're cold."

They reached the church. As daunting as it was impressive, its spires stretched into the night sky like spear tips. The doors were locked, but clicked open at Tanith's touch.

With the main lights off, the inside of the church was creepy. They passed a tomb that had a carving of skeletons wearing shrouds. To the left of the massive altar was a shrine, the centrepiece of which was a pedestal that held a glass case ensconced in gold and surrounded by long candles. It was topped off with a brass spire that reached upwards for three metres. Resting inside the case was a mummified head, leathery and brown, with empty eye sockets and tiny yellow teeth. Tanith peered at it.

"Who's this guy?" she asked.

"Oliver Plunkett," Valkyrie told her. "In sixteen hundred and something, he was hanged, drawn and quartered for practising Catholicism in Ireland. By the English, of course."

"Of course," Tanith responded solemnly. "And we're all very sorry about that."

Valkyrie nodded. "As well you should be."

"And why is his head on display in a church?" asked Tanith.

"Where else would you display a head?"

"Doesn't it seem kind of gruesome to you? I mean, *we're* used to seeing stuff like this, but what about ordinary people just coming here to pray, kneeling and muttering and crossing themselves, and they look over and see someone's head in a glass box? That's pretty morbid, not to mention kind of weird."

"Excuse me?" said a voice from behind.

They turned. A priest stood there, paunchy and middle-aged. "I'm Father Reynolds," he continued. "Can I help you with anything?"

Valkyrie held her hands down by her sides, ready to push at the air should she notice even one black vein. "We're just passing through, Mr Reynolds," she assured him.

He stiffened slightly. "That's *Father* Reynolds," he said.

"Oh, I'm sorry," Valkyrie said. "And what's your first name?"

"My full name is Father Declan Reynolds, and you, young lady, have broken into this church."

"Pleased to meet you, Declan," Valkyrie responded, ignoring the accusation. "I'm Valkyrie, this is Tanith. You might be able to help us, actually. We're looking for something. It's a flat piece of gold, about the length of your hand. Would you have seen it?"

The priest frowned at her. "You lost some gold?"

"We didn't lose it," Tanith said. "We're just looking for it. A friend of ours told us it'd be somewhere near the head in the box. We're assuming that he meant *this* head in the box, unless you have another one stashed away somewhere?"

"I may be new to the parish, but as far as I am aware, this is the only head in a box that we have. I'm sorry, if this is a joke, I fail to see how it is funny."

"The flat piece of gold," Valkyrie said. "Have you seen it?"

"I don't know what you're talking about," the priest said,

turning to walk away, "but maybe you can explain yourselves to the Guards when they get here."

If he expected them to protest, or to run after him, he was disappointed. When he'd walked a few steps and they still hadn't reacted, he whirled, to find them examining the box. "Come away from there at once."

Valkyrie ran her hands along the base. "In a second," she said.

"You are not allowed to touch the cabinet!" the priest shouted, storming towards them. Valkyrie's fist caught him just under the chin. He stumbled back, his legs wobbling and his eyes already closing. He slumped to the ground and lay there, unconscious.

"Oh," Valkyrie said. "I thought he was possessed."

"Sure you did," Tanith grinned. She pressed her hand against the golden base of the cabinet and they heard a soft *click*. She pushed, rotated her fingertips, and a flat piece of gold came away, dropping from the base into her palm.

"Damn," she said. "I'm good."

They called Skulduggery to let him know they'd found the first half of the key. He told them to walk to the bus depot and wait for him there.

Up through Drogheda, the streets were frozen and empty. The roads glistened, like someone had carelessly tossed down a hundred thousand tiny crystals. Parked cars were covered in frost, windshields thick with ice. Christmas lights gave it all an unearthly sheen, and somewhere far away a house alarm was going off.

Valkyrie and Tanith crossed the road and kept heading south, towards the bus depot. Valkyrie had her arms crossed, hands jammed under her armpits. Her ears were freezing and her nose was red and running. She stepped on an icy patch and her feet flew out from under her. For the third time in ten minutes, she landed on her backside. Tanith looked back and sighed. Even she had stopped finding that funny.

They crossed the bridge, staying off the pavements, sticking to the road, where it was less slippery. They hadn't heard one single moving car, let alone seen one. The lights at the depot were on, and the buses sat still and silent. They hopped the low wall and Tanith pushed open the glass door. An old woman looked up from where she was sitting.

Valkyrie nodded to her warily, while Tanith went to the ticket booth. It was almost as cold in there as it was outside.

"There's nobody else here," the old woman said. "I tried the office as well. Nobody here at all."

Tanith glanced at Valkyrie, and went to make sure. When she was gone, the old woman looked back to Valkyrie. "Have you been watching the news? Terrible, isn't it? All those sick people."

"It is," said Valkyrie.

"I've been sitting here for hours. I tried calling my son, but I couldn't get through."

"The phones are down."

"Is that what it is? I hope he's all right. I hope he hasn't got sick. He's got children, you know. A ten-year-old and a four-year-old."

"He's probably fine," said Valkyrie.

The old woman did her best to smile. "I just want to get home. It isn't right. This town is never this quiet. Where are all the people? Are they all sick? The man on the news said that the sick people are prone to outbreaks of violence. If everyone is sick, it's not safe here. I just want to go home."

"Us too."

"What's your name, child?"

The old woman didn't look like someone a Remnant would hijack. She was neither young nor strong. She was small, and her hair was white, and even though she was wrapped up against the cold, she looked thin and frail.

"My name's Valkyrie."

"That's an unusual name. French, is it?"

"Uh, Scandinavian, I think."

"It's very pretty."

Tanith came back. "No one here," she said.

"I told you," the old woman responded. "I've been here for three hours, and you two are the first people I've seen. I should just be thankful that you're not like the ones they showed on the news."

"Where do you live?" Valkyrie asked.

"Duleek," the old woman answered. "Do you know it?"

"I've seen signs for it."

"The Duleek bus was supposed to leave at ten past seven, but nothing out there has even moved. I haven't seen any drivers. I don't know how I'm going to get home."

"We're expecting a lift any minute now," Valkyrie said, "maybe we could give you a—"

"Val," Tanith interrupted, glaring at her.

"You're very kind," the old woman smiled, "but it's quite all right."

"We can't leave her here," Valkyrie said to Tanith.

"Why not?" Tanith answered. "Who's going to touch her? She's safer here than she would be with us."

"It's freezing in here."

"So? She has mittens." Tanith turned to the old woman. "Normally, I'd have no problem inviting you along. But for all we know, you might be sick."

"Me?" the old woman said, surprised. "But I'm not running around hurting people."

"No, you're not. But you could be about to start."

The old woman blinked at them, then seemed to shrink back into the layers of clothes she was wearing. "I should probably stay here anyway. My son might be looking for me."

Tanith shrugged at Valkyrie. "See? Problem solved."

Then the lights went out.

"Great," she heard Tanith mutter.

For a few seconds, they were in nothing but blackness. Then Valkyrie's eyes started to adjust, and she could see vague outlines in the gloom. The shape that was Tanith moved to a window.

"The whole town's gone dark," she said. "There's not a light on for miles."

"Maybe they have a torch in the office," said the old woman, sounding scared.

"I have a lighter," Valkyrie said, clicking her fingers. She cupped the flame, disguising the fact that it burned in her palm.

"Oh, that's bright," the old woman said, relieved. "I don't mean to be a burden on you, but is it at all possible to get a lift with you, when your friend comes? I don't really like the idea of staying here alone."

"I'm sure we can work something out," Valkyrie said. She could see Tanith in the flickering light. Her friend did not look pleased. "I'll look for a torch."

Valkyrie moved into the office, searched the two desks and then the shelves. She found a torch and clicked it on. The beam lit up the entire room.

"Found one," she called.

She heard Tanith gag, and fear shot through her. She ran out of the office. The old woman had her thin, frail hands wrapped around Tanith's throat.

Valkyrie gave a roar and the old woman cursed in a language Valkyrie had never heard before. Valkyrie was almost on top of her when the old woman's thin, spindly fist flashed out, almost taking her head off. The torch went spinning across the floor and Valkyrie went down, rolled by pure instinct, got up and didn't know what was happening. Her legs buckled slightly and she staggered, saw the old woman hurling punches down on Tanith.

Valkyrie's palm snapped against the air, and the space rippled as the old woman shot sideways, whooping as she went. Tanith sprawled across the floor, unconscious.

The old woman scrambled up. By the light of the torch Valkyrie saw her black lips and vein-ridden face.

"You can't escape," the old woman said. "And why would you want to? You have a glorious destiny."

"It's not destiny," Valkyrie seethed, stepping closer. "Even if it was, I've changed it. It's not happening."

"That's why we're here," the woman explained. "To make sure it does. Darquesse, we were aimless. We were nothing. We were anger and hatred and spite. But now? Now we have purpose. Now we have a future. With you."

"If you want me to lead you, then let's start right now. I have a pair of shackles in my pocket. I want you to put them on."

The old woman smiled and shook her head. "You need to be guided further along the path," she said. "Then you will assume your mantle. Then we'll obey. Right now, you still think you're Valkyrie Cain. You still think you have friends. Like this one." The old woman knelt by Tanith, and stroked her hair. "Let me be your friend. I'll leave this body, this old decrepit thing, and I'll join with her. Such a nice form to take, with that pretty face, with everything so hard, and strong, and firm. All this muscle, and all this leather."

"Stop describing her," Valkyrie said. "It's getting weird."

The old woman lunged, but Tanith raised her arm and tripped her, and the lunge turned to a stumble. Valkyrie slid into her, flipped her to the floor, got behind her and choked. The old woman squirmed like a fish, but Valkyrie held on. She didn't want to hurt her, didn't want to cause the old woman actual harm, she just needed her to go to sleep for a while. She tightened the choke and the old woman weakened, and then her head drooped forward. Valkyrie turned her on her side, and got up.

"Oh my God," Valkyrie said numbly. "We just beat up a pensioner."

"Evil pensioner," Tanith corrected, coughing slightly as she dragged herself to her feet. "What was she babbling about? I heard her say Darquesse."

"Yeah. Yeah, she did. Just, you know, more babbling. Couldn't make sense of half of it. You OK?"

"I'm good. A bit woozy. She has a pretty good right hook, you know. For a granny."

42

THE LESSON BEGINS

"Teleporting one thousand people is not that different from teleporting one person," Gordon said as they sped down the empty motorway. "The effort, the magic, goes into the initial opening of the rift in space. How wide that rift eventually opens is somewhat immaterial."

"What rift?" Fletcher asked.

"Do you actually know how your power works?"

Fletcher couldn't look at Gordon while they were in motion, so he kept his eyes fixed on the windscreen. "Sure. I think about a place I've been, and I go there. I don't open a rift in space or anything."

"Actually, that's precisely what you're doing. Emmett Peregrine told me how he got his head around it, and I think it might help you. Uh, Fletcher, I don't want to sound like a schoolteacher or anything, but could you look at me when I'm talking to you?"

"Sorry," Fletcher said, "I can't. You make me carsick."

Ghastly frowned. "How does Gordon make you carsick?"

"Well, he keeps slipping, you know, out of the car, kind of."

"That's hardly my fault," said Gordon. "Sometimes I don't notice a turn coming up, or Ghastly switches lanes without telling me."

"Sorry about that," said Ghastly.

"It's quite all right. Fletcher, I promise I'll try harder."

Fletcher exhaled, then nodded, and turned around in his seat. "OK," he said. "Carry on."

Gordon smiled gratefully, then the Bentley went over a bump and his face disappeared into the backseat. He had to lean forward to be visible again. The whole thing made Fletcher quite queasy.

"Instead of focusing on the distance travelled," Gordon said, "think of it like this. You're not the one moving."

"I'm not?"

"You're using your power to stay totally still, and the world moves around you until you are exactly where you want to be."

"Uh..."

"It's like me, right now. I'm tethered to the Echo Stone, and the Echo Stone is moving, but *I'm* not. The world is moving around me. And occasionally through me. For you, Fletcher, existence itself rotates and pivots according to your will. I'm sure someone of your self-esteem has no problem with the notion that the universe revolves around him, am I correct?"

"I think that all the time."

Gordon smiled. "I know the feeling well. Emmett used to say that he let the world do the travelling while he stayed in the same place. He focused on where he wanted the world to stop, and that's all he did. He didn't burden himself with thoughts of distance, or how many people he was taking with him, or how big a cargo he was transporting. He saw his destination as a clear point in a whirlwind, and he let it come to him. Do you understand?"

"I... I think so."

"That's good. Understanding is the first step. Acceptance is the second. Once you've accepted this as fact, the possibilities are endless."

43

BY THE SWORD

Burgundy Dalrymple didn't live in a very nice house. It was, in China's opinion, ramshackle to the point of dilapidation. It stood alone, a bungalow on a dead road. Two windows were lit up, and even the light was sickly. The garden was a jungle of weeds and long grasses. To be fair, China couldn't see much of it in the darkness, and for that she was grateful. Squalor held no appeal.

Valkyrie called just as Skulduggery turned off the van's engine. China waited while he spoke to her. They'd obviously succeeded in securing their half of the key. Skulduggery told

Valkyrie to wait for them, and then he activated his façade and nodded to China. They got out, and approached the house.

The front door opened slightly.

"Go away!" said a man's voice from behind it.

Skulduggery and China stopped, and Skulduggery's fake face smiled. "Hello, Burgundy," he said.

"That's not me," said the man. "That's somebody else. Go away."

"Burgundy," Skulduggery said, "we just want to talk to you. One minute of your time, and we'll be gone."

"I'm not Burgundy!"

"You're Burgundy Dalrymple," China said. "Master swordsman and war hero."

The man's laugh came out as something like a bark. "War hero? No one calls me a war hero!"

"Well," China said, stepping out of the shadows so that he could see her face, "I suppose it all depends on which side of the war you were fighting on."

There was a moment of silence, then his voice cracked as he said, "You're China Sorrows."

"I am, and this is Skulduggery Pleasant. We'd like to talk to you about Remnants, if you have the time."

"I... I suppose..."

"May we come in?" Skulduggery asked.

"Well... all right. But I don't allow people to bring in weapons. Are you armed?"

"No."

"Show me. Open your jacket."

Skulduggery hesitated. "Oh," he said, "*armed*. Yes, I am armed. I'm a *little* armed. I just have a gun. In some people's hands that's *barely* a weapon."

"Take it out and leave it there."

Grumbling, Skulduggery did as he was told.

"OK," said the voice, "come in."

They stepped on to the porch. The wood was old and rotten and creaked under their weight. Skulduggery pushed the front door open. The hall which greeted them did so with dim light. The moment he stepped through, his face rippled, and withdrew from his skull. He stopped immediately, and turned to her. "Be careful," he said, his voice soft. "This house has been bound."

China felt it too upon crossing the threshold – the invisible tattoos that graced her body went dull as her magic was dampened.

"In here," the man called.

They walked slowly into the living room. It was

surprisingly big, but barely furnished. There was a dining table in the middle of the room and a few chairs around it. A few lamps. That was it. The walls, however, were decorated with all manner of fencing swords, rapiers and sabres, and unlike their dusty surroundings, these swords looked like they were lovingly kept in perfect working order.

Burgundy Dalrymple stood on the far side of the dining table. He was a little too skinny and he needed a shave and a haircut and, China imagined, a wash.

"I'm Burgundy Dalrymple," he said nervously.

"We need your help," Skulduggery told him. "We know of your history with the Remnants, and we know how much it has affected you and how you live your life."

"OK," Dalrymple said. "Go on."

"We also know that you have tracked down one half of the Receptacle key."

"I'd have tracked them both down by now," Dalrymple nodded, "but people stopped talking to me about ten or fifteen years ago, so no one would answer my, you know, my questions. Why? What do you want?"

"We want your half of the key," China said.

Dalrymple's tone was firm. "No. No. I'm keeping it so that

no one will be able to trap the Remnants ever again. I would have destroyed it already if I'd been able to, but it's pretty durable. Why do you want it?"

Skulduggery tilted his head. "You mean you don't know?"

"If I knew, would I be asking?"

"We need it to turn the machine on, Burgundy. The Remnants are loose."

Dalrymple looked at Skulduggery, and for a long moment he said nothing.

"Where," he said at last, sounding like he needed a drink of water, "where are they?"

"We need the key, Burgundy."

"I thought you wanted to study it, or something. To run tests, to find out how something like that, how it works, but... But you want to *use* the Receptacle? Why would I help you do that? This is what I've been waiting for!"

"I don't want to threaten you in your own home," Skulduggery said, "so if you'd like to step outside, I can threaten you there."

"Outside?" Dalrymple sneered. "Where magic isn't bound? Where you can throw fire at me and take the key from around my charred neck?"

"Ah, so you have it *on* you?"

Dalrymple went to the wall, and grabbed a sword. "You want it? You're welcome to take it."

"It would really be much easier if you just gave it to me."

"Come on!" Dalrymple snarled. "Let's be having you!"

"I'd really rather not," Skulduggery said.

"If you can beat me, you can take the key from my blood-soaked corpse!"

"Again, not entirely appealing."

"Take up your steel!"

Skulduggery sighed, walked to the closest wall and chose a sword with a jewel-encrusted hilt. Dalrymple walked forward, and suddenly lunged. The blades clashed, and Dalrymple began circling.

"We really don't have to do this," Skulduggery said. "I mean you no harm. None at all."

"I mean you *acres* of harm," Dalrymple growled. "Untold *quantities* of harm. I will visit a whole *continent* of harm upon you before we are through."

"You are an odd fellow."

China watched Dalrymple come in with three quick jabs. Skulduggery parried the first two and sidestepped the third, responding with a riposte that Dalrymple blocked easily. They went at it again, blades flashing and singing together.

Dalrymple kept his left hand held high behind him in a classical fencer's stance. Skulduggery kept his free hand low and out in front – far less flashy, far more cautious.

"You're good," Dalrymple said.

"You're too kind," Skulduggery responded.

"I haven't faced anyone half as good as you in a hundred years."

"That's very nice of you to say so."

"Not really. I just haven't *fought* anyone in a hundred years." Dalrymple pressed forward his attack, and Skulduggery retreated, barely keeping the slashing blade at bay. "I'm rusty," Dalrymple continued. "Out of practice. My form is all wrong."

"It looks fine to me."

"It's sloppy." Dalrymple batted Skulduggery's blade down and swiped at his head. Skulduggery jerked away and stumbled. "In my prime that would have taken your head off."

Skulduggery scrambled to his feet. "How embarrassing for you."

"There was a time in my life when swordplay was the only thing that meant anything."

"Everyone needs a hobby."

"But it was an empty time," Dalrymple said, almost sobbed. "A lonely time." Skulduggery moved in, trying to take advantage of the distraction, but couldn't get through Dalrymple's defence. "And then the Remnant came into me, and that loneliness went away." Dalrymple slashed, cutting through the sleeve of Skulduggery's jacket.

Skulduggery backed off. "But you can't remember any of it," he said.

"I don't need to remember details. It was the *feeling*. The feeling of being *whole*. Being *complete*. That's what I remember. That's what I miss. That's what I want back."

"And have you ever tried just making friends?"

Dalrymple snarled again, and stepped in quickly, his blade seeking out Skulduggery, who was doing his best to remain elusive. "You mock me."

"I don't," Skulduggery insisted, on the retreat once more.

"You laugh at me."

"I find it rude to laugh at a man with a sword."

The blades scraped together and Dalrymple flicked his wrist. Skulduggery's sword flew from his grip, and he had to dive to the floor to escape. He rolled and came up, giving himself some room.

"Burgundy," China said, taking a rapier from the wall, "would you mind awfully if I replace Skulduggery for the remainder of this duel?"

Dalrymple looked around, his eyes narrowed. "I'm not going to spare you just because I've fallen in love with you," he warned. "I know about you. I know it's not real love."

"But of course it's real," she said, flourishing the rapier. "All love is real love." She sent out a light jab that he batted away. "Otherwise it's not love, is it? Otherwise it's pointless. A waste of time and energy. And I despise wasting either."

Now it was Skulduggery's turn to watch as Dalrymple came back at China and she blocked, replied with a swipe that *he* blocked, the shrill taps of blade on blade settling into a rhythm as they moved around each other.

"You're trying to confuse me," Dalrymple said.

"I am trying no such thing. The love you're feeling is a real and genuine thing. Just because it is not reciprocated in the slightest does not lessen its worth."

"You don't love me," Dalrymple sneered.

"Isn't that what I just said?"

He neared. "You wouldn't be fighting if you knew what it was like. When your body is a vessel for a Remnant, you don't need tricks to make people fall in love with you. You don't *need* their love."

China backed away, blocking and countering. She stepped up on to a chair, and then she was on the table, and he was following her up, the clashing of their swords only getting faster. It was dangerous up there, not much room to manoeuvre, and Dalrymple's strikes were increasing in strength. China was impressed. Her wrist was already aching.

She saw Skulduggery, out of the corner of her eye, retrieve his sword and walk towards them. "Burgundy," he said, "I am a firm believer in fair fights. I really am. But we did not come here to lose. We came here to get the half of the key that you stole, and we won't be leaving without it. So I'm afraid we must cheat a little."

While Dalrymple parried China's thrust, Skulduggery poked at his leg – and Dalrymple's blade clanged off his.

China blinked, then defended, and Skulduggery tried again to injure Dalrymple. But once again, Dalrymple's sword flashed down, faster than her eye could follow, and he batted Skulduggery's attempt away and then resumed his attack on China. She would have thought it impossible if she had not been there to personally witness it.

"Cheating against you isn't easy," Skulduggery murmured.

Dalrymple jumped down from the far side of the table. China followed him to the floor while Skulduggery moved around. They closed in, their swords cutting towards Dalrymple while he defended with startling alacrity. China went left and Skulduggery went right, and still they failed to draw blood. The entire affair was becoming completely unacceptable. Any moment now, China was about to perspire.

She leaned in with a deep thrust that was parried, but she responded with a flick that almost took Dalrymple's hand off at the wrist. Now the master swordsman was on the back foot. Skulduggery went low and China went high, and then they switched, and switched again, robbing Dalrymple of a chance to anticipate their next move.

"Surrender," Skulduggery said.

Dalrymple didn't answer immediately, too busy defending. "You seem to have me beaten," he said at last.

"So it seems. But if this is true, then why are you smiling?"

"Because," Dalrymple answered, "I know something you don't know."

"And what is that?" asked Skulduggery.

"I'm not right-handed," Dalrymple replied, and threw the sword into his left hand. China cursed and fell back under his renewed onslaught, and Skulduggery cried out as a sliver of bone was cut from his arm. China lashed out desperately to keep Dalrymple away, but his sword was moving much faster than her own, and she couldn't find her balance. She fell to one hand, continuing the fight with her other while she tried to scuttle out of range.

Skulduggery reared up behind Dalrymple and Dalrymple spun, thrusting through Skulduggery's ribcage. Skulduggery froze, looking down at the blade that pierced his clothing. Then Dalrymple twisted the sword and dragged it out so that it scraped across Skulduggery's sternum, and Skulduggery howled in pain and crumpled to the ground.

China slashed her rapier at the back of Dalrymple's neck, but he dodged, whirled, and his sword crashed against hers and suddenly her hand was empty. He kicked her in the chest and she went down.

He stood over her with the tip of his blade at her throat. "There," he said, panting a little. "You are defeated. Now it is *you* who will answer *my* questions. Where are they? Where are the Remnants?"

"I don't know," she said.

The tip pressed against her skin. "Tell me or I'll kill you."

Skulduggery was still curled up on the floor, his arms wrapped around himself. China sighed. "Fine. I'll tell you. But if you switched on a television or a radio, you'd already know all this."

"I don't trust modern technology," he informed her.

"Why doesn't that surprise me? In that case, you've missed the countless stories of riots that are breaking out all across the city. All across the country."

Dalrymple's mouth hung open. "They're all out? The Remnants? All of them? That's... That's..."

"That's what you've been waiting for?"

His eyes brimmed with tears. "Yes."

"For well over a hundred years?"

He nodded quickly. "Yes."

"Then tonight is your lucky night, Burgundy. But you better hurry or else there'll be none left to join with you."

"Yes," he said, his eyes unfocused. "Yes, I... I have to go."

The tip of his sword wavered from her throat and China lashed out, the toe of her expensive boot crunching into his knee. He fell back and Skulduggery rose, grabbed Dalrymple's sword-hand and wrenched it behind him, breaking it. Dalrymple screamed and the sword dropped, and Skulduggery threw him against the wall.

"Give me your half of the key," Skulduggery said, his voice cold, devoid of humanity.

Dalrymple sobbed in pain. He tried to run for the door, but Skulduggery kicked his feet from under him. He stomped on Dalrymple's broken arm and the poor man screeched until he passed out. China stood up as Skulduggery searched him, finally finding the key on a light chain around the unconscious man's neck.

"Are you OK?" Skulduggery asked China as he examined the flat piece of gold.

"I'm fine," she replied. "How are you? He hurt you, I see."

"Just a scratch."

"Just enough to make you lose your sense of humour?"

He looked at her. "Only temporarily, I assure you. I'm right as rain now, though. We have one half of the key, Valkyrie has the other. We might actually win this, you know, even against overwhelming odds."

China shrugged. "Stranger things have happened."

44

SIEGE AT THE HIBERNIAN

kulduggery and China arrived in Drogheda, and they all got into the nice warm van. Tanith immediately told them that Valkyrie had beaten up a priest and an old woman. China laughed, and Skulduggery handed Valkyrie the half of the key he'd recovered from Dalrymple. She pressed it against the half from the church and was unable to pry them apart again.

They got on to the motorway and drove without seeing another car until they got to the slipway for Balbriggan. Two cars were stopped in the middle lane – the doors open and no one around.

"A crash?" Tanith asked as they drove slowly by. Valkyrie could see no sign of collision, and she got the uncomfortable feeling that they were being watched.

Skulduggery pressed down on the accelerator. "We don't stop," he said. "For anyone."

Neither Valkyrie or Tanith said anything.

They reached the city centre and cut through the empty streets, ignoring traffic lights. At the entrance to Trinity College, a grit-spreader was pulled in to the side of the road with its lights on and its engine running, but there was no sign of the driver. They swung around St Stephen's Green and saw a man running up to them, waving his arms frantically. Valkyrie looked away as they left him behind.

The city was dead around them, killed by cold and fear.

"Checkpoint," Skulduggery said, as his façade flowed over his skull.

Valkyrie peered out at the flashing blue lights of the Garda squad cars ahead of them. Four cops in reflective jackets waved them down.

Valkyrie and Tanith lay flat in the back. Valkyrie's heart was thumping wildly by the time the van stopped. She heard the window whir down, and a cop asking Skulduggery for his driver's licence. China asked if there was a problem. The cop stammered a little when he replied that this was just a routine checkpoint, nothing to worry about. At least his love-struck reaction to China Sorrows was a normal response. That was a good start. But when Skulduggery told him that he didn't have his licence on him, the cop ordered him to step out of the van.

"Is there a problem?" Skulduggery asked.

"Just step out of the van, sir," the cop replied.

"We weren't speeding, Guard."

"Sir," the cop said, irritation creeping into his voice, "I'm telling you to step out of the van. You can either do as I ask, or we'll pull you out and arrest you."

"There's no need for threats," Skulduggery said. Valkyrie heard the door open, and Skulduggery got out. The door closed.

"There's four of them," China whispered from the front. "One on my side. Three around Skulduggery."

There was a knock on the passenger side window. China wound it down.

"Hello, there," Valkyrie heard a cop say.

"Hello," China said back, a smile in her voice.

Valkyrie noticed Tanith moving slightly. The streetlight

glinted briefly across the steel of her sword. Valkyrie swallowed.

There was a short cry from outside, then something slammed into the side of the van at the same time as China kicked her door open. The sound of the door hitting the cop's head was unmistakable. China closed her door calmly as Skulduggery got back behind the wheel, and they sped on.

"Trouble?" Tanith asked, sitting up.

"Nothing I couldn't talk my way out of," Skulduggery replied.

Valkyrie looked out the back window at the crumpled forms of the Guards. "Were they possessed?"

"I don't think so," China said. "They didn't seem especially strong."

"All it takes is one Remnant in a position of power," Skulduggery said. "For all we know, they could have the entire police force on the lookout for us. Everyone hold on – we're going to be moving a little faster."

He pressed his foot down on the accelerator, and the van roared.

By the time they reached the Hibernian, Valkyrie was scared and depressed. She worried about her parents, and for the first time she worried about her cousins. She wondered how they were coping with what they'd learned over the past twenty-four hours. The events they'd witnessed, plus the madness breaking out all over the city, all over the country, would be enough to freak *anyone* out, let alone two highly-strung teenagers.

According to the radio, the entire country was, understandably, panicking. The authorities were inundated with reports of missing people. Some commentators were saying this was a neurological virus, others said it was a biological attack, and still others were saying, and this was Valkyrie's personal favourite, that this was God's punishment for not going to church any more. Some of the attacks reported were genuine Remnant activity, but others were clearly down to Kenspeckle's time-released thought bomb.

Whatever the cause, the effect was the same. People were staying in, locking their doors and windows and isolating themselves from their neighbours. There were reports of scientists in hazmat suits walking the streets. The country was going crazy, and the rest of the world was just waiting for the sickness to spread to them.

Skulduggery parked Ghastly's van across the road from the Hibernian and out of sight. Making sure no one was watching, they hurried over to the locked door at the rear of the cinema.

A hidden camera picked them up, and a few moments later the door clicked. They hurried inside and the moment the door closed again it locked, sliding steel bars into place and activating an alarm system that Kenspeckle himself had designed.

"Ghastly called," Kenspeckle said when he saw them. "He said they're three hours away, if they're lucky."

Skulduggery sent Tanith to check defences on the upper levels, and he took Valkyrie with him as he checked the lower ones.

"When do you think the possessed will get here?" Valkyrie asked as they walked.

"Any time now. To be honest, I'm surprised they're not here already."

"I don't like waiting," Valkyrie said. "I think too much. I think of everything that could go wrong with this dreadful plan of ours."

"Surely not *everything*."

"You are of no reassurance at all, do you know that? If you were any kind of a friend, you'd be telling me that in a few hours the Remnants will be gone and everyone will be back to normal."

"You mean if I was a true friend," Skulduggery said, "I'd take this opportunity to lie to you?"

"Pretty much, yes."

"In that case, this dreadful plan cannot fail. In a few hours, the Remnants will be trapped in the Receptacle and everyone will be back to normal. People can carry on arguing about who should be the two new Elders, I can get back to tracking down this Tesseract character, and you can continue your lessons in Necromancy while you go on another date with Fletcher, as Caelan seethes with jealousy on the sidelines."

He tested iron shutters that were sealing off an old doorway.

"You notice everything," she said.

"Not everything, but a lot."

"He told me he loves me," Valkyrie said. "Caelan."

They resumed their walk.

"You don't want a vampire loving you, Valkyrie."

"He's not a bad person."

"Because he's not a person."

"Don't give me that," she said irritably. "That's all anyone ever says. *He's an animal. He can't be trusted.* That's what *he* says, too. He calls *himself* an animal, for God's sake."

"And what do you think he is? Troubled? Misunderstood? He's a killer."

"Caelan is different from the others."

"Yes, he is."

Valkyrie frowned. "You agree with me?"

"Absolutely. The other vampires are brutal, bloodthirsty animals barely held in check by their brutal, bloodthirsty code. But Caelan? He's much worse."

She sighed and shook her head, but he continued.

"He broke the first law of being a vampire when he killed his own kind. If he can't stick to that simple rule, how safe do you think you are? Do you know why vampires are known for holding grudges? It's because once a passion for something, in that case vengeance, starts to burn, it consumes them absolutely. Vengeance, hatred, or love. They each burn as bright."

"So you're saying he'll become obsessed with me?"

"If he told you he loves you, he's *already* obsessed with you."

"If you talked to him, if you sat down and gave him a chance, you'd realise how wrong you are."

Skulduggery didn't say anything. He just looked at her, then slowly cocked his head to one side. Valkyrie looked away, aware of the blush that was rising.

"What did you do?" he asked.

"I didn't do anything. What are you talking about?"

"Loath as I am to protect your relationship with Fletcher, you *are* still with the boy, aren't you?"

"Of course."

"You're not with Caelan, then?"

She shook her head.

"And you have no *plans* to be with him?"

"He's way too old."

"That's not an answer."

"Well, I don't know what you want me to say! Do you want me to say we kissed? Because OK, we did! Once! That's all. And I said never again because I'm with Fletcher, and he agreed. There. What else do you want to know?"

Skulduggery said nothing, just kept walking. She felt the flash of righteous anger fading fast, leaving her feeling stupid and childish and really wishing she hadn't said anything.

"I see," he said at last.

"I don't have to explain myself to you," said Valkyrie. "I don't need to get your permission to kiss Caelan, or Fletcher, or anyone."

"That's right," he said quietly, "you don't. But we still have the problem of a vampire being in love with you."

"I told you, it's *not* a problem."

"You can't afford to encourage him."

She glared. "I'm not encouraging him."

"Then kissing him probably sends the wrong signal."

Valkyrie looked away, unable to argue with him there.

"And what if Fletcher finds out?" Skulduggery continued. "Are you willing to lose your boyfriend over this? Caelan may be on his best behaviour with *you*, but by now, I can assure you, he is *hating* Fletcher. A hint, a suggestion, that's all it would take to ruin things between you two."

"Caelan's not going to say anything," she said, without conviction.

Then the lights went out. Before Valkyrie could even click her fingers, the emergency generator activated.

"Power cut?" she asked. "Or...?"

"Remnants," Skulduggery said. "They're here."

They ran back to the others. Kenspeckle had a screen set up in the Medical Bay that showed multiple shots of the building's exteriors.

There were hundreds of them – men and women and even a few children, mortal and sorcerer, all of them out there in the freezing cold with black-lipped smiles on their black-veined faces. Valkyrie could see Wreath and Shudder and Ravel, and a few other people she recognised. There was movement in the crowd around the main door, and Tesseract walked forward. He looked straight up into the camera.

Valkyrie felt the fear in her gut, and the cold, cold guilt. A part of her, a despairing part, wailed and cried that they were here for her, that all this was her fault.

It wasn't, of course. The Remnants getting free had nothing to do with her, as far as she knew. If they hadn't come after her, they'd still be out there, still hurting people and taking over bodies. This way, at least, they weren't targeting mortals. For the moment.

They watched the screens as the possessed spread out, wrapping around the building like a noose on a neck.

A few of them approached the perimeter on the west side. One of them waved a stick at the air until it hit the invisible dome Kenspeckle had set up. The dome glowed blue at the point where the stick touched it, and the blue rippled outwards and gradually dissipated, like a pebble thrown into a still lake. The possessed let out a chorus of appreciation for such fine defensive work.

On the street-facing side, a sorcerer hurled a stream of energy that was soaked up into the blue without causing damage. A ball of fire exploded against it, bullets hit and dropped harmlessly, and a fist of shadows broke apart on impact. All those attacks did was send ripples of blue around the little building.

A group of the possessed broke off from the rest, started using their magic to blast away at the ground.

"They're digging under," Valkyrie said.

"They're going to have to dig deep," Kenspeckle told her. "We're not encased in a bubble, but the dome does continue down into the earth for about ten metres. It's not going to be easy for them."

"How long till they break through?" asked Tanith.

"The dome will not fail completely," Kenspeckle said, "but some gaps may start to appear. We can expect some of them to get through before the dome repairs itself."

"Don't mind that at all," Tanith shrugged. "Just don't want to get bored."

Valkyrie didn't say it, but looking down at the hundreds of murderous, black-lipped faces, she didn't think there'd be much chance of that.

"Spread out," Skulduggery said, "but not too far. We go where we're needed, but we don't go alone. Is that understood? Our aim is to defend and repel attacks until Fletcher teleports back to us. Until then, we do not rest and we do not stop. Let's go."

Under sustained attacks, gaps were appearing, and sorcerers were getting through to the building itself. There were further defences there, of course, and even more inside, but little by little, the building was breached.

Valkyrie was down in the morgue, watching helplessly as a large hole was blasted through the wall and three sorcerers jumped through.

Skulduggery ran to intercept the intruders. He pushed at the air and sent one of them back to the dome. The other two were Elementals, and knew how to meet the rush of air without losing ground. The biggest of them, an ugly man with curly black hair, slammed into Skulduggery and took him down. The other one, dressed in a suit and tie splattered with mud, went for Valkyrie.

She dropped right before he reached her, sweeping his feet from under him. He hit the floor and she gripped him with shadows, threw him spinning to the side of the morgue. The *smack* his head made against the concrete was wet and sickening.

The man with the curly hair punched Skulduggery's head, grunting as his hand broke. Skulduggery kicked him away and rolled to his feet, slid sideways to avoid a lunge from the third intruder. His hand came around, caught the guy behind the ear, sending him stumbling. Valkyrie pushed at the air, directing it at the guy's feet. His legs flew out behind him and he fell, and she ran up and volleyed his head like a football.

Skulduggery whipped an elbow into the curly-haired man's

nose. The Remnants were strong, and their sensitivity to pain was lessened, but they were still in human bodies, and human bodies had certain reactions to certain things. An elbow to the nose causes the eyes to water, which blurs the vision. A kick to the shin sends signals shooting into the brain, which in turn brings the hands down to protect the injured area. And a knee to the chin rocks the head back, which makes the brain slam into the wall of the skull, which results in blackout.

The man with the curly hair dropped like a sack of ugly potatoes.

Through the hole in the wall, Valkyrie could see the blue energy of the dome, and the possessed on the other side. She barely resisted the urge to shout, "That all you got?" The urge came from fear and the expectation of the inevitable, like when she was a kid playing hide-and-seek and she'd be consumed by the need to lunge from her hiding place as the seeker grew close and shout, "I'm here! I'm here!"

She wasn't a kid any more, and those kinds of self-destructive urges had no place in her life, especially now.

The possessed looked at her and smiled. A few of them chanted her true name. She just stood there beside Skulduggery and waited for the next lot to break through.

45

FRIGHTENING

Tanith knew the sorcerer striding through the laboratory towards her. His skin was dark as ebony, his body big and broad and his eyes burning. He had taken the sword that fitted so comfortably in his hand from a vanquished opponent on a battlefield long ago, and it had served him well ever since. He was an Adept, his name was Frightening Jones, and they had briefly dated back in the 1970s.

His sword came for her and she slipped to the side, tried to sweep her own blade along the back of his leg, but he was already pivoting. Steel clashed and Tanith backed off.

"I've missed you," he smiled.

"How've you been?" she muttered.

He shrugged, and sent the tip of his sword whistling for her throat. She dodged away.

"I'm doing all right," he said, continuing his advance. "I was just over here for a bit of business, and then, well, you know..." He tapped his head. "It's really not as bad as you think, sharing space with a Remnant. Although, to be fair, this new joining hasn't made me appreciate Irish weather to any great degree. Still looking forward to being back in Africa."

He lunged and she parried, flicked her sword to his shoulder, but he raised his blade, and her cut went wide.

"What about you?" he asked. "Anyone special in your life?"

"Oh, Frightening, you know you're the only one for me."

He laughed, and she pressed in, and now it was he who was forced to retreat. His defence was strong, the steel of his blade backed up by muscle and sinew. It flickered where it needed to flicker and his feet moved where they needed to move. He was still good. He hadn't let his skills diminish. Tanith wondered if he was still better than she was.

He blocked a cut and shuffled forward, using his shoulder to knock her sideways. She flipped backwards to avoid the swipe to her knees, parried the follow-up and avoided the next strike altogether.

"When you've quite finished dancing," China said as she strolled by.

Frightening moved round so that he could keep both of them in view. "Miss Sorrows," he said, "so good to see you again. If you wait right there, I'll get around to killing you as soon as possible."

China folded her arms. "I haven't got all day, Mr Jones."

Frightening brought his sword down on Tanith's, nearly ripping it out of her hands. He stepped up and booted her in the gut. She staggered, half bent over, and barely managed to roll away from the next assault.

"Well?" Tanith gasped to China.

China's eyebrow raised. "Well what?"

"Are you going to help me or not?"

"Nonsense, you don't need my help. You're doing fine."

Frightening feinted low, then brought the sword high. Tanith blocked, replied with three strikes in quick succession. The first two he batted aside with ease, but the third he let sail overhead as he ducked below it, bringing his blade dangerously close to her ribs. She darted away just in time.

Three more possessed sorcerers came through. China

turned to them, arms still folded, her fingers briefly touching the invisible symbols carved into her forearms. Her arms flew wide and the nearest possessed caught a wave of blue energy at point-blank range. His bones broke and his flesh ruptured even as he was sent flying backwards. The other two Remnants rounded on China, just as Frightening renewed his attack on Tanith.

Tanith stumbled as she parried and blocked, trying to regain her footing and give herself some space at the same time. An almighty swing from Frightening took the sword from her hands. Instead of retreating further, she surprised him by leaping forward.

They struggled with his sword, Tanith kicking and kneeing at his legs the whole time. She sneaked a boot around his foot and pushed into him. He went back, tripping over her, but bringing her with him. He grunted as she landed on top of him. Using her full weight, she pressed the sword down against his throat. Teeth gritted and perspiration dotting his forehead, he resisted.

Out of the corner of her eye, she saw China fling a dagger of red light into the chest of one of the possessed. He gasped and sagged, fell to his knees and keeled over. The remaining sorcerer grabbed China and slammed her against the wall.

Frightening was pushing back, the blade moving away from his throat with agonising slowness. It was all Tanith could do to watch the inevitable happen. In another few seconds, the blade would be far enough away for Frightening to start squirming beneath her. He'd throw her off, the battle would resume, and she'd more than likely die.

She thought of Ghastly, of the brief kiss she'd given him. All that time wasted. To die here and now, killed on this cold ground by a man she had cared for yet never loved, it was almost more than she could bear. She had thought she had all the time in the world to find the right moment with Ghastly. The curse of immortality, she reckoned, was procrastination.

Tanith flipped her body vertically, till she was in a handstand with both hands still on the sword. Frightening's eyes widened as her full weight bore down on him, but her balance was easily shifted. She sprang away before he could try anything tricky, snatching up her sword as he got to his feet.

China, meanwhile, was getting down and dirty with the remaining mage. They rolled across the ground, China's hair in her face. Finally, China simply grabbed the sorcerer's head and slammed it down on the concrete, once, twice. Satisfied that her opponent was no longer a threat, she got up, breathing hard and looking angry.

The pupils dissolved in Frightening's eyes, leaving them pure white and glowing. Tanith cursed, had to dive to avoid the stream of white light that burst out. She got behind a metal desk, felt the heat and heard the metal sizzle all around her. Abruptly, the light moved, and she peered out, saw Frightening closing in on China. China's forearms were pressed together, forming the sigil that erected the shield between her and Frightening's eye beams. Tanith had always thought those eye beams were among the coolest of Adept powers to have. She didn't think they were quite so cool today.

"Keep the shield up!" she shouted. "He can't sustain that level of intensity for more than a few seconds!"

"If you're bored," China shouted back, "you could always lend a hand."

"Nonsense! You're doing great!"

Frightening swivelled his head, the twin beams scorching towards her, forcing Tanith to duck back behind cover. She felt the heat die, and the brightness falter, and risked another peek to see Frightening blinking his pupils back into service.

"Now!" she called, lunging from cover.

For a few moments after using his power, Frightening was

left blind as his magic recharged. China hit him from the side and Tanith leaped, both boots crunching into his jaw. He sprawled, his sword clanging to the floor. In an instant, China was leaning over him, her hand pressing against his forehead. He screamed, then went silent, but China kept her hand on his forehead, making his body jerk. Tanith grabbed China and yanked her back.

China's elbow cracked against Tanith's cheek and Tanith held up her hands.

"Stop! Wait! What the hell was that?"

China narrowed her eyes. "You attacked me."

"No, I didn't."

"Yes, you did. You're one of them."

Tanith stared at her. "Did you see a Remnant slide down my throat? No, you bloody didn't!"

"Then why did you stop me?"

"Because you were going to kill him!"

"He was going to kill *us*, you stupid girl."

"No, China, he was going to lie there and be unconscious. Once that thing is out of him, he's a good guy again. The same goes for most of these people that you don't seem to have a problem using lethal force against."

Without taking her eyes from Tanith's, China tied her hair

back off her face. "If it's a choice between them or me, I pick me. Your little concessions of mercy are going to get you killed."

Tanith wiped blood from her lip and didn't respond.

46

ACCORDING TO PLAN

The shield held.

Its colour deepened with each impact. With each attempt to break through, it would darken, then fade, and then the attacks would begin again and the Hibernian Cinema would be covered by a blue dome of energy.

The sorcerers outside were taking turns, fifty of them each time, throwing everything they had at Kenspeckle's defences.

The defenders went where they were needed – constantly repelling attacks and forcing back intruders. It was exhausting.

Valkyrie fought her way from one side of the building to the other and back again. She was cut and bleeding and bruised and she couldn't catch her breath.

There was a crash from a corridor behind her, and she heard Tanith shout, "They're in!"

Valkyrie ran to help. Tanith was locked in a struggle with a black-lipped sorcerer, the pair of them rolling amid the debris around the massive hole in the middle of the floor. Another sorcerer was climbing up, and Valkyrie snapped her palm at the air, sending a rock hurtling into his face. The sorcerer fell back with a scream of pain, but another one took his place before the scream was even half done.

A flash of red light blinded her and she felt something hot sizzle by her cheek. She stumbled back, hands out against the air. There was a disturbance, something big coming for her. She clicked her fingers and flicked out a fireball, heard rapid cursing in response. She blinked quickly, able to see shapes now, and she saw the figure as he batted out the flames on his shirt. She gathered shadows and sent them roughly to where his head should be. His blurred form spun in mid-air and dropped.

Valkyrie squeezed her eyes shut, then opened them, vision clearing, in time to see Tanith rising off the unconscious sorcerer she'd been struggling with. Another black-lipped man climbed up into the room and Tanith met him, ducking the swipe of a knife and firing back three punches in return. The man grunted and the knife dropped. Tanith caught him with a kick that toppled him backwards into the hole.

Skulduggery ran in, fire in both his hands. He stopped in the middle of the room and sent twin streams of flame down into the hole. Valkyrie heard screams and shouts and a lot more cursing. Suddenly he doused the flames and crouched, fingers splayed out on the ground. The floor rumbled, cracked, and belched clouds of dust into the air as the tunnel caved in beneath them.

Skulduggery looked up. "Everyone OK?"

Tanith nodded. Valkyrie raised an eyebrow. "Another one of your new tricks?" she panted.

"Just the natural progression of earth manipulation. I'll have to teach it to you sometime."

"It won't hold them for long," Tanith said.

The possessed were inside the cinema and they were trying to get through into the science-magic facility. Valkyrie heard a terrified scream, and she split off from the rest. She rounded the corner to see a woman with wild, bushy hair closing in on Clarabelle. Valkyrie dived on her.

"Run!" she said to Clarabelle, and Clarabelle did.

The woman elbowed her and Valkyrie heard a crackle, just as the woman brought up a stun gun. Valkyrie dodged back, stumbled and fell backwards. She was so tired, her body so drained, that when she hit the ground it actually felt good to be lying down. Then the crazy woman jumped on her and it didn't feel so good any more.

The stun gun crackled centimetres from her neck, and Valkyrie did her best to keep it away. "You'll thank me for this later," the crazy woman said through gritted teeth.

Valkyrie braced her forearm against the lower half of the woman's face and slowly forced it back. She was running on pure adrenaline, and she was down to her last reserves. The crazy woman grinned, and Valkyrie's strength failed. A moment before the stun gun pressed into her skin, Fletcher grabbed the woman and yanked her off. They vanished and Valkyrie sank back. Slowly, and with a moan, she raised both arms up. Fletcher reappeared above her, took her hands, and pulled her to her feet.

"I'm getting pretty good at this nick of time stuff, aren't I?" he asked. She would have hit him if she wasn't so tired.

Skulduggery ran over, China and Tanith behind him. "Fletcher, did you make it to the mountains?"

"Yes, we did," Fletcher said. "We don't know where the cavern is exactly, but I can definitely teleport to the general area."

"You're the only one immune to the Remnants," China said to Skulduggery. "When we get there, we'll do our best to hold them off while you activate the machine. From this point on, you're the only one who matters."

"I got Kenspeckle to open a few doors," Ghastly said, hurrying over, "so they're all flowing into the cinema. We need them in one place, and we're not going to get a better chance than right now."

Skulduggery turned to Valkyrie. "Are you ready?"

She nodded. "I can do it."

"Fletcher, they're going to be focused on the screen, trying to get through. You need to teleport us behind them, and then be ready to teleport everyone to the MacGillycuddy's Reeks. Can you do that?"

"I can," Fletcher said. "Everybody hold hands, now."

Suddenly they were in the cinema, watching two thousand crazy people as they shouted and laughed and cursed.

"Valkyrie," Skulduggery said. "*Now.*"

She reached out, allowing the coldness of the ring to spread to her fingertips. The shadows swirled and rose like a dark mist. The noise gradually died down, as the possessed swiped at the mist, expecting an attack. When none came, they looked around, confused. Valkyrie felt the shadows drift between them, and concentrated on spreading it out further. She opened her eyes, saw them all looking at her.

"Fletcher!" Skulduggery barked.

"Everyone hang on," Fletcher said. His hand gripped Valkyrie's shoulder. The others formed a chain on the other side of her.

"I'm not the one moving," she heard him murmur. "It's the universe that revolves around me..."

Valkyrie saw it out of the corner of her eye, a sliver of blackness reaching from behind Fletcher's shoulder. Before she could warn him, the Remnant scampered up to his face and he stumbled back, trying to tear it away. He fell to one knee, but it was already in his mouth. He reared back and it was gone from sight, and his body arched in pain, then relaxed.

All around them, the possessed were laughing. Fletcher raised his head, and smiled with black lips.

Skulduggery's gun leaped into his hand, but Fletcher disappeared.

"Over here," Fletcher said.

They spun. Ghastly pushed at the air, but Fletcher was

already gone. He appeared beside Tanith, who whirled in an instant, her sword slicing through nothing but empty space.

"You can't beat me," Fletcher said from behind them.

Skulduggery fired and China hurled daggers of red light.

"How stupid are you?" Fletcher called from the stage.

"I can be everywhere and anywhere," Fletcher said from ten paces away.

"You can't stop me," Fletcher laughed from right beside them. He grabbed Valkyrie, pulling her from the others, and teleported her to the middle of the possessed sorcerers. The dark mist was already gone. The sorcerers around them started to chuckle. She glimpsed Skulduggery and the others through the gaps, but they were being ignored now that the Remnants had their prize.

"I love you," Fletcher said, holding her close. "I was pretty sure I loved you before this, but now? Now I know. I love you more than anything, Val, and please trust me. When you're joined, you'll like it."

Valkyrie punched him right across the jaw, elbowed a woman who reached for her and kicked out at a man. Someone tripped her and she fell. The people laughed, and then she felt hands grabbing her from *beneath*, and she sank into the ground. The sorcerers dived for her, but it was no use, and she shut her eyes as she was pulled down, underground.

"Hello, li'l darlin'," Billy-Ray Sanguine said in her ear.

47

STRANGE BEDFELLOWS

The rumbling stopped and Valkyrie felt the cold, hard earth all around her. It was pitch-black and the familiar fears rose in her throat. Her thumb pressed against her index finger.

"If you're plannin' on clickin' those fingers and generatin' a little flame to see by," Sanguine said, "may I suggest an alternative that will not burn up our remainin' oxygen?"

Yellow light flooded the small space that surrounded them, and Valkyrie found herself looking at her own reflection in his sunglasses. He handed her the narrow torch.

"Got this for you," he said, his perfect white teeth flashing in a smile.

"What are you doing?" she whispered.

"I ain't exactly sure on this," he replied, "but it looks to me, and I may be wrong, but it looks to me like I'm savin' your life. Yep, I... I think that's what it is."

She frowned. "You're not one of them?"

"The Remnants? Naw, they haven't got me yet. Creepy critters, ain't they?"

Valkyrie shifted a little. A half-dozen rocks were sticking painfully into her. "Why are you here?"

"Now, before you get all aggressive, let me say that I *do* remember the last time we met, and I *do* remember the promise you made me."

"I said I'd kill you."

"I *told* you I remembered, didn't I?" Sanguine said crossly. "No need to threaten me again, just because you can. Fact is, I was plannin' on leavin' you alone for a while, but a job came up, and I needed my... payment."

"How are you mixed up in this?"

"For once, I'm on the side of the angels, if those Roarhaven folk can be described as such. They hired me to help out against the creepy critters. I had a look, saw that they seemed to be goin' after *you* all the time, so I figured the best way to hurt them is to take away the thing they want.

"I admit, the thought did enter my mind to kill you, and so take you away from them on a more permanent basis, but two factors stopped me from that course of action. The first factor is that for all I know, the reason they want you so bad is to kill you, and so by killin' you myself, I'd be doin' them one hell of a favour. The second factor is that I don't want you dead just yet. I'm quite lookin' forward to all the pain and torture I know you got comin' to you."

"You're on our side?"

"That appears to be what I'm tryin' to say."

"So... you'll be fighting beside us?"

"It'll be strange, not tryin' to cut your throat all the time, but yeah."

Valkyrie pushed questions and suspicions and misgivings out of her mind. "OK, fine. We need to get into the Medical Bay to get Kenspeckle and Clarabelle, and then we have to get to the van on the other side of the street."

"In a sec."

She glared. "Let's go."

"You ain't my damn boss, Cain. For your information, whatever force field thing you guys cooked up means I have to go deeper than usual to get around it, which means I have to work harder. We'll move when we're able to move."

"You're still injured."

"Yes," he said, his mouth twisting into an ugly sneer, "I'm still injured from when you cut me with a damn *sword*. I am still unable to move with my usual efficiency. Now, if this inconveniences you, please accept my heartfelt apologies. But once again, I must let it be known that this is *your* damn fault."

The look on his face and the hate in his voice told Valkyrie to tread cautiously. He was a killer and a psychopath, and although he may have temporarily switched sides, she knew it wouldn't take a lot for him to abandon her down here.

"Bet you never thought we'd end up on the same side, huh?" he asked, a new smile crossing his features. "Bet you never thought I'd save your skin."

"What?"

"Just makin' small talk. Got to distract myself from the pain, y'know? Life has a funny way of workin' out, don't it? Take your friend, for example. The sword-lady."

"Tanith?"

"First time we met, we were tryin' to kill each other,

remember that? But every time subsequent to that there's been a kind of a *frisson* between us."

"A what?"

"*Frisson.* It's French for... To be honest I don't really know what it's French for, but I know what it means in American. A sort of electrical undercurrent of emotion."

"I know what *frisson* means, but I really don't think Tanith would share your view."

"You're a kid. You don't know the ways of menfolk and womenkind. All those threats she fires my way? That there is the mark of flirtation."

"Oh, dear God," Valkyrie said, the colour draining from her face. "You fancy Tanith."

"I don't *fancy* her, I—"

"You have a crush on Tanith. That is disgusting."

"What? Why would it be disgustin'?"

"Because you're a hired killer."

"That don't make it disgustin', just makes it... unusual. Does she talk about me?"

"Somebody shoot me."

"What does she say? I'm a formidable foe, right? Does she say anythin' in a kind of a more... wistful voice?"

"I don't want to talk about this."

"Does she ever say, 'If only he were good...'?"

"Stop your talking. Stop it right now. Stop it. She has a boyfriend."

His face fell. "Someone I know?" he asked morosely.

"He may have punched you a few times, yes."

"She's not... She's not datin' the skeleton, is she? How would that be even possible, let alone... nice? He's got no skin, or lips, or... or nothin'. And he talks. Good God, he talks and he never shuts up."

"It's not Skulduggery."

"Well then, who else could it...? It's not the ugly fella, is it? It couldn't be the ugly fella."

"Don't call him ugly."

"It *is* him! But he's all scars! I mean, I know I ain't got no eyes, but once you get past that, you got my face. And my face is all right. Better'n his. His is a mess, like he was dropped head first into a blender as a kid. Seriously? She's with him?"

"Seriously, and you're not going to break them up. Not because you won't try, but because you won't be able to. Look, are you ready yet? Can we move now?"

"I'm ready," he snapped. "But this conversation stays between us, understand? My romancin' ain't gonna work if she knows it's comin'."

"Believe me, I never want to speak to anyone about this ever again."

Sanguine took a breath and clenched his jaw, and Valkyrie clung on tight. They burrowed through the ground, the rumbling like thunder in her ears. She spat out dirt, keeping her eyes closed. Eventually she felt their trajectory shift. They were headed upwards now, but moving slower and slower with each passing second.

They broke through to light. They weren't in the Medical Bay, but they were close enough. She left him panting on the ground.

"Stay here," she said, "and catch your breath. I'll be back in a minute."

"Missin' you... already," he managed.

Valkyrie took off running. She called Kenspeckle's name, then Clarabelle's. She knew Kenspeckle wouldn't allow himself to be taken over again, but didn't know quite how far he'd go to stop that from happening. Would he hurt himself? Would he do worse?

"Kenspeckle!" she shouted. "We have to go! Clarabelle!"

Getting no answer, she ran the length of the corridor and turned into the next one. She called again for Kenspeckle, and passed yet another darkened room.

Drip.

She stopped, and turned. Slowly, she retraced her steps. She listened intently.

Drip. Drip. Drip.

Valkyrie pressed her shoulder to the wall, centimetres from the doorway.

"Hello?" she said softly. "Kenspeckle? Clarabelle?"

Drip.

"Kenspeckle. It's me. It's Valkyrie. Are you in there?"

Still no answer. Still no sound, apart from that irregular dripping.

"I'm coming in," she said, and stepped into the room. She poured her magic into a flame and it burned fiercely, throwing light across the countertops and equipment to each of the four corners. A warm, flickering light that illuminated Kenspeckle Grouse as he lay on the table, and Clarabelle, his assistant, as she crouched on top of him, a scalpel in each hand. Kenspeckle's eyes were open and unseeing, and the work Clarabelle had been doing reminded Valkyrie of her own dissection just a few days earlier. Blood covered him, and dripped to a puddle on the floor.

Clarabelle screeched, her lips black and her skin riddled with veins. She leaped off the old man's corpse and fell on to Valkyrie. They sprawled out through the door, landing in the corridor, those scalpels whipping at Valkyrie like snakes. Valkyrie seized one of Clarabelle's wrists, held the blade away from her, tried to block the other one, but it bit into her face and scraped along her cheekbone. Warm blood flowed. Valkyrie cried out, and anger coursed through her, giving her the strength to throw Clarabelle off.

She got up, grabbed a metal tray and swung it into the back of Clarabelle's head. She hit her again, and again, and wouldn't let her up. Valkyrie battered her until Clarabelle dropped to the floor and didn't move. Valkyrie threw the tray to one side and ran.

The corridors twisted and turned. Valkyrie's hand was at her face, the blood pouring through her fingers. She slowed, panting, and heard voices. She crept forward, peered round the corner. Shudder and Tesseract were heading her way, followed by several other sorcerers, including Fletcher.

"We're going to have to break her," Fletcher was saying. "You don't know her, not like I do."

"Leave Darquesse to us," Tesseract said.

"But that's it, right there, that's your problem. She's not Darquesse, not yet. She's still Valkyrie. We'll never convince her to embrace her inner mass-murderer unless we cut off the things that she clings to."

"And your suggestion?" asked Shudder.

Valkyrie ducked into a doorway as they neared.

"I'll go pick up her parents," she heard Fletcher say, and her stomach lurched. "I'll bring them back here and kill them in front of her."

"And what will this accomplish?" Tesseract asked. "Apart from making her hate us so much she never gives in? No, Valkyrie must become Darquesse willingly. We leave her family alone, for now."

Valkyrie stayed where she was, crouched in the darkness as they walked away, trying to get her breathing under control. Her hands were shaking as she took her phone from her pocket. She thumbed a button and called her reflection.

"Take my parents out of the house," she whispered.

The reflection's voice was as cold and uninterested as ever. "Why?"

"They're in danger. Fletcher's been possessed. Take them somewhere. Not to Beryl's, Fletcher knows where they live. I don't care where you take them, just get them out of the house."

"Hello, baby," said Fletcher from right behind her.

Valkyrie twisted, but he was already gone. Something hit her hand and her phone went flying. She swung a fist in an arc, but didn't catch him, and then he was behind her again and his fist crunched into the back of her head. She dropped to all fours, hair in her face, stunned. He grabbed her and hauled her up, threw her over a table and teleported to the other side as she landed on the ground. He kicked her, the Remnant inside him adding to his strength. She curled up, struggling for air.

"I thought I heard you," he said. He was smiling. That cute smile she liked so much. "When I said I wanted to kill your folks, I thought I heard something, a little gasp. I knew it was you."

Valkyrie turned over, gave a moan of pain.

"I'll bring you to the others in a bit," Fletcher said, "don't you worry about that. I just thought it'd be nice if we spent a few minutes alone. I thought you might want to talk or something."

She moved quickly, pushing at the air, sending the table hurtling to the other end of the room. But not Fletcher. Fletcher wasn't there any more. She sensed him behind her, but was too slow to do anything as he grabbed her under the jaw with both hands and started dragging her across the floor.

"Knew you were fooling," he said. "I know you too well, you see. Can't bluff me, babe."

Valkyrie grabbed his wrists to ease the pressure and swung her legs up and over in a backwards somersault. Her boots caught him in the face and he let go, cursing. She was up now. She took hold of the shadows in the room and they lifted him up and slammed him to the ground. She glanced at the door, but she couldn't outrun a Teleporter and she knew it.

She aimed a kick at his head. He moved at the last second, rolled away, tried to come up, but her knee caught him under the chin. He fell back and she pressed in. If she gave him even a moment to recover, he'd teleport. She got behind him and wrapped one arm around his throat, braced it with the other, going for a choke. Fletcher reared back, but she hung on. He heaved forward, lifting her off her feet, trying to shake her loose. She tightened her hold. The Remnant might not need air to function, but the body it was using sure did. Another few moments and Fletcher would be unconscious.

He stopped trying to pry her fingers back, and instead, staggered to a chair that stood against the wall. He put one foot up on the seat. Valkyrie wriggled, did her best to throw him off balance, but didn't dare loosen the choke. Grunting, Fletcher shifted his weight forward, and slowly stood up on the chair, taking Valkyrie with him.

She screamed a thousand curses in her mind, but there was

nothing she could do, as Fletcher stood on shaky legs, and then propelled himself backwards. They fell in silence, Valkyrie shutting her eyes and waiting for the impact. She hit the ground and her head smacked off it, and stars burst behind her eyelids. She wasn't even aware that she'd lost the choke. She wasn't even aware of Fletcher getting to his feet beside her. She just lay there.

"Wow, you're tough," she heard Fletcher say. His voice sounded dim. "I'm not mad. I'm not. This is good. Darquesse is going to have to be tough, am I right?"

His image came into view. "But, wow, you nearly got me there. You nearly had me. If I didn't have all this extra strength, I'd be out cold. I think I like that, you know, my girlfriend being stronger than me. I'd never admit it – well, the old me wouldn't – but the new me is a lot more self-assured."

Valkyrie moaned, and Fletcher knelt beside her. He gently raised her head off the ground, then slammed it back down again. His hands moved over her, checking her pockets.

"You know, I fancied you the moment I saw you. I didn't want to admit it, because you were young and, you know, really annoying, but yeah, I liked you. We had something, didn't we? A connection? I liked the way you took all of this so seriously. I found that really funny. Ah, here they are." He dangled her own handcuffs over her. "I've really liked being your boyfriend, actually. I love all the fun stuff we do. But that's *nothing* compared to the fun we're going to have."

He clicked the cuff on to her right wrist, and was going for the left when someone collided with him from behind. They crashed against the chair in the dark.

Valkyrie rolled slowly on to her side. Her head hurt and she felt sick, but she brought her legs in and got them under her. In the dark around her were more crashes, the sounds of struggle. Two figures, throwing each other into walls. She took a deep breath, then another, willing herself not to throw up. Strength was returning with each moment that passed. The world was becoming clearer. She stood.

Fletcher came stumbling from the shadows. There was a snarl and he turned just as Caelan leaped at him, and they both vanished.

Valkyrie frowned, and even as she started to wonder what Caelan was doing here, a wave of dizziness nearly pitched her on to her face. She managed to stay upright and staggered out into the corridor. She slumped against the wall and stayed there, gathering her strength. She took a small key from her pocket, opened the handcuff and put both away. Warm blood trickled down her face.

Her phone was on the floor nearby. She held out her hand. She could feel the air, but it took a few seconds before she could focus enough to pull it towards her. The phone lifted into her hand, and she slipped it into her jacket, then pushed herself away from the wall. Her balance was back. Her strength was back. She was hurting, but she'd get over it.

Valkyrie found her way back to Sanguine, who raised an eyebrow as she approached, but didn't say anything. He took her underground, and they moved slowly through the earth and under the street. He was breathing hard, straining against the pain.

Finally, she heard shouting. Hands gripped her, pulling her from the ground. They were on the other side of the road, away from the Hibernian. She opened her eyes to see Ghastly dragging Sanguine to his feet, his fist pulled back, ready to punch. She called out and he looked around, puzzled.

"Our side," she coughed in Skulduggery's arms. "He's on our side."

Ghastly frowned at Sanguine and let him go. The Texan dropped to his knees, exhausted and in pain. Valkyrie heard shouting.

"They've noticed us," said Tanith.

"Everyone get to the van," Skulduggery ordered.

They ran, the Remnants behind them. Ghastly jumped in behind the wheel and they took off, tyres spinning.

"Are we going to *drive* there?" Tanith asked. "I know this thing is fast, but I don't like the idea of a five-hour car chase on icy roads. And they have Fletcher now. He could teleport them all to any one of a hundred places he's been between here and Kerry, and we'd drive right into them."

"Fletcher's distracted," Valkyrie said. "I don't know for how long. Caelan was there. He helped me. Kenspeckle's dead."

There was a moment of awful calm, that Skulduggery quickly dispelled. "We need to stay ahead of them just long enough so we can find somewhere to pull in. We'll let them overshoot, get to Kerry ahead of us, and we'll take our time, approach it right."

"It's going to be tricky," Ghastly murmured.

"It usually is."

48

PLAN FALLS APART

Valkyrie chewed on a leaf to numb the pain as Tanith stitched the cut on her face as best she could. When Tanith was finished, Valkyrie sat back and closed her eyes. After an hour of driving, they turned off the main road and bounced down narrow lanes of potholes and ice for twenty minutes, then headed north, moving perpendicular to their destination. Valkyrie kept her head down. The van was warm, but it was no comfort. After everything she'd seen and been through, she just wanted her boyfriend's arms around her. Sometimes the most comforting thing in the world was a hug.

It got dark, and Ghastly turned the headlights on. They passed three cars in two hours, and with every one they'd ready themselves for an attack. But the drivers were human, and mortal, and no threat to them.

Skulduggery asked questions. Sanguine answered them in his lazy drawl. Valkyrie didn't pay attention. She lay down in the back, her head on Tanith's lap, and fell asleep.

She woke to a conversation Skulduggery was having with Ghastly about abandoning the van and getting another. Ghastly was insisting on speed. Skulduggery was of the opinion that they should pick the first suitable vehicle they came across – there was no telling when this van would be recognised and reported.

Valkyrie dozed off again, only opening her eyes when the van pulled into an all-night petrol station. There was snow outside. Tanith took a few food orders and got out, hurried up to the bored man at the station window. Ghastly activated his façade and went to keep an eye on her, in case the Remnants had spread out this way. Valkyrie got out to stand beside Skulduggery while he filled the tank.

"I know he hid it well," Skulduggery said, "but Kenspeckle really liked me."

She surprised herself with a small smile. "No, he didn't," she said.

"No, he didn't. But he liked you."

"I don't really want to talk about this. What is there to say? I can't believe he's gone? Can't believe he's dead? Obviously, it's a shock. I don't need to *tell* anyone that."

"Sometimes it's not what you say, Valkyrie, it's just the fact that you're saying it."

She shook her head. "We don't have the time. Fight now, mourn later. That's our thing, right? If we stop and consider the implications every time something bad happens, we'd never get anything done."

"Kenspeckle was your friend."

"When all this is over, we'll see who's alive and who's dead, and then I'll cry, OK?"

He put his hand on her shoulder. "OK."

"Clarabelle's going to feel so bad when this is done with," Valkyrie said quietly, then shook her head. She had to focus. "How far are we from the Receptacle?"

"We're less than an hour from the mountain range, but we should wait until morning before approaching. Once we're there, that golden key in your pocket will guide us to where we need to go."

"Do we have a plan?"

"Plans are an invitation to disappointment."

"And yet we're probably going to need one. The Remnants are going to be all over the place to stop us from reaching the machine. Are you going to fly us in over their heads?"

"They'll be expecting that. Now that we have Sanguine on our side, we could always *burrow* right under them."

"I don't think so. These days he can't go 3 metres without needing a rest."

"So we can't go above, and we can't go under. Looks like we're going to drive in as close as we can, and just walk right in."

"The direct approach."

"The only approach we have left."

Morning was slow in coming, and failed to bring with it warmth. Valkyrie's nerves jangled beneath her skin. She noticed Tanith clenching and unclenching her fists beside her, and Ghastly had gone scarily quiet. Only China and Skulduggery seemed unperturbed by the danger they were about to walk into. Valkyrie couldn't have cared less about how Sanguine was coping.

They drove deeper into a small town, which seemed to be hibernating under all the snow. Valkyrie longed to see normal people out walking, or buying the morning paper, or even sitting at traffic lights. She didn't like this ghost town thing that had struck and spread, turning Ireland into a ghost *country*.

The van slowed suddenly, pulling in to the side of the road. Valkyrie peered over Skulduggery's shoulder. A police car lay on its side at the junction ahead of them, its lights still flashing.

"The rest of you stay here," Skulduggery said. "Valkyrie, you're with me."

They got out. She slid the door closed, and pulled the bandage away from her face. "How does it look?"

He peered at her. "It's healing. The swelling has gone. It's a nasty scar, but with everything Tanith applied to the wound, it should disappear in a day or so."

She glanced back at the van, and her voice lowered. "You don't trust them."

"Not entirely," he admitted.

"You think one of them's possessed?"

"We have no way of knowing until they reveal themselves. You're to stick with me, OK? Do not allow yourself to be caught alone with any of them."

She nodded. Skulduggery held his gloved hand out in front as they approached the car, turning the ice to steam, allowing them a firm grip on the road. Valkyrie wished she could have done that while she was slipping and sliding all over Drogheda.

They reached the junction. Two cops lay on the far side of the car. Valkyrie went to one, Skulduggery to the other. She hunkered down, felt for a pulse.

"This one's alive," she said.

"This one isn't," Skulduggery replied. "But I don't think the Remnants are out this far any more. I'd say they're panicking, keeping everyone back."

"So they're content to just sit around and wait for us to show up?"

"Why not? They know we have to go to them eventually. They probably have a few scouts flying around, checking the perimeter. We'll have to be very careful from here on out."

They turned, and retraced their steps. Sanguine walked towards them.

"Get back in the van," Skulduggery said.

"We may," Sanguine responded, his words slurring like he was drunk, "have a bit of a problem."

And then he collapsed. A stream of red light hit Skulduggery and blasted him back, all the way to the junction, where he hit the overturned police car and flipped over it. Valkyrie jumped sideways. She could see Ghastly, lying on the road beneath the open door of the van, and then China, strolling towards her with a beautiful, black-lipped smile.

Valkyrie raised her hand, but China flicked a dagger of red light into her. It hit her jacket and it was like she'd stuck her fingers into an electrical socket. She jerked back and fell to her knees.

"It's time to come with me," China said. "You've impressed all of us, but really, you didn't need to. You're Darquesse. That's all we needed to know."

China crouched over her, and took the golden key from Valkyrie's jacket, and put it in her own pocket. "I don't think this is going to be much use to you, to be perfectly honest."

Someone moved around the van. Valkyrie's vision cleared, just as Tanith collided with China from behind. They slipped on the ice and went down, but Tanith instantly sprang to her feet. China kicked out, catching her in the leg and knocking her back, then came up and tapped her forearms and flung them wide. Tanith dodged the wave of blue energy and got in close, her fist smacking against China's cheek. Tanith's hands blurred. A punch caught China in the ribs. She staggered back, gasping for breath, but managed to block the kick that followed. She tried to give herself some room, but Tanith was already closing in.

China knocked her knuckles together, and the tattoos glowed briefly red. She swung a punch that missed, but the next one caught Tanith in the chest. Tanith went sprawling, and slid across the ground.

Valkyrie glimpsed the glowing symbol on China's right palm a moment before she seized Tanith's wrist. Tanith screamed in abject agony, kicking out by pure instinct. Her boot crunched into China's ribcage. China grunted and released her hold, and Tanith scrambled up and charged.

She went low, her shoulder against China's stomach while her arms wrapped around her legs. She lifted China and then slammed her to the ground, falling on top of her. With her left arm, China held Tanith close, not giving her the room she'd need to throw damaging attacks. Tanith was concentrating on keeping China's right hand, with that glowing symbol, away from her.

Feeling returned to Valkyrie's legs, and she started to get up. Her brain struggled to sort itself out.

Tanith shoved China away and they parted, coming up on their feet at the same time. Tanith was the first to strike, but China parried the blow and chopped at Tanith's bicep. Tanith back-peddled, her right arm hanging uselessly, and China stepped in quickly and caught her with a solid haymaker to the jaw. Tanith spun and fell to her knees.

Sanguine leaped at China, wrapping an arm around her

throat. They stumbled back, but instead of trying to break the choke, China's hand went to her belly. Blue energy crackled through her, throwing Sanguine off. He dropped to the pavement, and China turned her attention back to Tanith. She activated the symbols on both of her palms, then stepped up to clamp her hands on either side of Tanith's head. Tanith arched her back and screamed.

Valkyrie pushed at the air, but her focus was off, and all she could do was stir up a breeze that played with China's hair. China looked at her and let go of Tanith, who collapsed beneath her. Valkyrie's legs gave out and she fell. She saw a Remnant flitting down towards Tanith, but China held out her hand.

"No," she commanded. "Leave her. She annoys me. Take the scarred one."

The Remnant hovered as if reluctant, then darted for Ghastly. China turned back to Valkyrie. "Come now," she said. "Your disciples are waiting."

49

FOLLOWING THE KEY

Tanith raised her head, and watched China and Ghastly drive off in the van, taking Valkyrie with them. Tanith's head was buzzing and every joint was sore.

"Is someone gonna help me up?" Sanguine asked as he lay spreadeagled on the pavement. Tanith ignored him. Skulduggery came over, pulled her to her feet, and a wave of dizziness overtook her. She stumbled back against a lamp post.

"They have Val," she muttered, waiting for the world to stop spinning. "Why didn't China just kill her? Why do they want to keep her alive?"

"Valkyrie is Darquesse," Skulduggery said.

"What?"

"It's a long story, one that we're going to help her make sure never comes true. Our only chance is the Receptacle. Are you OK? Can you fight?"

"Always." Tanith pushed herself away from the wall, managing to stand by herself. "But China has the key. Can you activate the machine without it?"

"Hello?" said Sanguine. "Anyone hear me?"

"According to Gordon we *need* the key," Skulduggery said. "We have to get it back."

"So we fight our way through all the possessed to China, and then fight our way back to the Receptacle? I like a good scrap as much as the next girl, Skulduggery, but we'd never make it. We need another plan."

"We don't *have* another plan. The Remnants are in place right *now*. We don't have time to mess about trying to hotwire a machine that none of us have ever *seen* before."

Sanguine grunted. "Fine. Don't help me up. See if I care. I'll just lie here an' freeze to death."

Tanith spun to him. "Will you shut up?"

Sanguine smiled. "You are finally succumbing to my charms, ain't ya?"

"Unless you have something constructive to add," Skulduggery said, anger biting the edges of his words, "then I agree with Tanith. Shut. Up."

"Oh, but I *do* have somethin' constructive to add. Swordlady, help me up now an' I'll solve all your problems an' woes, I swear on my dear dead momma, may she rest in pieces."

Tanith stalked over to him, grabbed his outstretched hand, and twisted his wrist until he leaped up, howling.

"There," she said. "Happy?"

The Texan scowled at her. "We got to work on our communication skills, honey bunny."

"This constructive thing you were going to add to our conversation," Skulduggery said. "Now would be a good time to share it."

There was a sound, like a car backfiring in the distance. Sanguine frowned, and his hand went to his shoulder. When he took it away, it was covered in blood. "Hey," he said, surprised. "I think I been shot."

Tanith looked past him, and saw a man running towards them, his left arm in a sling, his right holding a gun. He was firing as he came.

"That guy shot me!" Sanguine exclaimed.

The man's aim wasn't improving, but the closer he got, the closer the bullets whined. Tanith ducked behind Skulduggery as he held up a hand, creating a solid wall of air. Sanguine took a deep breath, and the ground swallowed him.

"Remnant?" Tanith asked.

"Dalrymple," Skulduggery replied.

The man, Dalrymple, threw the gun away and took a sword from his belt, yelling a battle-cry. A hand emerged from the ground, snagged his foot, and Dalrymple sprawled onto the road. Sanguine rose up behind him, kicking the sword from his hand. Dalrymple lunged, but Sanguine caught him with a knee to the gut, then grabbed his ear. Dalrymple cried out, and Sanguine dragged him over to the pavement. He dumped him at Skulduggery's feet, then turned his full attention to clutching his injured shoulder.

"This really hurts," he muttered. "I hope we're gonna kill this guy. We *are* gonna kill him, right?"

"Please," Dalrymple sobbed. "Let me close to them. I'm sorry I shot at you. You were just in my way. I thought you were going to stop me."

Skulduggery turned his head, looking behind them. Tanith followed his gaze. The possessed would have been preparing to stop anyone from reaching the Receptacle – so that probably meant that the place where they gathered was directly outside the chamber. She looked at Skulduggery and knew he was thinking the same thing.

"Leave the weapons here," Skulduggery said. "We won't stop you."

Sanguine looked up. "What? We're lettin' him go?"

"This has nothing to do with you, Sanguine."

"I'm the one he shot!"

"Dalrymple, go. Now."

Dalrymple looked up, tears in his eyes, like he was waiting for Skulduggery to change his mind. When nothing more was said, he scrambled up, and sprinted past them.

"I don't believe you guys," Sanguine said, shaking his head. "I bet if he'd shot *you*, you wouldn't be nearly so forgivin'."

Tanith looked at him. "How stupid are you?"

Sanguine looked offended. "Not very."

"Think about it, moron. None of us know where the Receptacle is, do we? None of us know where the Remnants are. They could be anywhere. It's a big mountain range."

"It ain't *that* big."

"He's going to lead us right where we need to go. And you notice he's on foot? So he knows a short cut."

"And... we're gonna follow him?"

"Do you need me to explain it to you slower?"

"Hey, enough with the attitude, OK? I been shot, an' my insides are still all twisted up, and I'm sufferin' from blood loss. But I ain't no moron. Fact is, both of *you* are the morons. You're plannin' on followin' him to the creepy critters an' the machine that'll save us all, but you can't start it, can ya? What're you plannin' on doin', lookin' at it awhile? Remarkin' on how pretty an' shiny it is? Call that a plan?"

"Do you have a better idea?" Skulduggery asked.

"Course I do. I'm from Texas. We all got better ideas in Texas. My idea is to follow that fool who shot me, get into the cavern where the giant Soul Catcher is kept, and turn it the hell *on*, usin' this key I picked from the pocket of Miss China Sorrows." Sanguine held up the golden key, and tossed it to Skulduggery. "Now tell me – what do y'all think of *that* particular plan?"

They kept at a safe distance, but they needn't have bothered. Dalrymple was so intent on getting to his precious Remnants that he didn't even glance back once. Sanguine spent most of the time complaining about his arm. He was chewing on a leaf to numb the pain, but it was obvious, just by looking at him, that he was getting weaker with each step. Halfway there, Skulduggery slowed down to help him traverse the rocky terrain. Sanguine was too tired to question the sudden change of heart, but Tanith knew that Skulduggery must have one last job for him to do before he fell by the wayside.

"Hold on," Skulduggery said at last, as they watched Dalrymple disappear from sight. The golden key was glowing. He moved it around, and the glow strengthened. "This way. Tanith, check on Dalrymple."

He half-carried Sanguine up an incline to their right, and Tanith jogged to where she had last seen Dalrymple. She crouched as she approached an outcrop, and peered over it. Below her, in a wide-open space of grasses and gorse bush, were two thousand possessed people. She saw Dalrymple running towards them, then ducked down before anyone saw her. Keeping low, she hurried back, and rejoined Skulduggery just as he sat Sanguine down next to a sheer wall of rock.

"I'm feelin' distinctly woozy," Sanguine mumbled.

"It looks like they're all there," Tanith told Skulduggery. "And I mean, all of them. There's an *army* down there. Is this the cavern? Where's the door?"

"I think this *is* the door," Skulduggery replied. "Notice how sharp the angles are on this section? See? Less weathered. Less beaten down by the elements."

"So... what? What does that mean?"

"They're resistant to damage. And the door to the cavern would have to be *very* resistant to damage."

"Hey," she said, nudging Sanguine with her foot, "can you take us inside?"

"Let him rest," Skulduggery told her. "We're going to need him soon enough. I'm sure we can get in here by ourselves."

"So how do we open it? Is there a magic word or something?"

"I hope not. I'm assuming this key will activate the machine *and* open the door, but..."

"But where's the keyhole?"

"Indeed."

He tapped the key against the rock wall. Nothing happened. She pressed her hand flat against it, the way she'd open any locked door. Still nothing.

"Are you sure this is the door?" Tanith asked. "I can't see any join, or hinge, or anything like that. How does it open? Does it swing, or rise, or sink, or what? If we knew that, we could work our way back from there."

Skulduggery examined the rock anew. "It wouldn't be easy

to open, but at the same time it should be straightforward. Anyone who needs to access the Receptacle ought to be able to do so, once they have the key."

"So maybe it's a combination of both," Tanith said. "A magic word spoken by whoever's holding the key."

"It's possible, but that doesn't exactly help us. Any one word in any language, magical or mortal, could unlock it."

"Well, you're the detective. You figure it out."

Skulduggery sighed, and considered the rock wall again. "Open," he said loudly. "*Oscail. Oscailte amach.* Enter. *Mellon.* Open Sesame. Remnant. Soul Catcher. Receptacle. Danger."

"Wow," Tanith breathed. "We could be here a while."

Sanguine looked up from his seated position beside Skulduggery. "There's somethin' written on it," he said, slurring his words. "The key. Look."

Skulduggery turned it over and Tanith stepped up, but all she could see was flat gold. "I can't see anything," she said.

"I can," Skulduggery murmured. He tilted the key till it caught the light. "It's faint, but it's there."

She peered closer. "You sure it's not just your imagination playing tricks?"

"When my imagination plays tricks," Skulduggery answered, "they're a lot more elaborate."

"I swear, I can't see anything."

"That's because you're lookin' with your eyes," Sanguine said, his head drooping. "Me an' the skeleton, we ain't *got* eyes."

"It says *erode*," Skulduggery said.

Tanith looked at the rock wall. "Nothing's happening."

Skulduggery thought for a moment, then said, "*Creim*," and the wall started to rumble.

Tanith looked at him. "It worked. It's working. What did you say?"

"*Creim*," he repeated. "It means *erode* in Irish."

Relief swept through her and she smiled, and the rock exploded into a cloud of dust that stung her eyes and got into her mouth. Tanith stumbled away, coughing and spluttering. The dust was in her hair and in her clothes. Her vision finally cleared and she saw Skulduggery, standing there in a dust-free air bubble.

"Oh," he said, noticing the state she was in. "Sorry."

The cloud parted for him as he walked through it. Tanith scowled and followed, helping Sanguine up and entering the newly-formed cave mouth.

"Maybe you should put your arm around me," Sanguine said. "I'm feelin' faint."

"If you faint, you fall," Tanith responded.

Torches flared in brackets as they passed. The tunnel went on for twenty metres, then opened out into a cavern. Skulduggery stood just ahead, waiting for them to catch up.

"Well?" Tanith asked. "Is it there?"

He didn't answer. He didn't have to.

A globe, like a small glass moon, 100 metres high and 100 metres wide, sat in a cradle of metal and wooden struts, lashed together with rope and chains. The architects, the engineers, whoever had built this, had used the rocky outcrops to border the machine, to supply its foundation. The cavern itself seemed to be an extension of the massive device, designed to accentuate the size and shape, giving the Receptacle an air of something that had always been here, a natural formation of magic and old science, deep within the mountain.

"Cool," Tanith said.

She left Sanguine leaning against the wall, and joined Skulduggery as he hurried to what looked like a control centre. There were dials and gauges and levers, and a narrow rectangular slot. Without wasting time on ceremony, Skulduggery slipped the key into the slot. Immediately, a gauge came to life. Skulduggery grabbed a lever and pulled it down sharply.

And nothing happened.

"Well," Tanith heard Sanguine say, "that's kinda disappointin'."

"No," Skulduggery said, "look. It's moving."

Tanith could see it now. The globe was beginning to rotate – very, very slowly. It creaked as it did so.

"It hasn't been used in over a century," Skulduggery said. "It needs some time to warm up. In order for the Remnants to be dragged into it, we've got to make sure that the possessed stay close by."

"An' just how," Sanguine asked, "are you plannin' on doin' *that?*"

Skulduggery looked at him, and his head tilted.

Sanguine's mouth turned down. "Aw, hell," he muttered.

50

MACGILLYCUDDY'S REEKS

Her surroundings were quite beautiful – a snow-covered mountain, layers of mist rising from the valleys, a pale blue sky. They had passed a lake on the way here, and the roads were narrow and winding, occasionally edged with low stone walls. Altogether very pretty, with the effect only ruined by the two thousand black-veined people waiting for her when she was pulled out of the van.

China marched her to a small hill in the middle of the

clearing, all the Remnants gathered round in their hijacked bodies. China removed the shackles from Valkyrie's wrists. Anton Shudder and Tesseract joined them on the hill. The crowd was silent.

"Valkyrie Cain," Tesseract said, "I am very glad I didn't kill you. What a mistake that would have been. I would have robbed us of our saviour."

"Let me go," Valkyrie said. "If I'm your saviour, then do as I command. Let me go."

"You're not our saviour. Not yet. But with a little help from us, you soon will be."

"I don't know what you expect me to say. Do you think I'm just going to agree to all this? I'm not going to hurt innocent people."

"If we torture you enough," said Tesseract, "you'll do anything we tell you to."

Valkyrie said nothing.

"I'm the one who saw you. I saw you through the eyes of Finbar Wrong, laying waste to the world. That's all we want. We want a dead world, where we are free, where we don't have to hide in flesh suits. You give us that world. From the moment I saw you I knew we had to help, to guide you on your path. Now, I am not so sure I was right."

"So you're going to let me go?"

There was a ripple of laughter in the crowd.

"No," Tesseract said. "You see, we have been talking, all of us, and we wonder if we are taking the correct approach. It was China who thought of it, actually."

China smiled. "We're friends, aren't we, Valkyrie? That's what you said. And because we're friends, because I know you so well, I can see that it would take a lot to make you hurt the people you love."

"I'm not Darquesse," Valkyrie blurted. "I've changed all that. That future doesn't happen any more."

"How can you be sure?" asked China.

"I've sealed my name."

"Ah, I see. So you think the only reason you kill everyone is because someone is forcing you to, yes?"

"Of course. Why else would I do it?"

"Because you want to, perhaps? Because something happens, something so awful that it drives you to the edge, and the only way out you can see is if everybody dies?"

"That's insane."

"All kinds of people want to kill the world, Valkyrie."

"Not me."

"Not yet." China laughed. "But I agree with you. I don't

think you have it in you. So I came up with an alternative. What if, Valkyrie, what you say is true? What if you *would* never do this? What if, in fact, it isn't even you?"

"What?"

"I think Darquesse is like *us*, you see. I think Darquesse has a Remnant inside her."

Valkyrie shrank back. "No."

"I think in order for our messiah to come out, one of us is going to have to bond with you."

"No."

"And we already have a volunteer," China said with a smile.

Fletcher appeared at China's side. "I love you," he said to Valkyrie. "And now I'm going to *be* you."

Hands grabbed her and she struggled against them, but there were too many. Her head was pulled back and there were fingers in her mouth. She bit down and tasted blood, heard a howl of pain, but her jaws were forced apart and she saw it, the Remnant, darting from Fletcher's mouth as he dropped to the ground, unconscious.

The Remnant latched on to her face and it was cold. The hands released her and Valkyrie staggered back, lost her footing. She fell, rolled down the small hill, all the while trying to pull the darkness away from her. She felt it slither down into her throat. Her hands clutched at her chest as the Remnant dissipated within her. Tendrils of cold slithered through her body and pierced her brain. Something burst within her mind and the fear went away, and Darquesse stood.

The others were watching her expectantly, eyes filled with hope and hunger, mouths twisted in smiles.

Ghastly was the first to step forward. "My Lady?" he asked, voice shaking. When Ghastly had been Ghastly, before the Remnant shared his being, he had been a good man. Darquesse remembered their first meeting, when he had told her that magic wasn't a game, and that she should walk away and leave this behind her. He had said those words for her own good, but of course she hadn't listened. This was a path she had always been meant to walk.

Destiny? She didn't believe in it. But she had seen into the future and they had seen herself burn the world. And *that*, she believed in.

She took her eyes off the people around her and looked at the world. The mountains and the snow, and the rocks and the sky. She tasted the air. Why would she want to destroy all this? What was it that could drive her to annihilate an entire planet? And what would she do, once everyone and everything was dead? Who would there be to talk to?

Darquesse smiled at the questions she found herself asking. No doubt, when the time came, she would fully understand why she was killing everything. When the time came, she was sure it would all make perfect sense.

"Lady Darquesse," someone said, barging through the crowd to throw himself at her feet. His left arm was in a sling. "I am yours to command. You have given me purpose. You have given me a reason to exist. What is your will?"

He looked up at her, tears in his eyes.

She kicked him under the chin, marvelling at her strength. His jaw splintered instantly, but her boot continued upwards and his head came apart around it. Some important piece of him, possibly his brain, shot into the sky like a football. His body crumpled and she laughed and turned to the others. The shock over what she had just done made some of them step back, but there were plenty of others who were laughing along with her, and there were a few who actually applauded. She despised them all.

She leaped for the nearest one, a sorcerer she had once spoken to in the old Sanctuary. Her fingers closed around his throat and she tore out his windpipe. The woman beside him clapped, and Darquesse put her fist through the woman's chest, then flung the body behind her.

The laughter was dying. No one was cheering any more.

Darquesse swept through them, their screams like a lullaby, making her smile. As she moved, she could sense the Remnant inside her. She could sense its presence and its confusion. This was not how it was meant to be. It had slithered its way inside and opened her up, allowed Darquesse to surface. But they had not, as the Remnant had expected, become one pure being. They were still two separate entities, and she felt its fear and it brought a chuckle to her lips.

Her soul was sealed, Nye had seen to that. It was hers, and hers alone. All the Remnant had managed to do was break down some walls between Valkyrie Cain and the source of her magic. It may have tainted something along the way, Darquesse couldn't be entirely sure. Not that it mattered. It was Darquesse who was in control here.

The Remnant wanted to get out. It was trying to bring itself back together and crawl out of her, but Darquesse wouldn't allow it. She kept it where it was, isolating it, draining its malevolence to add to the magic that was pumping through her body.

The sorcerers were attacking her now, trying to subdue her, trying to save themselves. She used the air to fling three of them upwards, then sent three spears of shadows after them.

Hands seized her from behind, trying to choke her. She poured darkness through her skin into his, and the man shrieked and fell back, his hands melting away to stumps. A stream of energy sizzled to her and she caught it in her palm, countered its effects without even knowing how she was doing it, and threw it back. The stream hit its owner, and its owner split apart in a fine red mist.

She crushed the skull of a handsome man and tossed him away from her. His body spiralled over the angry crowd. Things were not going as they had planned.

Darquesse clicked her fingers and flame enveloped her. Her skin and hair and clothes all burned, fiercely and brightly, but the fire didn't damage her. People scrambled to get away. She held out a hand and fire leaped at them. They rolled and writhed and screamed. She laughed. A man tried to run. Tesseract caught him by the throat.

"You run from your saviour, you ungrateful wretch?"

"She's killing us," the man gasped.

"This is what we call warming up." Tesseract shoved him back. "Darquesse, please accept my apologies. Kill as many as you like. When you are ready to begin the decimation of the world, please know that we will be ready to serve, to help in any way."

Darquesse used the fire to kill the man who had run, then let the flame go out and stalked towards Tesseract, wondering how long he would stay faithful once she started pulling out his spine. But then the ground started to crack, and Skulduggery Pleasant and Tanith Low burst up in a shower of dirt and rock. Billy-Ray Sanguine collapsed behind them and didn't move.

"Valkyrie," Skulduggery said, "stop this."

Darquesse looked at him, then looked at Tanith. Tanith looked scared, and shocked, and upset, and worried. She held her sword like she was ready to use it on anyone who got close. Darquesse could see her own reflection in the blade. A pretty girl with a scar on her cheek, fifteen years old and dark-haired. Her pale face splattered with other people's blood. Her eyes, dark-ringed. Is this what they all saw, she wondered, or did they see something else? Something magnificent and terrible? Something monstrous?

"Valkyrie," Skulduggery said. She looked back at him. "You're not yourself. Do you understand me? You're confused. You are Valkyrie Cain. You are not Darquesse."

"You cannot change who she is," Tesseract said from behind him.

"Shut up," Skulduggery said without looking around. "Valkyrie. Listen to my voice. I'm your friend. I'm your partner. I promised you I'd help you with this and I intend to. You don't want this to happen, I know you don't."

A man lunged at Tanith and Darquesse gestured, took his head off with a shadow.

"Val," Tanith said, her voice shaking. "Please. It's me. It's us. You don't want to hurt anyone. Come back to us."

"I could kill you," Darquesse said. She didn't have to talk loudly to be heard. "I could reach out, take hold of your face and squeeze, turn your head to mush. In your last few seconds of life, what would you think of me? Would you still love me? What about you, Skulduggery? I could kill you just as easily."

"You're not going to kill me, Valkyrie."

"Valkyrie is gone."

"No, she's not," Skulduggery said. "I'm talking to her."

Darquesse shook her head. "You don't understand."

"I understand perfectly. Darquesse isn't a separate entity. She isn't another person. She's you. If you make the wrong choices, if you stop loving the people who love you, if you allow the world to twist and turn and change you, then yes, the future we've seen will come to pass. But if you fight, and if you kick, and struggle, and refuse to give in to the apathy, or the anger, or the hopelessness, then you'll change the future, and you'll walk your own path. And I'll be right there beside you, Valkyrie. I'll always be beside you."

She felt the Remnant inside her, its anguish, and she grew tired of playing with it. It had come into her so eagerly, impatient to share her being and help her fulfil the fate that the psychics had foreseen. But now it understood that there would be no sharing. The Remnant's presence was merely offering her a peek at what was to come – but she would get there on her own. She didn't need any help.

It squirmed and fought and its screams filled her head, and when she was done enjoying it all, she flooded her body with heat, and the heat burned away the cold that the Remnant had brought. She purged it from her body, and purged it from her mind, and then it was gone. And with it, for the moment, went the bad thoughts and the emptiness.

Valkyrie's legs folded beneath her and Skulduggery darted forward to keep her from falling. "Thanks," she mumbled, as the crowd surged around her.

"No problem," Skulduggery said softly, then pressed his gun into her temple and said loudly, "Any of you take even one more step and Valkyrie dies."

51

THE RECEPTACLE

The crowd froze. Tesseract stared.

"You're bluffing," he said.

"Try us," Tanith told him, her sword flashing to Valkyrie's throat, where it lay cold against her skin. "You're not going to kill her," Tesseract said. "Put the weapons down."

Skulduggery thumbed back the hammer of his gun. "Valkyrie would rather die, here and now, than allow another one of you to possess her and drive her to become the monster that kills the world. We'd be doing her a favour, she knows we would."

Wreath came up beside Tesseract, smiling. "Don't be ridiculous. She's your friend. She's your partner. She's an honest, decent, innocent girl with her whole life ahead of her. You're not going to kill her in cold blood."

"Ghastly," Skulduggery called. "Are you here?"

The crowd parted, and Ghastly made his way forward.

"You've known me a long time," Skulduggery said. "Do you think I'd be willing to kill Valkyrie to save the world?"

Ghastly's fist clenched, and he looked at Tesseract. "He'll do it," he said.

"I agree," said China, gliding easily through the throng of people. "To be perfectly honest, I'm surprised he hasn't pulled the trigger already."

Wreath's lip curled in a snarl. "Then we'll take her from him."

"I don't like your chances," Skulduggery said. "There are some among you who could probably take down either myself or Tanith before we could act. But both of us? You don't have a hope. We're giving you ten seconds to vacate the people you've possessed."

"I'm not going back to prison," Ghastly said. "If you're going to kill Valkyrie, then go ahead. We might not get our dead world, but anything is better than going back to that room."

"We're not telling you to," Tanith said. "Vacate those people and leave. Neither side is going to win here today, so we're calling it a draw. Try your luck again tomorrow, and tomorrow we'll kick the hell out of you."

"You expect us to give you back these people?" China asked. "I think not. I rather like this body and this mind, and all the magic that comes with them."

"Those of us who are inhabiting the forms of sorcerers are *weapons* now," said Tesseract. "We're not going to relinquish these weapons so you can use them against us the next time we meet."

"I'm afraid you don't have a choice," Skulduggery said. "Those ten seconds start now."

Tesseract glared at him with hatred in his eyes, and then he looked at Valkyrie. "Your friends are prepared to kill you, Darquesse. They fear you. As well they should."

"Five seconds," Skulduggery said.

"This isn't over," Tesseract said.

He pried his mask away from his face and opened his mouth wide, as all around him his companions did the same. The Remnant squirmed out and flitted to the sky, and Tesseract collapsed, unconscious, the mask snapping back into place. All around Valkyrie, Remnants crawled out of the mouths of their vessels to emerge as a cloud of writhing blackness that filled the air with angry shrieks.

Valkyrie looked up at Skulduggery. "The Receptacle," she whispered.

"Don't worry, Val," Tanith said. "We already found it. See that little cave over there? That's the entrance." And even as she spoke, the ground started to rumble.

The Remnants' movements grew erratic, as the first of them felt the pull. Three of them suddenly whipped out of the cloud, yanked by an invisible hand to the mountain, their screeches turning from anger to terror. More followed, in greater numbers, forming a continuous stream of howling darkness.

The Remnant that had vacated Tesseract's body dived down, clinging on to the collar of the assassin's coat, fighting the pull. It dragged itself towards his masked face, stopping only when Skulduggery went to stand over it.

"The moment you inhabit that man," Skulduggery said, speaking loudly to be heard over the shrieking and the rumbling, "I'll kill him and you'll be destroyed. Do you think I'm bluffing?"

Tanith lowered her sword from Valkyrie's neck, and Valkyrie started to breathe again. The stream ended, disappearing into the mouth of the cavern. The Remnant clinging defiantly on to Tesseract was the last one. And then it too let go.

But instead of allowing itself to be pulled into the mountain, it veered off and lunged at Valkyrie. Tanith shoved her out of the way and the Remnant collided with her instead. Tanith went rolling down the embankment, and Valkyrie and Skulduggery leaped down after her. Tanith tried to pull the Remnant from her, but it was no use. Her throat bulged, and she stopped gagging.

Immediately, she spun on to her back, her boot striking Skulduggery's leg with a sharp crack of breaking bone. He yelled in pain and Tanith was up and jumping, spinning in mid-air to deliver another kick to his ribs. Skulduggery stumbled and went down.

Tanith reached for Valkyrie, who stepped back and slapped the hand away, struggling to adjust to Tanith as an enemy. Tanith had no such qualms. Her elbow smacked into Valkyrie's jaw and Valkyrie sprawled in the gorse brush. She got up and blocked a kick that drove her back, tried to respond with one of her own, but Tanith just laughed.

The air rippled and Tanith hurtled off her feet.

"Run!" Skulduggery shouted as he tried to get up.

Valkyrie sprinted for the cavern. The Receptacle was still active, she could hear the rumble and feel the ground tremble beneath her boots. If she could lure Tanith into the cavern, the machine would rip the Remnant out of her, but she didn't have much time. It was already slowing down. She glanced back to see Tanith flipping over Skulduggery's head, landing to scoop something off the ground. Skulduggery's gun.

Valkyrie turned to run back. Tanith fired twice and Skulduggery jerked, stumbling on his bad leg. He went down and Tanith threw the gun away, then looked up to grin at Valkyrie.

Cursing, Valkyrie resumed her run to the cavern. Tanith was behind her and gaining fast, and Valkyrie realised just how much her friend had been holding back during their time training together. Tanith was always stronger, faster and better, but she had never made it too obvious. There were occasions when Valkyrie had even fancied that they were becoming equals. Now, with the effortless way Tanith was closing the distance between them, Valkyrie could see what a self-deluding fool she'd been.

She reached the cavern before Tanith caught up to her. The deep roar from the Receptacle was almost deafening, dust falling from the rock ceiling. The orb in the machine was alive with swirling blackness. Valkyrie turned, panting, as Tanith staggered in behind her. The grin was gone, replaced with a strained determination. The Remnant inside her must have been screaming in pain.

"Let her go!" Valkyrie shouted.

Tanith kept coming, lurching with each step. Valkyrie pushed at the air, just hard enough to hurt and maybe loosen the Remnant's hold, but Tanith sprang, catching her by surprise. Valkyrie fell back, whipping the shadows to cover her retreat, but Tanith cartwheeled on one hand and ran to the wall, running up and disappearing behind a jagged outcrop.

Valkyrie kept stepping back, searching for a place to stand that wouldn't leave her vulnerable. She saw movement out of the corner of her eye as Tanith dropped behind her, but she was too slow to do anything about it. Tanith wrapped an arm around her throat, going for a sleeper hold. Panic flashed in Valkyrie's mind. Her hands moved of their own accord, snapping flat against the air, the way she used to do at home to boost herself up to her windowsill. This time, she shot backwards, hearing Tanith's surprised yell as they both went sprawling.

She expected Tanith to already be on her feet by the time

she looked up, but the effect of the machine was becoming more noticeable. Tanith's lips were black, and the veins were spreading as she dragged herself up off the ground.

Valkyrie ran at her, intent on piling on the pressure until the Remnant couldn't take any more. Tanith blocked the first punch and dodged the second, but Valkyrie kicked at her shin and connected with the third. She followed it with a side kick, shooting it out like Tanith herself had taught her. Tanith doubled over and Valkyrie pulled her head down to meet her knee. Tanith snapped back on impact and staggered away, tripping over her own feet and falling in the dust.

"Leave her," Valkyrie demanded.

Tanith laughed, and spat blood. "You're going to have to kill me, Val."

Valkyrie went to move forward, but she could tell Tanith was trying to draw her in. Instead, she grasped a trail of shadows and flicked it. Tanith dived and rolled, the shadows missing her completely. She kicked out, sweeping Valkyrie's legs from under her. Valkyrie hit the ground, felt Tanith's hands on her, and then her jacket was yanked off. Tanith hauled her up and threw her against the wall. A fist flew at her face and suns exploded before her eyes. Another one came in low, swooping into her side. Without the protection of her jacket her lungs turned sharp and painful and she knew a couple of ribs were broken.

Her eyes were blurred with tears and she couldn't see what she was doing, but she knew roughly where Tanith was, so she launched her head forward. She felt the impact and heard Tanith's howl of pain. She wiped her eyes, saw Tanith holding her nose. She shuffled forward with a kick that would have felled anyone without Tanith's abdominal muscles. As it was, all the kick did was to give her a little more room.

Tanith grimaced suddenly, and gasped, and for a moment the veins went away and Valkyrie knew it was her friend looking at her through tortured eyes. Then the eyes turned narrow as the Remnant regained control.

Valkyrie stepped up with a punch that jarred her whole body and sent Tanith to the ground. "Fight it!" she screamed. "Tanith, fight it!"

Tanith rolled over. She tried to get up, then collapsed.

"Force it out of you!" Valkyrie called. "Do it now!"

The Receptacle was starting to slow down. They only had a few more seconds before it deactivated. Valkyrie grabbed Tanith's ankles, started dragging her closer to the spinning orb. Tanith kicked and struggled, but she was weakening. Valkyrie dropped the ankles and bent over her, slipping her hands under Tanith's arms and pulling her up. Grunting with the effort, she shoved Tanith the last few metres to the machine. Tanith grabbed on to an outcrop to keep herself upright and stood there, gasping.

"It's over," Valkyrie said. She didn't have to shout any more because the rumbling was dying down. "Please. Leave Tanith alone. You've lost, OK? You're not going to win this so please leave her. Rejoin the others."

"Now why..." Tanith managed to say, "would I want to do that?"

"Because you've lost!"

"No, Val... I'll only have lost if I get stuck back in that room."

Valkyrie stalked up. Tanith raised a hand to stop her, but Valkyrie pushed it down, and her fingers closed around Tanith's throat. "If I have to choke you out of there, I will."

Tanith's black lips parted in a weak laugh that Valkyrie cut off by squeezing.

The rumbling was now nothing but a low, rhythmic throb. The orb was spinning on nothing but its own momentum, and that was slowing with every turn. Valkyrie squeezed tighter, and Tanith's free hand tapped uselessly at her.

"Get out of there!" Valkyrie screamed.

The orb stopped spinning, and the rumbling stopped, and the Receptacle deactivated.

"No," Valkyrie whispered.

Tanith smiled, grabbed Valkyrie's t-shirt and pulled her closer, and her elbow cracked against Valkyrie's head. The next thing Valkyrie was aware of was a gunshot. She was on the ground – she couldn't remember falling – and she was watching Tanith run up a wall of rock and vanish into the darkness.

Skulduggery limped over, keeping his gun-hand trained on where Tanith had last been.

"Are you OK?" he asked.

"No," Valkyrie whispered.

52

NEW YEAR'S EVE

Ireland was under quarantine, all flights in and out of the country cancelled. There were no boats or ferries, not even the fishermen could leave port. Europe was on high alert, even now that a cure had been found for the so-called Insanity Virus. The scientists had a technical name for it, but because they didn't have a clue how it started, no one bothered with them.

A small group of researchers had stumbled on to the cure, and they were getting all the attention and all of the praise. They had saved the country from a bizarre and mysterious new pathogen which had baffled experts from around the world. The virus had struck, receded, and was now eradicated.

Some thought it had been a terrorist attack. Others blamed secret government experiments, which drew much mirth from government representatives. People had been hurt, property had been damaged, and memories had been wiped. The number of dead, it was reported, was much lower than it could have been, for which everyone should have been thankful. But there would be no big parties or celebrations this New Year's Eve. After the last few days, it seemed like the whole of Ireland just wanted to lay low.

Valkyrie wasn't feeling especially thankful either. It was still freezing cold, still harsh and unforgiving, and Roarhaven was the last place she wanted to be tonight. She wanted to be back at home, where she'd been spending most of the last few days, keeping an eye on her parents.

Skulduggery had arranged for a squad of Cleavers to provide protection, in case Tanith decided to pay Haggard a visit, but Valkyrie was still worried, and in no mood to watch other people play politics.

Roarhaven Sanctuary was a mass of corridors that spiralled inwards to its centre. It was smaller than the old Sanctuary in Dublin, and less concerned with charm or, indeed, heat.

Heavy doors led off into rooms of varying sizes and functions. Many of the corridors were swamped in darkness, and others too dimly lit to be of any real use.

They arrived at the centre room. Skulduggery pushed the doors open and Valkyrie and Ghastly entered after him. Ravel nodded to them, but didn't break off his conversation with Geoffrey Scrutinous and Philomena Random. Valkyrie saw many people she recognised from the first meeting before Christmas. They were quiet, and looked tired.

The Necromancers stood off to one side, talking among themselves. To their right the Torment stood alone. The mood was sombre. Eyes were cast down. Gazes were not met. The atmosphere hung heavy with shame and regret and guilt.

Corrival Deuce was one of the dead. Who had killed him was unknown, and virtually impossible to establish, but it had sent all their plans and schemes into a spiral. Valkyrie hadn't known him for long, but she recognised the loss as much as anyone. He had been their great hope, a leader strong enough to convince the international community that Ireland could stand on its own, without interference from others. And now that hope was gone.

Gradually, the conversation died down. Ravel cleared his throat. "I suppose we should start, then. Welcome, all of you.

We've been through a lot in the last week, and I am immensely glad to see so many of you here tonight. We have lost friends and family, we have seen the whole country plunged into a nightmare we can only hope it will recover from – but of course, we don't have the luxury of time in which to lick our wounds and grieve for the departed.

"We have a state of emergency. According to a trusted source in the German Sanctuary, in those few days when we were compromised, the international community, headed by the American Council, was about to swoop in and save the day. While it could be seen as reassuring to have such good friends around the world, the unfortunate fact of the matter is that if they did swoop in, they would never swoop out again."

"Which means we need to consolidate our power as soon as possible," Scrutinous said, "and *that* means choosing a new Council of Elders."

"A vote," said Shakra. "Now. Tonight. We need to show them we're strong and decisive in the wake of what happened."

"Erskine," Skulduggery said, "I think the obvious thing would be to have you as the Grand Mage."

Ravel frowned. "What?"

"I agree with Skulduggery," Ghastly said. "You know how the game works. In fact, I'd say the internationals would actually find you *better* to work with than Corrival. You were his right-hand man for years – you share some of his views, but you aren't nearly as extreme."

Ravel rubbed his forehead wearily. "And does it matter at all that I have absolutely no interest at all in doing this job?"

"Not really," Skulduggery said. "Desperate times, desperate measures."

"A vote," said Scrutinous. "All those in favour."

Ayes filled the room.

Ravel sighed. "Fine. And in that spirit of desperation, Skulduggery can be my first Elder."

Skulduggery shook his head. "Not a chance."

"And how come you get to pass on the job offer and I don't?"

"Because I'm me."

"I have a suggestion," said the Torment. Everyone looked at him. "We have already given you the Roarhaven facility to use as your new Sanctuary, which you have gratefully accepted. However, some of the citizens of our fair town have voiced misgivings. They feel that our good will has been taken advantage of."

"Go on," Ravel said, suspicion in his voice.

"It is our opinion that the Council of Elders should be comprised of three mages of firmly different sensibilities. For too long, the members of the Council have all thought the same way, held the same view, and clung on to the same prejudices. If Erskine Ravel is indeed elected Grand Mage, it is my feeling that the first of his Elders should be Madam Mist."

Ravel actually recoiled at the suggestion. "But... Madam Mist is a Child of the Spider."

"As am I," the Torment said. "You would dismiss us all because of this?"

"No, of course not, it's just... Children of the Spider have always been reclusive. Even more so than the Necromancers."

The Torment nodded like a wise old man. "And it is time we changed our ways. Madam Mist would not only be a representative of the people of Roarhaven – and you would need their support for this Sanctuary to succeed – but she would also be a voice for the few, and the marginalised."

"Everyone gets heard in the Sanctuary," Ravel countered.

"And Madame Mist will ensure that valued tradition continues," the Torment said. "Unfortunately, this is not open to discussion. If our request is denied, we will be forced to withdraw all assistance – this very building included."

"You're holding us to ransom," Flaring said. "There's no way we'd ever agree to that."

"Excuse us for a moment," Skulduggery said, drawing stares from everyone in the room. He walked to the side, followed by Ravel and Ghastly and Valkyrie.

"You can't be serious," Ravel whispered. "You can't seriously expect me to work beside Mist."

"It's what they've been planning all along," Skulduggery replied. "When they offered us this building, we knew there was going to be a hitch."

"Mist is more than a hitch," said Ravel.

"Your Council is going to need her in order to survive here."

"If they planned this," Valkyrie said, "then we're just going along with their plan. How is that a good idea? This is the Torment we're talking about."

Skulduggery shook his head. "Their plan was for Mist to be an Elder alongside Erskine, with Corrival as Grand Mage. But that isn't the case any more. Now Erskine is the Grand Mage, and so whatever schemes they've come up with are going to have to change."

"Then we need another Elder who's on our side," Ghastly said. "To make sure Mist is kept in line."

"Yes, we do," Skulduggery nodded. "Which is why it should be you."

Ghastly's eyes widened. "Have you lost your mind?"

"Why not? You're liked, you're well-respected, and everyone knows about your bravery on the battlefield. This could be your chance to make a real difference."

"I'm not a politician," Ghastly said. "I'm a tailor."

"You can still make my suits in your spare time, but we're really going to need you to do this."

Ravel nodded solemnly. "Destiny is calling, my friend."

"That's not destiny, that's you. And if it's bravery on the battlefield you're after, why not ask Anton, or Vex, or any one of the Dead Men? There were more than just you, me and Skulduggery in our little group, if you remember."

"Anton Shudder scares people, and Dexter Vex is halfway around the world, living the life of an adventurer."

"Ghastly, think about what this will mean," Skulduggery said. "As Elder, you could track down Tanith, capture her without harming her, and authorise a team of experts to figure out how to get rid of the Remnant inside her. Who else is going to take the time to do that? Who else is going to care enough?"

Ghastly closed his eyes. "Fine."

"Well?" the Torment asked as they rejoined the others. "Have you reached a decision?"

"Yes, I have," Ravel said. "I will need to meet with Madame Mist to discuss a wide range of matters, but it would be an honour to have her beside me, providing no one has any objection to my own nominee, Ghastly Bespoke. No? No objections? Excellent. In that case, we have a new Council of Elders. I think applause is due."

They started to clap, and Valkyrie joined in. She waited until they were on their way out, when she was alone with Skulduggery, before speaking again. "Is it possible?" she asked. "To help Tanith?"

"No," he said. "From what we know of Remnants, it's permanently bonded to her. There's no helping her, not any more."

"So you lied to Ghastly."

"Ghastly knows," Skulduggery said, his voice sad. "He just doesn't want to believe it."

Fletcher was waiting outside. When Skulduggery left them, Fletcher gave Valkyrie a pair of sunglasses.

She frowned. "Where are we going?"

"Australia," he smiled, and took her hand. In an instant they were standing in a park on a sunny Sydney morning, obscenely bright despite the sunglasses, and the heat hit her like a fist.

"Woah," she breathed.

She turned, saw couples and families strolling in the sun. She saw the edge of the Opera House, half-hidden by tall trees, and she turned again and saw the city.

"Thought you might appreciate the change," Fletcher said, slipping on his own pair of sunglasses.

Valkyrie took off her jacket and sat on the grass, then lay back, smiling broadly despite everything that had happened. "I should get you to bring me places like this more often," she said. "Pack a pair of shorts, a bikini... I'd be set."

Fletcher sat down beside her. "And how'd you explain a tan to your folks in the middle of winter?"

"I'm sure I'd find a way."

"So why don't you?" he asked.

"Why don't I what?"

"Get me to take you to places like this more often?"

"I don't know. I should. I suppose I'm always busy."

"Well," he said with a laugh, "it's either that or you'd rather spend your time with Skulduggery than me."

"You know that's not true."

"Really?"

"It's partly true," she admitted.

Fletcher nodded. "I don't blame you, actually. He didn't try to hurt you like I did."

Her smile dropped. "That wasn't your fault."

"It still happened."

"And you can't remember any of it."

"Does that mean I don't get to feel guilty?"

"We all feel guilty, Fletch."

He looked at her, and she looked away. To her right, a bright green bird, some kind of parrot, was feasting on a discarded sandwich. Valkyrie watched it until it had eaten its fill, and then it hopped closer. She stayed very still. The bird hopped on to her folded jacket. It was so close she could sit up and touch it, but she didn't move.

Fletcher looked at the bird and smiled. "This is what I love about Australia. If we were in Dublin or London, this would be a dull old pigeon, and we'd be shooing it away. But here, everything's brighter, more colourful. More fun. I should take you down to the Gold Coast. Take you surfing."

"Wait till I'm better at manipulating water," Valkyrie replied. "Then I'll surf."

"But that takes the fun out of it."

The bird hopped on to her leg, and she laughed. It travelled north, and stood on her belly, its head twitching as it surveyed its surroundings.

Fletcher grinned. "You've made a friend."

"It's waiting for me to give it some food. I haven't got any food, birdie. Look, it's completely ignoring me. If it perches on my face, I swear to God..."

"Give me a smile," Fletcher said, moving his phone up slowly. He took three pictures, and on the third the parrot or cockatoo or whatever it was looked around, and Fletcher nodded. "That's a good one," he said. "That's one you can never show your family."

The bird flapped its wings. Valkyrie yelped and turned her face to the side as it lifted off, and when she looked back, it was sitting on Fletcher's head. She burst out laughing and rolled away, fumbling with her own phone before the opportunity was gone. Laughing so much her hand was shaking, she took a half-dozen pictures of an increasingly horrified Fletcher.

"Please don't poo," he muttered.

The bird flapped its wings and he yelled as it leaped from his head and dropped down on the other side of him. Immediately, his hands went to his hair, fixing and straightening where the bird had flattened. Then he lunged, trying to grab the phone from Valkyrie's hand, but she held on to it and curled up into a ball, laughing too hard to form words. Finally, he gave up, and lay back.

"Please don't show that picture to anyone," he said.

She slipped the phone into her pocket and lay against him. "No promises."

Fletcher put his arm round her. "We should do this more often. You need a break, Val. A holiday. When was the last time you had a holiday? I bet it was years ago, wasn't it? You need a week away from everything. A week where people aren't trying to kill you, where you're warm and happy and safe."

She kissed his cheek. "You're always looking out for me, aren't you? That's why I love you."

She felt his body stiffen. "You love me?"

Her smile faded. "Pretend I didn't say that." Fletcher sat up to look at her, but she closed her eyes. "It's a beautiful day, and it was a nice moment. Don't spoil it."

"OK," he said. He hesitated, then lay back down. "Sure."

They lay there, on the grass, in the sun.

"So when do you want to go back?"

"Let's give it a half-hour," she said. "I'm just getting warm."

*　　*　　*

They stayed an hour, and then teleported back to Ireland. The cold came in at Valkyrie from all sides, and she groaned as she handed Fletcher back the sunglasses. She called Skulduggery to pick her up, and as the sun went down, they arrived at the Necromancer Temple.

53

TENEBRAE

Melancholia led them to the High Priest's private meeting room. She looked tired, and thin, and didn't even take the time to glare at Valkyrie like she usually did.

"The High Priest will be with you shortly," she mumbled. She swayed slightly, like she might faint, but regained her composure and left them in the room.

"She looks sick," Valkyrie said. Skulduggery nodded, but didn't comment.

The meeting room was a circular chamber with a domed

ceiling, lit by dozens of candles. Valkyrie sat at the round table and waited. Fifteen minutes later, High Priest Tenebrae walked in, and she stood. She was so used to seeing him flanked by Craven and Quiver, that meeting him alone was a little jarring. It was like he'd turned up without his clothes on.

"Detective Pleasant," Tenebrae said, "Miss Cain, what can I do for you? We're all very busy here, dealing with the fallout from the Remnant attacks."

"You weren't at the Sanctuary meeting," Skulduggery said.

"I felt my time was better spent in an environment where I wasn't despised. From what I hear, however, you all seem to have managed without me. Ravel and Bespoke and Mist – strange bedfellows. But I must ask why you are here. I am, as I have said, very busy."

Skulduggery's lunge was so sudden that Valkyrie jumped back in shock. He shoved Tenebrae against the wall.

Flustered, the High Priest tried to break the hold. "What the hell do you think you're doing?"

Skulduggery pointed his gun into Tenebrae's face. "Where's the Remnant?"

Tenebrae froze. "The Remnants are trapped. You said so yourself."

"I mean *your* Remnant. The one you had trapped in your

own little Soul Catcher. The one who inhabited Kenspeckle Grouse, who tortured Tanith Low. Where is *that* Remnant?"

"I... I assume it's with all the others..."

"Three months ago, Solomon Wreath took possession of the Soul Catcher with that particular Remnant inside. We were assured it would be returned to the Midnight Hotel. Anton Shudder said that never happened."

"There's obviously been a mistake..."

"Finbar Wrong can't remember much, but he can remember Wreath turning up with the Soul Catcher a few days before all this started."

"You're saying Wreath released the Remnant on purpose? To what end? To inhabit this Finbar Wrong person?"

Skulduggery stepped closer. "I'm saying you ordered him to."

"Preposterous. This man is a Sensitive, isn't he? Why would I order such a thing?"

"Maybe because you wanted a glimpse into the future."

"In which case," said Tenebrae, "I could have merely paid a Sensitive to do so."

"Not if there was something in that future you wanted to keep secret."

"Detective Pleasant, you're accusing me without one single shred of proof that I had anything to do with this."

"Where's Wreath?" Skulduggery asked.

"I'm afraid I don't know."

"He's in hiding?"

"I told you, I don't know. We haven't seen him since the Remnant attack. I fear he may have been killed."

"Which would be very convenient for you."

"Quite the contrary. If Cleric Wreath were here, I'm sure he could explain why he didn't return the Remnant to the Midnight Hotel as per my instructions. I neither like nor appreciate being accused of something I did not do. And if you're going to shoot me, then shoot me. Otherwise, put down the gun and stop this ridiculous posturing."

"I should shoot you. I should kill you."

"Cold-blooded murder? In front of your protégée?"

"It wouldn't be murder. It would be a justifiable execution."

Tenebrae's eyes flickered to Valkyrie. "And are you prepared to let him? If he kills me, it all changes for you. You'll be banished from the Necromancer Order. You'll never be able to fulfil your destiny. You'll never become the Death Bringer—"

Skulduggery smacked the gun against Tenebrae's head. "Stop calling her that."

"Why?" Tenebrae snarled, his hand rising to his forehead. "Because you don't want to hear it? Because it offends your delicate sensibilities? If she is who Cleric Wreath thinks she is, she has a chance to save the world."

"From what, exactly? You've never been too clear on the *threat*, have you? What does the Death Bringer save us from?"

Blood was trickling through Tenebrae's fingers. "These are matters I will not speak about to outsiders."

"Then you'll tell Valkyrie?"

"When she's ready to hear it."

"And when will that be? When it's too late for her to turn back?"

"Detective Pleasant, are you worried that Valkyrie will slip from your influence? I would never have guessed you'd be so insecure."

"This has nothing to do with me."

"Which presumably means that this is all to do with her, am I correct? And yet you haven't once allowed her to speak for herself this entire conversation."

"I enjoy listening," Valkyrie said.

Tenebrae's smile was not particularly good-humoured. "You're not usually so shy, Valkyrie. When you're on your own, you talk an extraordinary amount, don't you? You have opinions on everything. But when Detective Pleasant is here, you seem content to let him do all the talking for you. Have you noticed this?"

"Can't say I have," Valkyrie said.

"But now that I've pointed it out, I assure you that you're going to. He's afraid, you see. He's terrified that you'll turn out to be the next Lord Vile. Isn't that true, Detective?"

Skulduggery's voice lowered. "Valkyrie's path is her own."

"And if she does, in fact, turn out to be the next Lord Vile? What then? Will you still be so philosophical? Or will you hunt her down and kill her?"

"If it comes to that," Skulduggery said, putting his gun away, "you'll be dead long before you get to see if you're right."

Tenebrae took his hand away from his forehead, and looked at the blood. "Just so you know, I will be making a formal complaint about you to the Sanctuary. Not that they'll take any notice. Two of your best friends on the Council of Elders, Detective – this couldn't have worked out better for you if you'd planned the whole thing."

The mood in the car on the drive back was sombre.

"What are you thinking about?" Skulduggery asked.

She shook her head. "I don't know. Everything. My

thoughts can't seem to settle. Too much to think about. Have you heard anything about Clarabelle?"

"No," he said. "No I haven't."

"We shouldn't have allowed her to return to the Hibernian alone. We should have realised she'd find Kenspeckle's body."

"Valkyrie, we were organising the teleportation of two thousand people – most of whom were still unconscious. We didn't have time to consider each and every one of them."

"We let her go, Skulduggery. We didn't even think about what she'd find. Do you think she's figured out what she did?"

"She won't remember it, but..." He sighed. "The evidence is there. We made a mistake."

"And now Clarabelle has run off."

"If she wants to be alone, we should respect that. She's lost someone who meant the world to her. She needs time to grieve. How are you coping?"

"I'm grand."

"Have you mourned? Fight now, mourn later. Like you said, that's our thing. And now is the time to mourn."

"I don't know. I don't know how to feel or how to, to process it, you know? Kenspeckle reminded me of my granddad. Grumpy and grouchy and not approving of the people I hung out with. I felt safe with him. Every time he was around I knew that whatever happened, he could fix me. He'd shuffle in, complain, make me feel guilty about getting into another fight. Then he'd insult you, make me laugh, and fix me. And right before he left he'd say something really nice, to make sure I'd know he cared."

"You're going to miss him."

She looked out the window. "Please don't make me cry."

"Of course," Skulduggery said. "I'm sorry."

She didn't say anything, and they drove on in silence until another name drifted, unwelcome, into her thoughts. "Scapegrace," she muttered.

Skulduggery turned his head to her. "What about him?"

"He's still locked in Kenspeckle's examination room. They both are."

"And?"

"Well, we should probably let them out?"

"So they can make more trouble for us?"

"We can't just leave them there. They're looking for a cure, and Kenspeckle said it might be possible. We ought to let them out so they can find someone else to help them."

"Like who?"

"How about Nye? This'd be right up his alley."

"We don't want anything to do with Doctor Nye."

"And we won't *have* anything to do with him. We'll give them his name, let them find him. We can't leave them locked up in that room, Skulduggery. You know we can't. Just stop by the Hibernian. I'll be two minutes."

He grumbled about it a little more, but fifteen minutes later, Valkyrie was hurrying from the Bentley into the Hibernian. The place was a mess. The walls were scorched and rubble littered the walkways. The screen was off, but a hole had been blown through the wall, and she climbed in. Lights flickered in the corridors. Her footsteps were loud. Suddenly, coming in alone didn't seem like such a great idea. What if a Remnant had stayed behind?

She reached the examination room, but the transparent door stood open.

"They said they—"

Valkyrie shrieked and leaped away, spinning in mid-air to face her attacker. She landed and stumbled, and all the while Caelan watched her with a raised eyebrow.

"My God!" she gasped. "Don't do that!"

"Don't do what?"

"Don't sneak up on me!"

"I wasn't sneaking."

"You nearly gave me a heart attack!"

"I wasn't sneaking. I was walking."

"You should wear a bell round your neck!"

"Are you finished hyperventilating?"

"No!" Valkyrie shouted, then felt stupid. "What? What do you want?"

"I was just going to say, before you started screaming, that I released them. The two zombies. They said they were friends of yours."

"They said that?"

"I suspect they may have been lying, but the taller one would not shut up, so I opened the door and asked them to leave me alone. I hope you don't mind."

She forced herself to calm down. "No. No, I don't mind. I came to let them out anyway, so..."

"The crisis is over, I take it?"

"Yes. You didn't hear the details?"

"I'm a vampire without a pack. Nobody tells me anything."

"Ah," said Valkyrie. "Right. Yes, the crisis is over. And now that, you know, you're here, I suppose I should thank you for arriving when you did."

"You were in danger. I had to save you."

She nodded, and smiled. Out of gratitude, she knew she should have just let that one go – but then she found herself saying, "Well, thank you for *helping* me. *Saving* me is a bit... strong."

"Have you seen him since? The boy?"

"You mean Fletcher. Yes, of course I have."

"Even after everything he did?"

"That wasn't him – that was the Remnant."

"If what happened to him had happened to me, I would never have hurt you."

"It couldn't happen to you," Valkyrie said, "you're a vampire. Remnants can't possess the dead."

"Is that how you see me? As a dead thing?"

"No," she admitted.

"How do you see me?"

"As a friend."

"Nothing more?"

He touched her arm and she smiled, but moved away. "Caelan, I don't want you to think that this is going somewhere. You've been a really good friend to me, you've really come through, but I am firmly and absolutely with Fletcher. And even if I wasn't, I still don't think it'd be a good idea."

"Love is rarely a good idea."

"You don't love me."

"Yes, I do."

"Please, stop saying that."

"What will it take for you to love me?"

"I can't love a vampire."

"Because we're monsters? Because when the sun goes down, we change? You realise, of course, that the sun went down a few hours ago."

Valkyrie's eyes widened, and she immediately backed away. "What are you doing?"

"Don't worry," he smiled, "I'm not going to change." He took a syringe from his pocket. "Dusk used this, remember? It's a mixture of wolfsbane and hemlock and various other herbs. He'd inject it a few times a night, and it'd stop him changing. I've spent the last few days searching for it. The old man had manufactured more. Dozens of vials of it, for whatever reason."

"Kenspeckle hated vampires," Valkyrie said softly.

"I took every last one of the vials. I didn't think he'd mind, now that he's dead. I read his notes too, so I know how to make my own." Caelan's eyes closed. "I can feel it. It wants to get out. It doesn't understand why it can't." He looked at Valkyrie. "I don't have to be the monster. For you... For you, I can be normal. I can be human."

"If this is how you're going to live, you have to do it for yourself, not for me."

He smiled again. "You're my reward."

"No, Caelan, I'm not."

"Not yet, maybe. I have to prove myself. I'm willing to do that."

"Listen," said Valkyrie, "I'm trying to be as clear about this as I possibly can. I don't want to be with you."

"I can hear how fast your heart beats every time you look at me."

"Well," she muttered, "that's hardly fair."

"You are a strange girl, Valkyrie Cain."

"And I've got a Skeleton Detective waiting for me outside."

"You'd better get back to him, then. I'll see you soon."

Valkyrie thought he might step closer, try to kiss her, but instead, he just smiled. She walked away, and tried to ignore the fact that she was disappointed.

She didn't tell Skulduggery about Caelan. She got in the Bentley, told him the zombies had already escaped, and they drove back to Haggard.

"It's not over," said Valkyrie.

"What isn't?"

"This whole Darquesse business. I didn't stop it, did I?"

Skulduggery hesitated. "It doesn't look like it, no."

"No one else remembers what they did when they were possessed, but I do. I remember more and more all the time. The Remnant wasn't controlling me, it just... opened a door. Those people who died. I did that." She took a breath, and let it out slowly. "Don't worry. I'm not going to start crying or anything. If I had been in control, it wouldn't have happened. Obviously, I wasn't in control."

"I'm glad you realise that."

"But now we have proof, right? That there is something in me capable of doing everything we saw in that vision. So what are we going to do about it?"

"What do you suggest?"

Valkyrie looked straight ahead, at the road. "You could kill me."

"I have no intention of killing you, Valkyrie. Something turns you. Something triggers the change from the Valkyrie Cain we all know and tolerate to Darquesse, evil witch-queen of Dublin."

"It's going to be something tragic, isn't it?" she said. "Something awful happens to me or to someone I love, and I go nuts and seek revenge on the whole world."

"That's a possibility."

"Any idea what this awful, tragic event might be?"

"I don't know. But whatever it is, I'll be looking out for it, and so will you. When it comes, we'll be ready."

He dropped her off at the pier, and she gave him a wave and watched him drive away. She took out her phone as she hurried to her house, making sure the reflection was still out at a neighbour's party.

According to the message it had left her, it was standing in the corner not talking to anyone. The party itself was a complete flop, with no one being in the mood to make merry. Valkyrie, however, managed a smile at the thought of walking through her own front door for once, and letting the reflection be the one to climb up to the window.

She felt bad about the Cleavers, forced to keep watch out here in the freezing cold. Their van was parked on the far side of the road, with the engine off so as not to arouse suspicion. She had never engaged a Cleaver in conversation, had never even heard one speak, not really, but she approached the van anyway. She could sneak them out a couple of coffees if they needed warming up, and possibly give them some straws so they wouldn't even have to take their helmets off. She didn't know if they even drank coffee. She doubted it.

The front of the van was empty, so Valkyrie rapped lightly on the side door. The windows were darkened. When there was no sound from inside, she frowned. There were three Cleavers stationed here – one stayed with the van at all times, and the other two took regular patrols around the area. She gripped the handle. To her surprise it wasn't locked. She slid the door open. Three Cleavers lay dead inside.

She turned and ran to her house. She slipped on the road and fell, rolled, lunged up and kept running. She jumped the low wall around her front garden, landing in the shadows, staying out of the light that shone from the living room window. The fire was roaring and the TV was on.

Valkyrie saw her mum and dad chatting, and her knees went weak with relief. But they were talking to someone, a woman in jeans and a heavy sweatshirt. Valkyrie didn't recognise her until she turned her head to laugh. Valkyrie ran into the house and burst through into the living room. They all looked round, surprised at the dramatic entrance.

"Hi, Stephanie," Tanith said.

54

ENEMIES

"Heat," Valkyrie's mum said. "Heat!"

Her dad got up, hurried out into the hall. She heard him close the front door to stop the draught, but couldn't take her eyes off Tanith. "What are you doing here?"

"My car broke down," Tanith smiled. "I remember you said you lived here, so I thought I'd stay somewhere warm until my lift arrived. Are you OK? You look like you're in shock."

Her dad came back in. "Born in a barn, were you? I

swear to you, Tanith, I don't know where she gets it from."

Tanith laughed. "Don't worry, Des, she's exactly the same in school. I may only be a substitute teacher, but I've been around long enough to know that Stephanie swans in and out of class expecting doors to close all by themselves."

They all chuckled, except for Valkyrie.

"Tanith," Valkyrie's mum said, "were you caught up in this Insanity Virus thing? Wasn't it awful?"

"Oh, Melissa, it was. My neighbour got it, actually. He went nuts. Didn't hurt anyone, thank God, but it was so scary. Just like the reports on TV. He's fine now, though."

"It was an attack," Valkyrie's dad said. "Something like this just doesn't happen in nature. I bet you that whoever did this was using Ireland as a testing ground. It'll be America next, you wait and see. Or London."

His wife shook her head. "Some people are saying now it was hallucinogenic drugs pumped into the water supply. They're even saying it started out as a prank. A *prank*!"

"I'm sure you're right," Tanith said, nodding. "But it was terrifying. I stayed home the entire time – there was no way I was setting foot outside."

"Wise woman."

"Oh, excuse me," Tanith said, taking out her phone and reading the screen. "My lift is here."

"That was quick."

"That's the good thing about boyfriends – they come when you call. I'm not too sure how to get back to my car, though. It was on *one* of these roads..."

"Oh, I'm sure Steph won't mind walking you back."

"No problem," Valkyrie said. "You ready to go now? Let's go now."

Tanith stood up, and smiled again. "So eager to get a teacher out of her house. Des, Melissa, thank you so much for your hospitality. Hopefully I'll see you at the next parent-teacher meeting."

While her parents said their goodbyes, Valkyrie ushered Tanith out of the house.

"If you're going to set me on fire," Tanith said quietly, "you might want to wait until we're around the corner."

Valkyrie glanced back. Her dad was on the front step watching them go. After another few moments of letting the heat out, he closed the door.

Immediately, she stepped away from Tanith. "Why are you here?"

Tanith kept walking, forcing Valkyrie to keep up. "We're friends, Val. I just wanted to drop in, say hi."

"Ghastly's an Elder. He's getting everyone to figure out a way to help you."

She smiled. "Why would you think I need help? Look at me – don't I seem happy to you?"

"You're a Remnant."

They were around the corner now, out of sight and heading down to the pier.

"And we Remnants are happy creatures," Tanith said. "So Ghastly's an Elder, is he? Well, I'm glad. I wouldn't have liked to see him spend the rest of his life in that little shop, never making any new friends. Maybe now he'll meet a nice girl, settle down..."

"He loves you."

"He *is* a sweetheart."

Valkyrie stopped walking. "What do you want, Tanith?"

Tanith turned to her. "I'm here to tell you that I'm not going to kill your folks. That's what you're worried about, isn't it? Well, you don't have to be. I had a perfect opportunity to kill them, right there, and I didn't. The fact is, I'm going to leave your family alone."

"Why?"

"I've been a few people these past few days. I've been Finbar, Shudder, Tesseract. I have to say, though, and I'm not being biased, that I prefer being me. I prefer being Tanith. I'm just *prettier*, you know? And I smell nicer.

"But when I was Finbar, I saw that vision of you, in the future, and I got so excited. I started thinking of all the different ways we could help. First we were worshipping you, then we tried possessing you, and that didn't work. Have you talked to any psychics lately? They're still having dreams about Darquesse, did you know that? Whatever you did, Val, it didn't change anything. You sealed your name, but that just means you decide to kill the world all on your own, with nobody controlling you. It means you kill your own parents, of your own free will.

"So now you see why I don't want any harm to come to your folks. I want you to get there naturally – I want things to happen as they're meant to happen. And that means your parents stay alive and stay healthy, right up until the moment you kill them."

"And what are you going to do?" Valkyrie asked. "You're just going to sit around and watch?"

"I'm not the sitting around type now, am I? I'll be getting into all sorts of trouble, don't you fret. I'll be guiding you, nudging you. Every so often I'll give you the occasional push, just to keep life interesting, to make sure you're not straying too far from your path."

"I will never become Darquesse."

"You already did, Val, for three minutes, and it was beautiful. And I understand it now, why she turned on my brothers and sisters. Darquesse is indiscriminate about who she kills. She is a true, pure force of destruction. The next time she comes out, I don't plan to be anywhere nearby."

"I'll die first," Valkyrie said. "I'll kill myself."

"No," said Tanith, "you won't."

"I'd rather die than hurt my family."

"But you won't kill yourself. You don't have it in you."

"You don't know what I have in me."

"But we're all going to find out." Tanith smiled. "How is *my* family, by the way? My *other* family?"

"The Remnants are trapped and locked away. We're finding somewhere new to keep them. You'll never find them."

"Maybe I will, maybe I won't. But that's all yet to come, isn't it? We have all that to look forward to. For the right now, though, for the here and now, the most we can do is enjoy the time we have left." She held out her arms. "Hug?"

Valkyrie stayed where she was, and eventually Tanith dropped her arms.

"You really need to lighten up, you know that? I've lightened up completely, now that I'm sharing this mind. Now all I want to do is have fun."

"Tanith," Valkyrie said, "please. We're your friends. *I'm* your friend. I love you like a sister."

"And I love you, Val. I really and honestly do. Back when I was me, alone in here, without the Remnant, you were my favourite person in the whole world. I would have died for you. And now that the Remnant's here with me, I love you even more. Now I'd kill for you."

Valkyrie couldn't help it. Tears came. "I know you don't want to hurt anyone."

"No," Tanith smiled gently, "I really, really do."

"I want my friend back. I want my sister back. I don't want you to be the enemy."

"Oh, Val, in a few weeks, you're probably going to have a *proper* sister, a *real* sister. Then you won't need me any more. And I'll be OK. I'm good at making friends. Speaking of which, would you like to meet my new boyfriend?"

The wall beside her cracked and crumbled, and Billy-Ray Sanguine stepped through. Valkyrie moved back instinctively, but he barely paid her any attention. Tanith turned to him and they kissed, and Valkyrie's insides went cold. That act, the simple act of a kiss, was more powerful than any violent demonstration. Tanith was gone now. She was lost.

"Don't look so upset," Sanguine said, and Valkyrie realised he was grinning at her. "I'll look after her."

"Thanks, sweetie," Tanith said, resting her head on his shoulder. "Will you be all right to get us out of here?"

"So long as you have some more of that painkiller, honey bunny."

Tanith dipped into her pocket, came out with a leaf that Sanguine put into his mouth and chewed. "OK," he said. "I'm ready."

Valkyrie watched them step back against the wall. Thousands of tiny fractures spread outwards behind them. Sanguine went first, the wall sucking him in.

"We'll come after you," she said.

"I know you will," said Tanith. "What are friends for? Oh, and Val? Happy New Year."

The wall swallowed her, too, and Valkyrie was alone.

55

THE RETURN

Tesseract couldn't understand what all the fuss was about – it really wasn't that cold. Russia was cold. Parts of Siberia were especially cold. Ireland, during the winter, was practically tropical.

He was looking forward to going home. He'd spent far too long here, had been delayed time and time again. But now his return journey was close. All he needed to do was take care of one last piece of business, and then he could put Ireland behind him.

He had been watching the Torment for days, but the old man

never allowed himself to be caught outside alone. Syc and Portia were always with him, and occasionally Madame Mist joined them for a stroll through the streets of Roarhaven. Tesseract wasn't keen to take them all on again, so he watched and waited.

He knew there was an underground tunnel leading from somewhere in the town to the Sanctuary. Twice now the Torment had exited the Sanctuary without re-entering. Tesseract returned to his trailer, where he examined plans of the town and read back over its history. An underground tunnel was not mentioned in any of his research.

He took a different approach, focusing instead on the Torment's known associates. Like many of Roarhaven's citizens, the Torment hadn't been born in the town. He had retreated there, no longer prepared to tolerate the mortal civilisation that showed no sign of stopping its global spread. Roarhaven was a town of prejudice and bigotry, of bitter sorcerers and magical malcontents. The Torment, and later on the other Children of the Spider, found a home there that welcomed them and their views.

Beneath his mask, Tesseract smiled. He found a mention of Vaurien Scapegrace in a story from the Torment's past. Scapegrace had once been a citizen here, before he'd been kicked out. He'd even owned a tavern for a few years.

Tesseract put the files away, and chose a new mask from the wall. This one had rivets over the brow and a long slit at the mouth. The needles sank into the puckered wounds around his face as he left his trailer. He walked for fifteen minutes before he reached the edge of the town.

Using the night as cover, he stole through the streets, moving so silently even those he crept behind didn't hear him. The tavern was dark, the door locked. He forced a window at the back and climbed through. He found a trapdoor behind one of the bars, and followed the steps down into living quarters. The lamps were on, but no one was there. Tesseract waited.

A little under three hours later, he heard a low rumble coming from the bedroom, the sound of a wall sliding apart. He didn't move. The wall slid shut again, and now he could hear shuffling footsteps moving into the small living room. Music began to play. He knew the group, it was The Carpenters, but he wasn't sure of the name of the song. 'There's a Kind of Hush' perhaps. The last song the Torment would ever hear. Tesseract hoped he liked it.

He moved silently to the living room, but when he stepped in, it was empty.

"I don't wish to alarm you," Skulduggery said from behind him, "but I have a gun pointed at your head."

Tesseract spun, flailing one arm, and managed to knock Skulduggery's hand to one side just as he fired. He batted at the gun-hand again, sent the revolver flying, and Skulduggery caught him with a right hook that almost sent him to the carpet.

"If you would just give yourself up," Skulduggery said as he kicked him, "you'd make this a lot easier on me."

Tesseract caught the second kick in the crook of his arm, and immediately Skulduggery sprang into the air, twisting from Tesseract's grip. He tried to push at the air, but Tesseract lunged, barrelling into him, forcing him back. Tesseract got an elbow in his ear for his trouble, and he fought a wave of dizziness that threatened to topple him. The skeleton snapped out two punches to the head, then sent a sneaky one to the ribs. Tesseract felt something pop, and he growled.

Skulduggery swayed away from one punch and blocked the next, but couldn't stop the third. Tesseract grabbed him and pulled his head down to meet his knee, then hooked two fingers into his left eye socket and stepped back, swinging him around the room. Skulduggery hit the couch and went over. Tesseract picked him up and slammed him head first into the wall. He did it twice more, until he was sure the detective was dazed, and then he dropped him.

He heard the rumble of the parting wall, and left the living room. The Torment emerged from the bedroom, looked up and his old eyes widened for a moment.

"I see," he said. "There's no point in arguing with you, is there?"

"None," Tesseract admitted. "You tried to kill me, and you didn't pay me. I can't have that."

"I should have cut your throat."

"You should have."

Tesseract pressed his hand against the Torment's forehead and splintered his skull. The old man's body dropped, and Tesseract stepped over it. He could hear Skulduggery, on his feet again, no doubt with his gun back in his hand. Tesseract hurried into the bedroom and ran through the gap in the wall, into the tunnel beyond. A few moments later, he heard Skulduggery sprinting after him.

The tunnel was long and dark. It began to incline, the darkness giving way to an indistinct grey that became a door. Tesseract ran through into one of the Sanctuary's broad corridors. His natural inclination was to stick to the shadows, but the corridors ahead were brighter, and that meant they led to the exit. He ran on.

A bullet tugged at his coat at the same time as he heard the shot, and he dodged right, bursting into a room. He ignored the sorcerer inside and went straight for the opposite door.

He found himself in another room, filled with boxes and unopened crates. He grabbed a crowbar and stepped to one side. Skulduggery ran in and Tesseract swung for his legs. Skulduggery did a flip and crashed down. The crowbar hit him again and he grunted, and Tesseract helped him to his feet with a kick to the ribs. The crowbar cracked against Skulduggery's cheek, making him reel back.

"I haven't been paid to kill you," Tesseract said. "Lie down and don't get up. You don't have to die tonight."

Skulduggery clicked his fingers and a fireball sparked off in his hand. Tesseract hurled the crowbar. It struck the skeleton between the eye sockets and he went down.

The light in the room flickered, and Tesseract frowned. Shadows moved along the walls, in the corners, across the floor. He looked around, looked for whoever was doing this. The shadows whipped at him like a giant claw, its talons ripping deep into his back. Tesseract spun in almost a full circle, and for a moment he thought he might stay on his feet. But no, his legs collapsed from under him and he fell.

He'd once known a man who said that life hinged on the moment, that everything changed in the blink of an eye.

Tesseract knew the truth of that as well as anybody. It was in those moments that he struck, after all, snatching people's lives away. He'd always known that it was only a matter of time before one of those moments worked against him. The shadows had torn right through his body. He fancied he could feel his organs shutting down, one by one.

The room was quiet. The sorcerer in the other room, the one he'd passed, had obviously fled. Tesseract doubted there were any others working through the night. This Sanctuary wasn't fully active, after all. It would take a few weeks for that.

He watched Skulduggery pick up his gun, and stand. It took him a moment to see Tesseract, lying there in a pool of his own blood. The detective's head tilted. He was puzzled. Then he looked up, at something behind Tesseract.

Tesseract heard footsteps, but couldn't move his head. All he could do was watch Skulduggery as he backed away.

"No," Skulduggery said.

Skulduggery fired three times. The footsteps didn't even slow down.

Now Tesseract could see someone stepping into the edge of his vision. A shadow flicked the gun from Skulduggery's hand. The detective went to push at the air, but another shadow batted his arm down. Skulduggery charged, and the figure in black watched him come, and then the shadows swooped in.

They slid beneath Skulduggery's clothes – Tesseract could see them curl and writhe within him. They were in his very skeleton, wrapping around his bones, and Skulduggery screamed in agony as he was lifted off his feet. Darkness slipped from his open jaws to his eye sockets, leaked from his sleeves to between the buttons of his shirt. His body was rigid while the darkness investigated every part of him, and still he screamed.

The figure observed him without moving, letting the shadows do all the work. And then it was over. Skulduggery fell to the ground as the shadows retracted, melting back into the black armour their master wore.

"You can't be here," Skulduggery said. "You died. You're dead."

The figure must have said something in response, but Tesseract didn't hear.

"This is insane," Skulduggery said. He put all his strength into getting to his hands and knees. "You can't be here. This is... You can't be here."

The man in the black armour walked slowly around the detective, who was shaking his head, like he was willing this not to be true. "You're dead. You're not real. You're dead."

The figure stopped walking, and Skulduggery looked up at him, like he was listening. Tesseract thought he could hear the faintest of whispers, and then Skulduggery roared in anger, and leaped up. His fist struck the figure and there was an explosion of darkness, a wave of shadows that filled the room, and then it was gone.

Tesseract blinked, his vision returning. Skulduggery was on the floor, on his knees with his head down. The figure in black was gone.

Tesseract grimaced as he rolled on to his side. Moving slowly, he got to his feet. He could no longer feel the pain in his back. His legs were going numb. He was aware of all the blood he was losing, but he didn't dwell on any of it. Instead, he pointed himself at the door, and walked. Each step was a battle.

"Stop," said Skulduggery, from behind him.

Tesseract stopped. He didn't turn. He didn't have to. From the angle of the voice, he knew that Skulduggery was standing, and most likely the gun was back in his hand.

"Who was that?" Tesseract asked.

"No one."

"The gaping wound in my back tells a different story. I recognised the armour. It's the same armour Baron Vengeous wore three years ago, isn't it? But that wasn't Baron Vengeous."

"You're under arrest."

Beneath his mask, Tesseract smiled. "I'm dead, Detective. I have a few minutes left, if I'm lucky. He killed me most effectively, did he not? I would at least like to know his name. Did he give it?"

"He did."

"And what name did he give?"

For a moment, Skulduggery didn't answer. Then, "He said he was Lord Vile."

Tesseract gritted his teeth, and turned halfway, so he could see the Skeleton Detective. Skulduggery stood with his gun held down by his side. "And where is he now? Did you strike him down with one mighty blow?"

"He's gone. I don't know where he is. I hit him and he... vanished."

"What did he say to you?"

"What does it matter?"

"I'd really like to know."

Skulduggery shook his head. Tesseract waited, feeling those precious seconds slip by him so, so slowly. When Skulduggery spoke again, his voice was surprisingly empty.

"He said he came back for her."

"For Valkyrie?"

"He's building his strength. When he's strong enough, he'll kill her. He said he'll kill the Death Bringer, then all the Necromancers."

"And why did he choose to tell *you*? What connection do you have to him?"

Skulduggery didn't answer. He emptied his gun of spent shells.

"I know about you," Tesseract continued. "I make a file on everyone I am likely to go up against. I know about you, and I know there is no recorded instance of you and Lord Vile ever meeting."

"That's right," Skulduggery said. He slipped a fresh bullet into a chamber.

"You never fought him. Never faced him. When he arrived, you were gone. Why did you choose *then* to leave, I wonder? Did you know what was coming?"

"You think you know about me," Skulduggery said. "But you don't." Another bullet into the chamber.

"You're scared of him, aren't you, Detective? I know fear. I've felt it often enough, and I've inflicted it. You're terrified of him, so much so that you ran when you realised he was coming. Are you going to run this time, I wonder?"

Skulduggery clicked the chamber back into place. "No running. Not any more. I'm going to stand and fight."

"So what is your connection? Why do you fear him? What power does he have over you?"

Skulduggery raised the gun and thumbed back the hammer.

Slowly, Tesseract brought his hands up to the straps around his head, his numb fingers clumsily unbuckling the mask. Finally, it came free, and he let if fall, felt the air on his ravaged face. It felt so good. He felt like laughing.

"A dying man's last request," he said. "Answer me this. You were killed, yet you came back. Do you know how it happened? Do you know who would be powerful enough to hold back death, *true* death? Was it Necromancy that brought you back, Skulduggery? Was it Lord Vile?"

Skulduggery's gloved finger tightened on the trigger, but before the gun fired Tesseract's legs gave way beneath him once again. He stumbled to the wall, hit it with his shoulder and slid down to the floor. There was no pain, which was nice, because he could feel the rot spreading over his head. When he looked up, Skulduggery was putting his gun away.

"Not going to kill me?" he asked.

"Waste of a bullet."

"I realise I have no right to ask this, but would you help me outside? It's almost dawn, and I would like to feel the sun on my face."

Skulduggery tilted his head slightly. Then he came forward, stooped to wrap Tesseract's left arm around his neck, and straightened up, lifting Tesseract out of a pool of his own blood.

"The problem with living so long," Tesseract said, as Skulduggery walked him to the door, "is that we get used to it. We watch the mortals age and wither and die around us, watch the world change and decay... but no matter the hardship or the pain or the sorrow we suffer, we choose to continue living. Out of sheer habit, I think."

"You're quite chatty now that I've got to know you," Skulduggery said.

"I have a cat, you know. Back home."

"I know. You had cat hair on your lapel the day you killed Davina Marr."

"You don't miss much, do you? She doesn't have a name. She is just Cat. She curls up on my chest whenever I sit down, and goes to sleep. I hope she doesn't miss me. I'm going to miss her."

They emerged into the cold air of the morning. Dawn had yet to break. Skulduggery found a bench and he let Tesseract sit, facing the stagnant lake, and beyond it, the horizon. Then he sat beside him.

"Is there anything you regret?" Skulduggery asked.

"I regret being mortally wounded just a few minutes ago."

"Understandable."

"Apart from that, no. I lived. I killed. My life is my own."

The rot was seeping through Tesseract's body. He turned his hand over, but it was probably a good thing he couldn't see much in this dim light. He felt the flesh bubble, like he was being boiled from the inside out. It was an effort to look up again.

"What about you?" he asked, his words not much more than a mumble. "Regrets?"

"Many," Skulduggery said.

Tesseract's breath rattled in his chest. "That's the good thing about living. You get to make up for past mistakes."

"Or make brand-new ones."

Tesseract tried to smile, but didn't have the strength for it. His head dipped, and Skulduggery reached out to steady him. The sun cracked the horizon, split it with light that spilled through the sky in streaks of orange and deep red.

Read on for an exclusive
Skulduggery Pleasant short story...

This story was written for Charlie Smith, who won a competition to create a new character to appear in *Mortal Coil*.

The character Charlie came up with was Geoffrey Scrutinous, and this is how Charlie described him in his competition entry:

"Wears khaki shirts (Indiana Jones style), short trousers and maroon socks with leather sandals. Lots of beads and chains, lots of rings on one hand. Has a small goatee and wild frizzy hair with piercing blue eyes. A frantic, disbelieving nature and is very erratic in both appearance and personality. He sorts out disturbances in the non-magical population. He has the ability to get you to agree with anything he says, without you realising it."

You'll have seen Geoffrey in this book, of course. But as an added bonus, here's a little story all about him...

Thanks, Charlie!

The Wonderful Adventures of Geoffrey Scrutinous

The cop frowned. "But there's a dead body in there. I have to... I can't let anyone into the house. It's my job to preserve the scene for the forensics people, to investigate and, and solve the crime..."

Geoffrey Scrutinous nodded. "And you will do a wonderful job at preserving and investigating, I know you will. But for the moment, you want to delay all this hustle and bustle."

"I do?"

Scrutinous nodded. "Oh, yes, very much so. I have some friends coming, they're special investigators, and they have to look around a bit first."

"Who are they?" asked the cop.

"Just some friends. A tall man and a teenage girl. They're very good at this kind of thing."

"I'm not sure I should be allowing this."

Scrutinous smiled, maintained eye contact and poured more magic into his words. "It's perfectly fine. You know it is. You can feel it, that reassuring feeling that everything is going to be fine. You can feel it, can't you?"

"I... I suppose... They're good, then?"

"Very good."

"You think they'll be able to crack the case?"

"If anyone can, they can."

The cop nodded. "Good. I was hoping I wouldn't have to. I have no idea how someone could be run over by a train in their own living room."

Scrutinous patted the cop's shoulder. "Don't you worry," he said. "They handle this kind of thing all the time."

"I have to confess," Skulduggery Pleasant said as he took his hat off in the dead man's living room, "I have no idea what's going on here at all."

Valkyrie Cain nodded up to the corner of the room. "What's that bit?"

"It's his head," said Skulduggery. "You can see the rest of it there, hidden behind the curtain."

"Oh, yeah. That's disgusting."

"Nobody ever said being hit by a train was a neat way to die."

Valkyrie turned to Scrutinous. "And you're sure that's what they said?"

"Oh, yes," Scrutinous answered. "Neighbours reported hearing an old fashioned train. Like a steam engine, they said, with the 'choo choo' and everything. The walls of every house on the street rattled as it passed."

Skulduggery murmured something to himself. The living room was small and tidy, the furniture in place, the TV still on with the sound muted. It was three o'clock in the morning and the lamps gave the place a gentle, warm light. It would have been a perfectly good room in which to spend an evening were it not for the man who had been splattered across every imaginable surface.

"Well," Skulduggery said, "purely to get this out of the way, I'll just go ahead and say it. There does not seem to be any sign of a railway track on the carpet or, indeed, a train hiding behind the sofa. And I don't think one could have fit through the door."

"Maybe it was a ghost train," Valkyrie said. "Do ghost trains exist?"

"I've seen two," Scrutinous said. "But I've never heard of a ghost train that could run over anything living. A ghost train would be able to run over a ghost, not a man."

"And yet something big killed him," Skulduggery said. "And it was powerful and fast-moving. Just like a locomotive."

Valkyrie examined a couple of framed photographs on the mantelpiece. "Who was he? He wasn't a sorcerer, was he?"

"His name was Brendan Cassidy," Scrutinous said. "From what I can gather, he was a perfectly normal mortal. He worked as an assistant manager of a local store. Nothing whatsoever to do with us or anyone in our community."

Skulduggery took a bag of powder from his jacket and threw some into the air. It fell as a light cloud, shimmering with faint colour. "Definite traces of Adept magic," he said, "but I'm not getting a read on an exact discipline. Which only proves that he didn't explode of his own volition."

Scrutinous watched the two of them work, and tried not to get in the way. He wasn't a detective, after all. He worked in Public Relations – he convinced mortals that they didn't see what they actually saw. All this looking-for-clues lark was a tad beyond him. He liked to think of himself as a simple man.

He wandered over to a lamp. It was a very nice lamp. He'd seen better, of course he had, but this was a very fine example of a perfectly nice lamp. It suited the room. He approved. Beside the lamp was a fountain pen. He picked it up. It was an old pen, a classic. He wasn't an expert on pens, but he knew an old, classic pen when he saw one. He remembered when pens like this had first gone on sale, over a hundred and fifty years ago, when they were brand new and cutting edge. He'd probably owned a few. There was a pad of paper on which the pen had been lying, and he looked at it now, at what was written across the top page.

I'm going to be hit by a train, it read.

Scrutinous frowned. "Um," he said.

"Yes?" Skulduggery asked, from somewhere behind him.

"Um, I'm not sure, but I think I may have found a clue."

Skulduggery and Valkyrie joined him, and peered down at the pad.

"Ah," said Skulduggery. "I think you're right. That is indeed a clue. I don't know what it tells us, apart from the obvious, but it definitely tells us something. Valkyrie?"

"It tells us Cassidy knew what was going to happen," Valkyrie said.

Skulduggery nodded. "Anything else?"

"Uh..."

Skulduggery hunkered down and poked the pad with his finger. "The handwriting is very clear. Very legible. When he wrote this, he was calm. That tells us one of two things. Either he had already accepted his fate, or he didn't believe it would happen. Or he wasn't aware that he was writing it."

"That's three things," Valkyrie said. "How do we know it's even his handwriting?"

"There's a half-finished crossword by the armchair. Most of it is impressively wrong, but the handwriting is a match." Skulduggery straightened up. "Out of those three possibilities, Valkyrie, which one would you dismiss first?"

Scrutinous stepped away to let them converse. It was always fascinating watching detectives work.

"I don't think he'd accepted his fate," Valkyrie said at last. "There's nothing else here to suggest that he was preparing to die. There's no note to family or friends, the dinner plate in the kitchen hasn't been put away... He wasn't expecting this."

Skulduggery nodded. "Which leaves us with options two and three – he didn't believe what he'd written, or he wasn't aware he was writing it."

Scrutinous picked up the newspaper by the armchair and glanced at the crossword. He wasn't a fan of them, to be honest. There were enough confusing things in the world without crosswords.

"If Cassidy didn't believe what he'd written," Valkyrie said, "then why not tear out the page? This should be crumpled up in a bin somewhere, as just another bit of nonsense. But he didn't tear it out."

"So he wrote it, but didn't know he was writing it," Skulduggery said. "Which means something or someone was guiding his hand."

"Someone wanted him dead?" Valkyrie asked. "A sorcerer? Why?"

"There's something we're not seeing," Skulduggery said. "Geoffrey?"

Scrutinous looked up. "Yes?"

"What are you doing? I thought you hated crosswords."

"I do, yes."

"Where did you get that pen?"

"It was on the pad."

"What are you writing?"

Scrutinous laughed. "Writing? I'm not writing anything." And even as he said it, he heard the scratching of pen on paper, and looked down. "Oh," he said. "Oh, dear." He dropped the pen to the carpet.

Skulduggery held out his hand. "Let me see."

Scrutinous handed over the newspaper.

Skulduggery read what Scrutinous had written. "'I'm going to be eaten by a shark.'"

"Oh, dear," Scrutinous said again. "This does not bode well for me."

Valkyrie waved her hand, and the pen drifted up off the ground and hovered at eye level. "Haunted pen?" she asked.

"Cursed, more likely," Skulduggery said. "Physical contact seems to be enough for the curse to pass on. Geoffrey, you had no idea what you were writing?"

"I had no idea I was writing *anything*," Scrutinous replied. "I hate to be a pain, but do you think there's anything you can do to help me? I really don't want to be eaten by a shark tonight. The next round of my bowling tournament is on Wednesday and we're not doing too badly, all things considered. I'd hate to miss it."

"If a shark does come for you, it won't be tonight," Skulduggery told him. "The ink on the pad is at the very most a day old, Cassidy died four hours ago, and these kinds of curses really like the twelve hour rule. Any more than that and the power starts to wane."

"So I have twelve hours before a shark eats me?"

"Or you have twelve hours for us to save you, if you want to be glass-half-full about it. Cheer up, Geoffrey, you have our full attention focused on your dilemma. Wait, where's my hat?"

Valkyrie picked it up off the armchair and handed it to him.

"Perfect," he said. "*Now* you have our full attention."

Scrutinous smiled gratefully, suddenly reassured that everything was going to be all right. The skeleton detective and Valkyrie Cain were on the case, and they would stop at nothing to solve it.

"I'm hungry," Valkyrie said.

Skulduggery nodded decisively, said, "Then let's find you something to eat," and Scrutinous sagged.

They sat in the diner, Valkyrie doing her best to eat a burger that kept slipping from its bun. Skulduggery had activated one of his false faces, one which gave him a slightly bewildered look. He had placed the pen in a wooden box and was peering at it. Scrutinous sat in the booth and did his best not to worry. He had a glass of water in front of him that he didn't touch.

"This store," Skulduggery said, "where Mister Cassidy worked – where is it?"

"Donnybrook," said Scrutinous.

"Donnybrook," Skulduggery repeated. "Interesting. Do you know of any sorcerers living in Donnybrook? I don't. Thoroughly nice area, but no sorcerers."

"This burger is hard to eat," Valkyrie muttered.

"You're doing a fantastic job," Skulduggery said happily. He closed the box and put it in his pocket. "Now then, Donnybrook. No sorcerers in Donnybrook. No sorcerers around where Cassidy lived. So how did he meet the sorcerer who killed him?"

Scrutinous found it hard to know when Skulduggery was addressing him or merely thinking out loud. The eyes on his false face were slowly swivelling in every direction.

"Unless," Skulduggery said, "he never did."

Valkyrie asked a question with her mouth full.

Skulduggery's head tilted. "What I mean is, this is a curse that passes from one person to the next, yes? The pen keeps moving around. Brendan Cassidy may not have been the first victim, which means it's possible he had no contact *at all* with the sorcerer who started it. Which means that there should be more unexplained deaths that we haven't heard about. Excuse me for a moment."

Skulduggery took his phone from his pocket, then slipped out of the booth. He went away to make a phone call. Scrutinous looked back at Valkyrie. She had managed to shove half of the burger into her mouth but now froze, her eyes on his.

She mumbled something that sounded like "Sorry."

He looked away, and she munched on.

A few minutes later Skulduggery slid back into the booth. "Excellent news," he said. "There have been four unexplained deaths in the past two weeks. The first three were all sorcerers, and the fourth was a mortal woman who *knew* the last sorcerer killed and who lived in Donnybrook. Before she died, she could have left that pen in the store in which Brendan Cassidy worked. He picked it up, took it home, and got hit by a train."

"Who was the first sorcerer killed?" Valkyrie asked.

"His name was Elwood Satchel. Low level Elemental. If the curse did start with him, then the killer must has some connection. We find that connection, we find the killer, we save Geoffrey."

"Then let's do it," Scrutinous said. He paused. "How do we do it?"

"We talk to someone who knew Satchel well. He has a brother who's out of the country right now, and a friend who lives close by."

"So we talk to the friend," Valkyrie said. "Let's go."

They got in the Bentley, drove to the friend's house and knocked on the door. There was nobody home, so they went back to the Bentley and waited. Skulduggery didn't move for hours, and Valkyrie fell asleep. Scrutinous sat in the backseat and thought about sharks all night.

Satchel's friend returned home at ten the next morning. He was a sorcerer but, like Satchel, he wasn't a very powerful one. He worked nights as a security guard to pay the bills.

"It was a clear day," he said when Skulduggery asked him how Satchel had died. "The sun was shining. There were no clouds. But Elwood was... panicking. He kept running around, looking up at the sky. He ran into a café, ran right back out again, screaming something about how it didn't have a ceiling. And then... And then he jerked backwards, flew right off his feet. He was all twisted up, and you could smell burnt hair."

"He was electrocuted?" Skulduggery asked.

"Yeah. Apparently. The doctors said it was massive electrical current. But I didn't see anything, and he was running across the park when it happened. There was nothing electrical around."

"Did you find a note?" asked Valkyrie.

The man frowned. "What? How did you know about that?"

"Then you *did* find a note."

"Yes. Well, we think. A few days after he died, Elwood's brother found something written on the back of a receipt. It said 'I'm going to be struck by lightning'."

Skulduggery nodded. "Did Elwood have any enemies?"

"I... suppose. I mean, doesn't everyone?"

"Any enemies he had recently made?"

"Oh. Oh, yeah. One. Davit Maybury. They were friends once."

"What happened?"

"Ah, I don't know. The usual."

"I don't quite believe you," said Skulduggery.

"Look, Maybury's a weirdo, OK? He comes out with these weird things to say, and he looks... odd. He's got crazy eyes, you know? But Elwood grew up with him, they were childhood friends, and then... Elwood kind of stole Maybury's girlfriend."

"Ah."

"I suppose it was kind of a sucky thing to do. Maybury found it hard to talk to girls, because of his whole weirdness thing, and he finally found one who liked him and Elwood comes in and sweeps her off her feet... You think Maybury had something to do with his death?"

"Perhaps," Skulduggery said. "Do you know where we could find him? We just want a little chat."

Davit Maybury's house was quite nondescript from the outside. Skulduggery knocked a few times, then kicked the door in. It was quite a nondescript house from the inside, too. Skulduggery went first, hand open and fingers splayed.

"The air hasn't been disturbed for weeks," he said. "It doesn't look like anybody's home."

"So what are we going to do now?" Scrutinous asked. "It's almost eleven o'clock. I have one hour before a shark eats me."

"You'll be fine," Skulduggery said, poking around. "Everyone spread out. Look for clues."

Skulduggery and Valkyrie went wandering, examining things and muttering to themselves and each other. Scrutinous bit his lip and checked his watch.

Almost three quarters of an hour later, Skulduggery found something in the main bedroom.

"It's a door," he said, rapping his knuckles against the wall. "Very well hidden. Whoever installed it knew what they were doing."

"Where does it lead?" Scrutinous asked, and shifted his weight. The carpet in here was soggy, and water spilled through his sandals to wet his socks.

"It could be a stairway leading to a tunnel, or it could be a single room." Skulduggery stood back. "Maybury isn't the strongest sorcerer out there, and by all accounts he doesn't have many friends. It is therefore entirely conceivable that the moment he released the cursed pen upon Elwood Satchel he secluded himself away until it was all over. If something went wrong with the curse, if it didn't work, then Satchel might come after him."

Valkyrie peered at the wall. "So you think he's still in there?"

"Mister Maybury," Skulduggery said loudly, "we need to talk to you. If you can hear me, please open the door. I am a detective with the Sanctuary – we're not going to hurt you."

They looked at the wall and waited, and nothing happened.

"Um," said Scrutinous. "Where's that water coming from?"

Valkyrie looked around. "What water?"

Scrutinous splashed his foot a few times.

"That's the carpet," Valkyrie told him.

"And why is it covered in water?"

She frowned at him. "What are you talking about? It's not. It's just a regular carpet."

"It's a regular carpet covered in water, Valkyrie. You're standing in it too."

"No, Geoffrey, I'm not. My feet are perfectly dry, as are yours. Are you feeling OK?"

He stared at her. The water was rising. It was up to her ankles. It had completely covered his own sandals. It was cold and wet. "You can't see this?" he asked. "You can't hear the splashing? You can't feel it?"

She hunkered down, put her hand in the water, flat on the floor. Her eyes were on him the whole time. "Am I touching the water now?"

He nodded. She brought her hand up. It was perfectly dry. No drops fell.

"Oh, dear," Scrutinous said.

"Interesting," Skulduggery murmured. "The curse must deliver a reality that only the victim can experience."

"Which explains how a train fit into Cassidy's living room," Valkyrie said.

Scrutinous peered into the water, and his eyes widened. "I see a fish," he said. "A small one, a tiny one, but... it's a fish." He looked up. "When there's enough water, the shark will appear, won't it?"

"I'm afraid so," Skulduggery said. "Which means we have to get through this door."

Skulduggery and Valkyrie walked through the water without disturbing it, Scrutinous splashing noisily after them. They ran their hands all over the wall, feeling for imperfections.

"There has to be a lever here somewhere," Skulduggery

said. "The time and the effort was put into making this door virtually undetectable, not into making it impenetrable. At Maybury's price range, it's one or the other. So there has to be a lever somewhere nearby."

Even as he spoke, something clicked beneath his fingers. The wall shifted, the door swung open, and Skulduggery led the way in.

It was a small room, windowless, with an armchair and a side-table. On the side-table there was thick book and a scalpel. There was water in here too. Now it was up past Scrutinous' knees. His legs were freezing, and every now and then a school of tiny fish would brush past and he'd jerk away.

"We may have a problem," Skulduggery said.

Scrutinous stopped scanning the water and glanced up, saw a corpse in the armchair. Valkyrie had her hand covering her mouth and nose, but all Scrutinous could smell was the briny sea.

"That's Maybury?" he asked. "But... he's dead. He *is* dead, isn't he?"

"He must have trapped himself inside," Skulduggery said.

"He starved to death?" Valkyrie asked.

"I'm afraid he ran out of air long before that could happen. He obviously didn't think this through too well."

"But if he's dead," said Scrutinous, "how can he lift the curse? Who's going to lift the curse?"

"The important thing to remember is not to panic," Skulduggery said.

"How can I not panic? A shark is going to eat me!"

"It's really not as bad as it sounds. I was attacked by a shark once, back when I was alive. Well, not so much a shark as a rather large fish. And not so much attacked as looked at menacingly. But it had murder in its eyes, that fish. I knew, in that instant, if our roles had been reversed and the fish had been holding the fishing pole and I had been the one to be caught, it wouldn't hesitate a moment before eating me. So I cooked it and ate before it had a chance to turn the tables."

"That," Valkyrie said, "is one of the most useless stories you've ever told me."

"I'm just trying to make Geoffrey feel better."

"You went fishing, Skulduggery. That's not the same as being eaten by a shark."

"It shares similarities."

"Like what?"

"It was wet. Also, one eats the other. When looked upon like that, the main points are practically identical."

"Um," Scrutinous said, "could we start talking about how

we're going to lift the curse if the man who started it all is dead?"

"Yes," Skulduggery said, "of course. All is not lost. While it would have been easier to have Maybury simply cancel the whole thing, that is only one way to solve the problem. Davit Maybury was not an evil man. He was a weird one, by all accounts, but not evil. As such, it does not make sense that he would want many people to die, when all he was after was revenge on the one man who had stolen the woman he loved."

He took the wooden box from his jacket and opened it. Hesitating only a moment, he took the pen from the box. "Well," he said, "now we're in this together, Geoffrey." He held the pen in both hands, and twisted. The outer shell cracked and he pulled it away. He murmured something, then held up the pen for Valkyrie and Scrutinous to see. Four symbols had been cut into the inside. "The curse," he said. "I think Maybury made a mistake. Instead of the curse afflicting the first person to touch the pen, it has instead afflicted *every* person to touch the pen. Maybe he used the wrong symbol or misjudged the depth or the width... Every aspect of these sigils has to be perfectly judged."

"How does that help us?" Valkyrie asked.

"It means we don't have to lift the curse – we just have to correct his spelling."

"He carved the wrong symbol, so now we have to carve the right one?"

"In theory, once we do, it will mean the curse will have fulfilled its purpose the first time it was used, and all this will just... stop."

"In theory?" Scrutinous pressed. His teeth were chattering.

"Yes."

"That doesn't s-sound very certain."

"It's a very strong theory, Geoffrey. In much the same way that gravity is a very strong theory. It's almost certainly true. If I were you, I wouldn't worry about it."

"I have ten m-minutes left. The water has reached the ends of my shorts. There are f-f-fish swimming all around me and the floor has changed to a s-seabed. How do you expect me to not w-worry about this?"

"By taking deep, calming breaths."

"Do you know how to correct it?" Valkyrie asked.

Skulduggery picked up the scalpel from the side-table, before opening the book. "This is obviously what Maybury used to start it all, but because he got it wrong, I would be disinclined to trust the same instructions he followed.

We'll have to ask China."

Valkyrie raised an eyebrow. "But China isn't here."

"Your b-boyfriend," Scrutinous said. "He's a tele... porter... He can bring her."

"Fletcher's never been here," Valkyrie said. "He can't teleport anywhere he's never been."

"Well," Skulduggery said, taking out his phone, "where magic fails, technology prevails." He took a picture of the pen, then made a call.

Scrutinous glanced behind him, just in time to see a pale fin sink beneath the water's surface.

"It's here!" he screeched. "It's over there!"

Valkyrie jumped in front of him protectively.

"That won't do any good," Skulduggery said.

"I know!" she snapped. "But we can't just stand around while he gets eaten!"

Scrutinous took a deep breath and ducked his head into the water. The confines of the room did not exist down here. Down here, he was in the middle of the ocean. He saw a dark shape move out of the corner of his eye, and then it was gone. He came up for air.

"It's huge," he said. "Oh God it's h-huge."

"China," Skulduggery said suddenly. "We have a bit of an

emergency here. I just sent you a picture, did you get it? Excellent." He waited a moment, listening to her talk. "But that's just the thing. It *is* a mistake. The gent who set the curse didn't mean it to apply to *everyone* – he meant it to apply simply to the *first* one."

Scrutinous took another breath, and ducked down for another look.

The shark, and it must have been a Great White judging by its size, was visible in the distance, turning towards him. Scrutinous broke the surface, gasping for air. "It's coming!"

"But my question," Skulduggery was saying, "is how to correct the curse so that the original intent overrides the mistake? Really? Oh that's interesting."

"It's coming!" Scrutinous screamed.

"Geoffrey, please," Skulduggery said, "I can't hear what she's saying." He put the phone back to his head. "Carry on."

"Splash about," Valkyrie said. "Make a lot of noise. Scare it away."

Scrutinous splashed at the water and kicked his legs and screamed and yelled and hollered.

"A shark's coming for him," Skulduggery said into the phone. "Oh, have you? OK, I'll tell him." Skulduggery looked over. "China was attacked by a shark once, just like I was, except it was an actual shark and she was actually attacked. She says you're not to splash about, she says that makes you look like a seal, and sharks really like eating seals."

Scrutinous froze, and Valkyrie winced. "Oh, yeah," she said. "I saw that once on TV. Sorry."

"So it's just the upwards slash, then?" Skulduggery was saying, peering at the pen. "Is it too long or too short? How long should it be? No, shouldn't be a problem." He put the phone on loudspeaker and placed it in his top pocket, then readied Maybury's scalpel. "OK, making the cut now..."

China's voice came from the phone. "Has the shark eaten him yet?"

"Not yet," Skulduggery muttered, focusing on his task. "What happens if I do it wrong?"

"Geoffrey gets eaten," China said. "Am I on loudspeaker?"

"Yes, sorry, should have told you. Valkyrie and Geoffrey are here."

"Can they hear me?"

"Yes they can."

"Hello, Valkyrie," China said.

"Uh, hi," Valkyrie said back. "Is this going to take long? The shark's coming for him."

China said something in response but Scrutinous didn't

hear it. The shark came at him like a torpedo, its mouth open impossibly wide and all those teeth biting in at him. Scrutinous shrieked, dimly aware of Skulduggery gesturing, and then he was sent deeper into the water, tumbling head over heels, the shark missing him by inches.

Scrutinous turned, twisted, saw the shark flick its great tail and shoot back towards him, coming in for another go. In desperation, knowing it was useless but doing it anyway, he started to swim away from it. But there was nowhere to swim to, nowhere to hide, and then something snagged his right wrist.

An invisible force yanked him to the surface, the shark passing so close its rough skin scraped like sandpaper across his leg. He broke the surface, gasping, realising that Valkyrie had grabbed his arm and pulled, and for a moment he saw the both of them, the alarm in Valkyrie's eyes, Skulduggery still working on the pen, the room around them, and then he dropped again, below the surface, and Valkyrie and Skulduggery disappeared and there was only the shark down there in the middle of the ocean.

Oxygen bubbles filled his vision and he jerked his head from side to side, trying to get his bearings, trying to work out what direction the shark would attack from. Then he saw it, that huge mouth, those huge teeth, coming in on top of him and there was no way out, not this time, and the massive jaws closed over him just as the water went away and Scrutinous fell to the floor.

"There," Skulduggery said. "I think that did it."

Scrutinous sat up, gasping, looking around in astonishment.

"Is he dead?" China asked from the phone.

"Not even remotely," Skulduggery said. "He's back on dry land. Many thanks, China."

He hung up as Valkyrie helped Scrutinous to his feet. The water was gone, the shark was gone. Scrutinous wasn't even wet any more.

"It had me," he said. "The shark had me. I was, literally, about to be torn in two. You saved me. In the nick of time, you saved me."

"You're welcome," Skulduggery said.

"I was talking to Valkyrie."

Skulduggery's head tilted. "But I'm the one who worked the whole thing out."

Valkyrie grinned. "You're very welcome, Geoffrey, although I can't take all the credit. China helped, you know."

"But I carved the right symbol," Skulduggery said.

Scrutinous clasped Valkyrie's hand in his. "If there is

anything I can do for you in the future, anything at all, do not hesitate to ask."

Skulduggery looked at him. "Can I ask too?"

"No."

"Why not?"

"Valkyrie cared that I was being attacked. You told me to shut up."

"That's because your screaming was very annoying. How is that my fault?"

"If you'll excuse me," Scrutinous said, "I'm going to go for a walk. A nice, long walk, on solid ground."

He left them, heard them bickering behind him, and then Valkyrie was laughing and Skulduggery was acting offended. Scrutinous emerged into the midday sun, took a deep, calming breath, and headed off in search of some lunch.

Possibly seafood.

ALEX

* ALEX

alex

ALEX

ALEX

WOJTKIEWICZ